Praise for these other novels by *New York Times* bestselling author Allison Brennan

"If you haven't been reading Brennan's truly exceptional Lucy Kincaid/Sean Rogan series, then you have been missing out. . . . In this mind-blowing installment, Brennan also gives readers a fascinating look into the mindset of her epic villains. A chilling thrill-fest from beginning to end."

—*RT Book Reviews* (4½ stars, Top Pick!) on *No Good Deed*

"A fast-paced, suspenseful read with interesting characters and sinister twists that keep you turning the pages for more."

—Karin Slaughter

"Amazing . . . The interconnectivity of Brennan's books allows her ensemble of characters to evolve, adding a rich flavor to the intense suspense."

—*RT Book Reviews* (4½ stars, Top Pick!) on *Best Laid Plans*

"Brennan throws a lot of story lines into the air and juggles them like a master. The mystery proves to be both compelling and complex. . . . [A] chilling and twisty romantic suspense gem."

—Associated Press on *Silenced*

"All the excitement and suspense I have come to expect from Allison Brennan." —*Fresh Fiction* on *Stolen*

"The evolution of Lucy Kincaid from former victim to instinctive and talented agent continues in Brennan's new heart-stopping thriller. . . . From first to last, this story grabs hold and never lets go."

—*RT Book Reviews* (Top Pick) on *Silenced*

Also by Allison Brennan

Abandoned
Breaking Point
Shattered
Make Them Pay
The Lost Girls
Poisonous
No Good Deed
Best Laid Plans
Compulsion
Dead Heat
Notorious
Cold Snap
Stolen
Stalked
Silenced
If I Should Die
Kiss Me, Kill Me
Love Me to Death
Carnal Sin
Original Sin
Cutting Edge
Fatal Secrets
Sudden Death
Playing Dead
Tempting Evil
Killing Fear
Fear No Evil
See No Evil
Speak No Evil
The Kill
The Hunt
The Prey

TOO FAR GONE

Allison Brennan

TOO FAR GONE

For information address St. Martin's Press, 175 Fifth Avenue, New York, NY 10010.

ISBN: 978-1-250-16446-9

Our books may be purchased in bulk for promotional, educational, or business use. Please contact your local bookseller or the Macmillan Corporate and Premium Sales Department at 1-800-221-7945, ext. 5442, or by e-mail at MacmillanSpecialMarkets@macmillan.com.

Printed in the United States of America

St. Martin's Paperbacks edition / November 2018

St. Martin's Paperbacks are published by St. Martin's Press, 175 Fifth Avenue, New York, NY 10010.

10 9 8 7 6 5 4 3 2 1

Just because you're paranoid doesn't mean they aren't after you.

~ *Catch-22*

CHAPTER ONE

Charlie McMahon sat in the corner of Java Antonio where he could see everyone who walked in. He held the cup of tea in front of him, hands shaking, hot liquid spurting out the top. He put the cup down, absently wiped his burned hand on his jacket. The one sip he'd risked made his stomach ache. Every voice, every clink of cups, every spray of steam from the espresso machine, scratched the inside of his brain until he felt as if his head would explode.

He reached into the pocket of his jacket and retrieved the nearly empty aspirin bottle. He poured four into his shaking hand. One fell to the floor. He watched it roll into the corner then stop amid the dust and dirt and an empty sugar wrapper.

The remaining three he popped into his mouth and chewed, the bitter taste making him scowl. He sipped the tea again, a larger gulp, and burned the roof of his mouth. He barely noticed the pain because his damn head wouldn't stop pounding.

Paul was late. Two weeks ago Paul finally agreed to meet with him, but in a faraway place where there was no chance that anyone they knew would see them together. Paul refused to look Charlie in the eye, then told Charlie that he was paranoid.

"Maybe you should go on a vacation. Take a month and relax," Paul had suggested. "Maybe you're sick. You're acting crazy, and you have to stop."

Charlie knew that something was wrong with him. Physically, mentally. He knew what it was, it was on the fringe of his memory, but every damn time he tried to catch the thought it escaped. The more he chased the truth, the more his head ached and the thought, the memory, the truth faded away. Faded like he was fading.

He looked down at his hands. They seemed almost translucent. He could see them shake, but couldn't feel them. It was as if he was disconnected from his body.

He closed his eyes, opened them. His hands were there, normal, bruised on the knuckles. A healing cut across the back of his right hand.

How did that happen?

Charlie had pushed Paul, and his friend didn't push back. When Paul finally looked him in the eye, Charlie realized that Paul knew exactly what was wrong with him. Paul remembered what happened when Charlie couldn't, yet he wouldn't help him!

"What do you know, Paul? Dammit, I'm dying!"

"You're not dying. Just . . . you need help. Leave San Antonio. And stop trying to remember."

"What did I forget? You know, don't you? Why won't you tell me?"

He'd hit Paul. He remembered that . . . but that was nearly two weeks ago. Why were both of his hands bruised? And where was Paul?

Paul sent him a message late last night.

I found something. Can't talk on the phone. I'll meet you anywhere you want at 10:30 tomorrow morning.

Charlie picked Java Antonio because it was far from Clarke-Harrison. Far from home. Far from anyone who might know him or Paul. An anonymous coffee shop in the middle of the city. It felt safe . . . until now. Right now the walls were closing in on him and he couldn't *think*!

Leave, Charlie. Walk away. Disappear.

Paul was late. Was he dead? Had they killed him? Or had he become one of them?

Who the fuck are they? *You've lost your mind. No one is after you. Paul was placating you. He's going to call the cops. Or a fucking mental institution. He didn't believe you. The meeting is a setup. They're going to lock you up and you'll never know the truth.*

The overwhelming sensation to run, to go far away, hit Charlie and he got up too quickly, knocking over his tea. But the lid stayed on and only a small stream of amber liquid dribbled out. He picked up the cup, stared at it.

All Charlie wanted to know was what had happened to him. Why he had a journal in his handwriting but didn't understand what any of it said. Why he had the distinct feeling that he knew something important—something dangerous—but he couldn't remember what. He'd studied his calendar and his phone and email and knew that whatever had happened to him had happened at work.

Maybe. Because you're not really sure of anything, are you, Charlie?

That's why he needed Paul. They'd worked together for eight years before Charlie was fired. Paul was the only one Charlie trusted.

He lied to you. He didn't look you in the eye.

Charlie sat back down. He didn't know who else to turn to, he didn't know who he could trust. Memories scratched at him, trying to find a way to talk to him, to tell him the truth. But could he even trust them?

Every time he tried to listen, the whispers of truth disappeared in a wave of agony.

Voices drifted his way. He turned his head slowly, trying to figure out who was talking about him. Two teenage girls.

They're not talking about you.

Why weren't they in school?

It's July. School's out.

They laughed, both with their heads down looking at their phones. Something about that was familiar . . . was it the phone? The way the brunette girl was holding it? Something familiar . . .

Her face shifted, and she became someone else. She saw Charlie looking at her and quickly turned away and became a teenager again. She whispered to her friend. He'd scared her.

"Hello, Charlie."

Charlie jumped, looked left and right. A man he'd never seen before stood in front of him. But he wasn't looking at him. He was looking at a display. Had he spoken? Was it in Charlie's head?

"Who are you?" he whispered.

"You need to stop asking questions, Charlie. You won't like the answers."

"Where's Paul?"

He'd spoken too loud. People glanced at him, then quickly turned away. The teenagers shifted away from him, their heads together.

Now they *were* talking about him. Now they sounded scared.

Charlie didn't want to scare anyone. Especially kids. His daughter was fifteen. He hadn't seen her in almost three months, because Lisa said he needed help. She was scared of him, that he would hurt her. Hurt the kids.

I would never hurt you, Lisa. I would never hurt the kids. I love you.

He'd tried to get help, but only felt worse. More paranoid. More . . . forgetful.

He wrote hundreds of pages in code and didn't know what it meant. He'd showed Paul his journal two weeks ago and Paul knew. But he said he didn't.

He lied to you. Why can't you see that there is no one to trust?

"Where are your notes, Charlie?" the stranger asked him.

Charlie hadn't seen his lips move. What if he wasn't talking? What if Charlie was hearing things?

Again. Hearing voices again.

Everything was bright, too bright. His body and mind disconnected. Impossible.

Just a reaction to . . .

Charlie turned, chasing the memory. Reaction to what? What?

His head ached and the memory turned black.

This man had answers. This man knew what *THE FUCK WAS GOING ON!*

remember remember remember remember remember

It was so close . . . but he couldn't grasp it.

Remember or you'll be dead.

"Where's Paul? Did you kill him?"

Silence fell around him. Was he still talking too loud? Shouting? He could barely hear himself. Everything inside was suppressed by cotton, as if he were speaking through a vacuum.

The girls got up and walked to the other side of the coffee shop. They were talking to someone behind the counter. Because of him? Had he scared them?

Forget the girls. This man has the answers you need. Make him talk!

Someone was walking toward him. Who? Who knew him?

Charlie hit his head with his palm. It hurt, but he had to remember!

"Sir."

Charlie looked up again. A young black kid stood there. He wore an apron. Charlie's vision was blurry and he couldn't make out his name tag. The kid looked nervous.

This kid is just a guy doing his job. Doing his job and you're freaking out his customers.

"I'm sorry," he mumbled.

"Can I help you? Would you like me to call someone for you?"

He wanted to talk to the police, but he didn't remember what he needed to tell them. He had tried talking to his wife, but she wouldn't let him in, wouldn't let him see their children. He didn't blame her. He'd yelled at her . . . He'd talked to Paul . . . Paul was supposed to be here!

Paul had answers.

They'd killed Paul.

Charlie looked at his watch.

"Are you waiting for someone?" the manager asked.

"Paul's late," he said. "I think he's dead."

The belief that Paul was dead hit him so hard he wondered if he really knew that his best friend, his former colleague, was in fact dead. Had he seen him dead? Had he . . . God, had he *killed him*?

You didn't kill Paul. You haven't seen him in two weeks.

But Charlie couldn't remember where he'd been yesterday. Just flashes of images. Of alleys and hiding and a one-room apartment in the middle of nowhere.

And numbers. So many numbers and formulas . . .

"Sir, are you okay?"

"No!" Charlie jumped up and the table fell over. He didn't care that the lid popped off his tea and it splattered everywhere. Several people walked briskly out of the coffee shop. Two more had their phones to their ears. What were they doing? What were they saying?

Charlie knew what he had to do. This might be the only way to figure out what was wrong with him, what he knew that he couldn't remember, why his head felt like it was going to go off like a fucking Roman candle!

A gun was in his hand. How did it get there? He didn't remember putting a gun—two guns?—in his jacket. Why was he wearing a jacket? It was *July* in *San Antonio*. No wonder people were looking at him strangely.

People were screaming. Several ran out of the coffee shop. No, no! This wasn't happening.

He fired a bullet into the ceiling.

"Everyone down! You!" He grabbed the manager and held the gun to his head. "Do you have a cell phone?"

"Y-yes."

"You need to call Paul. Right now. Right the fuck now!"

He pulled the manager away from the windows. Self-preservation kicked in. He ordered one of the employees to lock the door. He held a gun on her, made her lock the door. She did.

"Down! Get down, everyone!"

People fell to the floor and froze. Someone was crying.

Stop, Charlie. Stop. This is insane.

"No else leaves until Paul gets here, understand? I don't want to hurt anyone. I don't want to hurt anyone. Okay? Okay?"

He was repeating himself. But he didn't care. He would keep these people as long as necessary to get answers.

"Give me your cell phone," he told the manager.

Charlie had stopped carrying a phone because he feared *they*—

who the fuck are they?

—were tracking him.

The manager reached into his apron and handed Charlie a phone. His hands were shaking.

"Put it on speaker. Call Paul." Charlie recited his number by memory. He'd known Paul since college. Then eight years ago, Paul moved to San Antonio to work with Charlie. They were friends. Their wives were friends. They had barbecues and their sons were on the same baseball team. At least they had been before . . .

Before what? What, Charlie?

His head was about to explode.

The phone rang once.

Click.

A recording came on.

"This number is no longer in service. If you feel you've reached this recording in error, please check the number and try your call again."

"You dialed wrong! Again!" Charlie repeated the number slowly.

The recording repeated.

Paul really was dead.

CHAPTER TWO

FBI Special Agent Lucy Kincaid geared up in the back of the SWAT van and followed team leader Leo Proctor to the staging area kitty-corner to the coffeehouse that was currently under control of a gunman. Lucy wasn't part of the SWAT team. She was the newest trained hostage negotiator, though she would be second to Proctor for a minimum of six months. She wouldn't be talking to the suspect today; she was tagging along on her first official outing after completing Hostage and Crisis Response Training at Quantico.

As soon as she stepped out of the air-conditioned van and into the hot Texas humidity, she began to sweat. Fortunately, she wasn't decked out with an extra twenty-five pounds of SWAT gear; she was only required to wear her Kevlar vest and sidearm.

The FBI was here to back up the SAPD, who were taking lead in the hostage situation at Java Antonio, a small but popular independent coffee shop in downtown San Antonio.

Lucy followed Leo from the van while the rest of the team checked their weapons and gear.

"Lieutenant, sit-rep?" Leo said to the man clearly in charge who was directing personnel from the back of a police communications van. There were a dozen city and county vehicles filling all four streets that led to the intersection, which now held a tactical truck. Each street had been blocked off, and all businesses in a two-block radius evacuated or locked down.

"Proctor. Glad you're here." He glanced at Lucy.

"Agent Kincaid, hostage negotiator. Kincaid, Lieutenant Jordan Young."

They shook hands. Young was forty and had the aura of former military officer, and it was clear by how his officers spoke to him that he garnered respect from his men and women.

"I need you to negotiate, Leo—I've already set up a command, I'm the highest-ranking officer here."

"My people are your people," Proctor said. "Kincaid's my second."

Being second essentially meant backing up the primary negotiator. Listening to all communication, taking notes, passing along information between the negotiator and command and vice versa.

Generally the individual in charge of the scene was not the same person negotiating with the suspect. That SAPD and the SA-FBI worked well together was a testament to the men and women who led each department and the teams who cross-trained together.

"I have two snipers, one on each corner building," Young said, gesturing. "Two men in the back. If you can spare a pair I'd like to have them tag up with my team in the alley, and if you have a sniper we can use one back there. The rear is the only exit other than the front door."

Proctor said in his radio, "Dunning, take your team and secure the back with SAPD; Ramirez, find a roost with clear line of sight to the emergency exit. From here on out, Lieutenant Young is in command of this operation and you'll take direction from him, primary emergency channel."

"Roger," the team leader said over the radio.

"Suspect?" Proctor asked.

Young shook his head. "Working on an ID. No cameras inside, but we have a description from one of the hostages who escaped during the initial confusion. In fact, a dozen people got out before the shooter locked down. From preliminary statements, the guy was talking to himself and acting 'off'—*weird* was the word most used. He was wearing a thick windbreaker and it's over ninety degrees and humid as hell. When the manager confronted him, he snapped—per a witness. Another witness said he acted like he was quote, 'off his meds.'"

Unfortunately, Lucy knew that mental illness was one of the leading causes of spontaneous hostage situations. But generally, if the individual was mentally ill, they took people they knew hostage—family or friends—in a residence. This situation was distinctly different.

Young continued. "He fired two shots. Per witnesses, they both went into the ceiling. No one saw anyone injured inside. There are conflicting statements as to how many guns he has and what kind, though I'm going with one of the witnesses who stated he's a gun owner and identified a nine-millimeter in the shooter's hand, standard-capacity magazine, and a second handgun in his waistband, also a semi-auto—either a nine-mil or a forty-five."

"Number of hostages?"

"Best guess is fourteen. Do you have thermal imaging in your truck? Fire can set up as well, but they're still en route."

"We got it," Proctor said. "My tech just needs a minute."

"Good. We need to know where he is, get some sense as to what's going on in there."

"Is this personal?" Proctor asked. "Target an employee? Customer?"

"Don't know. We asked the witnesses for the basics, everyone said that he was alone and didn't appear to know anyone. They are all sequestered down the street, my people are working to get more information. He hasn't called out or made demands, but this whole thing started less than an hour ago. I need you to make contact, develop a rapport as we gather additional information. We need to de-escalate this as fast as possible."

Proctor listened to his com then said, "Roger, hold positions." He said to Young, "My team is in place, Ramirez has one hundred percent visual of the rear door."

"Excellent." Young handed him the bullhorn. "Work your magic, Leo. Godspeed."

Proctor took a breath, visibly relaxed, then turned on the bullhorn.

"This is Leo Proctor of the FBI. I will be calling into the coffee shop. I'd like you to answer, just to talk. Just see how you're doing, how the other people are doing."

He then nodded to Young's assistant, a uniform by the name of Jones, who handed him a phone already set to dial into the Java Antonio main number and record the conversation.

They let the phone ring more than thirty times. There was no answer and Proctor ended the call.

"Lieutenant," Jones said after listening to his radio, "we have an ID. Charles James McMahon, forty-six, address in Helotes per DMV. Two deputies are on their way now."

"Married? Kids? Employer?"

"Unknown, we're working on it."

"Work faster. Something triggered him, we need to know what so no one gets hurt."

"Yes, sir," Jones said, already on his phone.

Proctor got on the bullhorn again. "Mr. McMahon—Charles—this is Leo Proctor. I really need you to pick up the phone. I know you don't want to hurt anyone. We need to talk. You and me. We can work this out, but I'm sure you don't like shouting through a bullhorn any more than I do."

He dialed again, waited. No answer. He hung up. He didn't show any frustration, any rush. "As long as he's calm, we can get out of this," he said almost to himself. "Lucy, get Yancey out here. We need eyes in."

Lucy briskly walked to the tactical van. Tim Yancey was a technology analyst in their office and in charge of the equipment during tactical operations. He was a bit high-strung, skinny, and sharp on his feet.

"I know, I know," Tim said before Lucy could speak. "It's almost calibrated. Okay, okay," he said to himself and followed Lucy over to the staging area which had a direct line of sight to the coffee shop.

"I need to expand the range," he said as he walked up and put the thermal imaging camera on a table next to the SAPD tactical van. "Okay, okay," he mumbled again and pressed a few buttons to expand the field.

A blob of orange quickly took on distinct human shapes. Most were on the floor. Young immediately pointed to one on the left that was moving and had another shape close to him. "That's our guy. He's holding a hostage. I count . . . fifteen plus the gunman?"

"I concur," Proctor said.

Young asked Tim, "Why are these three shapes faded?"

"They're in another room," Tim said. "Probably the storage room, a bathroom—I don't have the exact layout."

Young motioned at one of his men. "Where are the blueprints I asked for?"

"Coming."

"I needed them five minutes ago."

"He didn't plan this," Lucy said.

Everyone looked at her. She didn't realize she'd spoken out loud.

"If he did," she continued, "he would have made sure that everyone was in the main room. Those three had time to hide in the back and he didn't notice? Others escaped? A dozen people ran out before he locked the place down. I think he would notice if he had a room full of customers and no employees."

"Point taken," Young said. "Don't know if that makes him more or less dangerous. Get him talking, Leo, I'm going to push my people to get us more intel."

Leo used the bullhorn. "Charles, this is Leo Proctor again. I'm calling you now. Please pick up the phone."

He hit REDIAL.

Lucy adjusted her earpiece and heard the ringing phone. She watched Tim's thermal imaging system and saw the suspect cross the room—with a hostage in tow—and stand next to what she presumed was the phone on the wall behind the counter.

"Answer it, buddy," Leo mumbled. "Pick it up, you want to."

The man put a hand on his head—more like he was banging the side of his head with his gun hand, as if flustered or frustrated. He walked away a couple of feet.

Leo hung up. He counted to ten. Then he hit REDIAL.

McMahon went back to the phone. He answered.

"What?"

"Charles, this is Leo Proctor. Call me Leo, okay? I just want to talk."

"No. No. This wasn't supposed to happen!"

"I'm sure you're right, Charles. Do you prefer Charlie?"

"They killed Paul, they killed Paul!"

"Is Paul a friend of yours? Maybe I can find out what happened to Paul."

"I can't think."

"That's okay, Charlie. We're in no rush. I just want to talk. Are the hostages okay? Do you need anything? Let me know what you need, I can help you. We both want the same thing."

"No, no, they killed Paul, that's why he's not here, that's why he—"

McMahon stopped talking, but he hadn't hung up.

"Who killed Paul, Charlie? Let me help you figure this out, okay? We have resources out here, we can find out what happened to Paul. Does Paul have a last name? Can you help us so we can help you?"

"No one can help. Stop calling!"

McMahon hung up.

Leo looked concerned. The key to being a good hostage negotiator was to be the optimist, the person who could calm things down, negotiate with the hostage-takers, figure out what they wanted and get them as much as feasibly possible, all the while talking to them and working to resolve the situation peacefully.

"He sounds paranoid," Lucy said. "Possible schizophrenic, or extreme paranoia. There would be medical records for that, if he was picked up by police at any time."

Leo said into his com, "Lieutenant, does McMahon have a record?"

"We're pulling everything," Young said. "Two minutes."

Lucy slid Leo over her notes. "He mentioned Paul three times. Said that's why Paul's not here—because 'they' killed him. A violent trauma, a sudden death, any number of things may cause someone to have a breakdown. But it didn't sound like he knew for certain—just that he *thinks* this might be the reason Paul isn't here."

They both watched the thermal imaging. McMahon paced with jerky movements. Two or three steps. Stop. Another step. Stop. Turn and walk two steps. Stop. Two more steps. Stop. He had the one hostage with him the whole time. That hostage was shorter and skinnier than McMahon.

One of the hostages was crawling toward the back and McMahon rushed over to the figure, aimed the gun.

McMahon didn't fire the gun, but the hostage stopped moving.

Leo redialed. "We've got to get him to talk, calm him down."

McMahon answered on the third ring. "Stop calling! I can't think with all these distractions!" He hung up and fired his gun at the phone. They could hear the hostages screaming from inside. Another gunshot. That made four total—two at the beginning, and two at the phone.

"Does anyone have a shot?" Young asked the SWAT teams.

The answer was negative. No one had a visual of the suspect. The blinds were drawn and no one could see in. Shooting off thermal imaging was a last resort because it put too many hostages at risk.

"He didn't shoot anyone," Leo said. "Just the phone. I need an in. I need to find out what's going on. Who's Paul? Someone has got to know this guy!"

Jones rushed over to them and said, "McMahon has no criminal record until two months ago. He was arrested for breaking and entering his former place of employment in May. According to the responding officer, he had been fired the week before. He broke in after hours, refused to say why, was belligerent, and resisted arrest. He was given probation. Extenuating circumstances—his wife left him in April, took their two kids. Then he was fired in May, broke in a week later."

"I need to talk to the wife ASAP," Leo said.

"We're trying to reach her now. He also has a pending charge for assault and is currently out on bail. The court date is set for two weeks."

"When? Where?"

"Ten days ago, he attacked Paul Grey at a bar in Guadalupe County. Grey didn't press charges, but the bar owner did—McMahon hit him with a broken beer bottle when he tried to break up the fight."

Leo and Lucy exchanged glances. Leo said, "Find Paul Grey now. Dead or alive, I need everything on him."

"On it," Jones said.

Leo said to Yancey, "Do you have the mobile phone ready?"

"Yes, sir."

"Set it up to give us direct audio, I'll see if he'll let us bring it in to him."

If they could plant one of the FBI phones inside, they could hear everything that was going on, and hopefully find a way to de-escalate. Plus, they needed to be able to talk to McMahon. Cutting off communication so quickly was never a good sign. Worse, he didn't state that he wanted anything. Hostage-takers who didn't ask for something were the most dangerous to themselves and others.

Young came over. "The wife is on her way. Name's Lisa McMahon, kids are Rani, fifteen, and Joe, eleven. They've been married for eighteen years, separated officially nearly three months ago—two weeks before he was fired. She said he had become irrational, kept odd hours, stopped talking to her about work or the kids. She didn't want to leave, but gave him an ultimatum—to tell her what was going on or she was leaving. He then started yelling—she doesn't remember specifically about what, just that it seemed to make no sense. She left that day with the kids. She's only seen him a couple of times since—said he's lost weight and isn't himself."

"Anything happen that instigated this behavior?"

"She claims she doesn't know. There's no history of depression or mental illness with McMahon or anyone in his immediate family, according to the wife. She's a teacher at Saint John Paul the Second in New Braunfels."

Lucy asked, "How long before she left was he exhibiting strange behavior?"

Young looked at his notes. "A few weeks. She said small things were off in March, but it was Easter dinner that she knew something was very wrong. She confronted him April tenth, she said, then moved in with her brother and his family. Her brother is a sheriff's deputy in Travis County, lives in San Marcos. He's bringing her down in a squad car, but it'll be at least forty minutes before they get here."

"Can you get him to talk?" Young asked Leo. "Calm him down until the wife arrives?"

"I'm trying. Get her on the phone, I have some questions."

Leo took a deep breath, picked up the bullhorn.

"Charlie, I'm sorry the ringing phone upset you. I only wanted to talk, to find out how I can help. All I want to do, Charlie, is help you, but shouting over this bullhorn isn't any way to communicate. Your wife, Lisa, is on her way. She wants to talk to you, too. I'd like to send a phone into the coffee shop. Then you can call me when you want to talk. You'll have the power, Charlie. Calling is up to you. I'm going to send one of my people to the door. They will leave the phone just outside the door and walk away. You can send one of the hostages to retrieve it. My number is pre-programmed. Just hit SEND and you'll reach me directly. I'm Leonard Proctor, you can call me Leo. Everybody does."

He put the horn down. "I don't think he's going to bite, but I need to buy us some time here."

Jones said, "I'll have one of our men drop the phone at the door."

"Fully geared, no guns," Leo said. "I don't want him thinking we're coming in, but I'm not putting anyone in his crosshairs."

Young pulled off one of his men and gave the instructions. They watched in tense silence as the officer approached the door in full tactical gear. He left the phone right outside the door and retreated without incident.

Leo said in the bullhorn, "Charlie, the phone is sitting outside the door. Please send someone to get it. Then you can call me. We can talk, just the two of us."

They watched the thermal. No one was moving.

Charlie was agitated, but he was no longer pacing. He stood at the counter near where he'd shot the phone.

"This is okay," Leo said. "If we can keep him calm, get his wife here, she might have more information she doesn't realize. I need to talk to her."

"We're getting her on the phone," Jones said. "One minute, sir."

Lucy said to Leo, "She teaches at a Catholic school—ask if McMahon attends church, if he's close to his priest—we might be able to get his priest out here to keep him calm."

A few seconds later Young's assistant handed him a cell phone and said, "Lisa McMahon. She's with her brother, Trevor Olsen."

Leo nodded, took the phone, and stepped away, motioning for Lucy to follow him. When they had a bit of privacy, he put the phone on speaker and said, "Mrs. McMahon? I'm FBI Supervisory Special Agent Leo Proctor here with Agent Lucy Kincaid. I'm the hostage negotiator and I'm trying to talk to your husband, but he cut off communications. I need a way to keep him calm, to find out what he wants."

"I can't believe this is happening," Lisa said.

"Lisa—can I call you Lisa?—you told the first officer you spoke to that you left your husband shortly before he was fired. That his behavior had changed and you were fearful."

"Yes—he was secretive and agitated. He yelled at me—Charlie has never raised his voice to me or the kids in the eighteen years we'd been married. Never. And this was . . . not just an argument. It was like he was a completely different person. It scared me. I didn't know what was going on with him. I still don't. He's a good man, Mr. Proctor. I don't know why he's doing this."

"Where did he work?"

"CHR. Clarke-Harrison Research. He's brilliant, at least, he was. I don't know what happened with him or why they fired him. They built an entire division based on his research, and he ran it for the last eight years. They gave him a huge promotion and a raise."

"When was the last time you spoke to him?"

"A month ago he came to visit the kids. I wouldn't—I wouldn't let him see them. Oh God, he was a mess. I thought he'd been drinking, but he wasn't acting drunk—just irrational. My brother rushed home, almost arrested him, but I said don't. I told Charlie he needed to talk to someone. That I'd come back if he got help. But I don't think he did. I've called, left him messages nearly every day, but he hasn't called me back."

"Do you know a Paul Grey?"

"Of course—he worked with Charlie. They're friends. Went to college together. When Charlie started the new division, he brought Paul on. Our boys play baseball together. Tell me what's going on, Mr. Proctor. Please."

"We're going to find out."

"Did he really take people hostage? Is anyone hurt?"

"So far, no one has been injured, and my goal is to keep it that way. You teach at a Catholic school—is Charlie Catholic? Would he be receptive to talking to his priest?"

"I'm Catholic, Charlie isn't—his family isn't religious."

Leo made a note, then said, "When you get here, have your brother walk you through to Lieutenant Young, okay? We hope to resolve this situation peacefully."

Lucy had only been listening, but she wrote *Paul dead?* on her notepad and showed it to Leo.

Leo said, "Mrs. McMahon? Is Paul Grey okay? Do you know if he was recently killed?"

"Paul? No, I mean, I would have heard. I think—I just—Paul?"

"When did you see him last?"

"Early June I had lunch with him, on a Saturday. I asked him to check on Charlie for me, because Charlie hadn't paid any of the bills. Then I talked to him two weeks ago. He was as worried about Charlie as I was and told me he was meeting with him. That was the last time I spoke to him."

Leo got Paul Grey's phone number from Mrs. McMahon and hung up. He was about to dial it when Jones came over. "Paul Grey's wife, Diane, filed a missing persons report yesterday morning—he didn't come home after work on Monday and no one has seen him since. It's a Bexar County case, he lives in Helotes, near McMahon."

Paul Grey was missing? Could that have set McMahon off?

Or had McMahon killed him? Snapped, killed his friend, then couldn't live with himself and took hostages? Maybe completely blocked out the murder.

That didn't make sense to Lucy, but she'd seen stranger things. There were many things that could cause someone to completely change their behavior, but one of the least understood and undiagnosed was a brain tumor. It was fortunately rare, but there had been several criminal cases where someone who was otherwise a law-abiding citizen did something illegal or dangerous. A case that she'd studied in college was about a woman who'd been a regular churchgoer and had lived her life without drugs or alcohol, did a 180 and slept with more than fifty men in three months, picking them up at bars all over northern Virginia.

Or McMahon simply snapped under the pressure and stress of his wife leaving and losing his job. That was a far more common scenario.

Leo assessed through thermal imaging that the situation inside hadn't changed, then got back on the bullhorn. "Charlie, it's Leo again. The phone is still sitting outside the door. I need to talk to you. Please, send someone to get it. I can help you but only if we can talk to each other."

They watched. Charlie was pacing again, but now he wasn't holding the hostage close to him, though the hostage was walking with him, about six inches apart. Charlie was holding his head, as if he was in pain.

Young came over. "The wife is still twenty minutes out—and that's pushing it. He's on edge and I'm not going to lose a hostage today. Where are we?"

"He has no history of depression according to his wife, but he's been acting out of character for the last three months," Leo said. "His friend is missing, yet McMahon thinks he's dead. What do you have on the missing persons report?"

Young slipped him a copy. "Not much. On Monday

Paul Grey went to work. Called his wife and said he'd be home late—said don't wait up. When he didn't come home that night, she called his work, found out he'd left at four thirty the day before, and hadn't been seen by anyone since. That's when she called the police. His car is missing, his cell phone not registering on GPS, indicates it's not in service. I don't have phone records, the wife may have given them to the sheriff's department, but they're not in the report. The police haven't pursued this as foul play—he's been missing less than forty-eight hours. His credit cards haven't been used, however. Think our hostage-taker killed his friend?"

"I don't know what to think," Leo said. "I need to give him something—that I'm trying to help. But the bullhorn is bullshit. I need to talk to him one-on-one."

"I will not authorize you going in. He has fifteen hostages. We don't know what he wants, I'm not giving him a cop."

"I don't think *he* knows what he wants. Give me a second."

Young nodded and walked away. Leo took a deep breath, got on the bullhorn again. "Charlie, it's Leo again. I have news about your friend Paul Grey. I want to tell you, but not shouting like this. Please call me. If you don't want to get the phone we left at the door, find another phone in there and call me. My number is 555-1023. That goes to me only, 555-1023. I'll answer."

He put the bullhorn down and watched the thermal feed. McMahon had stopped pacing.

Lucy waited with Leo, hoping this worked.

McMahon crossed the room and a few seconds later Leo's tactical phone rang. He hit RECORD then answered.

"This is Leo Proctor."

"Tell me about Paul."

"His wife filed a missing persons report. He didn't come home from work on Monday. He didn't fly anywhere, he hasn't used his credit cards."

"They killed him."

"Who killed Paul?"

"I don't know!"

"We'll figure this out together, Charlie. I promise, I will find Paul. Did you see Paul on Monday?"

"No. He didn't show up and I knew he was dead. They killed him and I can't remember!"

Lucy frowned. Was Charlie thinking today was Monday? Or had he planned on meeting his friend Monday? Or was this all in his head?

"Did you talk to Paul on Monday?" Leo asked.

"No one understands. Paul had answers, now he's dead. You're next. You're all next!"

"Charlie, you need to calm down," Leo said. He hadn't raised his voice, but Charlie was talking over him and Leo kept his tone even in order to calm the gunman down. Lucy tried to make out what Charlie was rambling about, but it sounded nonsensical.

"I'm listening, Charlie, but you can't talk that fast," Leo said. "Slow down, explain what happened. It's just you and me right now. I'm listening."

"If I tell you," Charlie whispered, "they'll kill you, too."

"Tell me what?"

"I don't remember! Paul knew, he was going to tell me, and now he's dead. I knew, but I don't know anymore. But I'm dying. I might already be dead. God, I can't think!"

"Charlie, let's talk face-to-face, okay?"

Lucy winced. That was the last thing that Young would let the negotiator do—go in face-to-face with the gunman. Not without knowing exactly what his goals were. Lucy had taken risks in the past—most cops did when lives were on the line—but they hadn't exhausted all other avenues yet. The wife was on her way, and often family could help calm a suspect down to the point of surrendering—especially when the suspect wasn't angry with the family.

"Let the hostages go and I'll come in," Leo said.

Young heard that and shook his head. Leo turned his back on the commander and said, "Charlie, can you hear me? Let the hostages go and you and I will sit down and talk."

Silence. Leo glanced at the line and nodded. Charlie hadn't hung up, but they couldn't tell whether he was still listening. The thermal imaging had him pacing, but the phone was no longer to his ear. Either he'd left it on the counter—live—or was holding it in his pocket.

"Paul's dead," Charlie said, his voice sounding distant. "Who did he talk to? Who killed him? They did. They can get to anyone. No one is that powerful. They are!"

Charlie was having a conversation with himself. Leo glanced at Lucy and whispered, "Is he schizophrenic?"

She shrugged and shook her head. She didn't think he was; schizophrenia didn't spontaneously show up one day in a forty-six-year-old man. But there could have been early signs that no one picked up on. "Doubtful."

"Drugs?"

"Maybe. But I couldn't begin to tell you what. Honestly, based on the very limited information we have I don't think we can make any assessment on this. But everything he's done so far makes me think he has an undiagnosed mental illness or possibly a brain tumor. There's also the real possibility that something happened with his missing friend and that he hasn't processed that information. Nearly all of his conversation is about Paul Grey, directly or indirectly."

Leo glanced at the thermal screen, then nodded. "He's agitated, speaks clearly but isn't making sense—at least to us. It's like he's having a partial conversation. The talking-to-himself part is beginning to worry me."

"Is he going to hurt anyone?" Young asked. "Because right now, he sounds stressed and he has fifteen innocent people and more than enough bullets to kill everyone."

"I don't know," Leo said, a sliver of frustration shining through his voice. He took a deep breath. "He has no history of violence until two months ago with the break-in at his former employer. If Kincaid's theory is accurate, and he has a tumor or a mental illness, we can't predict his behavior—he could put down his guns and walk out, or he could shoot someone. Based on what he's said, I don't think he *wants* to hurt anyone—but I would be concerned he'll take his own life."

"I can't trust that he won't hurt an innocent in the process."

"I need to try again."

"Do it, but the first sign that he's crossed the line, we're breaching." He stepped aside and put his SWAT team on alert.

Leo closed his eyes. He tried talking into the phone. The line was still open, but they couldn't hear anything except some movement and Charlie's faint voice.

Leo said into the bullhorn, "Charlie, you put down the phone. I can't hear you. Please pick up the phone again, we need to talk. I have an idea where we can all walk out of this situation. But we have to talk."

To Young's assistant, Leo said, "Wife?"

"ETA ten minutes."

"Shit," Leo muttered. He then said in the bullhorn, "Charlie, Lisa is almost here, and I think you should talk to her."

Charlie picked up the phone. "She'll never forgive me."

"Love is powerful, Charlie. I talked to her only a few minutes ago. She loves you, she wants to talk to you."

"Tell her I love her and I'm sorry. They did this to me. I just don't know how! I don't remember why! I need to remember, but it's gone. Everything's gone."

"You need to tell her you love her," Leo said. "She wants to hear it from you, Charlie."

"Someone here is with them." Charlie's voice took on a low, conspiratorial tone. "I don't know who it is, but they're everywhere. There's here. They're inside. They're watching me. They're watching you. We have to stop them. I have to stop them."

"Charlie, please show good faith. Release some of the hostages, it'll—"

But he'd already hung up.

Young said, "I don't like his state of mind, Leo. You did everything you could." In his com he said, "On my command, execute Plan Delta. The gunman is alone in the northwest corner of the building—you have his description and photo. All hostages are prone on the ground, except one who is three feet to the gunman's left, sitting. On three, two, one—go, go go!"

Leo stared, his face twisted in a sharp sense of failure. Lucy stepped close to him, put her hand on his arm, and together they watched the body-cam feed from each of the team leaders. Two teams of six, one from the front and one from the rear, breached the coffee shop.

The hostages began to scream. Through the jerky body cams, Lucy saw hostages down on the floor and Charlie McMahon standing at the counter, his hands on his head, each hand holding a small firearm aimed at the ceiling. SWAT identified themselves, ordered him to drop his weapons. Instead, Charlie turned and aimed the guns toward the SWAT team who entered the rear. He fired one gun directly at the team leader, the small-weapon retort distinct. Before the echo subsided, several rifle shots were fired from three different SWAT team members, including the team leader. All three appeared to hit their target.

McMahon went down.

The team leader secured McMahon's weapons while the rest of the teams swept the room for more hostiles, then quickly brought out the hostages. Two men stayed with the body.

"Clear."

"Clear."

"Clear."

"Suspect down, hostages are free. I repeat, suspect is down and no hostages are injured."

Young nodded once.

Leo turned and walked back to the FBI tactical truck. Lucy almost followed—he looked shell-shocked. Yancey shook his head. "Let him be."

"He did everything he could," Lucy said.

Yancey nodded. "Proctor has been the lead hostage negotiator for ten years, I've been here nearly as long. This is only the second time he couldn't talk the guy down. He needs to be alone for a few."

Resisting the urge to sit with him, Lucy turned back to the scene in front of her. Fifteen men and women—including a mother with a toddler, and several teenagers—were escorted from the building and to safety.

It could have gone very, very wrong. And while Charlie McMahon made his choice when he took the hostages, she couldn't help but feel sorry for the man, who had clearly been suffering.

A faint cry from behind her had Lucy turning. She saw a woman faint into the arms of a man in a sheriff's uniform.

Lisa McMahon. Charlie's widow.

CHAPTER THREE

Cassidy Roth turned and walked back to her car, ignoring the commotion around her. Tears burned behind her eyes.

She'd failed her friend and mentor.

Charlie had been the only person she could really talk to. Not about personal stuff, but work. He didn't find her off-putting as so many people did because she didn't know what to say or do in social situations. He didn't find her weird or too smart like most of the guys she'd known in high school. By the time she got to college, she wasn't interested in talking to her peers at all. She really only connected with people in the biochem department.

She walked several blocks to her car sweating in the heat and humidity, because the police had blocked off all the streets leading to Java Antonio. When she got to her car, she left the area and found herself stuck in traffic because of all the police detours. It took her several minutes to break free, and then she was on her way to Charlie's apartment.

She hadn't been able to save him, but she would prove—somehow—that he'd been murdered.

And not by the police. They may have pulled the trigger, but someone else set Charlie up.

She called the only person she trusted.

"Yep," he answered.

"Adam, it's Cassidy."

"Hey, Cass, what's up?"

"I need your help. And I might need to use your lab." Though she had no idea where she was going to get Charlie's blood. She could get his hair follicles. Maybe that would be the way to go. And she had his writings. She had always been the smartest person in school, but she hadn't been able to make sense of the code Charlie seemed to be writing in. But between her and Adam they could figure it out.

She wished she had asked him sooner, but Charlie was so paranoid he wouldn't let her talk to anyone. And the one person she'd reached out to on her own was now dead.

"What's wrong?" Adam sounded concerned.

"It's a long story, Adam. I'll tell you everything on one condition. You can't go to the police."

"Are you in trouble?"

"No. But the police can't do anything. This is a situation where they think the case is solved. I have to find something to convince them that Charlie was poisoned."

"Whoa, go back, I have no idea what you're talking about. Dr. McMahon? Your boss?"

"Yes. He was murdered and I need your help to prove it."

CHAPTER FOUR

One hundred and twenty-six minutes after Charles McMahon took fifteen patrons and employees of Java Antonio hostage, the situation was resolved with the gunman dead and no major injuries to law enforcement or civilians. It was a win–win as far as law enforcement was concerned, but Lucy couldn't help but feel sad for what McMahon had been going through that led him to such a desperate act. Normally she didn't have a lot of compassion for people who took their ill fortune out on the innocent. But it was clear that something else had been going on in McMahon's head, and she hoped they could figure out what it was.

Lieutenant Young coordinated the aftermath of the SWAT takedown. He segregated the hostages into groups, had a paramedic look at each one, had his officers collect names, addresses, and photos of each hostage for the records, and take preliminary notes. SAPD crime scene techs went into the coffee shop to process the evidence. The body was guarded until the coroner arrived to take custody. A media information officer was already on scene to answer press questions, and two counselors as well as clergy were available to the hostages.

A thorough investigation was just beginning, which would include interviewing each witness for a formal statement in order to re-create the events prior to law enforcement involvement. Detectives would be assigned to talk to everyone in McMahon's life, search his residence, vehicle, storage lockers, computers, and phone, analyze his finances, and more.

Especially in a case like this where there was no known motive, the gunman may have said or done something that could give them information on this situation, as well as help them in future armed conflicts. He may have left a note at home. There could be internet browser history that might give them information as to what he had been thinking when he fired a gun in a public coffee shop. They might never know why, but they would do everything they could to uncover the truth.

Though this was an SAPD case, most high-profile crimes were handled by a joint task force. With diminishing law enforcement funding, many FBI offices worked closely with local police departments to pool information and resources. Lieutenant Young was taking lead, and the first thing he did was pull Leo aside.

Lucy didn't know what they were talking about, but it was a quietly intense conversation that lasted several minutes. Then they parted and Leo walked away from everyone. Yancey and Lucy focused on downloading the tactical videos for analysis. In a situation like this, deadly force wouldn't be questioned, but every officer-involved shooting was investigated fully. That meant talking to all SWAT members, and hostages, as well as reviewing the body-cam video and any verbal communications. All that was handled administratively. Each officer or agent who fired a weapon would have to surrender it, be put on mandatory leave for a minimum of three days, and be debriefed and cleared for duty by a medical professional, usually a psychologist.

Several minutes later Lieutenant Young came over to Lucy. "I tried to get your boss to walk away and let me handle the investigation, but he's stubborn. He talked to ASAC Durant and she cleared him to work on the joint task force. You and"—Young looked at his notes—"Lopez?"

"Yes, sir, Jason Lopez."

"You two are also assigned to the task force for the duration, and Yancey, if you can be available for any tech issues that may arise when admin reviews the video and transcripts. Plus, we need a write-up and analysis of the thermal imaging program. You know the drill."

"Yes, sir."

"Three officers took shots, one was yours—Dunning. They've all been relieved for the next three days pending debrief and psych eval. But tell Dunning it was a righteous kill, we don't have anything to feel bad about here. Other than the shooter, no one is hurt. That's a win."

"You've known Leo a lot longer than I have," Lucy said, "but I think he can handle this. He probably wants to find the answers—the why—to what happened with McMahon."

"He's tough, and I told him we had no other choice. The guy was unhinged. But the plan was not to fire unless he turned his weapons on us. My guys are good—they would have held off. But you saw the feed."

She nodded. "McMahon aimed two guns at the lead team member and fired one. He had no choice."

Young listened in his earpiece, said something into his radio she couldn't make out, then turned back to Lucy. "My people are interviewing all the witnesses," Young said, "with Detectives Tia Mancini and Keith Hastings taking point. All reports will go through them so we can coordinate our investigation. Lopez is with them. I don't know when we'll be done here—it could take the rest of the day. You talked to the wife—did she give an official statement?"

Lucy shook her head. "She asked for a couple of minutes to pull herself together. Her sister-in-law is getting her kids from summer camp, and until she knows they're home safe I don't think she's going to be much help. But we need to formally interview her—and if I may, possibly take over the Paul Grey missing persons case from the sheriff. It may have been the trigger."

"I've already talked to the sheriff, it's ours. FBI can take lead."

Leo returned to the group, and Young asked, "Are you sure you want to do this—McMahon could have killed Grey and blocked it out, or was playing us. You don't have to be part of the investigation."

"I'm in, Jordan, don't push."

"Just trying again. You want to take the wife?"

Leo nodded. "I just spoke to her brother, Travis County Deputy Trevor Olsen. She's talking to her kids now, but she wants to talk to us. Olsen suggested later—at his place—but I want to do it now, then follow up tomorrow. We need a clear direction here, and she might know something she doesn't realize. The guy was in distress and we owe it to him, to the hostages, and to his family to figure out what brought him to this point."

"Agreed. My people will handle the hostages; you handle the family and the Paul Grey disappearance. Tomorrow morning at oh-eight-hundred everyone on the task force will meet at SAPD to debrief and for follow-ups. Agreed?"

"Thanks, Jordan. I appreciate it."

Young put his hand on Leo's shoulder. "I meant what I said, Leo. You did everything you could to save that guy. I'm sorry it went south."

Leo nodded at his friend, and when Young left, Leo hit the side of the truck. "Lucy, find out about the autopsy. You have a good rapport with the ME's office, right?"

"Yes, Julie's a friend." As much as the prickly Julie Peters could be a friend to anyone. She was the deputy medical examiner.

"She's good, right?"

"The best."

"Okay—see if you can get her on it. Something was going on physically with that guy. Maybe mental, but a good ME can see that in the brain, right?"

"Possibly—they should be able to identify a tumor, or chemical imbalance."

"I asked Mrs. McMahon's brother to call me when she's ready to talk, and I'd like you to sit in. You're a psychologist, you might pick up on something that I don't. So be ready."

Lucy left Leo and Yancey at the tactical truck and walked over to where the hostages were being interviewed in a restaurant. Jason Lopez was talking to two teenage girls, but when he saw Lucy he wrapped up the conversation and approached her.

"Clusterfuck," he muttered.

"Did you expect anything else?"

"Those two girls—Cindy Oberman and April Forsyth—they're fifteen. Both were supposed to be in summer school today for flunking geometry, but ditched. Don't think they'll do that again. Anyway, they were sitting at the table next to McMahon and each had a different statement."

"You took them separately or together?"

"Together—Mancini said not to split them up because they were scared and we didn't want to further terrorize them. They're minors, their parents have been called, but that was a situation in and of itself. Both with divorced parents, everyone works, no one can get here for an hour, a lot of family stress. I'm going to follow up again with them tomorrow, though, because it doesn't make sense."

"What specifically did they disagree about?"

"Cindy—the blonde—said McMahon was talking to himself, she thought he was a homeless guy who panhandled enough for coffee. 'Off his meds,' she said. April, the brunette, said he was clearly not homeless, his clothes were too clean."

"Observant."

"Yeah, except she insisted that he *wasn't* talking to himself, he was having a conversation with someone else. Which doesn't make sense because no other witness said he was talking to anyone, but several said he was muttering to himself."

"Who?"

"She didn't see his face. A guy was looking at a display, but she said he was listening to McMahon and said something to him, but she couldn't hear what."

"Get a description?"

"Nope. Just a guy in a suit, old like her dad."

"How old is her dad?"

"Forty-six. But I've interviewed enough teenagers to know that he could be anywhere from thirty to sixty."

"But he would have to be in there, right?" She gestured toward the witness staging area.

"I asked her to point him out, and she said he wasn't here."

"Have any of the hostages been released?"

"Yes, but at the time I was talking to the girls, only the mother with her kids had been released. Mancini talked to her, she wasn't much help." He flipped through his notes. "We have identified eight individuals who fled prior to the doors being locked. Names, numbers, et cetera. He could have left with them; maybe he went to the police station or his car. We'll track him down."

"Are there security cameras in there?"

"Nope. But SAPD is canvassing the businesses in the area. Some have security feeds, we should be able to put together a series of events. If the guy left we'll find him."

Tia Mancini motioned for Jason, and he said to Lucy, "We'll be here all day, so I probably won't see you until the morning briefing. And thank Sean again for the Fourth of July barbecue. My son had a blast with Jesse."

"We were glad you could make it."

"Bobbie said when she gets the house in order, she'll reciprocate. I can't tell you how happy I am to have my family finally here."

"Family is why we do all this," Lucy said. "I enjoyed meeting Bobbie and the kids."

When Jason transferred from Phoenix to San Antonio six months ago, his wife didn't want to take the kids out of school in the middle of the year, plus they needed to sell their house. It had been hard on them, and while Lucy's initial working relationship with Jason had been strained, they'd developed a mutual respect. Sean hooked Jason up with a terrific real estate agent who helped make the relocation easier for the Lopez family. Bobbie and his two kids moved a month ago.

The barbecue on Saturday had been an easy way to introduce Sean's son Jesse to their friends. Most people didn't know Sean had a thirteen-year-old son—Sean himself hadn't known about Jesse until last year. Their relationship was short-lived because Jesse, his mother, and his stepfather had been put into witness protection, but a recent threat assessment indicated that the danger was low because those threatening the Spade family were dead. Jesse's mother agreed that Sean could have visitation rights, and Jesse was spending most of the summer in San Antonio.

Jason headed over to regroup with Tia Mancini,

and Lucy went back outside. She saw the coroner's van and looked around for which deputy coroner was scheduled. She was pleased to see Julie Peters.

She approached and said, "I'm glad you're the one taking lead on this."

"You want in?"

"I have a debriefing at eight, what time will you start?"

"Don't know yet—I have to move some bodies around, but SAPD says this is a priority. Sometime tomorrow morning. And I know what you need—full tox, complete autopsy. No stone unturned, yada yada. I'll put in a call to the hot doc."

"Excuse me?"

Julie grinned. "Dr. Dominic Moreno. Even his name is sexy."

"And he is what? An ME?"

"No, a brain surgeon. Literally—he's a neurosurgeon. He works out of the university medical center, transferred at the beginning of the year from Johns Hopkins to head up the department here. He's absolutely the finest specimen of male anatomy I've ever seen in my life."

"Ask him out."

"I did. He's gay."

Lucy laughed, then quickly covered her mouth. Not appropriate here.

"But he's so nice to look at, I really don't care. And brilliant. He's assisted me a couple of times when I found a brain anomaly, and since it's a research hospital, he's more than happy to help. I'll give him a heads-up and ask for an assist."

"If he does, I'll shoot him the audio files of Proctor's conversation with McMahon. It might help, from a neurological standpoint."

"I'll let you know either way. I'm outta here. It's too friggin' hot to stand around, and the body is only going to get riper. Sorry I couldn't make the party at your place this weekend. Truly, I thought about it, but people—living people, that is—make me break out in hives. I'm just not much for large groups."

Lucy could relate. While she didn't dislike groups—growing up as the youngest of seven kids, she couldn't avoid them—she was always exhausted after a big event like the party. She'd slept in on Sunday and then was lazy for the rest of the day—a rarity for her.

"Sometime you'll have to come over, just you, me, and Sean."

"That I'd enjoy," she said with a sincere grin and secured the back of the van, then she and her assistant climbed into the cab and drove off.

Lucy spotted Nate Dunning, her friend and colleague, leaning against the FBI tactical van. He looked angry—and for Nate, that was saying something. He rarely showed emotion.

She walked over to Nate. "How are you?"

"I did the job, Luce."

"I know."

"Be my friend, not my shrink."

"I am."

"Mandatory leave is bullshit."

"Agreed." Most of the time. "You took the shot on

orders, because you had to. I get it. It's only three days," she reminded him.

"I need to be in the field. I'm worried about Leo and want to be part of his team, but I'm going to be sitting around doing shit and talking to fucking shrinks."

"I'm on the task force, Nate. I'll keep an eye on him. I listened to every word of their conversation. Leo did everything he could to end this without gunfire. Something was going on with McMahon. I'm hopeful that the autopsy will give us answers."

"We couldn't have done anything different," Nate said.

"I agree. And if you need me—as a friend, either me or Sean—we're here for you."

He nodded, but he wasn't smiling. "Thanks, Luce."

CHAPTER FIVE

Yancey and one of the SAPD tech guys had collected all the raw security footage from every building in the area to create a viable time line for each hostage entering the facility, when McMahon arrived, and people who left after he arrived, up until he had the doors locked. Some of the images were clear, others fuzzy, depending on the quality of the security camera and where it was focused.

She watched over Yancey's shoulder as they fed the data into a program that would clean it up as much as possible. Unfortunately, some of the feeds were so bad they wouldn't be useful.

"This is going to take time," Yancey said.

She knew that, but she was always interested in the process.

Fortunately, Leo popped his head into the back of the tactical truck. "Lucy, Lisa McMahon and her brother are ready to talk."

Lucy walked with Leo halfway down the block to a

real estate office that had opened its conference rooms to law enforcement for interviews. Most of the witnesses were at the restaurant, but this afforded more privacy for Charlie McMahon's widow.

Lisa and her brother, Deputy Trevor Olsen, sat close together on one side of a table that could sit eight. Lucy and Leo introduced themselves and sat across from them.

"I think I can hold it together," Lisa said. She tightly held her brother's hand. "My sister-in-law has the kids, I just talked to them. They'd already heard on the news—not that it was their father, but what happened." Tears leaked out and Trevor handed her another tissue to go with the stack of used tissues next to her.

"We won't keep you long," Leo said. "I know you want to be with your family. But it's important to get your immediate thoughts, and then Agent Kincaid and I will follow up in a day or two to see if you remember anything else. I was the one talking to your husband, trying to negotiate a peaceful resolution. I'm really sorry I couldn't convince him to put down his guns."

"None of this makes sense to me. This isn't Charlie. It just isn't."

"When we talked earlier, you said you left him in April and shortly thereafter he lost his job. You said he'd changed, had become belligerent and violent."

"Not violent—he never hit me or the kids. He just—he wasn't himself. He yelled, was short-tempered, complained that he had a headache—I thought he might have migraines, wanted him to see the doctor, but he said it wasn't a migraine. He stopped talking to me about his work, about the kids, he was so . . . distant, I guess I'd say, when he was home."

"When did this start? April?"

"Early March, but it wasn't too bad. It was shortly after Easter—that was the first week of April—when I really noticed that something was wrong."

Trevor spoke up for the first time. "We were all over at Lisa's house for a meal. Charlie isn't close to his family, and it's just Lisa and me and her kids and my wife and our daughter. Lisa and I have always been close. Charlie didn't talk. He stared at a baseball game—he doesn't even like sports—and then went to bed before dinner. No explanation."

"I went upstairs to talk to him," Lisa said, "and he was sitting on the bed staring at the wall. He said he wasn't feeling well, but I knew it was something else. I didn't push then, told everyone he had a bug, but he just never got better. He would get up before me and go to work, and usually didn't get home until after midnight. I don't think he was sleeping much. When I tried to talk to him, he would snap at me. He was moody, but it was like a perpetual bad mood that sometimes was worse."

"What happened that led you to leave?"

"I gave him an ultimatum. That he tell me what was going on, why he was acting this way, or I was leaving. He yelled at me. I thought he was going to hit me—he didn't—but I had never seen him so angry. And he wasn't angry at me. He was angry at himself. He said he lost something important, began to tear the house apart and couldn't find it, but he wouldn't tell me *what* he'd lost. I said I'd help him find it, but he just . . . well, he'd cut me out of everything for weeks before this, but this was completely different and he scared me. I left with the kids."

"Have you seen him since?" Leo asked. "Talked to him?"

"At first, no—I didn't want to talk to him. But Trevor convinced me to go see him. We both went over to the house."

She glanced at her brother. He squeezed her hand in support.

"I mediated between them," Trevor said. He wasn't as emotional as his sister, he was doing his best to keep his cop face, but his eyes were rimmed in red and he was holding back his conflicted feelings. "We sat down and tried to work through what was going on. Lisa loves Charlie—I love Charlie. My daughter, she's only six, worshipped him. He was so great with kids. We came up with a plan to have Charlie for dinner, to figure out what was going on, and he thought he might need to see a doctor because he was having lapses in memory. At the time, he seemed remorseful, like he really wanted to figure out why he was having mood swings and forgetfulness. But he said he didn't want Lisa to move back, not until he figured out what was wrong."

"I was so hopeful," Lisa said. "I told him I wanted to come back, and I would be right there with him, no matter what it was. Then everything changed a week later—the first week of May. He was fired. I saw him after, reminded him that he was going to see his doctor, and he told me it was a trap. That made no sense. Then he said he couldn't see me or the kids, told me to stay away from him. And I . . . I didn't know what to do. I thought he was staying in the house, but I started getting late notices and realized he wasn't paying the bills. I took over all the bills then. Once, at the end of May, I went to the house, and there was rotting food in the refrigerator and I wondered—feared—that he was dead. I called his cell phone and it had been disconnected. I called Paul, and Paul said he'd track him down and find out what was going on."

"Paul Grey? You said he was a friend?"

She nodded. "Charlie and Paul were friends from college. They'd worked on a major research project together in grad school. They kept in touch, and when Clarke-Harrison expanded, Charlie brought Paul on and Paul and his family relocated from Los Angeles."

"What did they do for CHR?" Leo asked.

"Charlie is a neurologist, Paul a biochemist. They worked on Alzheimer's research. Did I hear that Paul is missing?"

"His wife filed a missing persons report yesterday," Leo said. "Were you aware that your husband was arrested for assault a week or two ago? He was released on bail. He assaulted Paul, but it was the bartender who pressed charges."

It was clear Lisa knew nothing about it. But Trevor did.

"I didn't want to tell you," he said to his sister.

She looked confused. "Why would Charlie hit Paul? They were friends. Colleagues. It doesn't make sense!"

"That's what we want to find out," Leo said. "What else do you know about your husband's work?"

"Not much. Charlie has been involved in Alzheimer's

research most of his career. He believed that in his lifetime he would find a cure. His grandmother was diagnosed when he was a teenager, she lived with his family until she died. It was really rough on everyone, especially the last couple of years. The only person in his family Charlie was close to was his grandmother, and then to lose her like that . . . Charlie wanted to make a difference—he *has* made a difference." Her voice trailed off and she looked away, her face clouded.

"Lisa," Lucy said quietly, "I know this is difficult for you. You need to focus on who your husband was, remind your children who he was before all this happened. But right now, we want to help you find answers, and the only way we can do that is to figure out what changed in March. Was he working on anything specific?"

"I wouldn't know. He used to talk to me about his work, but I didn't really understand what he was saying. I listened because he was excited. Until he just stopped talking about anything."

"Do you know why he was fired?" Leo asked.

"He wouldn't tell me. I asked Paul . . . he said he couldn't tell me because of a nondisclosure statement he'd signed. I got so mad at him—this is Charlie, his friend. I was so worried about Charlie—and mad. Mad at my husband because I didn't understand."

"There's no record of your husband having any history of mental illness?" Leo asked.

"None. Charlie has always been the most even-tempered person I know," Lisa said. "In fact, until April he never raised his voice, we never went to bed angry with each other, and we were happy. And now—my husband is dead, everyone thinks he's a bad person. And he wasn't. I want to know why this all happened."

"So do we, Mrs. McMahon," Leo said.

When Lisa and Trevor left, Leo and Lucy sat in the conference room. "Do you know anything about Clarke-Harrison Research?" Leo asked.

She shook her head. "I'll ask Zach to research them, but we should talk to McMahon's supervisor as soon as possible about both McMahon and Paul Grey's disappearance."

Leo glanced at his watch. "It's nearly five. We'll go over there after the debriefing tomorrow once we have more information about Grey. Are you up for talking to his wife tonight?"

"Better now than later."

"What do you make of all this?" Leo asked Lucy as they left the office and walked back to the staging area. Most law enforcement were gone; only a few officers and the forensics unit remained. "Three months ago Charlie McMahon was a normal, happy professional with a wife and two kids. He spiraled down to a paranoid hostage-taker."

"We need to search his house," Lucy said. "There may be evidence that will help us figure out what he was thinking."

"Let's do it now, since Grey's wife lives in the same area. I'll talk to the lieutenant and tell him what we're doing, he may have already sent a team to McMahon's. But I know how this is going to work—no one, other than McMahon, was killed or seriously injured. Young will want us to do due diligence, but this isn't going to be a priority."

"Meaning, do just enough to close the case."

"Exactly. We need to be prepared to dig in our heels, even though this isn't an official FBI investigation and we're here at the pleasure of SAPD. I'll work over Jordan—I've known him for years, I can convince him not to rubber-stamp the investigation. But he's going to want something tangible to justify spending time and resources. We'll have a day or three to put it together, because that's how long it'll take to process the statements and get the coroner's report, but we might need more time."

"My gut impression, based on what Mrs. McMahon said and what McMahon said to you, is that he was seriously paranoid, possibly drug-induced paranoia or some sort of neurological disorder. I talked to Julie Peters, and she's bringing in a neurosurgeon to assist with the autopsy. Maybe that will give us the answers we need. Except for what happened to Paul Grey."

CHAPTER SIX

Sean Rogan had never been as happy and content as he'd been the last three weeks.

He was finally getting to know his son.

For nearly a year Jesse had been in witness protection with his mother and stepfather. On June 1 the US Marshals determined that the threat to the family had diminished. While they might never be 100 percent safe because of Carson Spade's criminal activities and then his turning state's evidence, everyone he had worked for was now dead.

Carson avoided jail because he agreed to work with the DEA and FBI to show them how he had used banking laws and shell corporations to launder money for a drug cartel. His knowledge was vast and would help law enforcement develop the skills and tools to go after other criminals. One of Sean's close friends, ASAC Dean Hooper of the Sacramento FBI, was working directly with Carson, and the terms of his deal required the family to relocate into Hooper's jurisdiction.

Sean was from Sacramento, and his brother Duke still lived there. Rogan-Caruso-Kincaid main headquarters was located in Sacramento, and it was an easy flight. Though Sean's ex-girlfriend Madison had lied to him about Jesse, then tried to thwart Sean from seeing him, she'd finally come around. From guilt, Sean figured, for lying to him about something so important. Sean could visit Jesse whenever he wanted in Sacramento with twenty-four-hour notice, and she agreed to let Jesse stay with Sean for six weeks this summer. Sean flew to Sacramento to pick him up after Jesse's thirteenth birthday.

They were now in the middle of those six weeks, Lucy was finally home from training, and Sean felt like he was on top of the world. So even though Lucy called to say she'd be late, Sean didn't mind. He and Jesse sat back down to play more video games. In this heat there wasn't much else to do, though Jesse could spend just as much time in the pool as playing games.

"You beat me again," Jesse said, frustrated that he'd never beaten Sean at *Halo Reach*.

"I'm the best."

Jesse frowned.

"Would you rather I let you win?"

"No, but—"

"You're getting better. It took me two minutes to beat you the first time, and today it took me nineteen."

"I'll never win."

"You'll go home and beat all your friends. Isn't that good?"

Sean didn't believe in letting a kid win just because

he was frustrated, but he also didn't want to kill Jesse's spirit or excitement for games.

"Yeah. I guess I'll have to settle."

"You never *have* to settle. I've been playing video games for longer than you've been alive. I designed a couple games. Maybe tomorrow we can check out some new games—something neither of us has played—and we'll start off on equal footing."

"Really? That might be fun."

"Hungry? I'm starving." Sean looked at his watch. Eight o'clock and Lucy wasn't home. After the intense hostage situation and subsequent takedown of McMahon, he hadn't expected her to leave work on time, but it was getting late. He sent her a text message.

"Can we go to that barbecue place again? The Rib House?"

"My favorite. We'll go pick it up. We don't have to wait for Lucy—she doesn't know what time she'll be back—but I'll get plenty. And there's nothing I love more than leftovers for breakfast."

Sean whistled for Bandit, who was sleeping on the dog bed in the game room where they were playing. The golden retriever immediately came to him, alert and eager. Sean scratched him behind the ears. He liked bringing Bandit with him when he went out—he'd given Lucy his Mustang because Bandit's claws would damage the leather seats, and he'd bought a Jeep Wrangler with durable seats that wouldn't be easily destroyed by the eighty-pound dog. He'd spent months training Bandit after they adopted him in November while on their honeymoon, and while Bandit was still learning—it was hard to break him out of eighteen months of no training whatsoever—he had made great strides. Sean was taking him to a tactical training class to learn how to search and rescue. Bandit was a natural, and Sean enjoyed working with him. He wasn't ready to go out on an assignment, but the instructor was confident by the end of the summer Bandit would be prepared.

But it was too hot to leave Bandit in the car, even with the windows down, so Sean closed him in the sunroom, which was off the laundry room. Sean had wanted to give him the run of the house, but he was still a puppy in many ways and when he was bored he chewed shoes, paper, belts—anything he could find. The sunroom was dogproof, and fortunately Bandit didn't chew furniture.

Sean's phone vibrated with a message. He glanced down. Michael Rodriguez, one of the boys at St. Catherine's Boys' Home, asked if he was coming over this weekend.

Some of us were wondering if you were going to come by this weekend, since you haven't been around in a while. Are you still out of town? Too busy?

Sean felt bad—he usually went over to the boys' home once a week to talk to them, help with homework, or just have dinner. But with Jesse in town, he hadn't really thought about it. What kind of benefactor did that make him?

"Is something wrong?" Jesse asked.

"Nope, nothing. Just a friend of mine wanting us to come over this weekend."

"Are we?"

"Maybe." Sean responded to Michael that he'd get

over there soon. He didn't want to make a promise he couldn't keep, so didn't give a specific day or time. Maybe he should bring Jesse over there, introduce him to the boys.

They left, and Jesse chatted while Sean drove. Sean couldn't have been happier. He'd always been focused on his own entertainment—video games, driving cool cars, taking risks, flying planes. Before Lucy, he'd dated a lot of women as well. But he'd never been truly *happy*, he realized, until the last two years. Falling in love could do that, but it wasn't just Lucy. It was a contentment that he'd never had before. A sense of security. That even though he hadn't raised Jesse for the first thirteen years of his son's life, they were okay—they'd already gotten over the hard part.

He'd also had three weeks of just him and Jesse while Lucy was training at Quantico. That time really helped them both adjust to the changes in their lives. Since Lucy had been back, Sean realized he'd been unjustifiably nervous. He wanted time with Lucy, but didn't want Jesse to think that he didn't want him in the house. And while Jesse had of course met Lucy, they hadn't spent enough time to really get to know each other. What would Jesse think of her? Would he think she was trying to replace his mother? Would Lucy feel left out?

All Sean's fears were unfounded. The transition was seamless. Lucy didn't play video games (well, she had tried after they started dating, but she didn't enjoy it like he did), but she was a whiz at board games and they'd developed a very comfortable habit of playing games after she got home from work. And on Saturday, they had a big Fourth of July party at the house—the first party since their wedding reception—and it had gone smoothly. Jesse had befriended a couple of kids in the neighborhood, and Sean let him go to the park with them.

Sean didn't tell Jesse that he kept his eye on him at the park. Jesse was old enough to go out on his own, but Sean was still concerned about the people Carson Spade had turned against. They might all be dead and buried, but there could be others they didn't know about. Or someone who thought Carson had more information or money that would benefit them. Diligence would keep everyone safe.

Sean didn't want to return Jesse to Sacramento in three weeks. Less than three weeks, really—two weeks from the coming Sunday. Eighteen days.

He was going to miss his kid. It didn't seem fair, because he'd missed most of the first thirteen years of his life through no fault of his own. But Madison hadn't put Sean on the birth certificate, which complicated things, and he supposed that he was grateful that she'd agreed to give him liberal visitation rights and have him legally declared Jesse's biological father. He didn't want to push it and ask for more time.

Sean had set up a trust fund for Jesse with what he would have paid in child support for thirteen years. He wasn't giving a dime to Madison—she didn't need it, her family was well off, and she'd never told him about Jesse until she was forced to—but he wasn't going to shirk on his financial responsibilities to his son. Jesse would be able to access the money when he graduated from high school. And for the next five years, Sean would continue to pay into the trust. It'd be more than enough to get Jesse through college, or provide him with a cushion for virtually anything he wanted to do.

What the money wouldn't do, however, was make up for time lost. And the money Sean had put into the trust had drained almost all his accounts. He wasn't broke—he and Lucy owned two houses and he had a plane—but he wasn't fluid. He'd have to double down on jobs for RCK over the next couple of years to rebuild his savings—but he didn't mind. He liked working, and corporate and personal security was a good business.

They walked into the Rib House—a casual hole-in-the-wall restaurant that had the best BBQ Sean had found in the city—and ordered the largest family meal, two and a half pounds of meat and four sides. Sean was serious about wanting leftovers. They sat at a table while they waited.

"Dad, can I ask you something?"

Sean's stomach fluttered. Jesse had started calling him Dad more often than not, and every single time Sean felt goose bumps.

"Anything, you know that."

Jesse remained silent.

"Is something bothering you?"

"No—sort of. I want to change my name. To Jesse Rogan."

Nothing could have surprised Sean more, or made him happier. "Okay."

"So you're good with it?"

"I'm more than good." What could he say to Jesse?

He was ecstatic. Jesse was his kid—and Jesse was proud of it. Just like Sean was of Jesse. "You didn't think I'd be upset about it, did you?"

"No, but—well, I haven't told my mom yet. I looked on the internet about the rights of kids—kids don't have a lot of rights."

That was for certain. It had been a bone of contention between Sean and his brother Duke when Duke, as his guardian, made some decisions Sean didn't agree with that impacted Sean's life.

"Maybe if you talk to her you'll be surprised what she says."

"Maybe. But—well, I guess I don't want to hurt her feelings."

"I can respect that."

"But I don't want to wait until I'm eighteen—when I know I can do it without anyone's permission."

"So you want advice on how to talk to her?"

"I guess I wanted to make sure you were okay with it."

"I am *very* okay."

"And then—maybe you could be there when I tell her."

Sean didn't know how well that would go over. "If you think that would be easier. When I take you back to Sacramento, I can stay for a few days, no problem. But you need to think about it a little more. You don't want your mom to think that we're ganging up on her, or pressuring her." Sean didn't actually care—Madison had hurt him deeply, and his knee-jerk reaction was to hurt her back. But fortunately, he wasn't the brash, reactive man he used to be. He recognized that his son would look to him for guidance, emulate him in many ways. He wanted to be the best person he could be, even when he wanted to rub reality into Madison.

He frowned. "I didn't think about that."

"We don't have to make the decision right now. We have time. Just think about how you want to do it. You'll know what's the right choice. But Jesse? You could not have made me happier."

Sean knew he was being followed almost as soon as he left the Rib House.

There was little parking at the restaurant so he'd parked on the street around the corner. As soon as he turned onto Becerra, a dark sedan pulled out from the adjoining business. Normally Sean wouldn't think twice about it, except that this wasn't the best area of San Antonio, and the car was so shiny it was practically new. Still, the clincher was there was no front license plate—a no-no in the state of Texas.

Sean didn't normally run surveillance for RCK, but he was aware of the principles, and one of them was to avoid being identified by removing the front license plate.

It was also a tactic among criminals and stalkers.

That didn't mean the vehicle was following Sean. There could be a legitimate reason for not having a front plate. But Sean had learned to be cautious—and he wasn't going to take any chances with Jesse in the car.

He hopped onto the I-90 east in the direction he'd

take to go home. The sedan followed. Sean turned off at the next exit.

"Do we have another stop?" Jesse asked.

"I need gas. Should have done it on the way."

Sean pulled into a chain gas station and up to a pump. He did in fact get gas, though he had more than half a tank. As he watched, the sedan passed the station and was out of sight.

Still, Sean couldn't shake the feeling that he'd been followed.

He filled his tank and jumped back in the car. As soon as he merged onto the freeway, he spotted the sedan again—the same one, distinguishable only because of the missing plate.

Shit.

The windows were tinted and he couldn't make out the driver, but there were two people in the car, both large men. The passenger appeared black, the driver white or Hispanic.

Sean merged south on I-35 instead of north to go home. The sedan went south.

Shit shit shit.

"Hey, aren't we supposed to be going the other way? Or am I all turned around?" Jesse asked.

"You're right." He had promised Jesse early on that he would never lie to him, and he couldn't start now. "Don't look. We're being followed."

"Really?" Jesse almost looked, but stopped himself.

"I can lose them, they don't have a tag team." The best way to tail someone was with three vehicles. Two usually worked, but three was best. Either these guys were amateurs or they had targeted Sean to rob.

They picked the wrong mark.

Sean didn't know San Antonio as well as his hometown of Sacramento, but he'd lived here for a year and a half and had made a point to learn the streets and get a sense of his surroundings. He exited at SW Military and went east. The sedan followed. He kept his speed steady, but as he approached Roosevelt—where he knew there was a traffic camera—he slowed down, timing the light until it was about to turn yellow, then sped up and ran the yellow light.

Either they would stop at the red and Sean was free and clear, or they'd run it and Sean would beg, borrow, or steal the photo from SAPD.

They ran it.

If Jesse weren't in the car, Sean would engage rather than evade, but no way in hell was he putting his son in danger—especially since he had no idea *what* the danger was. He made a series of turns and then hit I-37 going north. Traffic was a bitch, the tail end of the peak commute hour, but Sean maneuvered better than the sedan and five minutes later he'd lost them.

Still, he wasn't taking chances. He continued north, then took I-10 west, and finally hit I-35 again.

No sign of the sedan, and there didn't appear to be a second car tailing him.

While he was relieved, he wasn't happy. He needed to figure out exactly what was going on. The first call would be to the US Marshals. They'd done a threat assessment that concluded the Spades were at low risk if they left WITSEC, but they refused to share the report with Sean.

He needed to see it. He considered that he might be able to sweet-talk his way into viewing it, but if not, he might have to hack into the marshals' database and retrieve it himself. But the marshals had some of the tightest cybersecurity of any government agency, and hacking them was a major felony. Sean didn't *think* he'd be caught, but he wasn't positive. He hadn't been a hacker in a long, long time.

But there was no way he was going to lose Jesse.

In the back of his mind, he wondered who he'd pissed off recently. He and Lucy had helped take down a human trafficking organization three months ago. If there was fallout from that, JT Caruso—the head of RCK—would be on top of it and give Sean a heads-up. Sean had taken a couple of security jobs, but they were all tech-related—increasing corporate security to prevent espionage. Nothing investigative. And he'd only taken one job—which he could do from home—since Jesse arrived three weeks ago.

There was also the issue that he looked like a younger version of his brother Kane, and Kane was always making the wrong people mad. Since Sean had been helping him out more, Kane had practically beat into him that he was at risk just because he was Kane's brother.

"Some idiots may think you're me, so always watch your back, kid."

But Kane had been keeping a low profile for the last year. He was living in a border town with his girlfriend—wow, that was something Sean hadn't thought would ever happen, since Kane was the epitome of the lone wolf—and was avoiding cartel entanglements. In fact, since Sean's wedding, he knew that Kane had only worked south of the border twice, both times to rescue ransomed tourists. Neither trip had been eventful.

The more Sean thought about it, the more he thought the tail was related to Jesse. But he wouldn't know for certain until he talked to the marshals.

"Dad?" Jesse sounded worried.

Sean glanced at him. "It's okay, we lost them."

"You look mad."

Sean tried to relax. "Just a little concerned. But you know that I would never let anything happen to you, right?"

"Right."

"So we're taking the scenic route back home." He was trying to make light of the tense situation, but he certainly wasn't taking it lightly.

He wouldn't, until he knew that his son wasn't in any danger.

CHAPTER SEVEN

Diane Grey wasn't home. Leo phoned her from outside the house, and she said she'd meet them in an hour, so Leo and Lucy drove to the McMahon house, which was less than a mile away.

The planned community meandered through the hills with two-story houses on large lots, though they seemed to repeat each other in style. An upscale division, Lucy guessed, and most of the homes were well maintained and on quiet streets. Definitely the suburbs, and seemed a good place to raise kids. Now that it was after six and the worst of the heat had passed, kids were playing in their yards, and the pools that they could see from the street were filled.

The McMahon house was on a cul-de-sac with several large trees helping shade the picture windows. The lawn had been mowed and hedges trimmed, but that was the extent of the work. "Did McMahon take care of his yard or did they have a service?" Lucy asked.

"I don't know. Would it matter?"

"If he was taking care of the house, his behavior would be even more odd. His wife said she came over a couple of times and the place was a mess, and she had to start paying the bills because he'd let them lapse. Mowing the lawn wouldn't fit with that behavior."

"I see your point."

Lisa McMahon had given them a key to the house and her permission to enter and search. They could have gotten a warrant just to cover themselves, but it wasn't necessary.

They first walked around the exterior, checking doors and windows for explosives or other booby traps. All the blinds were closed—not uncommon in Texas especially in the hot summer months when residents wanted to keep the house as cool as possible during the day.

There was no car in the garage—McMahon's vehicle, a Ford F-150, had been found parked at a meter two blocks from the coffeehouse. The McMahons also owned a Ford Explorer, which Lisa drove.

The house had an empty feel—no noise at all, no radios or air-conditioning unit or television running.

Leo said, "Proceed with caution, Kincaid. We clear the house room by room before we search."

She followed the SWAT leader's direction. He had her unlock the front door, and he kept his focus on any movement in the house. Nothing.

But as soon as she opened the door, she smelled death. She immediately drew her gun.

They cleared the living and dining room, then the

kitchen and family room. It was in the den they found the body.

"Well, shit," Leo said. "It's Paul Grey."

Paul Grey was long dead. He was on his back on the floor in the middle of the den that was clearly Charlie's home office—books on science, memory, Alzheimer's, textbooks, and more. Fiction ran to Michael Crichton and westerns. And Charlie's best friend, Paul Grey, was in front of his desk, as if they had been having a conversation and Charlie had shot him.

The house was hot, leaving him bloated. Though Lucy would have to inspect him to be certain—which she couldn't do before the crime scene team came in to process the house—she thought he was past rigor mortis, meaning he had likely been dead for longer than twenty-four hours.

She put on gloves, though had no intention of touching anything. She used a pencil to flip on the light switch, then visually inspected his body. Dried blood on his right temple and a larger, messier exit wound on his left indicated that he had been shot. But the blood on both sides appeared dry, and she looked all around the room. There was no blood spatter, and only a small amount on the floor beneath him.

"He wasn't killed here," she said. "At least, not in this room. There's hardly any blood."

"We need to clear the house and call it in," Leo said. "It's going to be a long night."

* * *

The FBI's Evidence Response Team arrived on scene. They were in the county, not the city of San Antonio, otherwise they would have had SAPD process the scene. But Leo didn't want yet a third jurisdiction—the sheriff's—in the middle of the investigation, so it was better to keep the evidence in house and share with SAPD.

Paul Grey hadn't been killed in the McMahon house. There was no visible blood in any other room or on the grounds, but no indication of how he'd been brought inside. Agents canvassed the neighborhood, and no neighbor claimed to have seen anything suspicious.

Lucy spoke to the next-door neighbor, a young stay-at-home mother of three children under six named Annie Greene.

"I'm shocked," Annie said. "Until Charlie lost his job, he was wonderful. He was out in the cul-de-sac every weekend with half a dozen kids playing baseball. Throwing with his son. For the Fourth of July every year we had a street party and Charlie is the one you always want around. He had a kind word to say about everyone, and he was funny. Kids especially loved him. This year we didn't even have a party because Charlie and Lisa always organized it."

"And after he lost his job?"

"When Lisa left he fell apart. Maybe before he wasn't himself—didn't say hi when he saw me, for example. Kind of in his own world, as if deep in thought. But when Lisa left—most of the time I didn't even see him."

Lucy didn't comment that Lisa left *before* Charlie lost his job. "When was the last time you saw him?"

"Weeks. Mid-June maybe? Austin—my son—finished kindergarten on June fifteenth, and it was a couple of days before then."

That surprised Lucy on the one hand—although, on the other, the house had an un-lived-in feeling. They'd found stale Chinese takeout in the refrigerator, and a receipt in the bag indicating it had been bought on June 12—four weeks ago. Had he not been here for four weeks? Where had he been living? Could the witness who thought he was homeless have been right? Maybe he was living out of his vehicle.

Lucy asked, "In the last two or three days, have you seen anyone at the house? A car in the driveway?"

She shook her head. "I'm here most of the time, I try to keep an eye on the street. We don't get a lot of traffic here. But I go to bed early—the kids wear me out. My husband doesn't get home until seven on most nights, so I get the kids to bed by eight and we have some quiet time, but I'm usually asleep before ten."

"Is your husband home?"

"No—he's out of town this week. Japan. He works for an oil company and travels a lot."

"When did he leave?"

"Sunday morning. He'll be back Saturday."

He wouldn't have been here when Paul Grey's body was dumped. They needed a better time line of Grey's day on Monday, but the likelihood was that he was killed after four thirty when he left work, but before Tuesday morning. But why would Charlie McMahon kill him—and then bring his body to his house? Maybe Charlie really did have a psychotic break.

Lucy thanked Annie for her time, then regrouped with Leo. "No one has seen him since a few days before June fifteenth, the witness isn't sure of the exact day."

Leo concurred. "The mail goes to a PO box and I talked to Lisa—she had it forwarded to a PO box in San Marcos in May when she learned Charlie had stopped paying bills. She also said that he hadn't accessed their joint bank account but has been living off his credit card—which she's paid off every month. She's going to bring the statements to headquarters tomorrow morning. It'll help us retrace his steps."

"And hopefully find out where he's been living. Because it certainly isn't here."

"Proctor!" Mike Jackson, the head of their Evidence Response Team, motioned for them to come over. Mike was tall and lean with dark skin and unusually attractive green eyes. He'd been in the San Antonio office for ten years, and had run the ERT for the last five. "I found out how the body came in. Oh, and while you were talking to the neighbors, the coroner arrived. You're right, Kincaid, he wasn't killed here—not enough blood. So I processed the garage—someone drove into the garage and brought the body in through the door that goes into the laundry room. There was some trace evidence on the doorframe and floor. The body had to have been partially carried and partially dragged—at least, that's my best guess based on the evidence we have."

"Carried? Or could one person have done the job?" Leo asked.

"I can't say. Grey was on the shorter side, but slightly heavy. One large person could carry him, I suppose, but he'd have been a deadweight. I'm leaning to two people, but I can't swear to that. He might have been dragged, but we'll have to wait for the autopsy. We'll print, of course, and finish processing, but I don't know what we're going to get. No smoking gun, that's for certain. But did you notice there's no computer?"

Lucy nodded.

"It wasn't taken recently—my guess is that it's been gone for weeks. There's dust on the desk. *But* there was no dust on the drawer handles. Someone went through them in the last couple of days."

"That's good, Mike," Proctor said. "Whatever you can get, let me know ASAP. And plan on being at the debriefing tomorrow at SAPD at oh-eight-hundred."

"So much for my beauty sleep," he said and went back inside.

"We need to tell Mrs. Grey," Leo said to Lucy.

She nodded. As they drove over, she asked, "Where's his car?"

"That's the million-dollar question."

CHAPTER EIGHT

Carson Spade hadn't actually *lied* to his wife Madison; at least he convinced himself it wasn't a lie. He *was* going to meet their mutual friend Jeremy Robertson for drinks. He just didn't tell her why. And it wasn't a complete lie that Jeremy was helping Carson find gainful employment. He wasn't allowed to work as an accountant or in any financial institution per the terms of his plea agreement with the Department of Justice. He'd also been disbarred and couldn't practice law. But he could work for a business as a consultant, as long as he didn't control any funds or have access to banking accounts, and Carson was smart. He and Jeremy had been talking for six weeks, ever since Carson left WITSEC and relocated to Sacramento.

Sacramento! Who on the planet wanted to live here? Not to mention there were Rogans and Rogan associates everywhere. But that was another term of his probation—that he had to work *for free* for the FBI analyzing money-laundering schemes and helping *them* do their job.

To say Carson was unhappy with the arrangement was an understatement. All because of that bastard Sean Rogan.

What Madison didn't know was that Jeremy Robertson had some friends who were less than squeaky-clean. And while Carson had lost nearly all his money when the FBI seized his bank accounts and assets, he had a few accounts here and there that they had never uncovered. True, if they found them his agreement would be null and void and he'd have to stand trial for his alleged crimes, but he wasn't overly worried about that. Because he *was* good at what he used to do for the drug cartel, and he'd used those skills to benefit himself.

He'd turned over one of his hidden accounts to Jeremy to help him with his Rogan problem.

And Jeremy was late. Which pissed Carson off. He was taking a risk meeting with Jeremy. What if the FBI was following him? They'd only been out of WITSEC for six weeks. What if they knew about the other accounts?

They don't. Not even Madison knows about most of the other accounts.

It burned him that he was living off Madison's money. He was supposed to provide for her and Jesse. He was supposed to be the man of the house. And he'd provided *very* well for years. Madison never complained, never asked where the money came from. Never concerned herself. And even when she found out, she wasn't overly interested . . . until Sean Rogan came back into her life.

You did it. You're the one who brought Jesse down

to Mexico. Madison only went to her ex because she was worried about her son.

But dammit, shouldn't she have been worried about *him*? Jesse wasn't in any real danger until Rogan and his people got involved.

What really bothered Carson, more than anything, was the disdain Jesse showed him. He'd raised the boy as his own, and now Jesse thought he was a pariah. And that feeling of Jesse's was rubbing off on Madison. When was the last time they'd had sex? A couple weeks ago? And Madison was barely into it, as if she was just going through the motions. She used to initiate sex, she used to have *fun* in bed with him. He remembered mornings when she'd roll over and take him in hand, get him horny, then do things he had only dreamed about before he met her. Now he had to suggest the idea and she seemed . . . resigned to accommodate him.

He wanted things back to the way they were before Sean Rogan ruined everything. And if he could get Rogan out of the picture, he could fix his marriage. They had a vacation house in Hawaii. One of the smartest things Carson had done was put most of their property in Madison's name only. The FBI couldn't touch them. Carson had a plan to convince the FBI that he and his family needed a new start, and they would relocate to Hawaii. He'd return once a month to assist per his probation, but why should he be at their beck and call? Hawaii was exactly what he needed, and if the only good job he could find was there, so what? The FBI couldn't prevent him from making a living.

That's where Jeremy came into the picture. He had

businesses all over the world, and one of his headquarters was in Honolulu.

Jeremy finally arrived and slid into the booth across from him. The waitress came over and Jeremy ordered a Scotch; Carson ordered his second.

"Rogan made my guys," Jeremy said once the waitress delivered their drinks.

Carson scowled. "Then your guys aren't any good."

"It's difficult tracking someone trained in security. And someone like Sean Rogan is always on edge. But there is another option."

"I'm all ears."

"Grab Jesse. Just for a day or two, let him escape."

Carson shook his head. "Absolutely not."

"Look, Carson, no one will hurt him. But your plan has holes. I went along with it to prove to you it's not going to work. Rogan isn't going to send Jesse back to Sacramento just because he thinks there's a threat. I've researched the guy. He'll keep the kid *closer* if he thinks there's a problem. Bring in his brother, the mercenary, which means two security-trained Rogans."

Carson hated Kane Rogan almost as much as Sean.

"The threat can't be to Jesse. I told you from the beginning, if Madison thinks that Jesse's in danger because of *Rogan's* job, then she'll bring him home and we'll be a family again. As it is, she's moping around the house completely miserable. And she blames me!" He took a deep breath. He couldn't lose his cool, not with Jeremy. If Carson showed weakness, Jeremy might exploit it. They were friends, but Carson was aware that even friendship had limits.

"It's not my fault this happened," Carson said, his voice calm. "She should never have gone to Rogan in the first place. Telling Rogan that Jesse was his kid? The worst of all worlds. Jesse has developed a mouth on him—he's been talking back to me, he doesn't do what I tell him, he ignores me half the time. And Madison won't lay down the law because she's afraid Jesse will like Rogan more than her. The kid is running the house and Madison is feeling guilty and just lets him."

"But if there's a threat to you or your family, they'll put you in WITSEC again. I could set it up—"

"I don't want to go back. I want my *life*. Freedom. Opportunity. The fucking American dream. And I'll have everything in three years when I'm done with this ridiculous probation." They'd originally wanted seven years. The one good thing Carson's lawyer did was get it down to three, even though that was three years too many. It wasn't like he was buying and selling drugs, and he never killed anyone. "What about Hawaii? I talked to you about it, can you make it happen? Or were you just blowing smoke up my ass?"

Jeremy waited until the waitress arrived with their refills and left before he leaned forward and said, "I'm working on it."

"I've paid you a lot of money, Jeremy. You know there's more."

"There might be another option."

"I'm listening."

"Rogan's wife."

Carson hadn't quite figured out where Rogan's wife fit in. All he knew was what he'd heard from his lawyer—

that she was one of the federal agents who'd investigated his employer and uncovered the shell corporations Carson had set up. But she wasn't a financial whiz or anything like that. She had been investigating human trafficking and stumbled upon the Flores operation.

"What about her?"

"I've been doing my research. She's been involved in several high-profile and dangerous operations. What if we stage an attack on her? Make sure that it gets in the press, or at least something that will force Rogan to tell Madison about it. Especially if Jesse's around—Madison would go ballistic."

That was true, Carson thought. She might demand that Jesse come home. Carson had to get the kid away from Rogan before he turned the kid against both Carson and Madison.

"Jesse can't get hurt. Not a scratch."

"Of course not."

"And she can't see it coming. Don't kill her—just shake her up. I can't have anyone at Rogan-Caruso-Kincaid investigating a murder—it'll make the whole thing far too hot. But if she gets shaken, it'll put Rogan on edge. In fact, if he's worried about his wife, he might send Jesse back on his own." That would be best—because then it's Rogan's choice, not even Madison pushing for it. Make Rogan seem like he's picking his wife over his son. That wouldn't go over well with Jesse *or* Madison. And maybe Carson could get part of his life back.

"She's working a high-profile case now. I'm going to head to San Antonio first thing in the morning to keep my eye on the situation. After all, you saved my ass. I'll never forget it, Carson."

Carson had told the FBI *almost* everything about his career as a lawyer and accountant for the cartels. But there were a few people he protected—people whom they would never even think to look at, like philanthropist multimillionaire Jeremy Robertson. Carson had long ago helped Jeremy hide money from his first ex-wife, and they'd been friends ever since.

Jeremy drained his drink. "And is plan B still on?"

"Of course. As soon as Jesse is back in Sacramento, Sean Rogan must die."

CHAPTER NINE

Lucy didn't get home until after ten. Bandit greeted her, but Sean wasn't in the kitchen. She tracked him and Jesse to the family room, where they were watching a movie. It was clear that they'd just gotten out of the swimming pool—the subtle scent of chlorine hung in the air—and they were still in their swim trunks, wrapped in towels, on the recliner chairs. She smiled. Jesse looked so much like Sean it was eerie. They had the same dark-blue eyes and solitary dimple. Jesse's hair was a lighter brown than Sean's, but there was no mistaking the resemblance.

"We just started the movie," Jesse said. "We can rewind if you want."

"No, I'm good. Finish watching, I'm going to shower and eat. Long day."

She leaned over and kissed Sean.

"Bring your plate in here," Sean said.

"I will."

Lucy showered, then went downstairs to warm a

plate. Sean was already doing it. "You don't have to stop the movie for me," she said.

"Jesse crashed ten minutes after you left," Sean said. "I left him in the family room with the movie going. I'll wake him up in a bit. You look tired."

"Long day. And I did a death notification right before I came home."

He rubbed her back and kissed her again. "I'm sorry. McMahon? The hostage-taker?"

"No—his wife showed up only minutes after SWAT took him out."

"I talked to Nate a bit about the situation—he hates being on leave."

"It was justified, he'll be cleared." Lucy grabbed a water bottle from the counter. "Leo and I went out to McMahon's house and found a body—his best friend." She drank half the bottle.

"He killed his best friend?"

"That's what people think, but I don't know." She sat down at the island and took a bite. Though she hadn't eaten much today, she wasn't that hungry. "There's a lot of things that don't add up. Yeah, on the surface he snapped. Wife left him, lost his job. But it's more than that. He was in pain—physically and emotionally. No one saw him at the house for weeks. That doesn't mean he wasn't there, but no one saw him there. We're going to interview his former employer tomorrow, talk to his wife again, find out where he was living since it wasn't the house. I'm really just too tired to think anymore tonight." Sean was listening to her, but he kept glancing down the hall.

"What's wrong?" she asked him.

"We can talk later."

"Tell me," she insisted.

He rubbed her arms up and down, sat next to her at the island. "I was followed leaving the Rib House."

"Followed? Like a tail?"

"Black sedan, no front plate, they were definitely following me. I lost them near the mission."

"That's nowhere near the Rib House, or on the way home."

"I wasn't going to lead them here. And I got them running the red light on Roosevelt and Military. Do you think you can sweet-talk one of your friends into getting me the photo? I have the exact time."

"Of course you do," she said. "I'll see what I can do."

"I might not need you to call in a favor. I called Jesse's handler in the marshals' office; I'm going to stop by in the morning. They still won't give me the threat assessment, but promised to answer my questions."

"I sense a but."

"I called Rick." Rick Stockton was one of the assistant directors in the FBI and a good friend of the Rogans. "I asked for a favor. He's going to make some calls. No promises, but I think he can get it done."

"The marshals would have never let the Spades out of WITSEC if there was any danger."

"Unless Carson Spade lied about potential threats."

"Why would he do that? He's in as much danger as Jesse—actually more."

"I know. But I don't like that guy."

Sean glanced over his shoulder as if worried that Jesse could hear him.

Lucy stepped into his arms. “You’ve done a great job with Jesse. I know this is difficult for you, but Jesse trusts you and you’ve really worked hard at forgiving Madison and Carson.”

“Madison—yeah. I’ll never be completely okay with missing the first twelve years of Jesse’s life, but she’s trying, so I can try. But Carson? No. There’s no forgiveness for what he did. I don’t like him and, more important, I don’t trust him.”

“For Jesse, maybe try keeping that under wraps.”

“I’m really trying.” Sean kissed her and smiled. “He wants to change his name. To Rogan.”

Tears of joy clouded her vision. “Oh, Sean—that’s wonderful.”

“He told me tonight when we were waiting at the Rib House. I almost started bawling right there. I just love that kid so much, and I love that he’s bounced back after everything he’s been through. I want to do right by him, and I don’t really know what I’m doing.”

“You love him, and that’s all that matters.”

“Are you okay with it?”

“Of course. I love Jesse. I wish—well, nothing. I’m just happy for you.”

She wasn’t going to spoil the moment for Sean. Lucy couldn’t have children, and it had taken a long time before she could accept it. She loved that Sean had a son . . . she just wished they could have a child together.

He leaned in and held her face. “I know, princess. I know this is hard for you.”

“This isn’t hard. Not what you think. You, Jesse, me, we’re good. We’re very good, and I’m glad he’s a part of our lives." She took a deep breath. "Carina is pregnant again. She's due end of November. She emailed the family today after her three-month checkup. I'm happy for her and Nick."

"But."

"No buts."

"We can start talking about adopting. It might take a while."

"We will—but not now. We're still newlyweds, and I'm enjoying being newlyweds very much."

Sean kissed her and ran his hands through her damp hair. "Me, too," he said, kissing her neck.

She loved this man, and she felt so lucky to have him in her life. Then he tickled her and she yelped.

"None of that here," she said with a laugh. "Let me eat, go put Jesse to bed, and then maybe you'll get some more kisses upstairs."

"I'm counting on a lot more than a few kisses," he said with a wink.

Sean wasn't asleep when his phone vibrated on the nightstand. He grabbed the phone before it woke Lucy and slipped into the adjoining room that Lucy used as her in-home office. He closed the door and answered.

"Rogan."

"It's Kane. Siobhan and I were in Arteaga helping the sisters finish repairs after the storm."

Sean didn't even know how to respond to Kane. He'd never apologized for not being accessible by phone, and he never explained why. Kane's relationship with

Siobhan, and her affiliation with the charitable organization Sisters of Mercy, had changed him.

"I was followed today. Don't have a clear description of the guys—two men, dark sedan, no plates. But what's been bothering me is I don't know where they picked me up. They followed me out of the Rib House off Becerra and I lost them around the mission—after I forced them to run a red light."

"Get the photos?"

"I'm trying to go through semi-legal channels. Lucy's going to talk to one of her contacts at SAPD, I'm talking to the marshals. I checked my Jeep for a tracker—it's clean. Checked my phone and Jesse's—both clean."

"Who knew where you were eating?"

"No one—I was picking up takeout."

"Did you call it in?"

"No. I go there at least once a week. They know me, they love Lucy."

"I know the place. Good business, good people, sketchy area."

"I must have missed a tail. I would have noticed the dark sedan in my neighborhood, but maybe there was a second vehicle. Then why didn't they tag-team me leaving the place?" he asked.

"Sweep the house and cars again. Do you think it's the Flores cartel?"

"I don't know. Carson pissed off a lot of people when he turned state's evidence."

"Jose is out of the business, and he's the lone surviving family member. I've kept tabs on him. He's relocated, and I'm certain he's staying clean—but I'll verify."

"I honestly don't know if Jesse's the target—or what we were involved with at the end of March. Zimmerman is still alive." Tommy Zimmerman had run an underage sex-trafficking organization from coast to coast that Sean and Lucy had helped shut down. But they'd worked on the periphery—there were others who'd be more realistic targets for revenge.

"He won't be getting out of prison, but it's a valid point. I'll talk to JT and he'll make sure there's no chatter coming from Zimmerman. I'll be up there tomorrow."

"Why? A job?"

Kane paused. "To keep my eye on you and Jesse."

"I've got it under control, Kane."

"Well, I don't have anything else to do. Siobhan is staying with the sisters for another week. I like the nuns, but I can only take them in small doses."

Sean chuckled. "They wouldn't let you and Siobhan share a room, would they?"

"What's with these people?" Kane said. "We live together."

"They're devout."

"It's ridiculous," he muttered.

"And how does coming back to Texas help the situation?" He paused when he realized the truth. "You came back because you got my message. You didn't have to do that."

"You're my brother. Jesse's my nephew. I'm not going to let these fuckers mess with what's mine. I'll see you by noon." He hung up.

Kane had a funny way of saying *I love you*, but his message was clear, and Sean was relieved. He could protect Jesse, but he recognized that it wouldn't be a lot of fun for the kid if he put him on house arrest—especially since there wasn't an explicit threat and Sean didn't know who to protect him from.

Sean went back to bed, but doubted he'd be able to sleep for a while.

"How's Kane?" Lucy rolled over and rested her hands on his chest.

"I'm sorry I woke you."

"You sounded worried."

"Just want to make sure no one thinks they can go after my kid."

"They'd be fools." She kissed him. "So is Kane on his way?"

"How did you know?"

"Because he's Kane." She rolled on top of Sean and kissed him again. And again.

"It's two in the morning."

"You're awake, I'm awake, and we're in bed. Almost naked."

"I'm almost naked." Sean slept in his boxers. "You have clothes."

She pulled her tank top over her head. "Now I'm almost naked, too." She pressed her bare chest against his. She touched him, his face, his arms, between his legs. He groaned and wrapped his arms tight around her.

Lucy was just what he needed.

CHAPTER TEN

Thirteen cops filled one of the conference rooms at SAPD—seven from SAPD and six from the FBI. Lucy was surprised so many people showed up, but realized several were present to give reports and wouldn't otherwise be involved in the investigation. Lieutenant Jordan Young started promptly. "We all have work to do, and you all know how much I love meetings, so we're going to make this quick. We know what happened yesterday, and our job is to figure out *why* it happened. The autopsy is scheduled this morning. My office is handling the press—the PIO is giving bare-bones information, and that includes information about the body at McMahon's house. Detective Mancini, start with the results of the witness interviews yesterday."

Tia nodded to CSI Ash Dominguez, who dimmed the lights and launched a computer program on the whiteboard. "I've distributed copies of all statements—these are eyes-only because they're unedited. Most are consistent, but there are a few anomalies that we're going to follow up on. Ash, Jason, and I were up into the wee hours putting together this computer model because I think it's important that we know as much as we can about what happened immediately prior to McMahon taking hostages, and why there are some discrepancies." She nodded to Ash, who clicked to the first screen, showing a diagram of the inside of the coffee shop. There were three different colors for the people, all displayed in silhouettes, and McMahon was in black. She used a laser pointer to direct.

"McMahon was sitting at this corner table near the window. The blinds were tilted up because the front of the store faces east and gets bright in the mornings. This is standard operation—they generally open them fully at noon according to the manager.

"McMahon's table had the best view of the door. He could see everyone coming in or out, but had little visibility of the counter or any other tables other than those immediately around him, because of this"—she pointed—"eight-foot-long, six-foot-high display rack that was used both for merchandise and to divide the sitting area. According to the time stamp on his tea, he ordered at ten twenty-four a.m. Witnesses concur that he sat at the table alone.

"At ten thirty-five, two girls entered the store—April and Cindy. They're fifteen and were cutting summer school. They went to the first half of their class and had a thirty-minute break, but decided they wouldn't return. They were drinking and discussing what to do for the day at the table next to McMahon. By ten fifty both girls agree that McMahon appeared agitated. He seemed to be debating whether to leave—he got up at one point, then sat back down. He began to talk to himself. They specifically heard, 'Where's Paul? Did you kill him?' Here's where this gets interesting. April's statement is that McMahon was talking to *another* man who stood by the display rack. She heard the man talk, but his voice was low and she couldn't hear what he said. But she swears that McMahon was talking to him and listening to him. No one else—not even her friend Cindy—remembers this man."

Tia pointed to a figure standing about three feet from McMahon next to the display rack. "April says the man was looking at the mugs. The manager, here"—she pointed to a figure in green—"approached McMahon and asked if he could help him, if he needed anything. McMahon grew more agitated and grabbed the manager, revealing that he had a gun. Several witnesses said they saw only one gun, but two witnesses said he held one and had another in his waistband, under his jacket. At some point after the manager approached McMahon, but before McMahon pulled his gun—which was less than a minute—the man at the display rack—we'll call him POI One—left.

"Here's where things get confusing, but thanks to Ash we've put together what we believe is an accurate series of events. As soon as McMahon drew his gun, eight people closest to the door fled." The screen showed which people bolted. "Several others took cover." The screen shifted and showed people hunched on the floor. "McMahon ordered one hostage to lock the door. The employees behind the counter hit the floor and crawled into the adjoining kitchen." Ash clicked and showed a new screen. "This is how the scene looked when the first nine-one-one call came in. The rest we've put together based on witness statements and Tim Yancey's thermal imaging program." As she spoke, the scene played out behind her. Mostly, people were still, but McMahon paced, holding the manager close to him.

Tia continued. "Most witnesses heard McMahon talking about Paul, whom we have identified as Paul Grey, his colleague and friend, who was found deceased in McMahon's house last night. Most witnesses claimed that he was 'rambling,' that he made no sense, but we've put together phrases that more than one person heard. They include multiple questions about Paul, that he must be dead, that 'they' killed him. 'They' are not identified by name, but McMahon talked about 'them,' and several people called him skittish and paranoid. He told himself to 'think' or 'remember' no less than twenty times. SAPD arrived on scene within seven minutes of the first nine-one-one call, and SWAT and Lieutenant Young were on site within eleven minutes.

"We identified and interviewed all eight people who left prior to the door being locked. We showed their photos to April. None of them are the man she saw. It could be that McMahon was talking to him and he left without making a purchase because he was irritated. But no one has come forward and in my experience, if someone is that close to a threat, they'll come forward afterward. Unless he was really clueless—possibly a tourist or passing through and didn't make the connection. Our best guess based on timing and witness statements is that the man left the coffeehouse as soon as the manager approached McMahon." She nodded to Ash, who switched the program to an image from a security camera on the street.

"This image is of the man we believe April Forsyth saw. He's wearing slacks and a button-down shirt. We showed her this image. She thinks it's the same guy, but couldn't swear to it. The timing, however, fits."

Young spoke up. "Any way to enhance the photo? It's crap."

Tia shook her head. "You can't add pixels that aren't there. This was a camera at the ATM machine two doors down. If he was closer, we'd get a great image, but the farther away the worse the quality—we cleaned up the distortion as much as possible, but there's no way to get an ID on him from this. However, it's clear that he has light hair, he's Caucasian, and Ash went out to measure landmarks so we can safely say he is six feet tall, but not more than six foot one. He's thin. April said 'old like my dad'—her father is forty-six. I'm going to peg this guy at between thirty and forty. We showed this image to the employees and no one recognized him—but we're going to show them again today, plus those off duty. They don't need to know his name, but if he's a regular customer, one of the employees should recognize him."

"But," Jason said, "we don't have any confirmation that he was actually in the coffeehouse, or that he spoke to McMahon. Only one witness made that statement."

"True," Tia said, "but April was emphatic, and didn't change her statement even when her friend chastised her."

"Eyewitness testimonies are notoriously unreliable," Young said.

"I agree," Tia said, "but both Jason and I talked to her. She may be in summer school for flunking geometry, but she's not a dumb kid. She's very observant. For example, several witnesses thought McMahon was homeless because he wore a bulky jacket, was unshaven, and talking to himself. April, as well as the manager, both said his clothes were clean and he didn't smell like he'd been living on the street.

"The manager spent last night at the hospital. We got his statement, but then he collapsed. Stress, fear, whatever—the guy had a gun on him for two hours, I don't blame him for falling apart. Jason and I are going to talk to him again today. He was the closest to McMahon, and perhaps McMahon said something else that might help us figure out what was going on with him, and if he killed Paul Grey."

"On that note," Young said, "Leo? What happened at the McMahon house?"

"That's the million-dollar question," Leo said. "First, no neighbor has seen McMahon in the last month. The earliest was a few days before June fifteenth, but we can't confirm an exact day or time. No one saw Paul Grey enter the house, and Grey's car wasn't found on the property or in the neighborhood. It's clear that McMahon wasn't living there full-time. There was a lot of dust, rotten food, and a Chinese take-out receipt dated June twelfth. We believe that was the last time he was at the house—or close to it. The leftovers were in the refrigerator."

"And the wife didn't come over?"

"She said the last time she was there was in May. He had stopped paying the bills, so she took over, and she also went to collect things for her kids. The separation was stressful and she didn't want to confront him. I believe her."

"And Grey?"

"He wasn't killed at the house. We'll know more after the autopsy, which is scheduled right after McMahon's. But Jackson has a report on that."

ERT leader Mike Jackson spoke up. "The coroner would have my hide for this, but based on the temperature of the house, air-conditioning off, and the last known time Grey was seen alive, my guess is that he was killed a minimum of three hours *before* his body was left at the house. This is primarily because there was very little blood found under his head—which had a gaping hole on the left side. The blood was dry or mostly dry by the time he was moved there. And my guess? There was a slight bend in his knees even though he was lying on his back on the floor. I think he was killed while sitting down, and left in that position for several hours before his body was moved to McMahon's."

"So," Detective Keith Hastings spoke for the first time, "McMahon kills him somewhere, doesn't know what to do with the body, takes the body home with him—in the middle of the night and the neighbors don't see—and leaves it. Then because he's looney-tunes or on drugs, he doesn't remember killing him and goes to the coffeehouse thinking he's meeting Grey."

"Sure," Jackson said, "that's one theory. And maybe that's what happened. But there could have been a second person. The problem is that I can't prove it—I've collected all the evidence I can, and I *believe* the body was carried by two people, but there were *some* drag marks, and one point where the victim's head hit the wall around the turn from the laundry room into the kitchen. But I can't prove definitively whether there was one or two people. There are no prints that shouldn't be there, but we're still processing a lot of evidence and it's going to take a while. But I concur with Leo—the guy wasn't living in the house."

"So where?" Young asked.

"We don't know yet," Leo said. "Lucy and I are meeting with the widow again today. She's bringing in all their banking and credit card statements. McMahon hadn't touched their joint bank account, but was living off their credit card. She didn't want to cut him off, so she paid the bill every month—averaging between a thousand and twelve hundred dollars."

"She can afford that every month?" one of the cops said.

"It was coming out of McMahon's severance when he was fired," Leo said.

"He could have had a weekly motel or an apartment," Hastings commented. "You can find some dives for five bills a month."

Jackson said, "One more thing that's important. Grey was dumped in the McMahon house within a few hours of his death. He went through full rigor right there in the den, wasn't moved for at least twenty-four hours. The coroner will be more accurate, but the guy was dead between thirty-six and forty-eight hours. I'm leaning closer to thirty-six, but the ME would rip me a new one if I wrote that as fact."

"He was killed midnight on Monday, take or leave a few hours," Lucy said.

"That's my educated guess, based on the evidence," Jackson said.

"We're processing McMahon's truck," Young said. He asked Ash, "Anything? Was he living out of it? Trace evidence?"

"We have it in impound and I'll be heading over there after this meeting. I told the team hands off until I get there. We have good people, but in something like this we want to make sure there's a clear chain of custody, especially since McMahon is a suspect in Grey's murder. All I can say is that it doesn't appear that he was living out of his truck. But there were a lot of newspapers and notebooks and I want to make sure each item is cataloged properly and look for any blood or biological matter. I should be able to prove or disprove if McMahon's truck was used to transport Grey's body. The coroner is drying McMahon's clothes and shoes and will be sending them to my lab for processing—if he killed Grey, there is likely evidence on his clothes or in his truck."

Young was taking notes. "Good—let me know as soon as you have a preliminary report. We have a full task force through the weekend, but brass is giving a preliminary press report today, and wants a full report Monday morning. I know that's asking a lot, but when we have a hostage situation like this—even though the only fatality was McMahon—we need to get answers sooner rather than later. Telling people that McMahon cracked isn't an answer. I want to know why. But truth is, the time and resources that we're putting into this aren't going to last forever. The shooter is dead. We need to confirm that he did in fact kill Paul Grey before we make that statement publicly."

Lucy spoke up. She'd been taking a lot of notes, but now she said, "I don't think that McMahon killed Paul Grey."

"Why not?"

"I think he suspected he was dead, but he didn't kill him. First, McMahon's state of mind yesterday tells me he was a loner—at least he has been since he started his decline around the end of March, and certainly since he lost his job in May. He was paranoid, and could have had an undiagnosed mental illness. But just because someone has a mental illness doesn't mean that they are violent or a threat."

"He took fifteen people hostage," Jason said.

"Yes, and I think that we need to put our weight on April Forsyth's statement. If we talk to anyone who looks like the man she saw, we bring her a picture. She was one of the few people who didn't believe that he was homeless, and he wasn't. His clothes were clean, his shoes clean, his hair clean. We know this based on the surveillance tapes and his body. I'll confirm with Julie Peters after the autopsy. And the POI leaves less than a minute before McMahon pulls a gun. Why? Why not stay in the area when he sees others fleeing the coffee shop? Or when it pops on the news? Something is off about his behavior. He could have a logical explanation—

maybe he was late for a meeting. But I want to hear that from him."

"Needle in a haystack," Hastings muttered.

Young said, "As of this point, Mancini, Hastings, and Lopez will continue processing witness statements and cleaning up this time line of events for the brass. Everything needs to be signed and sealed. They are on point to find the POI. Proctor, Kincaid—you're on Paul Grey's death. If you need someone else, Officer Jones is at your disposal, and you can tap Lopez—after today I don't think we'll need him. Ash, you're lead on processing the coffee shop and truck. Jackson, you and your team still have the Paul Grey murder, but if you need our lab for anything, it's yours."

Lucy slid a note to Leo. He read it, nodded. "Kincaid and I are also following up with McMahon's employer—who was also Grey's employer. We'll find out what they were both working on—McMahon when he was fired, and Grey recently. And according to the missing persons report Grey's wife filed on Tuesday, the last person to see Grey alive was his secretary, who claimed he left the office at four-thirty p.m.—even though his wife said he'd called at four to tell her he would be working late."

Young flipped through some papers. "Clarke-Harrison? Pharmaceuticals and research. You got it. Reports from everyone at the end of each day. Overtime is only cleared through Saturday, so use your time wisely, because Sunday you're on the clock."

They disbanded. The meeting took less than an hour, and they'd shared extensive information. If only all meetings were so efficient.

Lucy approached Ash Dominguez. She'd met him a couple of times when one of her cases collided with an SAPD investigation, but she didn't know him well. He was young and smart and obviously loved his job. "Ash, can you send me a copy of that PowerPoint?"

"Sure—I need to clean it up first. I'm making an animation from this, and Yancey is helping me overlay a few things. It'll be much more helpful. Yancey is more a tech guy than me. You'll have it by the end of the day."

"Thanks, Ash. I appreciate it."

Lucy tracked Leo down in the bullpen, where he was talking to Tia Mancini. Tia was saying, "I see your point, Leo, and we need evidence either way. The way I see it, he killed Grey somewhere else, panicked, brought him to his house. Maybe didn't know what to do with the body. Like you said, he was mentally ill—paranoid. Maybe he didn't know *what* he was doing."

"I don't want the word to get out that we think he's guilty. The press already jumped the gun and got half the story wrong."

"Because we gave them a no comment."

"Because we don't have answers!"

Lucy had rarely seen Leo frustrated, and she reflected that Nate had been concerned about him after the negotiations went south. Nate, as part of the FBI SWAT team that Leo headed, knew the man better than she did.

"We're going to get answers," Lucy said with confidence. "It's been less than twenty-four hours since this went down. A couple days and we'll know what happened."

"I've known Jordan for years. He is a great cop, but

he runs a tight ship," Tia said. "He meant it when he said no more overtime after Saturday."

"We don't have overtime in the FBI," Leo said. "We have a murder to solve, and neither of us believes that McMahon killed Grey. We need evidence either way."

"And if we don't find it, it becomes a cold case," Tia said.

"What are you doing about the POI?" Lucy asked.

"Nothing I can do at this point. We put out a statement that's running on the news, social media, and the papers. Specifically asking for anyone who was at Java Antonio yesterday morning prior to the incident to contact police to give a statement. Hopefully he'll see that and call. But short of that, I don't know what else we can do."

"Can April work with a sketch artist?"

"My gut says no. She saw him but didn't get a good enough look. My guess is that she might recognize him if she sees him, but she doesn't have anything more than a vague description. Jason and I are going to her house later to talk to her again, see if she remembers anything else. She more than anyone seemed to want to help, and everything she's said has been confirmed—except for that guy. I'm going to show her this picture again now that it's as enhanced as we can get it. The image might trigger something."

"Good idea," Leo said. "Thanks, Tia, for letting me vent."

Tia squeezed his arm. "Call me anytime, Leo. You know that."

CHAPTER ELEVEN

Lucy and Leo met with Charlie McMahon's widow at FBI headquarters. Again her brother, Deputy Olsen, came with her. It was clear Lisa McMahon hadn't slept much, if at all, and she kept apologizing for Charlie and herself.

"I should have seen it coming."

Lucy spent thirty minutes talking to her while Leo and Olsen went through the McMahon financial statements for clues about Charlie. At first Lucy just listened, then she tried to convince Lisa that unless she had put the gun in his hand, or had foreknowledge that he intended to take hostages, she was not responsible. Guilt was powerful, and any survivor went through myriad emotions.

"Lisa," Lucy finally said when McMahon's widow started circling back to her regrets, "we're just starting our investigation, and neither Agent Proctor nor I are jumping to any conclusions as to what happened. It's clear to me, however, that Charlie had something going on with him that he shared with no one, except maybe his friend Paul Grey. And in my opinion—based on the witness statements and the evidence we do have—I don't think Charlie went into that coffeehouse planning on hurting anyone."

"But he brought two guns with him. Two guns! A reporter showed up at Trevor's house this morning, as we were leaving to come here, and asked if I knew that he'd killed Paul."

"We don't know who killed Paul. We've just started our investigation."

"But Paul was shot. In m-m-my house." Her hand went to her mouth and her eyes filled with tears.

Lucy reached over and took her free hand. "Lisa, I can't tell you everything that happened because we don't know. The crime scene investigators believe that Paul was killed somewhere else and brought to your house."

"Why would Charlie do that?"

"We don't know that Charlie *did* do anything yet. Don't talk to the reporters. They can ask anything they want, but you have every right not to answer them. If they harass you at all, call the police."

"Trevor said he'd arrest them for trespassing. But—I don't know what to do. When can I go to the house? I can't bring the kids there, ever, but I want to get rid of it. Put in on the market, or just walk away. I don't know. But I have to go through it. We spent nearly twenty years there . . ."

"Don't make any major decisions right now, like walking away from the house," Lucy said. "Why don't you sleep on it for a few days and talk to your brother. You can hire someone to clean the house, pack it up, whatever you want. You don't have to do it yourself. It'll be another day or two before you'll be allowed back in at any rate. Someone will contact you when it's been cleared."

She nodded.

"A couple more questions if you are up to it?"

"Okay."

"There was no computer in the den, which seemed odd. Did Charlie have a computer?"

"A laptop. He had a computer, but when he was fired I assumed his work took it back. It was one of those state-of-the-art computers. But he had a personal laptop."

Lucy made note. There had been no laptop found in the house or Charlie's truck.

"Had Paul and Charlie kept in touch after Charlie was fired?"

"No—not really. Like I said, I reached out to Paul when Charlie wasn't paying the bills and Paul said he'd talk to him." She took a deep breath. "I let it go too long. I should have done something more to get him help."

"If someone who needs help refuses to get it, you can't blame yourself. He had a lot of time to get help—but until we know exactly what was wrong, we don't know that he didn't get help, do we? We'll figure it out, Lisa. The laptop," Lucy said, getting back to information she needed, "did it have theft protection on it?"

"No."

"Do you know the model?"

"Not really—it's a good one, but that information would be in his office, or wait—it would be in my insurance papers. We had to document all electronics."

"Good. If you can get me that information at your earliest convenience. Did you collect his email information?"

She nodded.

The FBI would access McMahon's emails and see if there was any indication of what his plans were yesterday. There also might be information about where he was living and who else he was talking to.

While Leo took all the files and information to the tech unit, Lucy walked Lisa and her brother out. She tried to reassure them that the FBI was doing everything they could to find the truth about what happened with Charlie, but she didn't think they believed her—or that anyone could ever learn the truth.

Lucy walked back inside the office, frustrated that she couldn't give Charlie's widow any more reassurances. Leo caught up with her as she made her way to her desk.

"Our cybercrimes team is going to hack into his email," Leo said, "but we already have a lead on where he was staying. Not a location yet, but he used his credit card multiple times in a six-block radius in the Harlandale neighborhood."

"Are there cheap apartments down there?"

Leo nodded. "I convinced Jordan we needed officers

to canvass the area. He agreed it was a good lead, so he's assigning Jones and someone who speaks fluent Spanish. Plainclothes, because cops in that area will get the cold shoulder. Let's go, we're meeting Cortland Clarke at eleven thirty."

CHAPTER TWELVE

Clarke-Harrison Research had two identical three-story buildings that connected through a skywalk only minutes from the San Antonio airport. The easternmost building was completely secured with two visible guards and perimeter fencing; the western building was open, and that's where Lucy and Leo entered the lobby. The only way to access the far building was through the guard gate, or the third-floor skywalk. The structures were elegant, sleek, functional, and a bit futuristic, which Lucy supposed was a plus in the field of advanced medical research.

They showed their IDs to the security guard who manned the camera-heavy front desk. Another guard was posted at the elevators and he had a view of both the elevator banks, sweeping staircase, and lobby.

Leo said, "We have an eleven thirty appointment with Cortland Clarke."

"I'll notify Ms. Clarke's assistant."

Lucy and Leo walked over to the front of the building

where they had a bit of privacy. "A lot of wasted space," Leo mumbled. The lobby itself was two stories tall and all windows. There were several sitting areas with couches and plush carpets on the cold cement floor, potted plants—Lucy touched one and noted they were fake, but high quality—and brightly colored artwork on sturdy easels since there was little wall space to hang anything. At first glance it appeared to be simple contemporary art. Lucy inspected the closest one to her—an intricate yellow-and-blue organism—and read the sign. It was the Ebola virus magnified more than one hundred thousand times. It was eerily beautiful.

"I read up on the company this morning," Lucy said. "Cortland Clarke and Garrett Harrison started CHR sixteen years ago with a grant from Clarke's grandfather, a philanthropist named Hiram Clarke. He died three years ago. Clarke has two master's degrees—in biology and marketing communications. Harrison has a medical degree from Johns Hopkins, specializing in neurology. He was working in a trauma hospital in New York when the elder Clarke approached him about a paper he'd published on amnesia. Clarke wanted to fund research into amnesia and memory loss. Another research company had gone through trials but lost their funding after a scandal, so Clarke used the grant to buy out the company and they were already ahead of the game when Harrison came on board. Three years later Clarke-Harrison had their first drug approved by the FDA for migraine headaches. They received a larger grant and expanded into Alzheimer's research—which is Dr. Harrison's focus."

"And is that when they brought McMahon on?"

"It doesn't say on their website—they could have scrubbed all mention of him after they fired him. They received FDA approval for a drug two years ago that has shown some success in slowing the progression of Alzheimer's, but I read some articles that indicate it wasn't as well received by the industry because it's very expensive for few benefits—or at least few benefits that the patients can see. They're working on what they call a breakthrough in Alzheimer's research that was approved for human trials earlier this year, and they hope to have it on the market by the end of next year. Early tests have indicated that the drug is able to completely stop the progression of Alzheimer's. You can't reclaim memories that have been lost, but the patients don't get worse."

"If that's for real, it could change the quality of life for millions of families."

Lucy had some knowledge of medicine, but not enough to fully understand Clarke-Harrison Research. But if what they touted on their website was true, they could become a household name in only a few years.

It was a good fifteen minutes—and Leo was growing increasingly frustrated—before Cortland Clarke's assistant approached them.

"I apologize for keeping you waiting," he said in a low, well-modulated voice. "I'm Edwin Bennett. Ms. Clarke was in the lab and the test took longer than we thought. Please, follow me."

He used his key card to get into the elevator and then to access the third floor. The elevator opened into a plush lobby with a view of San Antonio in the distance.

An airplane descended practically in front of them, over the freeway, landing on a distant runway. The soundproofing was as state-of-the-art as the building itself. Lucy could barely hear the plane.

Edwin led them to a set of double doors labeled with Cortland Clarke's name, which opened into a smaller waiting room with two secretaries. Four closed doors showed people through glass working on computers or talking on the phone. A fifth door with Edwin's name on it was open; he had the best view of the support staff. He passed his office and knocked on another set of double doors, then opened before waiting for a response.

"Agents Proctor and Kincaid are here. May I get either of you coffee? Water? Tea?"

"We're good," Leo said.

"Let me know if you need me, Ms. Clarke," Edwin said and stepped out, closing the doors behind him.

Cortland Clarke was a beautiful woman with long straight blond hair and dressed in a sleek black pencil-thin skirt and creamy silk blouse. Her makeup was impeccable and she walked in four-inch spike heels with the grace of a ballerina, something Lucy had never been able to master.

Behind her sat an older man in a conservative-cut three-piece suit and burgundy silk tie with matching handkerchief folded and placed precisely in his breast pocket. Lucy didn't know much about clothes—especially men's clothes—but the ensemble looked expensive.

She shook their hands. "I'm so sorry to meet you under such terrible circumstances." She motioned for them to sit at the conference table by the windows, then introduced them to Robert White. Before she even said *lawyer* Lucy knew he was the Clarke-Harrison corporate counsel. His whole demeanor practically screamed attorney.

"Please sit," Cortland said as she herself sat at a seat with a mug of coffee already half gone. She sipped. "Are you sure I can't have Edwin bring you something to drink?"

Leo sat across from them and Lucy sat next to the senior agent. All business, he declined the second offer for beverages, and said, "You're aware of the hostage situation yesterday morning downtown?"

Cortland nodded. "Horrific."

"How long had Mr. McMahon worked for Clarke-Harrison?" Leo asked.

"Nearly twelve years."

"And he was fired—according to his wife—in May of this year?"

"Yes, his employment was terminated."

"Why?"

"That's confidential."

"McMahon's dead. Employee confidentiality doesn't transcend death."

"In this case, I disagree. His termination related to an ongoing proprietary research project and thus I can't discuss any details with you."

"I can get a warrant."

White spoke up. "I doubt that. McMahon was terminated two months ago. The tragedy yesterday has nothing to do with his terminated employment. If—and I use this as a big hypothetical *if*—his termination led him down a mental slippery slope that resulted in him taking fifteen people hostage, we don't have even a tertiary responsibility for that."

"I didn't suggest you did," Leo said. "I'm trying to figure out why an otherwise brilliant scientist with a PhD took fifteen people hostage. Our investigation indicates his behavior changed around the time he was terminated."

Cortland put her hand on the attorney's forearm and said, "Agents, I am heartbroken over what happened. Charlie was a valued part of our family here at Clarke-Harrison. Other than myself and Garrett, Charlie was here longer than anyone. I can state without violating any confidentiality agreements that Charlie was going through a difficult time at home. He and his wife had been fighting, and he couldn't seem to leave his personal problems outside the office. Garrett and I went to him and suggested he take a sabbatical—we offer a six-month paid sabbatical to any employee every seven years, and Charlie has never taken one. He refused. His wife left him. His behavior got worse, and a series of internal events forced us to terminate him. It was our last choice, but at that point it was our only choice."

"And that, Agent Proctor," the attorney said, "is far more than either of us should say on this matter."

Cortland Clarke had said virtually nothing of substance in her long speech, but sat straight with a concerned expression, as if she'd been far more forthcoming than she actually had been. Lucy knew they wouldn't be able to rattle her or get her to slip up.

"Please explain the circumstances regarding Mr. McMahon's arrest for vandalism," Leo said.

"We filed a police report. You should be able to access that, correct?" Cortland said.

"I'd like to hear what you have to say on the matter. It was less than two weeks after he was fired, you had him arrested but then dropped the charges. Why did you drop the charges?"

White slid over a thin folder. "In case you haven't received the police report, here's a copy. Ms. Clarke's statement is in there, as well as the guard who uncovered the vandalism."

Leo didn't look at the information, but slid the folder over to Lucy. She glanced through it. There was nothing they didn't already know. "Why did you drop the charges?" he repeated.

"As I said," Cortland began, "Charlie is like family, and he'd devoted most of his professional life to our research. His behavior had been erratic, and I felt he needed help, that going to prison would not serve anyone's best interests. He paid for the damages out of his severance package, and Garrett and I felt that was sufficient. I made it clear to Charlie that if he came back to the property I would have him arrested for harassment. He didn't return. I had hoped he finally went to see a counselor or someone who could help him work through whatever he was going through, but it's clear he hadn't."

Leo paused, and Lucy wondered if they were done. She almost stood when Leo said, "I regret to inform you that Paul Grey was found dead yesterday."

The information was clearly not a surprise to Cortland.

"Another tragedy. Diane called me last night in tears. I'm stunned."

"Mrs. Grey filed a missing persons report Tuesday morning," Leo said, "and based on her statement, Mr. Grey called her Monday and said he would be working late. When the sheriff contacted your office, Mr. Grey's assistant said that he had left at four thirty Monday afternoon and had no plans to return."

"I verified that with his assistant, and it's correct. Our legal office offered security footage to the police if they needed to corroborate that."

"You can give it to us," Lucy said, speaking up for the first time.

Leo glanced at her. Was he surprised? Didn't matter to Lucy—that security footage would be the most recent image they had of Grey. They could determine whether he was wearing the same clothes as when his body was found, plus they might be able to get some idea of his state of mind.

"Of course," Cortland said. "But can I ask why? You've found him—I'm still stunned that Charlie killed his best friend."

"We didn't say that," Leo said, a thread of anger in his voice.

Lucy realized that Leo was taking this case personally. He'd felt a connection—as many hostage negotiators do—with the hostage-taker. Like Lucy, he felt there was something more going on than what appeared to have happened, and he wanted to get to the bottom of it. But it was far more personal for Leo, and now Lucy understood what Nate was concerned about. This hostility could create problems, especially with witnesses like Cortland Clarke and her attorney, who were extremely savvy.

"Nooo," Cortland said slowly, clearly catching on to Leo's tone, "but Diane told me Paul's body was found in Charlie's house. I apologize if I jumped to the wrong conclusion. But you should know that Diane is certain that Charlie killed him—she was quite hysterical. Her sister was with her, finally got her to take a Valium and calm down. Poor woman."

"We need to access Mr. Grey's office, schedule, what he was working on, and to talk to his assistant—and Mr. McMahon's assistant."

"Slow down," White said. "First, we can't allow you access to Clarke-Harrison's research. Mr. Grey was working on a highly sensitive and important clinical trial, and none of that information will be provided to the FBI or law enforcement. You can attempt a warrant, and I will quash it. Mr. Grey's schedule is included in that—though I reviewed the day he left early and determined there was nothing proprietary on the sheet, so I made you a printout." He slid it over to Leo.

Lucy glanced over. There was nothing on the calendar except at five thirty p.m.: *Meeting with C. R.*

"Who is C. R.?" Lucy asked.

"We don't know. We assume it was personal. But he did leave at about four thirty—four twenty-six according to his key card and the security cameras."

"We'd still like to talk to the assistant," Leo said. "She may know who C. R. is."

"We asked, she doesn't."

"We want to talk to her," Leo reiterated firmly. "To ask about his state of mind and anything he may have said about this meeting."

White sighed—it was clear he didn't want them to talk to anyone else at CHR.

"In addition," Leo said, "Mr. Grey is party to charges of assault against Mr. McMahon. His assistant may have pertinent information regarding their altercation. I can do this the hard way if you'd prefer, Mr. White."

Cortland pressed a button on the conference table phone. "Edwin, please bring Nina Okala in."

"We also need to speak to Mr. McMahon's assistant."

"Mr. Paine is no longer with us. We terminated his employment when we found he'd let Mr. McMahon into the building the night he was arrested, resulting in the vandalism."

"We need Mr. Paine's contact information," Leo said.

"We'll provide you with that, of course," Cortland said.

"Have you seen Mr. McMahon since he was fired?" Leo asked.

She seemed surprised by the question. "No, I haven't—Robert spoke with the police after the break-in."

Leo turned to the attorney. "Did you talk to Mr. McMahon?"

"Yes, briefly. To sign the agreement about damages."

"He didn't use an attorney?"

"To my knowledge, he didn't retain one. He appeared remorseful for his actions and apologized. The police detective was there, he can attest that the meeting was cordial. It lasted maybe five minutes."

There was a knock on the door, and Edwin brought in a petite older woman in a suit as trim and professional as Cortland Clarke's.

Cortland smiled and motioned for the woman to sit. "Ms. Okala, these are the FBI agents looking into Paul's murder. They were hoping you could answer some questions about Paul's demeanor on Monday when he left."

"Anything to help," the woman said.

Leo asked, "How long have you worked for Mr. Grey?"

"Two months."

Lucy didn't miss the fact that two months was about as long as Charlie McMahon had been gone.

"On Monday he called his wife at four and said he was working late and not to expect him for dinner, then he left the office to meet with someone with the initials C. R. Do you know who C. R. is?"

"I'm sorry, I do not."

"What did he tell you?"

"I actually didn't see him when he left. I knew of the meeting because it was on his calendar. I asked him that morning if he wanted to meet in his office or have me schedule a conference room, and he said it was off site."

"Did you ask why?"

"No."

"Did you schedule the meeting?"

"No, he put it on his calendar himself."

"Did he have any other meetings with C. R.?"

"Not to my knowledge."

"Wouldn't you know? Did you schedule all his meetings?"

She glanced at Cortland.

Cortland frowned. "Why these hostile questions, Agent Proctor?"

"I'm sorry you're taking this interview as being hostile," Leo said. "I can assure you, our sole purpose is to find Paul Grey's killer."

Ms. Okala cleared her throat and said, "Mr. Grey didn't have many meetings outside the building—he had a regular staff meeting twice a week with his division, and occasionally with other people in house. He was a research scientist."

Cortland said, "What Ms. Okala means is that Paul worked in the lab. It's public information that he was brought on eight years ago, on Charlie's recommendation, to help with our expanded Alzheimer's research program. Paul's specialty was scientific data analysis."

"No one thought it odd that he was leaving for an off-site meeting?"

"I assumed it was personal," Ms. Okala said, "and he put it in his calendar so he wouldn't forget."

Almost verbatim what Cortland had said.

"So you don't know who C. R. is?"

"No, sir," Ms. Okala said.

"Care to hazard a guess?"

"No, sir. I really don't have any idea."

Leo was frustrated, and Lucy changed gears. "What was Mr. Grey's state of mind when he left work on Monday?"

"I didn't see him when he left."

"Did you see him at all that day?"

"Of course."

"The last time you saw him, was he preoccupied? Happy? Chatty? Did he say anything to you?"

"Mr. Grey was always professional. He didn't talk much except about the work, and the last time I saw him we passed in the skywalk. I asked if he needed anything before I left for my lunch break, and he said no. So I imagine I last saw him between noon and twelve thirty on Monday."

"Was his office in this building or the research building?" Lucy asked.

Ms. Okala looked confused.

"It's not a difficult question," Leo said.

Cortland said, "He has an office in both buildings—a business office, and a research office off the main lab."

"Was Mr. Grey going to or from the research building when you saw him?" Lucy asked. It wasn't an important question, but she had a theory she wanted to test.

"Why is that important?" Cortland said.

"I'm curious where he spent most of his time, and whether he was leaving work or going to work while Ms. Okala was taking her break."

"I just told you he spent most of his time in the research building," Cortland said, more irritated than flustered. "None of this is relevant to whether or not Charlie killed Paul. We don't know why Paul left early, who he was meeting with, but I'm positive it had nothing to do with Clarke-Harrison."

"But you can't know that for certain," Lucy said.

She opened her mouth, then closed it and tilted up her chin. "Point taken."

Mr. White said, "We have our own internal security

reviewing every project Mr. Grey was involved with. If there was any hint of impropriety or if anything is missing, we will go through the proper channels to remedy the situation. If that's all? Ms. Clarke is a busy woman running a multimillion-dollar research facility."

"For now," Leo said and stood up. "If you would please direct us to Mr. Harrison's office?"

Cortland stared at them a second too long. Did she not think they would ask to speak with the other principal? The one who was directly involved with McMahon and Grey's research?

"You'll have to make an appointment for next week," she said. "Garrett is away on company business."

"When did he leave?" Leo asked.

"Monday morning."

"We need his contact information."

"Garrett hasn't been in town all week, and he's in the middle of securing a major funding source. Does he really need to be bothered with this?"

"We need his information," Leo repeated.

White said, "I'll send that to you along with the security footage, if that would suffice."

Before Leo could answer, Cortland said, "If that's all, we really have work to do. With Paul's death, we're in the middle of a complete project review. This has put us back weeks, if not months."

"Murder has a way of doing that," Lucy said.

She didn't like Cortland, and from the woman's expression, the feeling was mutual.

Lucy and Leo walked out of Clarke-Harrison a few minutes later.

"What do you think?" Leo asked.

"She's hiding something. They all seemed like they were hiding something, but I think that everyone is terrified of Cortland Clarke. Even the attorney, who acted tough. He glanced at her one too many times."

"She was a piece of work."

"Definitely had answers for everything, and that in and of itself is suspicious—except she told us *nothing* of substance."

"Exactly. We need to find out who worked with Paul Grey prior to McMahon's termination. It can't be a coincidence that Ms. Okala started after Charlie left. And McMahon's assistant was fired for letting him in? We'll reach out to both Mrs. McMahon and Mrs. Grey to find out what they know about the research assistants."

While Leo drove toward Guadalupe County, where they planned to talk to the bartender about Paul and Charlie's confrontation two weeks ago, Lucy called Lisa McMahon.

"Lisa, it's Agent Lucy Kincaid."

"Any news?"

"Like I told you this morning, investigations take time. When we were at Clarke-Harrison, Ms. Clarke said that she'd terminated Charlie's assistant for letting Charlie into the building in May. Mr. Paine?"

"I didn't know that—Charlie never told me."

"Do you know this Paine?"

"Vince Paine. I don't really know him, but he'd been at the house a few times over the last couple of years. Charlie and Paul had dozens of employees. I met very few of the people who worked at CHR."

"Was there anyone he was particularly close to?"

"Garrett Harrison—he and Charlie were very close, though they didn't work day-to-day together. Garrett travels a lot."

That was good to know. Lucy made a note.

"What about his research assistants? Anyone he worked with for a long time? Someone he trusted . . . or distrusted?"

"I don't know—well, there are two who were with him a long time, whom he trusted, and they both came over to the house for barbecues and such when things were—well, better. Tom Perez. Young, very bright, very introverted. Has a lovely wife and two little kids. He left last year, took a position at a research university in Arizona. And of course Cassidy Roth. She worked for Charlie for the last three years or so. He hired her right out of grad school. She's a brilliant chemist. She had a rough life, is a bit odd . . . she really took to Charlie. I adored her, too, but . . ." Her voice trailed off.

"What were you going to say, Lisa? Everything is important."

"When I left Charlie, she came to see me at the school where I work. She was angry with me, told me I couldn't abandon him. I flat out asked her if she was in love with him. I mean, it sounds crazy—I trusted Charlie explicitly, and Cassidy was nearly half his age. Yet . . . he had been acting off. Not like he was cheating on me, just that he was lost."

"What did she say?"

"She said she loved him like a father. That if I couldn't see that, I was stupid. Cassidy has always been blunt—

one of the reasons Charlie liked her so much. But she was young, and sometimes didn't realize or didn't care what she said. She didn't have much tact, I guess you'd say."

"Do you know how to reach her?"

"I really don't. But she's in her late twenties and graduated from the Texas A and M master's program in genetic engineering, I believe. She doesn't have any family—her dad was an alcoholic and left the family when she was young, and her mother died while she was in college. I think that's why she attached so strongly to Charlie. She needed someone. She could be intense, which made it difficult for anyone to get close to her if she didn't consider them her intellectual equal."

"Thank you, Lisa. If you can find out anything else about her—where she lives, her phone number—it would help."

Lucy hung up. "What do you think?" she asked Leo. "Cassidy Roth—C. R.?"

"We need to talk to Ms. Roth as soon as possible."

"Makes me wonder why neither Ms. Okala nor Ms. Clarke mentioned her as a possible identity behind the C. R. in Paul Grey's calendar."

"Doesn't make me wonder," Leo said. "They were lying, pure and simple. Now we have to find out why."

CHAPTER THIRTEEN

After lunch Sean walked into the small US Marshals' office in the San Antonio federal courthouse. His contact was Marshal John Jimenez, who had facilitated meetings between Sean and Jesse during the year Jesse was in WITSEC. He was privy to the Spades' new arrangement with the FBI in Sacramento, and Jesse's visitation with Sean this summer. Though the marshals' office considered the threat level against the Spades low, they were keeping the file open. After all, Carson Spade had worked for a brutal criminal organization for years. Sean's brother Duke had installed security in the Spade house in Sacramento, and Sean had tested it vigorously. Nothing was foolproof, but it was better than most home-based security systems.

"Thanks for meeting me, John," Sean said.

"You didn't give me a choice, did you?" John motioned toward the coffeepot in the reception.

"No thanks, and I really do appreciate your time."

John poured himself a cup and sipped. "I need ten

minutes, Mags," he said to the administrator. Mags Cortez scared Sean. She looked at him as if she could read his mind, which would rarely be a good thing. She ran the office and the four deputy marshals permanently assigned here. The director position was open, and had been for most of the time Sean had known John.

John closed the door to the conference room and sat down. Sean followed suit. John had Jesse's file in front of him.

"I can't give you the threat assessment, Sean. I told you that last month, and nothing has changed."

"Jesse and I were followed yesterday when we left the Rib House. I lost the tail and haven't seen them since. And I'll admit—it might have something to do with my business, and not Carson Spade, but I need to cover all bases here. I'm working with my people at RCK on our own internal threat assessment, but this situation could be related to Spade."

"Jose Flores is the lone survivor of the Flores cartel," John said, "and our contacts at the DEA are confident that the entire cartel has disbanded. Other cartels are gaining strength—as I'm sure you know, considering your brother's work—but they wouldn't be out for Spade's hide. The destruction of the Flores cartel gave them a bigger share of the pie, so what would be the reason?"

"Kane's making sure that Jose Flores is truly retired," Sean said, choosing his words carefully. "But you and I both know that Carson Spade was up to his eyeballs in money laundering. He may not have been completely honest with you." Spade was a liar, and Sean had been suspicious of him from the beginning. That hadn't changed.

"I can't talk to you about his plea agreement."

"Which was bullshit," Sean muttered.

John didn't say anything.

"I manipulated the tail into running a red light at Military and Roosevelt. There's a red-light camera on the corner." He slid over his business card with the time of the breach, and make and model of the car. "I can't legally get this information, but you can."

John picked up the card and sighed. He put it on top of his folder. "I can't give you the information, Sean. But I can pull up their images and run them against the criminal database. If something pops that may indicate that there is a threat, I'll call you."

"That's all I'm asking."

"How's Jesse?"

"Great. Irritated that I have him on house arrest today until I get this figured out."

"You left him alone?"

"He's well protected." Kane had arrived right on time, and they reviewed external security just to be certain Sean's system was functioning properly. But Sean wouldn't leave Jesse with just anyone.

John sipped his coffee. "We wouldn't have supported the move out of WITSEC if there was a viable threat against any member of the family. You know that, right?"

Sean conceded the point. John was a good guy—a stellar record, former military, and smart. "I don't trust Carson Spade. He hated the arrangement from the beginning. I can't help but think he either didn't know everyone he could have pissed off, or he didn't tell the US Attorney everything."

"I wouldn't go around making accusations you can't back up."

"It's my gut telling me something was off about what happened last night."

"They must not have been very good if you picked up on them."

"No front license plate. Dark sedan. Tinted windows. Two burly guys in the front seat. Yeah, definitely flagged for me. They weren't amateurs, but they weren't professionals. I don't think they wanted me to see them, but they didn't back off when I did."

"Who have *you* angered recently?"

The question angered Sean because he didn't think the tail had anything to do with his work, but it was still a valid point.

He said, "You heard about the human-trafficking ring that went through San Antonio a few months back."

"I did."

"My wife was involved in that operation, and I had a peripheral role through RCK." No reason to give John too many details of RCK's role in shutting down Zimmerman's human pipeline. "Most of the low-level operatives are in prison, they don't worry me. Most of the high-level operatives are dead. But there's always one, isn't there?"

"Prison?"

"He wasn't granted bail—a small miracle—pending trial. I've already put a call into the right people to find out if he's been making calls and to who."

"You have a lot of friends."

"When I need to protect my family, I'll call in every chit I have."

"Can I give you some advice?"

"Do I have a choice?"

John smiled, but it didn't reach his eyes. "You've been in security for a long time. You know what you're doing. But you also have only three more weeks with your son. Don't let this cloud your time with him. Be cautious, but have fun."

The more Sean thought about it, the more he thought that Carson Spade was somehow responsible for yesterday's tail. It was the only thing that made sense. If Spade hadn't been honest with the marshals, then there could be a threat they weren't prepared for. The family had been officially out of WITSEC for six weeks—more than enough time for the bad guys to figure it out and trace them.

He called FBI ASAC Dean Hooper on his way back to the house. Dean was a longtime friend of the Rogans. Kane had known his wife long before Dean came into the picture, when Sonia was an undercover ICE agent. When a threat emerged against Sonia and her family, Sean and Duke had provided bodyguard protection. They'd met Dean and had been close ever since.

"Rogan? Can I put you on hold a sec?"

"Sure." Sean had called Dean on his cell phone—he didn't need this call going through FBI channels.

Still, Dean was one of those straitlaced FBI agents that generally made Sean squirm. If they hadn't had a history, Sean didn't think he and Dean would like each other very much. Sean tended to skirt the law while Dean was diligent in upholding it. He had worked out of FBI main headquarters for years in the White Collar Crimes Division, moving to Sacramento so that he could marry Sonia, whose career and family kept her in Northern California. Though the relocation had necessitated giving up his assistant directorship, it seemed that over the last few years he'd become the point person for white-collar investigations and consulted with FBI offices all over the country. That Carson Spade was put on probation in Sacramento was no surprise—not only did it put him under the purview of one of the smartest FBI white-collar crime agents Sean had ever met, it kept Jesse close to the Rogan side of the family. A win–win.

"Sorry to keep you waiting," Dean said when he finally picked up the phone.

Dean sounded busy, so Sean got to the point. "I think Carson Spade is up to something. I can't put my finger on what. Last night Jesse and I were followed coming out of a restaurant. I'm not working on anything big right now, I don't think it's my job."

"Do you have any evidence?"

"Instincts."

"I trust your instincts, Sean, more than most. But it's a big leap from 'I'm being followed' to 'Carson Spade is up to something illegal.'"

"I want to set up a sting."

"Whoa. Stop right there."

"Look, he hasn't changed his stripes. I know it, you know it."

"I know nothing of the sort."

"If he's not up to something, then he wasn't honest with the US Attorney and he has more enemies than we know."

"We have no evidence that he wasn't completely honest."

"He's a good liar."

"Sean, you're grasping at straws. You're letting your emotions cloud your judgment."

Sean tensed. "That's not it."

"I get it, Sean—Carson Spade is guilty of a multitude of crimes, he put Jesse and your family in harm's way. I know this is difficult for you, but if Spade's attorney gets wind that you're accusing him of a new crime, everything goes back into the courts and I won't have any leverage. He could argue any number of points, including a conflict of interest because of our friendship. If Spade is transferred out of my jurisdiction, I have no way of keeping an eye on him."

Sean knew that Dean had done everything in his power to keep Spade in Sacramento, but his instincts were rarely wrong, even when his emotions were involved.

"So he's done everything you've asked?"

"I can't talk to you about the terms of his probation. You know that." Now Dean sounded angry. Sean didn't want to make him mad, but this was his son's life.

"I'll bet if you dangle a carrot, he'll go for it. If he thinks he can get away with it."

"You cannot dangle any carrot, Rogan," Dean said sharply. "You're too close to this. And I get it—he put your son in danger. I don't like the guy. But so far, he has met every term of his probation. I can't accuse him of breaking the agreement when I have no evidence, and I can't let *you* of all people set him up. This isn't a closed FBI operation. The marshals are involved. RCK has a lot of leeway because of Rick Stockton; that doesn't transcend to other branches of law enforcement."

"I get that, but—"

"Have you considered that Carson *or* Madison hired a private investigator to follow you? Madison gave you liberal visitation rights when she didn't have to—she could have tied you up in court until Jesse was eighteen. What if she's having second thoughts? Or wants to make sure her son is okay? She's been through a lot in the last year."

Sean didn't have a lot of sympathy for his ex-girlfriend. She'd lied to him for years. She never told him she was pregnant. When she first asked for help in finding Jesse, she didn't even tell him that Jesse was his son—he knew it only after he saw the boy's photo. Jesse looked just like Sean. Hair a little lighter, skin tone a bit darker, but Jesse had the same deep-blue eyes that Sean and Kane shared. She couldn't deny it then. Still, forgiveness was hard, because Sean had missed out on the first twelve years of his son's life, and then lost him again to witness protection for a year. It was only now that he could finally have a relationship with his only child.

"Maybe I should just ask her."

"Or not."

"She won't lie to me again."

"I wish I had your confidence in everything, Rogan."

"It's my gut, Dean. She feels guilty for keeping Jesse from me, she won't lie to me. She'll justify it, but she won't lie."

"Your call."

"And Spade?"

"You're still going with this?"

What could he say? He wanted to take him down, but Dean was right. If Sean's fingers were anywhere near a sting, Spade could use Sean's personal involvement against him. Sean didn't want to risk never seeing Jesse again.

"Just . . . please watch him closely, Dean. You're the fucking smartest cop I've ever known. If you think something is up, you'll do something about it."

Dean sighed. "Sean—look. I can't talk to you about Spade or anything that we're working on. But I'll take your warning to heart, okay? Let me handle this. I'm going to pretend this call was solely personal. Sonia is doing great, thanks for asking."

"Give her a kiss for me."

Sean hung up and called Madison before he could change his mind. She answered on the second ring.

"Sean?"

"Hi, Madison."

"Is Jesse okay?"

"Of course. We've been having a blast."

"Can I talk to him?"

"I'm not home."

"You left him home alone? After everything he's been through?" Her voice rose in pitch.

"He's with Kane."

"Oh."

Sean could hear her biting her nails. "Madison, Jesse is great and I'll bring him home two weeks from Sunday, just like I promised."

"I know. I just miss him. A lot."

"You talk to him almost every day."

"It's not the same thing."

"No, it's not—and I'm glad you recognize that, Madison."

"How many times do I have to tell you I'm sorry?"

"I don't want to fight, Madison." His heart wouldn't be in it. "I know you're sorry."

"Okay. Good."

"Did you hire a private investigator to check up on Jesse?"

"No, why would I?"

"Because you don't trust me."

"Trust you? What has that got to do with anything?"

She sounded confused, and Sean didn't think she had any knowledge of the tail. But it was harder knowing whether someone was lying if you weren't face-to-face.

"Someone followed me yesterday. I thought maybe you'd hired a PI to, I don't know, catch me doing something or whatever. I don't know how you think, I just know you weren't happy about Jesse wanting to spend so much time with me."

"Someone followed you? Who? Why?"

"I'll find out."

"Is Jesse okay?"

"I told you he was."

"Maybe I should come out there."

Odd. She didn't ask Sean to send Jesse back, but she wanted to come to San Antonio?

"Go right ahead, but you're not staying at the house. This is my time with Jesse, and I'm spending every available minute with him."

"I know. I get it, Sean, and I really *am* sorry."

This time, she sounded sincere.

"I'll have Jesse call you tonight."

"Thanks."

He ended the call as he drove into his neighborhood.

Madison was a good liar, but he didn't think she was lying about hiring a PI. How could he be sure?

And of course that didn't mean that Carson Spade didn't hire someone. Men like Spade had a lot of shady friends.

Sean would get to the bottom of it, and if Spade was behind it he would skewer him.

CHAPTER FOURTEEN

The bar where Charlie and Paul had their confrontation was well outside the city, in a rural area in the adjoining county. The jukebox blared country music with a twang, and the patrons wore faded jeans, cowboy hats, and T-shirts. At three on a Thursday afternoon it wasn't crowded—a dozen people drinking beer, playing darts, or shooting the breeze. And as was the case at many neighborhood bars, the bar stools held old-timers. Half the patrons openly carried guns, but Texas was an open-carry state. They needed to be licensed, but it wasn't a crime, and neither Lucy nor Leo was here to cause problems for the bartender or the patrons.

"You're here about that guy," the bartender said after Leo showed his badge. He had a cut on his forehead that was healing, but it would likely scar.

"You're Jim Crouch?"

"Yep."

"Do you have a minute?"

"Sure. Want a beer?"

"I wish," Leo said. "Still on duty."

"Have a seat. Coke? Water? On the house."

"A couple waters would be nice, thanks," Leo said.

He and Lucy sat at one end of the bar. Jim put two cold mugs with filtered ice water in front of them. "I saw the news. You're following up, right, because that guy caused a fight the other week." He pointed to his head. "I wouldn't have pressed charges, but the guy was off his meds. I needed to file the complaint or I would have had to pay for the hospital myself, and my insurance company needed the police reports. And I wouldn't have gone to the hospital at all, but he whacked me good and I saw stars for hours."

"Why don't you start from the beginning?" Leo said. "First, had you ever seen Mr. McMahon or his friend before?"

"Nope, they'd never been in here. That was another thing—sure, we get strangers in here now and again, but most everyone is a regular. Some people come in most days, others once or twice a month, but I know nearly everybody who walks through that door. Happy hour starts at three because most of my people start work before dawn, come here on their way home. I close down at eleven during the week, stay open as late as people want on the weekends. This was a Friday, the last Friday of the month, which is always busy—a lot of folks get paid on Friday. So it was crowded and they were talking at the table right there." He gestured to a small square table in the narrow space between the end of the bar and the emergency exit.

"It's a private little corner, not much room to maneuver, they were minding their own business, or so I thought," Crouch said. "McMahon had a beer, but he didn't even finish it. The other guy—I found out later his name was Paul—he had a couple shots, he was definitely drowning something, ya know? And then Paul gets up to leave and stumbles. McMahon jumps up and grabs him. I thought he was grabbing him to take his keys or something. I didn't think he was drunk, but hell, he had three shots and a beer and he wasn't a big guy. Lightweight. But then McMahon hits him. Right cross to the jaw, wham. Paul goes down. I got over there, told them to take it outside. Paul gets up, pushes McMahon, and McMahon hits him again. The guy just lost it. I stepped in and he walloped me. I wasn't expecting it—I've broken up a lot of fights in my day, never been hit like that. I hit my head on the bar, couldn't catch myself in time, and one of my regulars called the cops. Fortunately, we get a few of the deputies here after shift, they know me, they came fast and broke it up—some of my guys came to my defense, so it got to be a real brawl."

"Did you hear what McMahon and Grey were talking about?" Leo asked.

"Not really. It was busy, and it was just me and Sugar running the bar because my other girl called in sick." He rolled his eyes as if he didn't believe she'd been sick. He called over to one of the guys at the bar, "Hey, Dog, did you hear what those two guys fighting the other week were talking about? You were sitting right next to them."

An old man—he had to be in his seventies—wearing

a VIETNAM VETERAN baseball cap shrugged. "Not really. They were hush-hush."

Lucy asked, "You remember the fight?"

"Yep, my mind is all here. Oh—well, you know, that reminds me. They were talking about something that the big guy forgot. And the little guy said it wasn't important. That's what set the big guy off. He said something like, 'It's important, why won't you help me?' Or something like that." He sipped his beer.

More of the same, Lucy thought. Charlie McMahon was trying to remember something and he couldn't, and it bothered him. More than bothered him.

"How long were they here?" Leo asked Crouch.

"McMahon came in first, ordered his beer. The other guy, Paul, came in maybe twenty minutes later. I can't say for certain because it was busy, but something like that. Oh, and Paul paid for all the bar damages. The judge at the arraignment said that McMahon would have to pay restitution. Then on Monday, that guy Paul Grey came in with a check and said he wanted to pay, that it wasn't the big guy's fault."

That was interesting. Lucy asked, "Did he say anything else?"

"No—just that he wanted to cover it, the check was for five thousand dollars. I told him that was too much, I didn't think the damage would cost more than two thou, tops, but he said to keep it." He paused. "I wouldn't have, you know. I made a copy of the check so I have his address, I would have sent him the difference."

Lucy believed the guy. He had that vibe about him, that his honor was important.

"What was his mood? His demeanor?"

"Sad. Like his dog had died. He was quiet—I got the impression that he's just a quiet guy—but he said not to hold it against Charlie. I said something like I hope they work it out, and he just shook his head and walked out."

"Monday? A week ago?"

"No, this Monday."

"What time?" Leo asked.

"Seven, or thereabouts. Not later than seven."

Dog piped up from his stool. "Quarter to seven. I looked at my watch. And remember, I said you should give us all a round on the house."

"And I did, didn't I?"

"All ten of us," Dog laughed. "Mondays are fucking slow. Excuse my French, pretty lady," he added to Lucy with a wink.

Lucy smiled back, the harmless old man humoring her more than insulting her.

"Leo," she said quietly, "that would be after his scheduled meeting."

Leo said to Jim, "When Paul Grey came in, was he alone? Did he meet with anyone?"

"No. Didn't order a drink or anything. Just walked in, waited at the end of the bar until I came over, and gave me the check. Is something wrong?"

Leo said, "Paul Grey was killed Monday night. You may have been the last person to see him alive."

The last person, Lucy thought, except his killer.

* * *

"Can you be late?" Leo asked Lucy.

"Late?"

"It's nearly five. Julie Peters sent a message to both Tia and me to meet her at the morgue, but we won't get back to headquarters until after six or so."

"That's fine," Lucy said. She sent Sean a message that she would be home by seven. "Sean is having fun with Jesse, he barely notices when I'm late."

"What's your take about what happened at the bar?" Leo asked Lucy as he drove through rush-hour traffic.

"The fight? It shows that McMahon had the potential to be violent, but that it was targeted. Hitting the bartender wasn't the intention, hitting Paul was. Yet Paul seemed to think the fight was his fault, even though he didn't throw a punch. Paying for the damages—that was surprising. But more surprising is that he went back there on Monday."

"After his five thirty meeting with C. R. Do you have any information about McMahon's assistant Roth?"

Lucy scanned her messages. "Nothing yet."

"Paul lies to his wife, leaves work early, meets—we presume—McMahon's old assistant, pays off McMahon's debt at the bar, and then . . . what?"

"Maybe he felt bad for his friend. Thought that something was seriously wrong with him and didn't want the pressure of the debt on him." But as Lucy said it, she didn't believe it. Maybe if he paid actual damages—but paying more than twice what the bartender said the damages were? That was . . . odd. And his demeanor was sad? Why sad?

"But where did he go after?" Leo asked. "You know,

that bar is remote—way out in southeast Guadalupe County. I'm going to contact the sheriff over there and have them double down looking for Grey's vehicle."

Leo got on the phone, and Lucy read the text message from Sean.

I'm making spaghetti we'll eat at 7:30. Kane's here. Nate's coming by. I'll save you a plate. Love you.

She smiled. She loved Sean's spaghetti sauce. It had been the first thing he'd cooked for her.

Because they were in the middle of rush hour, it took them nearly an hour to arrive at the morgue. Tia was already there. They traded information—Tia didn't have much, but April Forsyth was certain the man in the grainy photo was the same guy who'd left the coffeehouse right before McMahon took hostages. "She said it was his build and clothes more than anything. She's willing to work with a sketch artist, and her dad is bringing her down tomorrow afternoon, so I called in our best guy. But I'm not holding out hope. It sounds like you had a far more productive day."

"More questions than answers," Lucy said, "but we're making progress. We know that Paul Grey was alive at six forty-five on Monday. Hopefully Julie has more information."

They walked in, put on protective shoes and gloves, and were led back to the main autopsy room. Julie Peters stood between two bodies covered with sheets talking to a tall, dark, and handsome man in a lab coat.

"The gang's all here," she said sarcastically. "Took you long enough." Before Lucy could respond, Julie continued. "This is Dr. Dominic Moreno with the university. Brain expert. Moreno, FBI Agents Lucy Kincaid and Leo Proctor, and Detective Tia Mancini. They're probably the only cops I like."

He smiled warmly and nodded. "You certainly caught a most fascinating case," Dr. Moreno said in a deep, well-modulated voice. Julie looked at Lucy with an expression that said, *See what I mean?*

Lucy gave her a nod and focused on Moreno.

"How so?" Tia asked.

"I've already sent Mr. McMahon's brain to my lab, but Julie thought I should explain what we found during the autopsy."

"A tumor?" Leo said, sounding hopeful.

"No, there was no sign of a tumor, but there was another anomaly. Something I have never seen before—either professionally or in medical journals. I need to do more tests, and we've requested some very specific blood tests, in addition to the standard toxicology screens."

"Don't keep us in suspense, Doc," Tia said.

"The preliminary report indicated that McMahon was complaining that he couldn't remember something important. He acted paranoid, possible paranoid schizophrenic. One sign of schizophrenia is a loss of gray matter in adults. I didn't see this in McMahon. However, an MRI showed that the nerves leading from his hippocampus—which is sort of like the control room for long-term memories—were damaged."

"How could that happen? A brain injury?" Lucy asked. "Blunt force?"

"There was no sign of a previous concussion—and it

would have to be a severe trauma to the back of the skull to result in this kind of deep tissue damage. No sign of any trauma whatsoever. I've ordered several hormone tests. It's just a theory at this point until I get these tests back, and it could take a week or longer before I have any answers."

"What's your theory?" Leo asked.

Moreno hesitated. "I can't say this with any authority. And I need to study the brain further, get the tests back, consult with my colleagues. I was serious when I said I have never encountered anything like this. If I can't find an external cause, it could be genetic—and then I would want his children to come in for an MRI."

"Okay, off the record then," Tia said, just as curious as the rest of them.

Moreno frowned, glanced at Julie. "Don't look at me, Dom. I told you they'd want to know what we think."

He sighed.

"We understand," Lucy said. "This is just a theory."

Dr. Moreno said, "First, the hippocampus isn't the only place memories are stored. Long-term memories are stored all over the brain, and the hippocampus helps pull together those memories into recollections. Such as seeing a friend from high school ten years later at a grocery store. You don't expect to see that person, you recognize them but don't know why. Your brain sends signals from different parts until you recall exactly how you know the person. But if you saw that same person at a high school reunion, you wouldn't have to 'think' about it, because you expect to see your high school friends at a high school event, even years later.

"There is far more we *don't* know about the brain and how it works than we *do* know. We know that the amagydala, for example, controls core emotions like rage and love. We know that memories need nerves to travel back and forth within the brain. Based on the MRI, McMahon's nerves had severe damage. He may have experienced debilitating headaches, as bad as the worst migraine you've ever had. His memories could have been gone as a result of this nerve damage."

"Like amnesia?" Tia asked.

"In a way. I listened to the audio file of the negotiations, and there were a few things that caught my attention. He *sounded* paranoid, but the key point was that he didn't *remember.* We've all had that happen to us, and it's irritating, right? When we know we should know something, but can't put it together. A word on the tip of our tongue. A person we recognize but don't remember why. I think that process of trying to recall information physically pained him. Fingers-on-a-chalkboard irritation, but where the pain is real and long lasting. This inability to recollect something he deemed important turned into a form of paranoia. *They. They killed him.* He bonded with you, Agent Proctor. The way he spoke. He feared that anyone who sought out the answers *like his friend Paul* would die."

"Why did he fire his gun?" Leo asked. "If he'd put his gun down, SWAT wouldn't have fired."

"I can't answer that. Reaction? Panic? Fear? The core emotions that I mentioned—rage, love—that also would include fear. Fear is, in fact, the most elemental—primitive—emotion and drives us in ways we don't always recognize. I suspect Mr. McMahon's fear level was higher, he was reacting to everything he saw and heard, but he couldn't make connections."

"Wouldn't people have noticed this?" Lucy asked. "Schizophrenia, for example, rarely hits older adults."

"I don't believe he was schizophrenic. But based on his actions, and the lack of a brain tumor, a severe hormonal imbalance impacted him. According to the preliminary report, his wife said she noticed a change in his behavior in late March or early April? Around Easter?"

"Yes," Lucy said.

"I would look for some sort of trauma in the weeks—maybe months before that. We couldn't find any physical evidence, but I'm going to study the brain with more sensitive equipment."

Julie said, "I've also asked for a full genetic profile. If his genes told his body to stop producing glutamate for some odd reason, that might contribute to the deterioration of his nerves. It would get worse over time."

"Thank you for your work on this," Leo said. "I want to tell his wife what happened, and even if we don't know for certain, it sounds like it is likely a medical condition that spurned his behavior."

"I won't put it in writing yet," Julie said, "but I'm leaning that way. But now for the big news."

"That wasn't big enough?" Tia said. "It's more than I thought you'd be able to get from the corpse."

"Not McMahon, but Paul Grey."

Julie was practically jumping up and down.

"You know who the killer is," Lucy teased.

"Yes!"

Lucy wasn't expecting *that* answer.

"You have forensic evidence that proves McMahon killed him?" Tia asked. "I knew you were good, Julie, but you're the absolutely best."

"Yes, I *am* the best," Julie said, "but McMahon didn't kill Paul Grey."

They all stared at her. Julie milked it for several seconds before Leo broke down and said, "Then who?"

"Grey killed himself."

"How can you be certain?" Tia asked.

"Do you doubt me?"

"No, but—"

"It sounds like you doubt me."

"We don't," Lucy said, "but Grey's body was moved after he was killed. He didn't move his own body."

"No need for sarcasm, Agent Kincaid," Julie said. "That's your job, right? All I can tell you definitively is that Paul Grey killed himself. The angle of the gunshot wound is consistent with a self-inflicted gunshot. It's very difficult to plan a homicide as a suicide and get the angle right."

"Unless the victim is drugged."

"Even then, it's difficult, but yes, it's possible. I've asked for a wide array of tests in case I'm wrong—but I don't think I am. The victim will jerk, turn away from the gun, and the angle is generally straight-on—this was angled precisely, as if he was holding the gun. Plus, he had gunpowder residue on his hand *and* on his clothing. I've seen homicides where the killer attempted to make the murder look like suicide, but it's actually harder to do in real life than it is in the movies. But I have another piece of forensic evidence. Well, it doesn't prove suicide, but it does tell you *where* he was killed. He had glass embedded in the left side of his skull—I've sent it to the lab, but I'm pretty certain it's automotive glass. I think he was sitting in the driver's seat of a car, killed himself, the bullet went through—it was a three fifty-seven, which carries a wallop—shattered the glass, and he slumped against the broken window. Well, the glass didn't shatter—it was safety glass—but it crumbled enough that a few chunks found their way into his head. Possibly when whoever moved him got him out of the car."

"He killed himself," Leo said, stunned.

"Yep, I'm one hundred percent positive. Well, I'll say I'm ninety-nine percent positive. I had my boss run through it with me, and he concurs. No alcohol in his system. He hadn't eaten for more than eight hours—my guess was a salad and steak, likely between noon and one the day he died."

"Do you have time of death, too?"

"That's harder. It was hot, humid, and his body was moved. But based on his stomach contents, rigor mortis, temp, and adjusting the best I can for the conditions at the McMahon house? He died between eight p.m. and midnight on Monday. I'd put it closer to eight, but we just can't be positive."

"This is—surprising," Tia said. "I didn't see that coming."

"He killed himself and then what? McMahon moved his body?" Lucy said. "Why?"

"I'm not a psychiatrist," Dr. Moreno said, "but maybe that was the trigger. Seeing his friend dead snapped something in McMahon. Maybe he took his friend's body to his house in a way to protect him—and then forgot. Thought he was meeting him. And then in his own way remembered that he was dead."

"But there was no evidence on McMahon that he moved Grey's body."

"Not on his person. SAPD has his clothing and shoes," Julie reminded him.

Tia said, "Grey killed himself, McMahon snapped, case closed."

"No," Leo said. "It's not that simple."

"Sometimes it is," Tia said.

"This time, I don't think so," Lucy said. "We immediately assumed that Grey was murdered—largely because his body was moved, no gun was found at the scene, and it was a close-range head wound. Why would someone want a suicide to look like murder?"

"Insurance," Tia and Julie said simultaneously. Tia continued, "Most life insurance policies don't pay out for suicides."

"Not just staging the suicide to look like murder," Leo said, "but bringing the body to the McMahon house."

"Which points to Charlie McMahon," Tia said. "Maybe McMahon tried to talk him out of it, couldn't, Grey dies, Charlie doesn't want his wife to lose the life insurance policy, stages it to look like a murder."

This was getting too complicated, Lucy thought. And considering McMahon's state of mind at the time he took the hostages, she didn't think he could formulate such a complex plan.

"We need to step back and take the investigation one step at a time," she said. "I don't think that McMahon could have done this, at least not after witnessing his behavior the day he died."

"I'm inclined to agree with Agent Kincaid," Dr. Moreno said. "Based on my preliminary findings, I believe that McMahon was in severe pain. Julie, his stomach and liver?"

Julie nodded. "The guy didn't eat in more than twelve hours before he died, but he had six times the recommended dosage of aspirin in his system, and his liver showed early signs of Salicylate poisoning. I think he was eating aspirin like candy."

"Did it give him any relief?" Lucy asked.

"I doubt it," Moreno said. "And it may have contributed to his symptoms of paranoia and confusion."

Tia said to Leo, "You solved your case, and if Moreno and Peters can point to a medical reason for McMahon's actions yesterday morning, SAPD will close this case."

"We don't have proof that McMahon moved Grey's body," Leo said. "We don't know where he killed himself, where his car is, or *why* he killed himself."

"And what's the crime? Tampering with a crime scene? Misdemeanor. Sometimes, a spade is a spade."

"And sometimes, a conspiracy is a conspiracy," Leo snapped. He rubbed his eyes. "I'm sorry."

"It's been a long two days," Tia said.

"I'm pursuing this," Leo said. "There was something odd at Clarke-Harrison. They pretended they were being forthcoming, but it was all an act and we got nothing of substance from them. When are you releasing the cause of death?"

"The first bullet was fatal on McMahon, the other two would have been fatal as well. That's cause of death. We're pending medicals, but that's just paperwork. If there was a neurological or drug component, that goes to his actions prior to death, not cause of death—though we'll add it to the file as a mitigating factor. As far as Paul Grey? Self-inflicted gunshot wound. My boss will sign it tomorrow and we'll release it, but I can hold it until the end of the day. Who's telling the family?"

"We will," Leo said. "In the morning. It's seven o'clock, we've been working straight through for twelve hours. Mrs. Grey already knows that her husband is dead—tomorrow morning is soon enough for her to learn how."

CHAPTER FIFTEEN

Lucy rushed home after Leo brought her back to FBI headquarters, but she still didn't arrive until nearly eight. Sean was dishing up the spaghetti.

She gave him a quick kiss. "I told you not to wait for me."

"We were playing pool."

Sean had bought a pool table when he found out that Jesse was going to be spending six weeks with him this summer. They'd all had fun with it.

"Nate won," Jesse said. "I didn't think anyone could beat my dad."

Nate ruffled Jesse's head. "It's because your dad's too cocky and thinks he can't lose."

"Not cocky, confident. And I don't lose very often."

Lucy could see Sean swell with pride every time Jesse called him dad. It made her doubly thankful that the Spades had been taken out of WITSEC.

"I saw that, Dunning," Sean said.

"What?" Nate asked innocently. He scratched

Bandit behind the ears while the golden retriever licked his lips and looked up at Nate adoringly.

"You're fucking impossible," Sean muttered and brought the bowl of spaghetti with his amazing meat sauce to the table. When it was just two or three of them, they ate on stools at the center island, but five required the kitchen table. Lucy could still count on one hand how many times they'd eaten in the formal dining room. Why even have it?

Kane brought over several beers and a basket of fresh garlic bread. Nate grabbed a bowl of Caesar salad.

"If you want to run upstairs and change or anything, it's fine with me," Sean said.

"I'm starving," she said. "It's been a long day, and the last ninety minutes we were at the morgue." She sat down, glad to get off her feet.

"The morgue?" Jesse asked, sitting between Sean and Kane. "That's like, both cool and totally gross."

"Not that gross. I worked at the morgue for a year in DC. But it's probably not appropriate dinner conversation." Just what Sean needed, she thought: Jesse going home and telling Madison all about the violence and death Lucy surrounded herself with.

"Maybe after dinner," Sean said. "I for one want to know what happened with that McMahon guy. The press wasn't kind to him—he's fired, his wife leaves him, he takes a bunch of people hostage."

"It's more complicated than that," Lucy said. She glanced over at Nate. He was dishing up, either ignoring the conversation or thinking about the shooting. Nate was a tough guy and had been trained in the military.

McMahon wasn't the first person he'd shot and killed. But every life taken, even if it was justified, scratched away at your soul. She was really glad he was here to-night. He might not realize it, but he needed friends.

They dished up and ate, chatting about the pool table, video games, and music. Nate was a die-hard country music fan, which irritated Sean—it was probably the only thing they argued about, other than Nate feeding Bandit scraps and letting him sleep on the bed when Nate house-sat.

"Truce," Lucy said. "I'm stuffed." She got up and started to clear the table.

"Jesse," Sean said.

"Right!" Jesse jumped up and started stacking plates. Lucy came back to take them, and Jesse said, "I got it. I lost a bet today, I have KP duty."

"KP?" She glanced at Sean.

"He lost, he has to pay the piper. In this case, rinse the dishes. It's not like I'm making him clean the bath-room with his toothbrush."

"Betting with a teenager. Good example there, Ro-gan." She smiled and kissed him.

Kane got up to help Jesse with the kitchen, and Lucy, Sean, and Nate went to relax in the living room. She kicked off her shoes and curled her legs underneath her. Sean handed her a glass of wine. "My second glass? And it's a work night. You're a bad influence on me, Mr. Rogan."

"You'll sleep well."

She sipped, put the glass down. Nate sat on the floor with Bandit. "There were some anomalies in McMahon's brain, but no tumor. It's something so unusual that even the neurosurgeon Julie brought in hadn't seen it before. He won't go on record yet, but he thinks that the nerves that connect the hippocampus to the rest of the brain were severely damaged, but he can't imagine what caused it because there was no sign of physical trauma. The symptoms would be severe headaches and memory loss. Which explains not just a lot of what McMahon said to Leo during negotiations, but what the witnesses observed. His behavior suggested intense paranoia, but it may have been caused by whatever was going on in his brain—which was likely hormonal or genetic. Though I took advanced biology, this is way out of my skill set. They're going to need a couple of days."

Nate asked, "Did Julie tell you which shot was fatal?"

"The first, though all three would have resulted in a fatality. Does that make you feel better?"

"Not better or worse. I just wanted to know."

She didn't ask which shot was his—she knew he took the first shot, but the other two came simultaneously a second later. All three men had decided to fire at the same time, Nate was just faster.

"How's Jagger?" Lucy asked. The SWAT team leader for SAPD had been shot in his vest.

"Fine. Bruised. He's on mandatory leave, too. The guy should never have been able to get off a shot. If he was a better shot, he could have hit Ben in the head. Our headgear is good, but not bulletproof."

"Now for the real surprise," Lucy said. "Paul Grey committed suicide."

She explained what Julie had said, and that they were now perplexed about who would have moved his body. "The other consideration," Lucy said, "is that someone forced him to kill himself."

"That would be hard—unless someone he cared about was in jeopardy," Sean said. "Still, self-preservation is hard to fight."

"Everything we know about Paul Grey was that he and Charlie had been friends since college, Charlie hired him eight years ago and he relocated here from Los Angeles, and he was a smart, quiet researcher. But something was going on with him, and I think he planned to kill himself. He paid Charlie's debts—the bar fight that they were in two weeks ago. Immediately before that, he met with someone—we believe it was Charlie's former research assistant, but we haven't been able to locate her."

Sean rubbed her leg. "You just have to ask."

"Maybe I will, but our cyber team is on it. Yes, you could do it faster, but they'll find her."

"So he killed himself," Nate said, "and someone moved the body to McMahon's house? Who? Why?"

"Maybe McMahon himself, but so far there's no evidence of that. SAPD is processing his clothes and truck—if a body was moved in his truck, they'll find trace. Until then, we follow the path wherever it leads." Lucy glanced toward the kitchen. The water was running and Jesse and Kane were talking, though she couldn't see them from here. She kept her voice low and asked Sean, "Did you talk to Jimenez?"

Sean nodded. "He's going to pull the camera feed from that corner. He may or may not give me the information."

"He can't legally share it," she said.

"Unless he thinks there's a direct threat."

"What did you tell Jesse?"

"I'm not lying to him." Sean glanced over to make sure Jesse wasn't in hearing distance. "I called Madison and asked if she hired someone to check up on me and Jesse. She didn't."

"You *what*? Sean—I would be furious if I were her."

"She didn't, and she wasn't mad—she was apologetic that I would think she would do something like that. But I wouldn't put it past Carson. I didn't suggest it to her—I don't think she thought of it—but he doesn't like me."

"Big surprise there," Nate said.

"I called Dean."

Lucy didn't know if that was the smartest move, either. "Dean can't have you involved with Spade's probation."

"I know—but I don't trust Spade, and something about the tail yesterday—it just felt like him. His attempt to unnerve me or something."

"Which it has."

"Not like he thinks."

"Why now?" Nate asked. "And not three and a half weeks ago when Jesse first came?"

"Good question," Sean said. "Maybe he thought I would know it was him. Or maybe—and I've thought about this—he has been keeping an eye on us all along but I didn't notice."

"That's doubtful," Lucy said. "You've been hyper-aware of potential threats because you weren't allowed to view the threat assessment."

"True, but maybe it wasn't overt. Or maybe he's getting worried because Jesse's having fun or Madison is mad at him. When I went to pick Jesse up in Sacramento, the tension was pretty thick between them. Madison was all ready to defend him—even after she knew the truth—but time may have helped the truth sink in. I'm really just guessing here."

"What's Dean going to do?" Lucy said.

"I told him I don't trust the man, and I think he should be cautious. Dean is honestly way smarter than me."

Nate laughed out loud. Bandit shot his head up and thumped his tail against the floor.

"Shut up," Sean said, tossing a couch pillow at his friend. "I can admit when someone is smarter than me."

"Have you considered that Carson isn't behind this?" Lucy asked.

"Yes," Sean admitted. "JT is making sure that there's no fallout on us from the human-trafficking sting. But so far all is silent on that front. And Kane says Jose Flores is keeping clean. If Kane believes it, it's true, because he thinks the worst about pretty much everyone."

"Then put it out of your mind for now. Enjoy the time with Jesse. I'll probably be working most of the weekend, but I'll grab a comp day next Friday to make up for it. Think you can get tickets to the Rangers or the Astros? We can make a weekend of it."

Kane and Jesse came into the living room grinning.

Kane handed Nate another beer, even though he hadn't asked. They exchanged a look, and Lucy wondered what they'd talked about before she got there. Nate didn't have close family—his parents were both dead, they'd been much older when they adopted him. His adoptive sister was substantially older and they rarely talked. When he sought out his birth mother he learned she'd died of a drug overdose long before he found for her. He'd adopted the Rogans. Both Sean and Kane welcomed him without reservation and treated him like a brother.

"Want to go to a baseball game next week?" Sean asked Jesse. "I know you're more into soccer, but—"

"I love baseball."

"Well, the Rangers are outside Dallas and the Astros are in Houston."

"Aren't they like hours away?"

"Not by plane."

"Like, we can fly in your plane just to see a baseball game?"

"We'll do something else, too, make a weekend of it."

"Totally cool. You coming, too, Lucy?"

"I wouldn't miss it. My brother Patrick played in college. I went to almost all his home games."

"Can Kane and Nate come, too?" Jesse asked. "It'll be my last weekend here, unless I can convince my mom to let me stay another week."

Lucy looked over at Sean. His face fell. Not because he didn't want his brother and Nate to join them, but because he didn't want to think about taking Jesse home.

"Sure," Sean said. "The more the merrier. And then you guys can go off and do stuff so I can spend quality time with my wife." He wrapped his arm around Lucy and kissed the top of her head.

"I can't," Kane said. "I'm flying down to Arteaga on Wednesday to pick up Siobhan."

"Nate'll come," Sean said.

"I will? Who'll watch Bandit for you?"

"We'll figure something out."

"I'll think about it. Bandit and I like our time alone."

"Yeah, I know—I find dog hair on the guest bed."

"I'll wash the comforter next time."

"You're ruining my dog."

Nate leaned over to the golden retriever. "Don't listen to him, Bandit. He's just jealous because you love me more."

Sean rolled his eyes.

Lucy said, "I have an early day, and I'm dragging. Have fun, don't call it an early night on account of me."

She went upstairs. Sean followed a minute later. "You okay?" he asked.

"I'm good."

"You seemed—I don't know, upset that I called Dean."

"No, more Madison."

"What?"

"What if you're right and Carson did hire someone to tail you? Why wouldn't she tell him that you called?"

"I don't know—I don't think she will."

"But you don't know."

"What do you think will happen?"

"I don't want to give Madison any reason to keep Jesse from you. You are so amazing with him, and he's really thrived here. He worships Kane—I know partly because of what happened last year, but partly because Kane's as good with him as you are. I couldn't bear to see your heart broken again."

"I'm okay, Luce," he said and kissed her. "I don't trust Carson, but I'm not going off the deep end. I know I can't investigate him. It pains me, but I'm keeping my hands clean. But we both have to be diligent here. If Carson is not involved—if the tail was something else—we both need to be careful."

"I will be. Promise. Now go downstairs. I'm going to shower then crash. I wasn't kidding about the early morning."

"I love you, Lucy."

She smiled and kissed him. "I know."

CHAPTER SIXTEEN

On Friday morning, Lucy drove back out to Helotes with Leo to talk to Paul Grey's widow. Leo had given a status report to Lucy's boss, Rachel Vaughn. Though Leo was technically part of the counter-terrorism squad, because he was the SWAT team leader for the San Antonio office, he worked with all units as needed. Lucy had never worked this closely with Leo on a case, and she liked his style. He reminded her a bit of her mentor, Dr. Hans Vigo, though Leo was former military and looked like it. He was easygoing in many ways, but dogged. He worked logically—point A, to point B, to point C. He wasn't one to dwell on what-ifs, which was perhaps Lucy's only problem with her temporary partner. She liked running through different scenarios, bouncing around ideas to see what fit and what didn't.

However, she would take Leo as a partner over almost anyone else since Nate was on leave. She'd been an FBI agent for just over eighteen months, and while there were ups and downs, she finally felt like she was in her groove in the office. She and her new boss had gone through a rough patch (understatement) but had developed a cordial working relationship. Lucy never saw them being friends—she still walked on eggshells around Rachel, keeping their communications completely professional.

Lucy missed Ryan Quiroz, a seasoned agent who'd transferred to the Austin Resident Agency at the beginning of the year so he could be closer to his two young sons. There had been several new agents who'd joined the Violent Crimes Squad to fill open slots, and Lucy was most often assigned with Jason Lopez—who had come from the Phoenix office with Rachel. Jason had previously been tasked with spying on her, and Lucy was trying to get past that but found it harder than she'd thought. Trust was so important in their work, and that was the one thing that she needed to figure out with Jason and Rachel.

"You're quiet," Leo said as he drove.

She smiled. "Not enough coffee." She didn't want to share her office problems with Leo.

"We'll pick up something on the way back. I saw Nate come in this morning. Shrink debrief. He seemed to be doing good."

"He is, just irritated with mandatory leave. You know how he is."

"Yeah, he's still a soldier at heart. He mentioned that he was over at your place. Having friends helps. Before you and Sean moved here, Nate didn't really connect with anyone."

That surprised Lucy. Their friendship had been easy and comfortable from the beginning.

"Sean's brother Kane is visiting, and he and Nate talked. Worked through whatever was on Nate's mind. Kane is good at that."

Because they were going against commute traffic, they made good time reaching the suburb of Helotes. Diane Grey had made coffee and offered it to them. Lucy was going to decline, but Diane said, "Please—it makes me feel better to just do something. My son is still sleeping—I didn't have the heart to wake him up. He's having a hard time with Paul's death and everything that happened with Charlie—I just can't believe any of this. Charlie was his best friend."

Leo said, "Coffee would be great. And a private place to talk?"

"Of course."

She brought a tray into a den off the living room that had likely been her husband's office. She closed the doors and went through the ritual of pouring coffee and handing out mugs. "I fell asleep in here last night. It still smells like Paul."

This was going to be so much harder than Lucy thought. Telling Diane that her husband was dead had been difficult. But suicide? It was worse.

Leo said, "Late yesterday Agent Kincaid and I talked to Julie Peters, the chief deputy coroner and one of the finest pathologists in the state, who completed your husband's autopsy. She called in the medical examiner himself to confirm her findings. They're ruling Paul's death a suicide."

Diane stared at him. "No. No." She shook her head empathically. "Paul would never in a million years kill himself. That doesn't make any sense whatsoever. I want to talk to this woman. She's absolutely wrong."

"You can review the report, and Ms. Peters will go over it with you if you would like," Leo said. "But the evidence is conclusive."

"But—but you *said* that Paul was found in Charlie's house, you *said* that he'd been shot somewhere else and brought to Charlie's house. See? That doesn't make sense. Were you wrong then? Or maybe you're wrong now?"

"We don't have all the answers, but we will find them," Leo said. "Someone did in fact move your husband's body. We know that he died between eight p.m. and midnight on Monday, and his body was moved at some point before dawn Tuesday morning. We don't know *who* moved his body or why."

"But—I don't understand."

She sounded so lost—far more lost than she had yesterday when her anger fueled her responses.

Grief was a complicated emotion.

"Does Paul own a gun?" Leo asked.

She nodded, tears falling.

"Do you know where it is? What kind?"

"A small gun. I don't know anything about them, I don't know what kind. We have a gun safe."

"Would you mind checking? I'll go with you."

"He—I—" She stood, at a loss for words. Leo walked out with her.

Lucy's heart went out to Diane Grey. Learning of

your husband's death had to be horrific; knowing he committed suicide was soul breaking.

They returned a few minutes later, Diane leading the way, her face a mask of shock. Leo walked behind her and caught Lucy's eye and shook his head.

"He killed himself?" Diane whispered to herself as she sat back down, her hands clasped between her legs.

"Diane," Lucy said, her voice low and calm, "Agent Proctor and I want to find out exactly what happened. Paul's car is still missing, his cell phone is missing and we haven't been able to locate it through GPS, and his behavior was odd on the day he died."

"H-how?" She was trying to pull herself together, but her expression was still of disbelief.

"Yesterday you indicated that you knew about the fight between Paul and Charlie two weeks ago."

"Yes—but only because Paul had a cut on his face and a bruised jaw. He had to tell me."

"The night Paul died, he went to the same bar and paid for the damages. Even though the bartender said Charlie was the one who started it, that Paul was only defending himself, Paul told the bartender it wasn't Charlie's fault."

"They were friends. I guess—I don't know. Paul has a good heart. I guess he wanted to help Charlie."

"He was at the bar just before seven on Monday. According to his schedule, he put a five thirty appointment on his calendar to meet with someone with the initials C. R. We believe that person is Cassidy Roth. Do you know her?"

"Cassidy? Yes, not well. She worked for the division, but mostly for Charlie. She was . . . well, she had few social graces."

"How so?"

"She was blunt. She could be mean, but not on purpose. It's hard to explain. Paul said she was on the autism spectrum, but honestly, I don't know. Sometimes I think that's an excuse for poor manners. She was a very smart girl, just didn't know how to interact with people who weren't as smart as she was. She worshipped Charlie. I said something to Lisa once—it was a barbecue at her house, we were there, Cassidy, a few other people. I said Cassidy had a crush on Charlie. Lisa said no, she already nipped it in the bud. I pushed—because it was an odd thing for her to say. But evidently, Lisa had a conversation with Cassidy and was about to establish some boundaries, when she said she realized that she had nothing to worry about."

Leo asked, "Do you know where Cassidy lives?"

"No, I'm sorry. Lisa might."

"Do you know what your husband was working on at Clarke-Harrison?"

"He never talked about work, other than in the general sense. Especially after Charlie was fired. Paul took over the entire division, and he didn't want it—not like this, at any rate. Charlie and Paul complemented each other. Paul was quiet and studious and liked sitting at his modeling computer working through complex problems and analyzing data. Charlie was the big-picture guy, he could explain to anyone—even if you didn't understand the science behind it—what they were doing and why. He was passionate about their work, everyone loved him. That's why we were all shocked when he was fired. But . . . well, with Lisa leaving him, I guess Charlie just . . . I don't know. I really don't. I haven't seen him in months. I know Paul changed, too . . . he grew more distant, and wouldn't talk about Charlie, so I just dropped it. But he was spending more and more time at work, and I know it's because he had to do Charlie's work as well as his own, and it was too much. Maybe that's why he . . . he . . ."

Her eyes drifted over to Paul's desk. Lucy followed her gaze. A family picture was there, of Paul, Diane, and their son.

"How did Charlie's termination affect Paul?" Lucy asked.

"He was upset. He had to work longer hours, often into the night, and he was tired. Cortland Clarke said they were looking for a replacement for Charlie, but two months later and they still don't have anyone."

Lucy hadn't thought of that, and when Leo glanced at her, eyebrows arched, she realized he hadn't either.

Why hadn't the company replaced the head of the division?

"Did they ask Paul to take over?"

"In a way—but they said it would be only temporary. Still, Paul never told me about interviews or anything. Is that why—is that why Paul k-k-killed himself? The stress? Why couldn't he talk to me? Why would he—oh God, what am I going to tell JJ?"

The tears came then, and Lucy slid over to where Diane sat and put an arm around her. "Can I call someone for you?"

The doors opened and young JJ Grey stood there. "Mom?"

"I just need time," Diane said. "Please—come back later? I need to be with my son."

"We'll call first," Leo said, and he stood up. "We're sorry for your loss, Mrs. Grey." He put his hand on JJ's shoulder. "Take care of each other," he told the boy and walked out.

Leo slid into the driver's seat and checked his phone. "I have a couple messages. Hold on."

He listened and wrote down an address. "Cassidy Roth." He listened to another message, then hung up. "So I left a message for Cassidy at CHR this morning, and then had Zach follow up. She's out sick, has been all week. But Zach got her address from human resources. Much more forthcoming than Cortland Clarke. And Tia has a possible location for where McMahon was living. She and Jason are headed there now. She'll call us if they find anything."

Leo drove back to San Antonio and to an older neighborhood just beyond the downtown proper. The neighborhood was well maintained, with neatly trimmed lawns and lots of old trees providing both shade and charm. Each property had a small house in the front with a carport, and a long driveway to a nearly identical house in the back with a one-car garage. They had been built post–World War II, and several houses boasted

American flags or veterans stickers. Not a surprise—the air force base wasn't far.

The address they had for Cassidy was 11440—but the house in the front was A and the house in back was B.

They knocked on the house in the front. A small dog immediately began to bark.

"Settle down, Poppy!" an elderly voice said. There was shuffling, the dog continued to bark, and then they heard a chain slide across the door. The door opened, the glass screen separating the old woman from Lucy and Leo.

"May I help you?"

She had pale-blue eyes behind huge glasses.

"We're sorry to bother you," Lucy said, "but we're looking for Cassidy Roth."

"Cassidy lives behind me."

"Thank you, we're sorry to intrude."

"She's not home."

"When did she leave?"

"I don't know, I don't keep track of her comings and goings. She's a young kid. Is something wrong?"

Leo said to Lucy, "I'll check it out. See what you can learn."

Leo walked toward the back and Lucy smiled at the woman. "I'm FBI Agent Lucy Kincaid. Do you have a minute to talk?"

"FBI! Oh my. Poppy! Enough of that!"

The woman stepped out and closed the screen behind her. "Let's sit out here, shall we? It's going to be so hot today, but right now it's quite pleasant."

The woman motioned for Lucy to sit in one of two chairs on the tiny porch.

When they were settled, Lucy asked, "What's your name, ma'am?"

"Emmaline Granger, you can call me Em. Everyone calls me Em." She waved to a neighbor who was walking his dog. The man waved back and smiled.

"Em, call me Lucy. Cassidy isn't in any trouble, but we really need to speak to her. Do you know the last time you saw her?"

Em sighed and considered. "I can't right say. Monday is garbage day, and Cassidy took my garbage cans out and brought them back. She's a good girl. Keeps this place spotless. The grass trimmed."

"She takes care of your home for you?"

"Well, it's hers. She owns the property—both houses. I moved in here three years ago, and hope to never leave. She's never raised the rent on me, either. I offered her fifteen dollars more a month last year when I got an increase in Social Security, but she wouldn't take it. She gave me a complicated answer about her mortgage and interest and dollars per square foot or some such thing. I didn't understand what she was talking about. Now I just don't offer anymore, but I make her cookies and pies when my arthritis isn't too bothersome."

"So Cassidy was here on Monday."

"Yes. I saw her bringing in my cans in the afternoon. She left, came back when I was going to bed. I think I might have heard her car drive off late Monday night. I can't right say for certain, I was sleeping, but it woke me up."

"Do you remember what time?" Lucy rubbed the back of her neck. She had the distinct impression someone was watching her, but she glanced around and couldn't see anyone. Maybe a neighbor hiding behind curtains. They were driving an FBI pool car, and in a neighborhood like this they might think police.

"No, I'm an early-to-bed, early-to-rise gal." Emmaline chuckled. "I was in bed by nine. It was dark, though, and quiet—I went right back to sleep. My sister—she's two years older than me, lives up in Austin—she has *such* trouble sleeping. Wake her up and she's up for hours. Not me!"

"You said you've lived here three years?"

"Yes, ma'am. Three years last February."

"Did Cassidy ever discuss her job with you?"

"Not really. She's a very smart girl, I don't understand half of what she talks about. It's an important research job, but honestly, I can't remember where."

Leo texted Lucy, told her to come back to the other house when she could.

"Did Cassidy ever discuss her employer with you? One of her supervisors?"

"Cassidy is very private," Em said, which wasn't really an answer, but Lucy didn't know if she was being deliberately evasive, or if the comment was her way of saying Cassidy didn't talk about work.

Lucy handed the elderly woman her business card. "When Cassidy returns, if you could please have her call me. It's important—it's about her former supervisor at Clarke-Harrison, where she works. We have a few questions, and her assistance would really help us."

"Of course, anything I can do to help."

"Are you concerned that you haven't seen her in a couple days?"

Emmaline shook her head. "Should I be? Because Cassidy, bless her heart, is not a people person. I'm a people person, I like people, I like talking to them. How can one find out about anything if you don't talk to people? But Cassidy—too many people make her nervous, I guess you'd say."

"Does she have any friends who come by? Someone she's close to?"

"Not that I recall."

But the woman didn't look at her. Why was that?

"Are you sure? Cassidy is young, she doesn't have a boyfriend? Girlfriends?"

"I'm sure she does, but I don't want to be a nosy neighbor. I respect her privacy."

"I understand. Remember, have her call me when she returns. It's important."

"Of course, anything I can do to help. I'm sure she'll be home soon."

Lucy walked down the stairs, then around back to where Leo was standing on the small porch in front of Cassidy Roth's unit.

"Something wrong?"

"I don't know," he said. "The house is buttoned up tight, but I walked around and there's a backyard. Someone was watering this morning—the flower beds are damp. And before you ask, I checked—there's no sprinkler system."

"Maybe the neighbor did it."

"What if she saw us drive up? Look here—security cameras by both the front and back doors. What research assistant installs security cameras?"

Lucy concurred that it was odd.

"I want to put a cop on the house, but she might not come back."

"I gave Ms. Granger, the neighbor, my card. Told her to have Cassidy call me as soon as she saw her. She was very forthcoming, said Cassidy left late Monday night—after nine p.m.—and she hasn't seen her since. But when I asked about anyone who came to visit her, I think she lied to me."

"How so?"

"She didn't look at me. She was chatty and friendly, and then it was a subtle shift."

"I want to get a warrant to search her place, but we don't have cause."

"We can swing by later, or wait until Monday and track her down at CHR."

"That might work, though I'd like to talk to her without a CHR lawyer breathing down our necks. She owns a white Honda Civic. They're a dime a dozen, but I'll put out a BOLO for it."

They walked back to the street. Ms. Granger was still sitting on the front porch. She waved as Lucy and Leo drove off. His phone rang.

"It's Tia again," Leo said. "You're on speaker with Lucy and me," he said when he answered.

"Okay, I found McMahon's second place and it's been cleaned out."

"Tossed?"

"No—there are some clothes here, personal items, food—but his computer and papers are gone. And get this: The manager said his *daughter* came by Wednesday and took out two boxes."

"Daughter? She was in San Marcos on Wednesday. She's not old enough to drive."

"Dark-blond hair cut short, dark eyes, between twenty-five and thirty, comes by once or twice a week since he moved in May sixth. Maybe she was a mistress but the manager assumed she was McMahon's daughter. Or maybe McMahon said it was his daughter."

"He moved in early May?"

"The day after he was fired. It's a month-to-month, a furnished studio. Kind of a crap-hole neighborhood, but the building is well maintained."

Lucy flipped through her phone and showed Leo Cassidy Roth's DMV photo.

"Could be her," Leo said.

"Who?" Tia asked.

"Cassidy Roth. We're at her place now, but she's not here. Talked to her neighbor—she left Monday night and hasn't been seen since, but I think she was here this morning. And she has security cameras on her doors."

"What time Wednesday?" Lucy asked.

"He wasn't certain—around one in the afternoon, maybe a little later."

"I know what you're thinking," Leo said, "but SAPD didn't release his name to the press until late Wednesday afternoon."

"I'll bet she was there, a bystander."

"That could make her an accessory."

"That's a stretch," Lucy said, "because there's no evidence that he planned to take anyone hostage."

"He had two guns on him."

"But he was sitting in there for over thirty minutes before he engaged."

"Working up the courage."

"I want to go over the video footage again. We should have photographs and video of the crowds as well as security videos."

Tia spoke up. "Did you forget I'm here?"

"Sorry," Leo said.

"I heard what you said, we'll have all that at headquarters. But we need to find this girl. If she took anything from his apartment because it might incriminate him—or her—that's serious."

"Can your people spare an unmarked car to watch her place?" Leo asked Tia.

"Maybe for a day or two. I'll call the lieutenant and run it by him. Shoot me the address."

"If you can get the manager to confirm that Cassidy Roth is the one who picked up McMahon's things, we might be able to get a warrant for her place," Leo said.

"I'll check and get back to you." Tia hung up.

Cassidy watched the FBI agents leave. Her jaw was so tight she was giving herself a headache. She rubbed the tension away, took a deep breath. She should have figured they'd come talk to her eventually; she just didn't think they'd be here so quickly. And why did they sit out front for so long? Were they watching the place? She needed to a safer place. Maybe Adam would let her stay with him. But that might be awkward. He was already doing so much for her . . .

She wanted to run Charlie's hair samples because she had a vague idea what to look for—she knew the chemicals and drugs available at CHR. But Adam wouldn't let her—he said that would be far riskier for him than if he ran the tests late at night. He had full access to the university lab. On Wednesday night he ran standard toxicology screens, even though Cassidy knew that wouldn't yield anything. Now he was running more advanced tests. She needed to prove that a drug that CHR was developing had somehow infected Charlie.

But waiting was killing her.

Charlie must have been terrified during the hostage standoff. He didn't know what he was doing, he couldn't have. He would never take a room full of people hostage. That wasn't him. He was the kindest person she knew. And smart. But who would believe her? The FBI didn't understand complex chemical reactions. They wouldn't know what to look for at CHR. If they even believed her, what would they do? Go to Cortland Clarke and ask if there had been an accident in the lab and what Charlie had been infected with? Like Ms. Clarke would ever admit to any problem at CHR. Not when problems cost them money.

She needed proof. Something solid, like a report from Adam—who worked at a top university laboratory—that said *exactly* what Charlie had been exposed to and why he took fifteen people hostage.

Em came back in the house. "Honey, maybe you should talk to that nice girl FBI agent."

Cassidy took the card from Em's hand. LUCY KINCAID, SPECIAL AGENT.

"I can't, not right now," Cassidy said. "Thank you."

"I told the truth, mostly, but I don't like fibbing, even a little."

Cassidy didn't like asking her friend to lie for her, but when she saw the car she ran from her house to Em's and begged her not to tell them she was here. Almost everything she said was the truth—Cassidy had left on Monday night, and she hadn't come back until today. She was trying to help Charlie, and then . . .

She swallowed. Cassidy wasn't an emotional person, but thinking about Charlie being shot by the police made her feel sick. Reading the newspapers—listening to those fools who thought he was a bad guy. She didn't know how to fix it. She didn't know if she could. She was relying on a friend who had no vested interest in the outcome, but she had no one else to trust.

She owed it to Charlie to find proof that Clarke-Harrison was responsible for whatever had happened to him. Paul Grey promised he would help . . . and now he was dead, too.

What if they weren't real FBI agents? What if they were from the company and sent to kill her?

If they wanted to kill you, they wouldn't come over Friday morning and talk nicely with your neighbor. They would come for you in the middle of the night and make you disappear.

She was so close to figuring out what Charlie had forgotten. So. Damn. Close.

She just needed to spend more time with his journals—the journals that were in code, journals Charlie barely remembered writing. She needed to push Adam for the lab results, convince him to let her help.

"I'll figure it out, Charlie, I promise."

That was the last thing she'd said to him, on Monday.

And she'd failed him. She couldn't protect him, and now he was dead.

I won't let them get away with this, Charlie. I'll find out what they did to you and expose them all.

CHAPTER SEVENTEEN

Jesse had been acting odd all morning. He didn't want to play video games; he swam for a while but got bored quickly, then sat on his phone doing something Sean wasn't sure about. He could ask—or covertly find out—but he didn't want to break Jesse's trust.

"What do you want to do for lunch?" Sean asked, sitting next to Jesse in the sunroom.

He shrugged. "Where'd Kane go?"

"To check out something for me."

That morning, Sean had received a call from Jimenez at the US Marshals' office. He wouldn't send Sean the photo he'd obtained through the red-light camera, but he did give Sean enough information about the driver Manuel Domingo—including a long and colorful criminal history—that Sean wanted to check him out. The criminal history was mostly work-for-hire, not human trafficking or drug running. He'd done five years for robbery—a warehouse where he and his team stole more than ten million dollars in microprocessors.

Because most had been recovered, he'd been granted a reduced sentence.

Sean wanted to go himself, but Kane convinced him to let him and Nate check it out. Nate had gone through his psych eval that morning and was cleared to go back to work Monday—but he was bored, and Sean understood how that felt.

"You're lying to me," Jesse said.

"No—why would you say that?"

"You promised you would always tell me the truth."

"I have."

"Then tell me *exactly* what Kane is doing. It's about those guys who followed us on Wednesday, isn't it? You think they work for the Flores cartel."

"Yes, it is about those guys, and no, I don't think they're working for the cartels." Jesse was thirteen—how much should Sean tell him? He'd already seen violence in his young life, and Sean didn't want to coddle him, but at the same time, did he have to know everything?

It was harder, Sean suspected, because he hadn't been around for most of Jesse's life. Sure, he was his biological father, but he hadn't raised him, and things they did together were what friends—what brothers—might do. Play video games. Go to baseball games. Swim. Watch movies. They played together. Sean wasn't going to be around every night to tell him to do his homework or help him with his math. He probably wouldn't even see him on his first date, or drive him to the prom.

That realization—that he hadn't been around for the

important moments in Jesse's life, and likely wouldn't be in the future—upset him.

And now Jesse was expecting him to lie. Sean could see it on his face.

"I don't want to scare you, but I don't want you to think everything is just fine," Sean said cautiously. "My life, Kane's life, even Lucy—well, none of us have taken the safe and easy road. Growing up, I was around guns every day. Both my parents had been in the military, and then two of my brothers. Security was like second nature to us. I learned personal safety because my dad wouldn't have it any other way, and working with Kane I had the best on-the-job training out there. You'll learn to protect yourself, to see potential threats, but it doesn't happen overnight, so yes, I'm worried about you."

"Why can't you train me?"

"I already am, in a way. But it's a long process. You can't just expect to pick up everything in a couple weeks. And you're a kid. I want you to be a kid for as long as you can."

"A kid." Jesse grunted. "I haven't felt like a kid in a year."

His voice cracked, and Sean wondered if there was more here that he wasn't seeing—that he didn't know how to see because he was new to parenthood.

"I was forced to grow up fast, too," Sean said. "It's not fun, and you feel like you've been cheated."

"Are you going to tell me why you're babysitting me? And why you sent Kane out? Why couldn't we do it together?"

"First, I don't know what these thugs are up to, so I'm not going to bring you on some reconnaissance mission when I don't have enough information to ensure your safety. Second, I'm not babysitting you."

"You aren't working."

"I chose not to work while you're here. I only get you for six weeks. I finished up a big job before I picked you up in Sacramento, and I have another job lined up after you go back. You don't have to worry about that. Unless you're bored with me."

"No, but it's just weird."

"I guess it is. To answer your question, I trust Kane to get to the bottom of whatever those guys are up to. That's why he's looking into it." Sean paused. "Are you bored? We can have another barbecue this weekend. Or—" He stopped and considered what he could do. He'd been thinking about taking Jesse over to St. Catherine's since Michael texted him the other day. Why was he worried about it? It would be good for Jesse to meet the boys. He was feeling sorry for himself and Sean didn't know how to quell that except to show him that there were other boys, his age, who were far less fortunate. He didn't want to diminish what Jesse had suffered, but he wanted Jesse to put it in perspective.

"What?" Jesse asked.

"Last year Kane, Lucy, and I rescued a group of boys who'd been used by the drug cartel to serve as mules. That means they brought drugs across the border. They were beaten, starved, threatened, many were killed. One of the boys escaped and through a series of events, we found him and he led us to the rest of those held captive. These kids have had a rough life—their parents are dead or in prison. They don't have any support from family. I usually go over there once a week to help them with their homework, talk, whatever. School's out, so I didn't think it was a problem, but one of the boys—Michael, the kid who escaped—texted me the other day and wanted to know if I was around."

"Go ahead. I'm okay here, I really am. Bandit and I will just hang out."

"I know you are—my security is the best. But why don't you come with me?"

"Really? You don't mind me coming?"

Sean put his arm over Jesse's shoulders. "I like having you around. You'll like the boys. They don't trust easily. They might be wary around you at first, but they'll warm up. Just be yourself."

Kane trusted Sean's instincts about security, but after he checked with his sources and was confident the Flores cartel was completely disbanded and no one had put a hit out on the Spades or his brother, he thought maybe Sean had become marginally paranoid. With good reason—the Rogans had made a lot of enemies in the drug trade, and with Jesse just coming out of WITSEC and Carson Spade helping the feds as part of his plea deal, someone could be biding their time.

Still, Kane trusted his contacts, and he had pulled in favors to ensure that both Sean and Jesse were safe—as safe as anyone could be in their line of work.

Nate was driving—he knew San Antonio better than Kane. Once they had Domingo's name it was easy to track him. They located him at a gym in a sketchy warehouse district southeast of downtown.

"He's a gun for hire," Kane said. "We'll find out who hired him—if anyone."

Nate glanced over as he parked. "You think Sean is overreacting."

"I'll flush him out," Kane said in lieu of an answer. "There's an exit back and front but if he rabbits, he'll go to his vehicle."

"I got it."

Kane walked into the gym while Nate staked out the black Lincoln. It was hot and humid, the swamp cooler doing little to cool the sweltering gym. A dozen men and a few women worked with weights, but most of them stood around sweating.

Manuel Domingo was working with hand weights. He glanced at Kane but didn't look twice.

A short, muscular guy approached him. "Ten dollars a day, or twenty-five a week."

"I'm looking for Domingo," Kane said.

He shrugged. "Can I tell him why?"

"Friend of mine says he does odd jobs. I have an odd job."

He said it in a low voice, but Domingo was close enough to hear him. The manager glanced over at Domingo, who nodded.

The manager pointed to Domingo, and Kane approached. "You need a job?" Kane asked.

"Depends what."

"All you need to know is it pays two large to make a delivery."

"Not just any delivery."

"Special cargo."

"Who you get my name from?"

Jimenez had given Kane a list of known associates, and most were in prison. "Garcia. From McClelland."

"You were in the joint?"

"Short stint."

Domingo was suspicious. Kane held his ground.

"You want the job or not?"

"I need to make some calls."

"Or not," Kane said and walked away. Domingo hesitated, then followed.

Sometimes, it was just too fucking easy.

As soon as they stepped outside, Kane turned, elbowed Domingo in the gut, and flipped him to the ground. The guy was big but slow and Kane had a gun on the back of his head before he knew what happened.

Kane saw Nate approach out of the corner of his eye and he waved him off. Nate slipped back between the cars and watched.

Kane hauled Domingo to his feet and pushed him against the side of the gym. "So you wanted to do this the fun way," Kane said.

"Who the fuck are you?"

"Who hired you to follow the black Wrangler on Wednesday?" Kane asked. He didn't know how much Domingo knew about Sean—he might not even know his name, and Kane didn't want to give him any information he didn't already have.

"What?"

Kane punched him in the kidney. He knew from experience how much it hurt.

Domingo slammed his fist against the wall in pain. "Fuck!"

"Black Wrangler. Wednesday. The Rib House. Who hired you?"

"That? Oh, that was nothing."

Sean was right. Damn, Kane shouldn't doubt his brother.

"Why did you follow him?"

"No reason."

Kane applied pressure on Domingo's neck. "That's not an answer."

"Stop! I don't know, really—just a guy who paid me a thousand to follow this Rogan guy. That's it."

"Why?"

"I don't know why. I swear to God, I don't know!"

"What did you tell this guy?"

"That Rogan made the tail. I asked if he wanted me to tag-team, and no, the gig was over, I got my money, end of story."

"Who?"

"I. Don't. Know. A friend of a friend of a friend. Really, it was a handshake deal and I didn't even meet him!"

Domingo might be a big, burly guy but he was a wimp.

"How did you get him the information?"

"Message. The number's burned, buddy, you're not going to trace it or anything."

"How did you know where to pick him up?"

"Huh?"

Dear Lord, this guy was an idiot. "How did you know Rogan would be at the Rib House?"

"They sent me a text with an address."

How the hell did anyone know Sean would be at that restaurant at that time? Had to be a tracker of some sort.

"Stay away from Rogan," Kane said.

"Job's over. I swear."

"If you're lying, I will kill you."

Kane pushed him down and walked away. By the time he and Nate were in Nate's truck, Domingo had scurried back into the gym.

"What now?" Nate said.

"We wait and follow him. He was telling part truth, part lie."

"How can you tell?"

Kane just smiled. "I just know." He called Sean. "You were right, he was tailing you."

"I told you."

"I hate it when you do that."

"Don't doubt me."

"I didn't."

Sean snorted.

"We need to follow him, he might make Nate's truck."

"I'm at the boys' home with Jesse."

"Bring him. Good lesson."

"No. Lucy's leaving headquarters soon, I'll have her pick him up. Where are you?"

Kane told him. "But I don't know for how long."

"I'm ten, fifteen minutes away. I'll head there, let me know if you move."

* * *

When they first arrived at the boys' home a few hours ago, Jesse was more than a little nervous. He didn't know what to expect. When they walked in, several boys ran up to Sean and gave him a hug. They wanted to know where he'd been, if he'd been out of town on business, why he didn't come to Sunday dinner. Jesse felt both out of place and guilty. Apparently, his dad came here all the time to hang out with the boys, but he hadn't in weeks—because Jesse was here.

"So," Sean said to the gathering, "I wanted to introduce you to someone. This is my son, Jesse. He lives in California with his mother, but is staying with me for a few weeks this summer. Hey, Tito, why don't you and Brian show him around?"

Tito was the smallest kid in the group and walked with a limp. He had a big grin on his thin face. "Hi, Jesse! I'm Tito. Want to see the pool Sean built for us?"

"I didn't build it," Sean said.

Tito took Jesse's hand and pulled him outside. Brian was less friendly but followed them.

Tito continued talking. The kid looked really young, but Jesse learned he was eleven. He'd never gone to school until last year because his mother had been a drug addict and never enrolled him. When he was seven, she OD'd and he went to foster care, where he learned that his dad was in prison. When he was nine, he was sent to work in Mexico for friends of his father's. "But Michael came back like he promised and brought help."

"Shush, Tito," Brian said.

"Oh, you probably already know," Tito said.

"Know what?" Jesse asked.

"I don't want to talk about it," Brian said.

Jesse really wanted to know, but he said, "It's okay, the pool is really neat. Thanks for the tour."

"Do you play video games?"

"Sure."

Tito lit up. "Come to the game room! Sean got us some really cool games."

For an hour, Jesse played video games with Tito and Brian, then they had a snack in the kitchen and he met Sister Ruth, who took care of the boys and the house. A couple other boys came in and asked Jesse questions, and then it wasn't weird anymore. Jesse still wanted to know exactly what his dad had done, and why he'd bought a house for these kids, but Sean had gone off with an older kid named Michael. Probably the Michael he'd talked about earlier.

After snacks, they all went swimming—Brian found an extra pair of trunks for Jesse—and that's when Jesse saw the scars.

There were scars on all the boys. Even little Tito. His leg was really messed up—probably why he limped—but there was a big round, puckered scar that looked like it was from a gunshot.

"Were you shot?" Jesse asked without thinking.

Tito nodded. "I almost died but Sean saved me. I couldn't walk and he carried me really far instead of leaving me behind."

Jesse waited until Brian jumped into the pool. Tito seemed to be the most talkative and forthcoming, and

Jesse thought he'd answer anything. "Everyone here has scars. Were you—did someone hurt you?"

Tito nodded. "We were all locked up in a jail in Mexico, except when we were working." He paused, then lowered his voice. "I don't mind talking about it, Father Mateo says that it's good to talk because then the bad stuff doesn't stay inside. But it's hard for Brian and some to talk about it, even though we got out a long time ago."

"How long?"

"Over a year."

"Got out of where?"

"The jail. Where the general kept us when we weren't working. He was really bad and now he's dead."

Someone locked up little kids in a prison? In Mexico? Jesse didn't want to believe it . . . but he did. He'd seen some pretty awful things when Carson took him to Mexico when he worked for the Flores cartel. Jesse hadn't known it at the time, but then he learned the truth. And *these* boys were forced to work for a cartel? They were all about his age. Was it the Flores cartel? How could his stepfather have been party to anything like that? Maybe it wasn't the same criminals, but it was the same *type* of people—they were violent and they didn't care who they hurt.

"Hey, Tito!" one of the boys called from the opposite side of the pool. "Watch this!"

He jumped off the diving board and made a huge cannonball splash, soaking everyone within a foot of the pool. When he surfaced, Tito yelled, "Frisco! Do it again!"

Sean came out then. He was with the same boy he'd gone off with more than an hour ago.

"Hold it, Frisco," Sean said, "wait until I get out of here."

Sean walked over to them. "You show Jesse everything?" he asked Tito.

"We played video games, we ate, we swam, can you stay for dinner? Please?"

Sean squatted. "I can't. I have to go. But Jesse can stay for a while. Can I talk to him for a sec?"

"Sure." Tito limped off.

Sean stood and said, "Jess, this is Michael Rodriguez, a good friend of mine. We were just catching up, I didn't realize how much time passed."

"It's okay, we were having fun out here."

"Good. I have to go and help Kane with that project we talked about earlier. I called Lucy, and she'll pick you up on her way home. Can you hang here for another hour or so?"

Jesse looked at Michael. The kid was the oldest in the house, at least fifteen, and he looked like he'd seen everything and didn't like any of it.

"That's okay, Michael, right?" Sean continued.

"Sure," Michael said.

Jesse didn't believe it. Sean didn't, either, but he put his arm around Michael's shoulders and said, "I'm counting on you, okay?"

Michael nodded. "I have meal prep this week. You can help," he said to Jesse and motioned for him to follow.

Jesse glanced at Sean, who was watching closely. What was he supposed to do? Stay? Beg to go with Sean? He didn't know if he wanted to stay here, but if he made a scene, Sean would think he was immature.

He followed Michael inside, and changed back into his clothes in the bathroom. Sean was standing outside the door when he was finished.

"Jess, I'm sorry. I didn't mean to put you on the spot outside, but Michael doesn't trust many people. He'll come around."

"What's his story?" Jesse asked.

"I'll tell you later. I promise, okay? For now, just cut him a little slack. But not too much. Don't let him bully you, but realize that he's protective of the others, and even though you're my son, he's cautious."

"How did Tito get shot?"

His dad's face hardened. He'd seen this expression before—when they were escaping the Flores compound in Guadalajara. Hard and angry. Like his uncle Kane.

"A bastard shot him and left him. It got infected. He nearly died."

"He said you saved him."

"It was a group effort." Sean put his arm around Jesse and gave him a hug. "You're a good kid, Jess. So's Tito. Neither of you should have had to go through any of that bullshit down in Mexico. But it's over."

"I know."

But sometimes Jesse thought it would never be truly over. Just because Sean and Kane stopped the Flores cartel didn't mean that another group hadn't started up. It was like a never-ending cycle.

"You're okay that I'm going, right?"

"Is it about the guy who followed us?"

"Kane found him. We're going to track him, see what happens. Lucy will be here by six thirty. And Sister Ruth will insist you stay for dinner. But trust me—the food is always great. I'll be home before you go to bed, okay?"

Jesse was nervous, but he didn't want his dad to know he was worried. "Okay."

CHAPTER EIGHTEEN

Lucy got off the phone with Sean and immediately started writing up her report so she could get out of the office before six and pick up Jesse at St. Catherine's.

Every investigative road they took was a dead end, and both Lucy and Leo were frustrated. They'd gone over every possible scenario, but realized they didn't have enough information. If they took what they knew at face value—that Charlie McMahon had a damaged memory; that Paul Grey had committed suicide; that McMahon had *likely* moved his friend's body into his house—they still didn't know *why*. And they might never know.

However, Cassidy Roth was a very interesting potential witness. Why had she removed evidence from Charlie's apartment during the police standoff? Was there something incriminating? Why was she avoiding the police? Why hadn't she come to them now that Charlie was dead? Why had she called in sick, but wasn't at home?

Both Leo and Lucy believed that Cassidy had some of the answers they were looking for, but where was she? A cop was sitting down the street from her house, but considering she had a security system, Lucy was certain she would notice. The car may be unmarked, but anyone competent would know what to look for.

Why was she avoiding the police? Lucy didn't automatically assume that she was guilty of something. Some people were paranoid; some people had good reasons not to trust law enforcement. A few bad cops damaged the entire law enforcement profession—which unfortunately put innocent people at risk.

Lucy sent her daily report to her boss and was gathering up her things when Leo turned down the aisle and into the Violent Crimes squad room.

"Good, you're still here."

"Not for long," she said.

"I just got a call from Tia Mancini. Evidence is missing."

"What evidence?"

"The morgue sent three packages of evidence to the SAPD lab: one with McMahon's clothing, which had been dried and preserved; one with blood and tissue samples; and one with contents from his pockets—wallet, a bottle of aspirin, and his keys. Only his clothing made it."

"Do they know what happened?"

"No—Julie has samples of blood and tissue at the morgue and she's going to hand-deliver them tonight to the lab. But the physical evidence hasn't been processed. The evidence is documented, but that's it."

"There has to be some sort of mix-up."

"Peters has been tracking this all day and the shipping company is jumping through hoops but they can't find the packages anywhere."

"Is this an accident or deliberate?" Lucy asked.

"That's the million-dollar question. Tia Mancini is working on it now and interviewing the driver—maybe he lied through his teeth when he said they weren't on his truck."

"Julie has other samples, and wasn't McMahon's brain sent to the research lab at the university?"

"Yes, and she verified with Dr. Moreno that he implemented additional security measures. Only a handful of people have access to his lab; it's secure via key card, in a secure building. Good thing because McMahon's body was sent to the mortuary and was already embalmed."

"What if someone intentionally stole the samples?" Lucy asked.

"Who? Why?"

"I don't know," she said, thinking. "Maybe to destroy them."

"Which would mean that there was something in his blood that someone didn't want us to find?" Leo asked, skeptical. "If someone is smart enough to manipulate the system to destroy blood evidence, they'd know that the morgue would keep samples of everything sent to the lab."

"Not necessarily," Lucy said. "We know he was acting oddly for the last three months, and seemed to be getting worse. He could have been poisoned. Or maybe it wasn't the samples but evidence in his wallet."

"That's a stretch."

"Perhaps," Lucy admitted. "But Cortland Clarke was acting suspicious, and she was less than forthcoming. Clarke-Harrison is a drug research company, maybe there was some sort of accidental exposure."

"A cover-up?" Leo nodded. "I can see that. But an accident that didn't affect anyone else?"

She could see his point.

She said, "They specialize in Alzheimer's research. Memories. And Charlie was losing his memories."

"No judge will give us a warrant on that theory. We need something solid—like testimony from Cassidy Roth or Vince Paine. One more piece of news—you were right. Roth *was* at the hostage standoff. She was in the crowd in photos taken at eleven fifteen and eleven forty-five, but not at twelve thirty—which was after SWAT went in. She could have moved to another location and been missed, but Tia thinks she was gone by then."

"She may have left as soon as she knew he'd been killed," Lucy said. "No one has been able to find Paine?"

"He moved shortly after he was fired. Left no forwarding address. SAPD is working on locating him."

"So both Roth and Paine are in the wind."

"I won't go that far—yet. But it does seem unusual."

"One of them may know exactly what Charlie was researching and what was going on at Clarke-Harrison."

Leo sat down at his computer and typed rapidly. "I'm

sending a memo to the task force for a full background on the principals at Clarke-Harrison. I also didn't get Garrett Harrison's itinerary from CHR, and when I called it was after five and it went to a fucking answering service. Believe me, I left a message about the importance of speaking with Garrett Harrison as soon as possible."

"Why do they think delaying the inevitable is going to work? Harrison will be back in town at some point, and if not we can track him down."

"Another in a long line of questions," Leo mumbled. "Go—we may be working this weekend, we both need a night off to clear our heads."

Lucy was happy to pick up Jesse. She hadn't had much alone time with Sean's son, and this would give them the chance to really talk. It would be just her and Jesse alone for hours, and she didn't want the kid to worry about what Sean and Kane were doing. They could play games, walk Bandit, maybe make cookies. Lucy wasn't skilled in the kitchen, but she could follow a basic recipe. Besides, she really wanted to put the McMahon case out of her head for tonight. She could look at it fresh tomorrow, after a good night's sleep.

The conversation about the missing evidence had delayed Lucy, and she didn't arrive at St. Catherine's Boys' Home until quarter to seven. Everyone was eating at the large table in the dining room. Father Mateo had taken to eating with the boys more often than not, and of course Sister Ruth, who ran the home and cared for the boys, was there. She was supposed to stay for only six months, but Father Mateo had enlisted the help of every priest he knew, including a bishop or two, to make Sister Ruth's appointment permanent. Having continuity for these boys—ranging in age from ten to fifteen—was critical to their emotional and spiritual well-being, Mateo argued.

Jesse was sitting in the middle of it all, listening to the chatter. Everyone looked up when Sister Ruth led Lucy in.

"I'm sorry to disturb dinner," she said.

"There's always enough for one more," Sister Ruth said. "Please sit."

Lucy knew better than to refuse food from Sister Ruth, so she sat at the end of the table, next to Tito—the youngest boy who had been rescued more than a year ago. There had been seven they'd saved, plus Michael Rodriguez, the boy who started it all.

Michael was watching Jesse closely, Lucy noted. Was he a little jealous? Suspicious? Sean had spent a lot of time at the boys' home since he bought the house for the church, but hadn't been over as much since Jesse arrived . . . Lucy could see how Michael might feel neglected. Or worried. How much did Sean share with Michael about Jesse and his situation?

Lucy enjoyed listening to the boys. The younger kids, like Tito, had bounced back. They accepted their new life without question. They seemed happy, something Lucy didn't think was possible after what had happened to them. Time, and love, healed the deepest wounds.

Michael and a couple of the older boys hadn't regained their youthful exuberance, but they did find a peace that Lucy knew was hard-fought. They looked out for the others, obeyed Father Mateo, and focused on school. They were all in summer school to catch up from the time they'd lost. Some of the boys, like Tito, had never had formal schooling until last year.

By the time the boys cleared the table and those on KP duty were cleaning, Lucy realized that it was after eight. "We should be going. Thanks for having us, Father."

Father Mateo walked them to the door. "It was a pleasure. Very nice to meet you, Jesse."

"Nice to meet you." Jesse looked sheepish, not certain how to address the priest.

"Sean calls me Mateo. You can call me Mateo or Mr. Flannigan or Father, whatever makes you comfortable."

Jesse nodded. "Thank you, Mr. Flannigan."

Lucy walked Jesse out. "That was awkward," he said.

"It wasn't." They pulled out of the driveway. "You're not Catholic, Father Mateo understands."

"You are?"

"Yes."

"I've never even been to church. We just never do that stuff."

"No one holds it against you."

"But you go."

"Yes. Not every week, like when I was growing up, but often. There's a certain peace in the tradition that helps ground me."

Jesse didn't say anything for a minute. "Sean said that all those boys were held prisoner by a drug cartel. That they were forced to work for them."

"That's true."

"Was it the people that Carson worked for?"

"No."

"Are you just saying that to make me feel better?"

"No. Different people. Both criminal organizations, but not the same one."

"But the people Carson worked for sold babies."

Lucy knew that Sean had pledged not to lie to Jesse, but there were some things that were difficult to discuss with a thirteen-year-old. What exactly should she say?

"I know he did," Jesse said. He was angry, and Lucy didn't blame him. "Remember, I was down there. I heard a lot. And Kane and my dad talked about it."

"I'm not trying to shield you or sugarcoat the truth. But I don't know how much you want to know."

Lucy merged onto the freeway. One good thing about staying for dinner at the boys' home was that she missed rush-hour traffic.

"Jesse?" she prompted when he didn't respond to her.

"Tito, the little kid? Sean said he'd always walk with a limp because he was shot and it got infected and he needed two different surgeries but that leg isn't going to grow like the other one. And when we got to the house, Sean went off with the kid Michael—the one who stared at me all through dinner like he wanted to kill me. I don't know what they were doing, but Sean said that Michael had been through hell and Sean was the only one Michael would talk to about it. When Sean left, I helped Michael in the kitchen, but he didn't talk much."

"Michael might feel a little displaced. He didn't know about you. He's protective of the boys in the house. If it weren't for him, we'd never have found them."

"What happened to him? Tito said they were in jail. But that can't be right, is it?"

The truth, Lucy decided, was always the best recourse. But she didn't have to share all the horrid details. "A little over a year ago, shortly after I started with the FBI, I was part of a joint task force. Michael had been held captive in the basement of a drug dealer, escaped, and we had information that he was being used as a mule for one of the drug cartels. He didn't trust the police because he had been in foster care, and his social worker—a person he should have been able to trust—had turned him over to the cartels. When he escaped, he planned on going back to Mexico to rescue the boys who were used just like him. And yes, they were locked in an old jail every night so they couldn't leave."

"Foster care? Like they don't have parents?"

"Most of them had parents who were in prison. Michael's father is the one who turned him over to the cartel, in exchange for protection behind bars." She paused. "Michael's father killed his mother."

"That—that really sucks."

"Michael trusts Sean because Sean helped him rescue the boys. They would have died."

"Sean said Kane was there, too."

"Yes. Kane put together a small mercenary group who extracted the boys from a prison about an hour south of the border in the middle of nowhere. Sean carried Tito to safety. Michael sees him as a hero because he is a hero."

A car was following her too closely. Jerk. She pulled over into the far right lane. She wasn't the speed demon that Sean was on the road, but she was going a steady five miles over the limit.

She glanced at Jesse. "Are you okay?"

"Yeah. I just—my dad is overprotective, and I get that, but I was thinking he was just going overboard. I didn't know all this other stuff. You know, like about Michael and Tito. It just—I guess, well, I'm selfish."

"You're not selfish, Jesse. Why would you even think that?"

"Because I was just thinking about what I wanted to do and how mad I was. Kane came over yesterday and was like babysitting me. I thought it was stupid. I mean, I really like him, and he doesn't talk to me like I'm a kid, but he's not as fun as my dad. But now, well, I guess there was a reason."

"Sean and Kane are very protective of their family. You're family. It's as simple as that."

"I want to stay, Lucy," Jesse said, his words coming out fast, tumbling over each other as he got a lot off his chest at once. "I *don't* want to go back to Sacramento. And then I feel bad because I'd miss my mom a lot, but then I get mad at her because she lied to me *my entire life* and I think, I don't care at all whether I hurt her feelings. And then I feel guilty for thinking that! Isn't that stupid? I just don't know anymore."

Lucy was going to respond, but Jesse kept talking.

"And then I went over to Saint Catherine's today and my problems are *nothing*. My problems are petty and childish and stupid. One of the boys, I don't remember his name, his arm is all scarred and twisted and Sean said he'd been burned on purpose. And Tito will never walk right because someone shot him and just left him to die. All that they went through, and they don't complain, and Tito is like this totally happy normal kid except he's really small and he limps. And I feel like a total asshole."

Wow. Jesse was going through some deep soul searching, and she didn't think he'd shared all this with Sean. They were going to have to talk, but Lucy could at least try to make Jesse feel better about the situation.

"You can't compare yourself to Michael or any of the other boys," she said. "Yes, they had difficult lives, but they're going to be okay. They're in a much better place now with people who care about them. Sean has done a lot for them, true, but he wanted to. He found them in the jail. There were others—boys who didn't make it. That affected all of us, but Sean in particular. He doesn't like to talk about it, but he'll talk to you. Just ask him."

"He told me some things, but I know there's more. I've had everything just handed to me. I never had to work for it or worry about whether I would eat or whether I was going to die. They all have scars. Like . . . like they were whipped. I didn't think anything like that happened anymore."

"You went through your own crucible, Jesse."

"I don't know what that means."

"Finding out that your stepfather was working for a criminal organization wasn't easy for you. Finding out that your mother lied about your biological father wasn't easy for you. You have to find peace in that knowledge, and that's difficult."

"But none of that hurt me."

"It did hurt, and you have to realize that before you can forgive them. Just because you don't have external scars doesn't mean it didn't affect you. Cut yourself a little slack, okay? You're a great kid—and yes, you're blessed. You have a home and parents who love you and want you and would do everything in their power to protect you. Sean didn't introduce you to the boys because he wanted you to feel bad about what you have. He did it because they are an important part of his life and he wants to share his entire life with you. Do you understand that?"

He shrugged. "Maybe."

Lucy didn't know if she was getting through to Jesse, but she had an odd feeling that the car behind her had been following her too closely. She was still in the far right lane—and there were three lanes he could use to pass her. She was only a mile from her exit, but she merged left and sped up. The car followed. It was nearly dark, and the headlights made it difficult for her to see details.

Jesse noticed. "What's happening?"

"A car is on my tail."

She moved over to the next lane to the left and rapidly accelerated.

The car followed.

She pressed a button on the steering wheel and her speaker turned on. "Call nine-one-one," she said.

A moment later an operator came on the line. "Nine-one-one, what is your emergency?"

"This is FBI Special Agent Lucy Kincaid Rogan. I'm in my private vehicle and being followed by a dark SUV. No front license plate. I have a minor child with me. I have tried evasive maneuvers and the vehicle is still following."

"What is your location?"

"North on Thirty-Five, just past the I-Ten split."

"I will dispatch highway patrol to your location. The closest police station to you is on San Saba, less than two miles from your location. Do you know how to get there?"

"Yes. I'll head there now." It was behind her, but she could get off at the next exit and backtrack.

One of the best ways to shake a tail was to drive directly to a police station. If someone was a stalker or potential attacker, they wouldn't stop at the station. If the police knew that you were coming, they would meet you out front and, if lucky, could pursue the tail.

"I'll inform dispatch that you're on your way. From your location, I estimate ETA three to five minutes."

This section of the freeway was wide with lots of arteries going on and off. Lucy couldn't immediately get over to the right because of a barrier as another freeway merged in. As soon as she was able, she cut through traffic into the far right lane. The SUV followed. She sped up, weaving around slower cars. At the last minute, she exited. The SUV cut across three lanes and horns blasted. Then he was right on her bumper. She tried to speed up, but the truck rammed her.

It took all of her self-control not to immediately brake, which would have thrown her into a spin and likely flipped the car. As it was, the SUV came up next to her, slammed to the right and sideswiped her. She couldn't avoid going onto the shoulder. The embankment had a steep drop. If she could just get another twenty, thirty feet the grade was less sharp.

Her attacker jerked the wheel and pushed her car over the embankment.

She would have flipped completely if her passenger-side wheels went over first. As she realized what the SUV was doing, she turned so she was heading straight down the embankment, front-end first, using momentum to drive down, which thankfully prevented the vehicle from flipping. She slammed into the drainage ditch and the airbags deployed.

"Jesse!" she screamed.

She thought she heard the 911 operator talking, but her ears were ringing and she couldn't make out the words. She reached over to Jesse, feeling for him.

"Jesse, are you okay?"

At the same time she was trying to figure out if Jesse was hurt, she reached for her gun. She kept it in the center console when she was driving because it was easier to access than the glove compartment, in the event of an emergency.

And this was an emergency.

She didn't know what the bastards wanted, but Jesse

was her responsibility and she would not let anyone hurt him.

She brushed away blood that dripped down her face. Her nose was bleeding, and her head ached, but she couldn't think about that.

Streetlights shone into the car and she saw Jesse. He looked stunned, but he was breathing.

Her door was stuck, but Lucy couldn't stay here. She'd be a sitting duck if the SUV parked and gunmen came for them. She didn't see anyone, but her vision was fuzzy from the airbag powder.

"Jesse, can you open your door?"

"Agent Kincaid?" she heard over the speaker. "Are you there?"

"We were rammed off the road." She gave her location. "Jesse, open your door. We have to get out of the car *now*."

Jesse pushed aside the airbag and opened the door. His nose was bleeding, too. He could be injured, and Lucy shouldn't move him or herself, but she also knew they needed cover.

Jesse climbed out and tried to stand.

"Down," Lucy shouted, mostly because her ears were ringing and she had no idea if Jesse could hear her.

Jesse got down.

Lucy climbed over the center console and crawled out Jesse's door. She squatted next to him, using the V that the open door made as partial cover, and gave him a quick hug. "Are you okay? Jesse, is anything broken?"

"No. No—my nose is sore."

"It's from the airbag." Lucy's nose was bleeding. She

didn't think it was broken, but something had cut her head. She wiped more blood from her face and focused on her surroundings.

Sirens cut through the air, and Lucy breathed easier.

She risked glancing over the car; the dark truck was nowhere in sight. They must have bolted as soon as they pushed her car over. The drop wasn't deadly—most people would survive. Had they only wanted to scare them?

If anything, it pissed her off. Who were these people?

She glanced at Jesse. Sean had been followed the other day when Jesse was in the car. Now her. How had they known? Had they followed her from St. Catherine's? Or picked her up when she got on the freeway? She hoped Sean and Kane got answers tonight from the guy they were tracking, because if they didn't, she was going to call in every favor she had coming to figure out what was going on.

CHAPTER NINETEEN

Sean and Kane sat in Nate's truck outside a bar on the outskirts of San Antonio. Sean had parked down the street, since Manuel Domingo knew what his Jeep looked like. Sean needed to get a back-up car for situations like this.

It wasn't a bad neighborhood, though Sean wouldn't call it much of a neighborhood at all. The bar was on the corner, set back at a four-way stop. Beyond the bar were a few warehouses behind tall chain-link fencing. A two-pump gas station and quick stop stood open on one corner with no customers, and a strip mall took up another corner. None of the six businesses there were open this late. The fourth corner was a weed-strewn lot bordered by a cinder-block wall separating the lot from a dilapidated mobile home park.

Nate was inside the bar; Domingo would make either Sean or Kane, but Nate was a new face. They had ears through Nate's phone so they could come in if Nate got into trouble. All they knew at this point was that

Domingo had arrived here at eight forty-five and seemed agitated. It was clear, according to Nate, that he was waiting for someone.

Sean said to Kane, “I can’t believe you doubted me.”

“When it comes to your kid, you’ve been paranoid.”

“Justified.”

“You haven’t let him go two feet outside of the house.”

“Your point?”

“Security is smart; sitting on the kid now? Not so smart.”

Sean considered what Kane was saying. “Did he say something to you? Is he bored?”

“Curious,” Kane said. “He doesn’t know why you don’t go to work.”

Sean snorted. “I explained to him—I took a big job before I got him, I have another lined up in August.”

“It’s not the same as how normal people go to work.”

“Like Carson Spade? Who laundered money for the drug cartels?”

“Don’t bite off my head. He knows about the trust fund you set up for him. I know you have money, but you have to be running on fumes right now.”

“I’m fine. I appreciate your concern, but if I get tight I can get a loan. I own two houses and a plane. And Lucy has a regular paycheck and benefits.”

Why was Kane concerned about his finances? Sean wasn’t seriously worried. He knew he could make money if he had to. Maybe taking a job he didn’t particularly want, but he could if necessary. He’d do anything he had to for his family.

"I opened Jesse's eyes up today. We spent a few hours at the boys' home."

"How'd he do?"

"I think he was surprised. Jesse's a smart kid, but until last year he was sheltered."

"Some people want to shelter their kids from the bad shit. You've done a pretty good job sheltering Jesse."

"That makes no sense. I told you—"

"Yeah, and that's a good thing. But Carson Spade is an asshole and I don't particularly like his wife, either, and you won't say word one about them to the kid."

"Madison is his mother."

"Who lied to him. Why does she get a pass?"

"She doesn't. But I'm not going to talk shit about her around Jesse. How could he respect me if I throw her under the bus?" Sean hesitated, then said, "He knows what went down. I don't have to spell things out."

Kane grunted.

Sean didn't know if he was doing anything right, but at this moment, he knew that Jesse was in danger, and if Kane was right—that someone hired Domingo to keep tabs on Jesse and Sean—then Sean needed to prove that it was Carson Spade. He was 90 percent certain he was right.

But that lingering doubt—that the marshals' threat assessment missed something—had Sean on edge, and he'd stay there until he knew the truth.

Nate said over their coms, "He's leaving. Whoever he's supposed to meet is a no-show and he looks pissed off about it."

"Follow," Kane said. "We'll have a little discussion with him outside."

Kane and Sean exited Nate's truck and hid in the shadows until Domingo approached his car. Kane stepped into view.

"Fuck," Domingo said. He turned to go back into the bar and walked right into Nate. "You—you're one of them?"

Nate made himself a wall and Domingo was forced to turn and face Kane. Sean stepped into view.

Domingo recognized him. "What the fuck is going on?"

"Who hired you to follow me?" Sean said.

Domingo looked confused. "The job just came through channels. You know."

"Which channels?" Sean said.

"I can't tell you." He was agitated. Worried.

"You will tell us," Kane said, dark and serious.

"Really, what are you going to do, kill me?"

"Jail."

"You're not a cop."

"We have friends."

Sean pulled out his phone and said, "One minute more, I call a buddy with SAPD. I tell him anything, he'll believe me. We go *way* back. He'll keep you on ice for the weekend. Give your life a rectal exam. We'll find out exactly what's going on. If you doubt it, then you have no idea who you were hired to fuck with."

"It's a legit PI! Watch and report. No bullshit, I swear."

"Name."

He was sweating. "Come on, come on, I didn't hurt anyone!"

Sean was close to belting the guy. "Name!" he demanded.

Domingo looked from Sean to Kane and back to Sean. "I—I—"

Sean glared at him.

Domingo was sweating. "Look, it wasn't a big deal." He turned to Kane.

Kane just stared.

"Fuck. Fuck! Okay, okay. It's all legit, okay? Bart—"

A crack cut through the night and Domingo's chest turned red. Before Sean could react, Nate and Kane had their guns out. Kane pushed Sean down as Nate dove for cover.

Domingo had been sniped right in front of them. He stepped back once and slumped against the wall of the bar, his eyes dazed.

A car squealed down the street and disappeared from view. How the hell had they missed a gunman?

Sean crawled over to Domingo. He wasn't going to make it.

"Bart who? Domingo? Tell me!"

"Va-Vas. Vas. Quez."

He labored for breath.

Bart Vasquez? Sean didn't know him.

"Hired. Just a j-j-job."

Blood dribbled out of the corner of Domingo's mouth.

Nate said, "An ambulance and police are on their way."

"Go," Kane told Sean.

"No!"

"Go home now, Sean. I got this."

"I can't let you both—"

"Nate is a fed. But Jimenez gave you this guy's name. You can't be anywhere around here. As far as you're concerned, you told me and I confronted him here. He was shot and killed by a sniper." Kane looked at Nate. They were still squatting behind Domingo's car.

"Black American sedan, tinted windows, license ended with six-seven-seven-zero. I couldn't make out the letters."

"Damn good," Kane said. "Dammit, Sean, get out of here before anyone sees you and you're stuck."

"Modified Remington 700," Nate continued. "My guess, anyway. Could be an M24, easy enough to get one if you know where to look."

"I concur," Kane said.

Sean didn't want to leave his brother to clean up this mess, but he didn't really have a choice. "Be careful. The sniper could come back."

"Go," Kane ordered.

Reluctantly, Sean left before authorities arrived.

He tried Lucy as soon as he was away from the bar. She didn't answer. He tried Jesse. No answer.

His heart skipped a beat. It was after nine at night; they should be home by now. She would have sent him a message if they were going to a movie or something.

He sped up. He heard sirens, but they weren't coming from the direction he was headed. Through his phone, he logged into his home security system. Lucy hadn't come home. It had been set at one thirty that afternoon—when he'd left with Jesse for the boys' home.

Something had happened. He knew it before he got a call from an unfamiliar number on his cell phone.

"Rogan," he answered, forcing his panic down.

"Sean. It's Lucy."

"Where are you? Why aren't you answering your phone?"

"We were run off the road. We're both fine—your Mustang is not."

His heart thudded. "What happened?"

"Black truck, Ford F-250 with a camper shell. I originally thought it was an SUV, but it broadsided me and I saw the shell. They'd been following me, I did evasive maneuvers and was heading to the closest police station . . . they hit the car and we went off an embankment. We're fine. I want Jesse to go to the hospital for X-rays though. Just to be safe."

"Where are you now?"

"At the scene—it happened fifteen minutes ago."

Right before Domingo was killed. Same team? Dual attack? Something completely different? Sean hated that he couldn't figure out what the fuck was going on.

He said, "I'll be there as fast as I can."

CHAPTER TWENTY

Sean called Madison. He didn't want to make this call, but he had to. Jesse was her son. He looked over at Lucy. She approached, rubbed his arm, kissed him. "It's going to be okay," she whispered.

She'd been hurt, too. She had a cut on her forehead, and her nose and jaw were bruised as if she'd been in a fight. He wanted to punch someone. Instead, he squeezed her hand, then kissed it. As soon as Madison answered, he turned away. He had to focus on this conversation, not think about almost losing both his wife and his son.

"Hi, Sean," Madison said. "I'm surprised you're calling. I thought for sure you were avoiding me."

He had been. But not for the reasons she thought. Now he had no choice. He had to talk to her.

"First, Jesse is fine."

"Why wouldn't he be fine? What happened?" Panic filled her voice.

"There was a car accident. We're at the hospital just

as a precaution. He's getting X-rays, but the doctor doesn't think that anything is broken. He has a swollen nose from the airbag in the car."

"You've always driven too fast! Always, Sean. Dammit, were you racing? Racing with my son in the car?"

Did she think that he was seventeen again?

"Lucy was run off the road," he said through clenched teeth. "And I think your husband hired someone to do it."

He shouldn't have said that. Why had he said that? He was a total idiot.

"I want to talk to my son *now*."

"I'll have him call you as soon as he's out of X-ray," Sean said. "He's fine, Madison. He didn't want me to call you, but you need to know."

"Damn straight I need to know! How dare you accuse Carson of *anything*. He's been working hard to prove that he's changed. He's doing the right thing. This has been hard on all of us, but especially Carson. What have you been telling Jesse? Are you attacking my husband? Is this why Jesse won't talk to him? Are you filling my son's head with lies?"

Sean snapped. Lucy reached for him and he knew what she was going to say so he walked away.

In a low voice Sean said, "Carson Spade laundered money for a violent drug cartel, and he only stopped because he was caught. I don't care how *hard* any of this is on your fucking *husband*, he got off easy. He should be spending the next fifty years in prison, instead he gets fucking *three years'* probation!"

"Don't—"

"I've never said word one to Jesse about Carson, but *our* son is not an idiot. He knows the truth."

"How dare you!"

"Jesse will call you later."

He hung up. He was shaking. He was so angry and scared; he knew he'd just lost all visitation rights with his son.

Lucy came over and hugged him tight. "Sean."

"I could have lost you. I could have lost you both." He blinked back hot tears. He wasn't a man who cried often. He remembered twice. The first when he buried his mother. The second when he thought Lucy was going to leave him when she found out he'd lied to her.

The thought that he may have lost both his wife and his son tonight terrified him.

"They didn't want to kill us."

"You don't know that!" He was trying to get his emotions together but he was falling apart.

When he saw Lucy and Jesse sitting in the back of the ambulance, he had been a rock. He'd hugged them, talked to the police, surveyed the damage, called his insurance company. But now, now that he knew they were safe, he was on the verge of exploding.

He let Lucy walk him over to a plastic chair in the waiting room outside X-ray. He felt stiff and awkward, and he didn't want to let her go.

She held his face in her hands. Her head had been bandaged, and her nose was swollen. She had a bruise on her neck from the seat belt—it went under her blouse. It would be black tomorrow.

He leaned in and kissed her as the tears fell.

She held him and he worked on getting it together. For Lucy. For Jesse. They were okay. They were alive.

Someone had to pay for this.

"Sean, I think whoever hit us wanted to scare us, not kill us. They had time to come back and finish things, but they left long before I heard sirens. It felt like a warning, a show of force."

"The guy who followed me on Wednesday—he's dead."

"Dead? How?"

"Someone shot him outside a bar at about the same time you were run off the road." He would tell her everything about their conversation with Domingo later. "Kane told me to leave because Jimenez gave me information he shouldn't have. And now Domingo is dead."

"Jimenez gave you the information because he thought you needed it to protect Jesse."

"It's not that simple."

"For you, it is. It has to be. You didn't kill him."

"He was hired by a PI. But the way he described it, I don't think the PI even knew what he was doing. He was a hired gun, too. To keep tabs on me? Jesse? But then—you're run off the road. Why would Carson want to hurt Jesse?"

"You don't know that Carson is behind this."

"He is!" He swallowed his temper. "Who else?"

"I don't know."

"My gut tells me Carson wants something—but I don't know what! For me to send Jesse back? If I thought he was in danger, I'd never send him where I couldn't protect him. But Madison is livid, and I don't blame her. He might get exactly what he wants. I can't lose him, Luce. He's my son."

The thought of losing Jesse was as debilitating as the thought of losing Lucy. He loved them both so much he couldn't think.

"Sean, we're here," Lucy said. "We are fine. You need to focus on what you can control. You accused Madison's husband of something atrocious. Running her son off the road. Might not have been the thing to say under the circumstances, especially since we don't have any proof."

She was right. He'd reacted, he hadn't been thinking. "Oh God, Luce, what have I done?"

"We'll fix it. That's what we do, right? But we have to get to the bottom of this—whether it's Carson, or someone who wants to send Carson a message."

Again, Lucy was right. Maybe Carson had nothing to do with it, but was it a warning? Because Carson knew more than he told the feds? That would make sense, too. Someone sending a message to Carson to keep his mouth shut.

Why not just kill him? If he was a threat, it was safer if he was dead. That's how the cartels generally operated. Unless he had something they wanted.

Maybe it wasn't a cartel. Maybe it was someone else. Carson had been a lawyer for nearly two decades, he had other clients. What had the feds done to investigate them? Sean was pretty certain nothing Carson Spade had done professionally had been legal.

"Mr. Rogan?" a female voice said.

Sean and Lucy stood, hands entwined. The doctor stood in front of them.

"I'm Dr. Natalie Blair," she said.

"Where's Jesse?"

"Flirting with the nurses, I'm sure." She smiled. "He's fine. Broken nose, but there's not much to do for it other than tape it up. It's very common in car accidents like this. He'll be sore—he has bruises across his chest from the seat belt, and a mild concussion. I told him he should stay overnight, but he was adamant about going home. Are you familiar with concussion protocols?"

"Yes," Lucy said. "I'm EMT-certified."

"Good. Just talk to him every two hours, make sure he's coherent, call me if he complains of any sharp pains or if his head feels worse than a bad headache. I'd like to see him on Monday for a follow-up. Light activity, he probably won't feel like running a marathon tomorrow, but walking and moving around is good. If he experiences double vision, bring him to the emergency room." She handed Sean a card. "If you have any questions, call my service, they'll track me down."

"Thank you. He's really okay?"

"Yes. He was worried about you, Mrs. Rogan. Did you have X-rays?"

"Nothing is broken. Not even my nose. And I've had a concussion before; I don't have one now."

"I'll keep an eye on both of them," Sean said.

"I'm a pediatrician, but I think you should go see your doctor just to make sure."

Lucy didn't like hospitals or being fussed over. "I promise, if I feel any worse, I'll call my doctor."

"I need to sign the paperwork to discharge him, but you can go down the hall to the right and the nurse will direct you to Jesse."

"Thank you," Sean said, relieved.

He took Lucy's hand and walked as fast as he dared down the hall.

Lucy was worried about Sean, and not for the first time. She had rarely seen him so scared. He had always been a rock, always been strong—which helped her be strong. Now she needed to be *his* rock, because he was facing fears he didn't know he had.

They found Jesse lying down on a hospital bed.

He sat up as soon as Sean and Lucy walked into the room. "Can I go?"

"We're just waiting for the doctor to sign you out," Sean said, trying to put on a brave front.

Jesse stared at Sean. He saw what Lucy saw: the intense emotion that was clouding Sean's usual mischievous and cheerful expression.

"They said nothing was wrong. Except my nose. But it'll heal straight, she said, as long as I don't mess with it."

Lucy smiled. "You're going to be fine." Lucy glanced at Sean, but he was still staring at Jesse as if he didn't know what to do. "Besides," she said, "a crooked nose is attractive to girls."

"I'm sorry," Sean said suddenly.

Jesse frowned. "What?"

"You were safe, and now you're not because I wanted you with me."

"Sean," Lucy said. She knew exactly where he was going with this, and this wasn't what Sean wanted to do. "We all need a good night's sleep."

"Maybe you should go home."

"I don't want to go home. I want to go to *your* house."

Jesse was on the verge of tears. He didn't understand Sean's pain and guilt, and Lucy had to fix this.

"Of course," she said. "No one is making any decisions about *anything* tonight."

"I need you safe, Jesse. It could have been so much worse."

"I don't want to go back to Sacramento. I want to stay here. With you. And Lucy. *Please.* You talked to Mom, didn't you? What did she say? She can't make me leave, can she?"

"I need to talk to the doctor," Sean said suddenly and left.

Jesse looked stricken.

Lucy took Jesse's hands. "Honey, he's worried about you. About this situation."

"I don't want to *ever* go home."

"You don't mean that."

"Yes I do! Why doesn't he want me?"

She didn't know if the trauma of the night was making Jesse more emotional, or if this was a deeper-seated fear. For twelve years Jesse believed that his father didn't want anything to do with him because that's what his mother had told him. Sean explained that wasn't true, that he hadn't known about Madison's pregnancy or Jesse's birth, but sometimes, fears didn't easily disappear—especially when you'd believed something your entire life that turned out to be a lie.

She sat next to him on the hospital bed and took his hand. "Jesse, Sean loves you so much. He wants you, never think that he doesn't. Having you here this summer has made him so happy. Happier than I've ever seen him. That doesn't change the fact that he's worried about your safety. We don't know what's going on, but we *will* find out. Between me, Sean, Kane—we have a lot of resources and people to help. None of us are going to stop until we learn the truth."

"I don't want to stay if he doesn't want me."

Had Jesse completely missed what she said? "He wants you, Jesse. More than anything."

"Then why does he want me to go back to Sacramento?"

"Why would you think that?" Sean didn't want Jesse to go to Sacramento ever, but it wasn't his choice. "He wants to spend every minute of the time you have left. He just said what he did because he called your mom and she's worried."

"I told him not to. I knew she would do this."

"She needed to know what happened."

"I knew she'd freak."

"She loves you. We'll go home and figure this out. That I can promise."

Jesse didn't look convinced.

Lucy didn't know what else to say to get through to him. Then she realized she couldn't say anything—Sean was the only one who could. And Sean was so racked with guilt that he wasn't thinking straight.

* * *

By the time they were back home, it was after midnight and everyone was exhausted. Jesse wasn't talking, and he went straight to bed. Lucy told him that she and Sean would be checking on him every couple of hours.

"Sean, you need to talk to Jesse," Lucy said. "He thinks you don't want him around."

"He knows that's not true. I've told him every day I'm glad he's here."

"You told him tonight that you want to send him home."

"Because it's not safe for him! I can't keep him safe."

"If someone is after Carson Spade, Jesse is much safer here than anywhere else. You *know* that."

"What about this case you're working?"

Lucy had to shift gears. "It's pretty straightforward." It wasn't, not anymore with evidence missing, but there was no reason anyone would come after her.

"Sean," Lucy said, "this guy Domingo followed you and Jesse, then someone else followed me and Jesse. Jesse is the only common factor."

They had to figure out how they'd been tracked.

"What did you learn from Domingo?" she asked.

Sean stared at her for a second. "What?"

"Domingo. You followed him to a bar. He was killed. But he told you something."

"He mentioned a local PI, Bart Vasquez. I've never heard of him. Nate had the wherewithal to get a partial plate and description, but that's all we have. And as far as anyone is concerned, I wasn't there. Kane and Nate handled it."

"Nate."

Sean's face fell. "I didn't think. He's on leave."

"It'll be okay." She wasn't positive. But Nate hadn't shot anyone.

There was a knock on the door and Sean looked at the security pad. "It's Kane," he said, sounding hugely relieved.

He let in his brother. "Are you okay?" Kane immediately said to Lucy. "Jesse?"

"Yes."

Sean locked up and they sat in the living room.

"What happened at the bar?" Sean asked.

Kane hesitated a second, unusual for him, as he looked Lucy over.

"I'm okay," Lucy said. "Jesse's sleeping. Broken nose. He's fine."

Kane nodded, marginally relaxed, and said, "Nate knew the responding officer, we gave our statements and he let us go. We kept as close to the truth as possible—Domingo was spotted following my brother and nephew, so we just wanted to have a chat. He'd told us that a private investigator hired him, and as we were trying to convince him to tell us who, he was shot and killed. The partial matches a truck that was stolen only hours before the shooting, they'll probably find it dumped."

"So we're back at square one," Lucy said.

"Not exactly," Sean said. "Domingo did name the PI who hired him."

"Nate and I did a little recon. Vasquez has an office not far from the bar, and a house in the Dominion."

"Nice neighborhood for a two-bit PI."

"Not two-bit. Former cop, suspected of being dirty, never proven. Retired after twenty years, with pension, became a PI. Works mostly for defense lawyers and makes a small fortune digging up dirt to discredit witnesses. We'll talk to him tomorrow. I told Nate he's out. He called his boss from the scene and she wasn't happy about him being in the middle of an RCK operation, especially when he's on mandatory leave. So Jack's on his way, catching the first flight out of Sac in the morning." Kane glanced at Lucy, then looked straight at Sean. "This is your kid—you decide who's doing babysitting duty. You or Jack. No offense, Lucy, but you're going to be feeling like shit tomorrow. You already look stiff and sore."

"No offense taken. I *am* stiff and sore. Sean, I think you stay with Jesse. You need to talk to him, he's upset."

"I have talked to him. And I'm going to lose him. I know it."

"We will let *nothing* happen to that kid," Kane said.

"You don't get it. He was in a major accident. Went to the hospital. Madison is worried and angry and I don't blame her. She wants him home, and I have no legal authority to stop her."

"If Carson Spade is behind any of this, no one is going to send Jesse back."

"We can't prove it!"

"You can't. But Dean Hooper can."

"Dean?"

"Sean, for a smart guy, you're being a fucking idiot."

"Screw you." Sean ran his hands through his hair.

"You called Hooper to push him on Spade—Hooper can't tell you shit, and you should know it. But Rick? Hooper can share anything with Rick since they're both high-ranking feds. Rick will talk to him first thing in the morning and see exactly what Carson Spade has shared and how helpful he's being. He's also going to tail Spade and do a deeper run on known associates, outside of the Flores cartel. Spade gave up his rights per the plea deal, so his life is an open book as far as the feds are concerned. Trust them to do their job, Sean. You might not get the answers, but they'll do whatever it takes to protect Jesse."

Sean didn't say anything. Lucy didn't know how to make him feel better. The only thing would be if he found out exactly what was going on.

"Kane's right," Lucy said. "Let's get some sleep."

"How did they find us? Both on Wednesday and tonight?" Sean asked. "I've been beating my head about it and I can't figure it out. Jesse doesn't have social media because of WITSEC—they scared him silly about how easy it is to track people through those apps. I know the cars are clean—I checked them both Wednesday night. And our phones."

"Jesse is the commonality," Lucy said.

"Oh shit." Sean jumped up. He strode down the hall and a minute later came back with Jesse's phone. It was cracked from the accident, but otherwise operable.

He unlocked the phone, searched something in the settings, moving quickly, and Lucy wasn't certain what he was doing. Then she saw it.

"Parental tracking," Sean said. "Dammit! I would never have allowed this."

"You think someone hacked it?"

"Carson Spade doesn't need to. It's hooked up to Madison's phone. She knows where Jesse is at all times through this app."

"But someone *could* have hacked it," Lucy pushed. "Don't accuse Carson without knowing for certain."

"I'll find out," Sean said. "It'll take me some time, but I'll find out if anyone hacked this app. So help me, I will kill that bastard if he put you and Jesse in danger."

"And this is why you have to stay far away from Spade," Kane said.

Sean glared at his brother, then turned and walked down the hall. He slammed his office door closed behind him.

"What the fuck, Lucy?" Kane asked. "He's unfocused. Hell, even when you were lost in Mexico and I had to shake sense into him, he wasn't this stupid."

"He's afraid that Madison is going to take Jesse away. Working on the problem will help. His mind will settle down."

"What happened out there? I couldn't get details from Sean."

Lucy told Kane everything, including her conversation with Jesse about the boys. "That kid has been through a lot in the last year. He went from being a sheltered, normal, upper-middle-class kid to being thrown into the middle of a cartel war. To learning that his mother lied to him, that his stepfather is a criminal, and that his dad didn't abandon him. He's processing a lot and I think knowing what happened to Michael and the others affected him deep down. He feels like the blind man in the Bible—he was blind and now he can see, but what he's seeing is disturbing. He doesn't know how to work through this onslaught of information."

"You think Sean should have held back?"

"No—I think Sean should have taken him to visit Michael and the boys earlier. Sean has made it his life's mission to make sure those boys have a chance at a future, and Jesse knows it, and somehow has worked himself up that he's selfish or demanding or that Sean didn't think he was mature enough to handle the situation—well, I'm not quite sure." Lucy had some ideas, but she really wanted Jesse and Sean to talk things out. They'd had a great few weeks, but it was all fun. There was no pressure—and both of them had put pressure on themselves but hid it from the other. "Jesse wants to stay. He has some major trust issues right now, and I don't know how it's going to play out. He's only thirteen, but this last year he's been forced to grow up. Jesse wants Sean to fight for him, and he thinks Sean won't."

"That's ridiculous."

"He's barely a teenager."

"Sean would do anything to make that kid happy."

"Sean doesn't have the confidence in himself to think that he'd make a good father. He's become Jesse's friend—which is great—but Sean needs to be his father *first*. And that's not easy coming into fatherhood late in the game."

"I think you're overthinking this."

Kane was very black-and-white in his way of thinking. He could analyze any situation and know tactically what to do, but when it came to interpersonal relationships, he didn't understand the nuances.

"I'm really not," Lucy said. "I'm going to check on Jesse, then get a couple hours of sleep."

"Are you working tomorrow?"

"Most likely."

"Be careful. Just in case it wasn't Jesse they were after."

She appreciated his concern. "I told Sean, and I'll tell you—they didn't want us dead. They had plenty of time to come back and kill us. The whole thing was an exercise in fear. I don't scare easily."

"Who's your partner on this case?"

Sometimes getting through to Kane was impossible. "Proctor."

"Head of SWAT?"

"Yes."

"Okay."

"And if it wasn't someone you approved of?"

Kane just smiled and walked toward the kitchen.

Lucy checked on Jesse. She woke him up, talked to him for a minute, and made sure he drank water. She then went to Sean's den. He was focused on his computer.

"Sean."

He looked at her. "Hey. I thought you went to bed."

"I'm going. I just checked on Jesse, he's good. Are you going to be up for a while?"

"Yes."

"Set an alarm for two hours and go check on him."

Sean picked up his phone and scheduled it.

Lucy wanted to share everything she and Jesse had talked about, but now wasn't the time. Sean was tense and worried and he wouldn't take the information the way she intended. She walked over and wrapped her arms around him. "I love you."

"Love you too. Sleep. I'll be up in a couple hours."

Two hours later, Sean had nothing. Well, not nothing. He was confident that Jesse's phone hadn't been hacked, but he had to spend a lot of time studying how the parental tracking program worked so that he could figure out if the program itself had been hacked externally. It would be much easier if he had Madison's phone. When he figured out the back end, he'd call her and walk her through how to check to see if the app was compromised. She'd damn well better cooperate.

His alarm beeped, and he got up and stretched. The house was quiet. He went upstairs. The master suite was upstairs, a small den, and a bedroom with its own bath. Jesse had moved into the second upstairs suite, and as far as Sean was concerned, it was now Jesse's room. They had two other bedrooms downstairs, but Jesse needed his own space for whenever he came to visit.

If Madison ever let him visit again.

Stop. Stop thinking that way.

Sean opened Jesse's door. Bandit was on the end of his bed. As soon as he saw Sean, he sleepily got off and curled up in the dog bed Sean had put in the room. No one followed Sean's rule that Bandit wasn't allowed on furniture or beds, except Bandit—when he saw Sean.

Sean scratched the dog behind his ears and sat on the edge of Jesse's bed.

"Jess, it's Sean."

Jess rolled over, opened one eye. "I'm fine."

"Okay. Do you need anything?"

"No." He closed his eye again.

Sean sat in the chair in the corner and watched Jesse sleep. *If* he was sleeping. Sean wanted to talk to him, to explain his reaction at the hospital, but didn't know what to say. He kept replaying the scene at the embankment over and over in his head, a waking nightmare, but instead of finding Lucy and Jesse safe, he saw them dead in the mangled car.

He rubbed his eyes. The fear of losing the two people he loved more than anything terrified him, and he didn't know how to make it go away.

"I'm sorry, Jess," Sean whispered.

I love you, Jesse.

CHAPTER TWENTY-ONE

Sean didn't come up to bed. Lucy woke at four, thinking he might have fallen asleep in his office. She found him instead sleeping in the chair next to Jesse's bed. They were both out. She went back to bed for a couple of hours, but didn't sleep well. When she rose at seven, she checked on them again and they were still sleeping. She woke Jesse up, he said he was fine and then fell right back to sleep.

She left Sean where he was. If she woke him, he wouldn't go back to sleep, though he certainly didn't look comfortable in the chair.

Lucy didn't want to work over the weekend, but she had a job to do and Sean and Jesse were going to have to work things out. She believed that they would. Still, sometimes even the smartest people had a blind spot.

Kane was already up and had coffee made—strong, as she liked it. Kane winced when she added cream and sugar.

She popped a bagel in the toaster and sipped her coffee. "What do you know?"

"Nothing that I didn't share last night."

"What do you think?"

He considered. "I think you might be right—that whoever is keeping an eye on you three wants to shake you up."

"It worked, at least with Sean. Please keep an eye on him today."

"He'll be fine."

"He's worried that he's going to blow it with Jesse. He has to know he won't, if he's just himself and honest. He usually listens to me, but on this, his fears are getting the better of him."

"I'll knock sense into him."

"I know you will." She grabbed her bagel out of the toaster, spread on cream cheese, put it on a paper plate. She poured more coffee in a go-mug and said, "Depending on what we learn, it shouldn't be a full day—I'll be back as soon as I can."

Lucy grabbed the keys to her car, scratched Bandit on the head, and left. She had taken to driving Sean's Mustang when he bought the Jeep; now she dreaded her old, practical Nissan. Sure, it was a reliable car that was only a few years old, but it wasn't half as fun as the Mustang.

She knew the car was totaled. She felt bad about it because Sean had loved that car, but at the same time the solid frame had helped protect them from the impact of the larger truck.

There was little traffic on the weekend, and she made good time. Lucy was surprised to find her boss, Rachel

Vaughn, in the office. She'd sent her an email about the accident because Lucy had to file a police report, but she'd kept it brief by necessity.

"I'm surprised to see you," Rachel said.

"Leo and I are following a lead on the Paul Grey case."

"I thought that was ruled suicide."

"It is, but there are other factors—such as who moved his body."

"I assumed it was McMahon."

"It may have been, but we haven't found any evidence to support or contradict that. Didn't Leo copy you into the memo he sent to the task force?"

"I haven't read it yet. I was wrapped up in another investigation—Kenzie and Emilio have been assisting cybercrimes on a child pornography case. We executed half a dozen warrants yesterday at city hall—all on staff members who downloaded child porn to their computers."

Lucy's stomach flipped. "Did we arrest them?"

"Five of the six. I think one was tipped off. The one I really wanted. The others were caught up in the sting—three of them had one child porn video, the same video, and all denied knowing about it. I suspect it was a virus they opened, but cybercrime is going through the devices as we speak. The other two we have are cooling their heels in jail. That's why I love executing these warrants on Friday afternoon—very difficult to get arraigned and out on bail before Monday."

Lucy was surprised that her by-the-book boss would say that—but it was *technically* by the book.

Rachel motioned for Lucy to step into her office and close the door. "I hesitate to ask you about this, because I know you and your husband are personal friends with Nate. Do you think he's okay after the shooting on Wednesday?"

"Yes," Lucy said without reservation. "He was cleared in the psych eval—at least, that's what he told me."

"He was," she said.

"He acted on orders, and McMahon was a clear threat."

"It was justified, there's no doubt in my mind—or anyone's—that there was no other option under the circumstances. You do know what happened last night?"

"Yes, Kane is staying with us." She didn't know how much Rachel knew, though she'd gotten the "official" story from Kane.

"The problem is not that Nate was helping your brother-in-law on a case in his spare time, but he's not supposed to carry a firearm while on mandatory leave, and he had two in his possession. I would let it slide—but because there's a police report, I can't. Which made me think that Nate is on edge. He knows the rules."

Lucy had to choose her words carefully. "Yes, and I doubt he expected the kind of trouble he found. Nate doesn't go anywhere unarmed. Maybe because of his decade in the army, or because he's been a federal agent for three years, but it's very natural for him." She paused. "I don't know exactly what you're looking for from me."

"His state of mind."

"I'm not a psychiatrist, and I can't evaluate Nate. I'm too close to him."

"Maybe that makes you the best one to evaluate him."

"Maybe. I think Nate is fine, he's frustrated because he doesn't like not working. He has friends—and I'll always have his back."

"That's good to know." Rachel shuffled a couple of papers. "Did I see an email that you were in a car accident?"

"Yes, I was run off the road last night. Jesse—Sean's son—was with me. We were coming back from dinner and a Ford F-250 sideswiped us as we got off the freeway. There's a police report on it—when I get a copy, I'll send it to you."

"I don't need it—unless it's related to a case you're working."

"I don't think so." Could it have been? She didn't think so, but she hadn't seriously thought that it was related the McMahon case. Why would anyone want to run her off the road? To scare her? They hadn't figured out what had been going on with McMahon, and with the lost evidence, they may still never learn why he took a room of people hostage.

"Was it intentional?" Rachel asked.

Lucy didn't want to admit to Rachel that it was, but she wasn't going to lie—not again. Lying to Rachel at the beginning of their working relationship had created a plethora of problems between them that they'd only recently really begun to work through.

"I believe it was, though I don't know why. You're aware that Jesse's family was recently released from the witness protection program when the marshals determined there was no longer a threat against them."

"You think there still is?"

"I don't know. Possibly. Sean's on top of it and talking to the marshals. I'm focused on the McMahon and Grey cases."

"Right—just recognize that for all intents and purposes, the cases are closed. We're just gathering additional facts for the reports. But you and Leo can't spend a lot of extra time on this."

"You really need to read Leo's memo. Evidence is missing, it appears to have disappeared during transport. SAPD is tracking it through the courier, but it's very odd that only one of three packages arrived."

Rachel was surprised, and it was clear she hadn't read anything from Leo all day. "I'm sorry, I should have known. I'm working today to catch up on everything I've neglected since those warrants came through."

"We're hoping to have at least some answers this weekend."

"I won't keep you, then. Thanks."

Lucy left and breathed a sigh of relief. Rachel was preoccupied, and that was probably a good thing. Lucy had expected her boss to say it was an SAPD problem because technically, Lucy and Leo weren't on the McMahon case.

"There you are," Leo said. "Ready—wait, what happened? How'd you get that bruise?"

"Car accident last night. I'll explain on the way to Cassidy's house."

* * *

Fifteen minutes later, they arrived at Cassidy Roth's house. Leo intentionally parked in the driveway—if Cassidy tried to flee, she would have to do it on foot.

"You sure you're okay?" Leo asked for the third time.

"I'm fine. Just bruised. Are we on the same page here with Cassidy?"

"Yes."

Lucy didn't want Leo to worry about her when they needed to be cautious about McMahon's assistant. While she might be harmless, she had been at the hostage situation, left, and took two boxes of possible evidence from McMahon's apartment.

Lucy wasn't taking any chances. She'd faced young female criminals before, and in some ways they were more dangerous than their male counterparts because many cops didn't consider them as threats.

They waited until the officer who was watching the house came over to them. "I haven't seen her," he said.

"When'd you come on duty?"

"Six a.m., sir."

"We'll go to the front, you watch the back. If she bolts, grab her. But she's a person of interest, not a suspect at this time."

They approached Cassidy's door and Leo knocked. "Cassidy Roth, this is SSA Leo Proctor with the FBI. We need to speak with you."

A prickly feeling on the back of Lucy's neck had her turning sharply around, just in time to see a blind shift back into place in Emmaline Granger's house.

"Leo, I think she's in Granger's house."

"We don't have enough people to cover all the doors."

"She's going to run. We need to go." Lucy made a move toward Granger's house and Leo stopped her.

"Do not pursue her alone." Leo called for the uniform. He jogged back into view. "Stay here. Eyes open."

"Yes, sir."

Leo and Lucy walked briskly to the front of the property. Before they even got to the front porch, they saw a white Honda Civic—Cassidy's make and model—speeding down the street.

"That's her," Lucy said.

Leo jumped into the FBI pool car. He turned the ignition, then tried to back out.

The car didn't budge.

He jumped out. "Well, shit!"

Lucy ran out and saw that there was a four-by-four wooden stake blocking the rear tires. She and Leo removed it, but by that time Cassidy was gone, and they had no way of knowing which direction she'd turned when she reached the four-way intersection at the end of the street.

"Dammit," Leo mumbled. He made a call and Lucy heard him putting an APB on Cassidy Roth, then he made another call. "I need a search warrant." He gave Cassidy's name and address. "Cause? Obstruction of justice, removing evidence from a crime scene, interfering with a federal officer in the line of duty . . . yes, I believe the evidence is in her house."

Lucy doubted it. She didn't know the research assistant, but she had been a step ahead of them on Wednesday when she cleaned out whatever was important in

McMahon's apartment; yesterday when they tried to interview her; and today. She'd expected them, and she had a plan to bolt.

But she didn't say anything.

"Anything related to the McMahon hostage situation, Clarke-Harrison, or Paul Grey's suicide," Leo was saying on the phone. "Grey's phone is missing and so is McMahon's laptop. She was seen removing two boxes of evidence from McMahon's apartment."

Lucy looked over at Emmaline's house. The woman was looking at them through the closed screen, a worried expression on her face. She knew something.

"Thanks, Abigail. We'll wait here." He hung up. "Abigail is going to talk to SAPD—she thinks we'll get a warrant faster through the county DA than going through the AUSA's office. She'll call me back."

"Cassidy was in Mrs. Granger's house."

"Let's have a talk with Mrs. Granger."

They walked up the stairs. The old woman opened the door. "Come in, please."

"You're in some trouble, ma'am," Leo said.

"I didn't mean to do anything wrong," she said. "Please don't hurt Cassidy. She's not thinking straight."

Mrs. Granger shuffled over to the dining table and sat down. "Please sit. My arthritis is bad this morning."

Leo sighed, and his angry face disappeared. "Mrs. Granger," he said quietly but firmly, "we need to talk to Cassidy about Charlie McMahon and Paul Grey and what she knows about the hostage situation on Wednesday, and Grey's suicide."

"Suicide?"

"We know that she saw Paul Grey, whom she used to work with, only hours before he killed himself."

"I don't know anything about that. Cassidy is a sweet girl. She would never hurt anyone. She takes care of everything here, takes my garbage out every week."

Lucy said, "When I was talking to you yesterday, was Cassidy in your house?"

"Yes," she said. "Everything else I said was the truth. She did leave late Monday night. She didn't come back until Wednesday afternoon. She was so upset. She told me to please not tell anyone she was here because she had more work to do."

"What kind of work? She called in sick to her employer this week."

"I don't know. I don't understand what she did at work, and she really didn't tell me anything. All she said was that if she didn't figure it out, Charlie would have died for nothing."

"Figure what out?"

"I don't know."

"Did she tell you about the hostage situation?"

"I saw it on the news. I'd met Charlie. I couldn't believe what he had done, especially when Cassidy looked up to him so much. Cassidy said he didn't do it, but of course he did. I saw it with my own eyes. I told her that because they were friends she might not see the truth. She said he was already dying and she was helping him figure out what happened."

"What happened? What did she mean?"

"I don't know. A lot of what Cassidy said didn't make sense to me, but I never graduated from high school. I married the boy next door when I was sixteen and we had a wonderful life. All my kids went to college, except Timmy. He enlisted in the marines. Died for his country, but I don't cry because he loved his country and loved being a marine." Her eyes flitted over to a family photo on the wall. Five kids. One was in uniform. "That was Timmy's graduation from basic training. We all went to see him. His dad and I, we were so proud."

Leo said, "Bless him for his service, and your loss, ma'am. I served in the marines for six years, right out of high school. What happened to your boy?"

"They couldn't tell me. He was part of a special forces team, I think they call it. He died during a rescue, saving a fellow soldier. His name is Danny. He still writes to me. He named his son Timmy, after my boy. Timmy would never have been born, if my Timmy hadn't saved Danny. It was meant to be, but I miss him."

She smiled at them, but it was sad. "Cassidy is a good girl. If she's done something against the law, she didn't mean to. She must have a good reason."

"We're getting a warrant to search her house," Leo said. "Did she leave anything here?"

"No, she stayed up all night at her place working. I know because her lights were on when I got up at five."

"How did she know we were coming?" Lucy asked.

"She didn't. She left early this morning."

"We had an officer watching the house."

"I think she knew that," Mrs. Granger said. "She started parking down the street in university parking on Wednesday. She left before six in the morning. She came back right before you got here. She saw you drive up, and as soon as you walked back to her house, she left. Told me she had more work to do and she promised me she'd call you, Agent Kincaid, as soon as she had answers."

"Em," Lucy said, "think hard. Where would she go? Was there someone she might reach out to? Someone who might take her in?"

"Cassidy didn't have a lot of friends. She talked about someone named Vince, but I don't think she liked him much. He wasn't returning her calls, that I know. And there was another boy, Adam—they went to school together, and I thought they might be dating, but when I asked she just blushed and said no. She likes him but probably never told him. She can be very shy."

"Do you know Adam's last name?"

She shook her head. "I'm sorry. I don't think he lives too far away, though. I remember a couple of times over the last year or so when she said she was going to have coffee with Adam."

Lucy made a note. It would be virtually impossible to track down Adam with no last name who graduated from the same school as Cassidy and lived in the Greater San Antonio area—but maybe they'd catch a break if they could get a warrant for her house and find his address or last name in her belongings.

"If she comes back, you need to let us know, Em. She wasn't in trouble before, but now she is. And if she knows anything about what was going on with Charlie McMahon, she needs to tell us."

"She doesn't think the police can help," Mrs. Granger said. "But I'll call you, I promise. And I'm sorry I fibbed to you yesterday. Everything else I told you was the truth, I just didn't tell you she was in my house. Am I in trouble?"

Leo reached out and squeezed her hand. "No, Em, you're not in trouble. Unless you do it again."

CHAPTER TWENTY-TWO

Sean had an awful night, and he didn't expect the day to get any better.

He woke up in Jesse's room just before nine, his neck stiff and his back sore. He woke Jesse like the doctor had told him to. Jesse said, "I'm fine," and closed his eyes again.

Sean didn't think he'd been asleep. Jesse just didn't want to talk to him.

Sean took a short shower and walked downstairs. He didn't like coffee, but he poured himself a cup, sipped, and grimaced. He needed the jolt but he didn't understand how Lucy could drink this stuff like water.

Kane was on the phone, and by the conversation it was clear he was talking to Rick Stockton. When he hung up, he said, "Rick knows what happened. He's talking to Dean now, and will be alerting the marshals."

"What does he think is going on?"

"If this is a threat to Jesse, their threat assessment is shit." Kane paused. "You need to be prepared that they may have to go back into WITSEC. The marshals are generally very good, but they could have missed something—especially if Spade wasn't forthcoming."

Sean's stomach twisted painfully. He'd been thinking about this exact situation all night. That now that he'd found Jesse, he would lose him again.

"If Spade didn't tell the truth, if he hid something about his activities or associates from the court, he won't be allowed back into the program. That's part of his agreement," Sean said.

"But they would put his wife and son back in."

"Stepson! Jesse is *my* son."

"Sean."

Kane didn't have to say it. Sean couldn't protect Jesse and Madison if someone wanted to get to Carson through them.

"I don't want to lose him, Kane," Sean said quietly.

Kane clapped a hand on Sean's back. "We're going to get through this, no matter what happens. He's safe here for now, Jack's on his way, and I'm going to do some recon on this Bart Vasquez. Did you learn anything about Jesse's phone last night?"

"I left a program running overnight."

They walked down the hall to Sean's office and he slipped behind his desk. At least here he had complete control. Here, he knew what he was doing and how to find answers.

He scanned the raw data of the app that told Jesse's mother where he was. These apps were supposed to be hackproof, but Sean knew nothing was foolproof. Yet Sean had found no evidence that someone outside had accessed the app. Now he had just the raw code and data. Everything meant something, but what he wanted was a list of IP addresses that had logged into the program to look at the tracking. One came up almost daily—but Sean had already determined it was Madison.

This was going to take time. Raw data was a bitch to pore through, even when you knew what to look for.

Kane said, "Work on that, call if you learn anything. Jack will be here early afternoon. We're going to find out exactly what's going on." He paused. "I told Rick Lucy's theory."

"What?" Had Sean missed something?

"That being run off the road was a threat, not a planned assassination."

"She doesn't know that."

"She's not only trained, but she has above-average instincts. It was a hit-and-run, on purpose, but they had time to finish the job if they wanted Lucy or Jesse dead."

Sean hated hearing those words.

"Rick's going to relay that information to the marshals and hope that they'll delay any relocation until we get answers."

"And what if she's wrong?"

"Do you think she is?"

"I won't take that risk with Jesse's life."

It was clear by his expression that Kane didn't agree with him, but Jesse wasn't his kid. Jesse was *Sean's* son, and Sean would do *anything* to keep him safe.

"I'm going to recon Vasquez. Did you run him last night?"

"Basics. Owns a million-dollar house in the Dominion. Has a yacht moored in Galveston and a condo on the beach. More property in Dallas, a few rentals locally, and a giant ranch in Tucson. And that's just the property in his or his wife's name."

"He's married?"

"Anita Vasquez. Maiden name Garcia. Going back twenty-some years. One grown daughter attends LSU."

"Is she home?"

"I found her working in New Orleans for the summer. What are you thinking?"

"Do you know how he got his money?"

"No. I would have to cross over to the gray area. I'll do it if you think it's important." Sean didn't like breaking the law—even if it was a gray area—unless it was life or death. Not now, when he was married to a fed and it might ruin Lucy's life. "I couldn't find any way that he could have legitimately gotten that money, but there could be an inheritance—him or his wife. There was no major case where he won a settlement in a federal court or in Texas in the last decade. Not all court cases are online, so it would take some legwork—especially if it was out of state. I only looked in Texas because he's never lived anywhere else. I was going to check Arizona next, because of that ranch he owns."

"No known source of income and he was suspected of being a dirty cop. Now he's a PI hiring thugs."

"Sums it up."

"I may or may not make contact, but Jack will call when he lands. You find out how Jesse was tracked, then dig back into Vasquez for criminal connections."

"I know what I'm doing," Sean snapped. He rubbed his eyes. "Sorry," he mumbled.

Kane squeezed his shoulder. "You're not in this alone, brother."

Kane walked out and Sean went back to work, running a deeper background on Bart Vasquez and his wife, letting the computer program do the work for him, while he refocused on analyzing the raw data from Jesse's phone.

Because he was preoccupied and tired, he didn't see the problem the first time he looked through. His head hurt, but he needed to find it. He knew something was there.

So he went back again. And again.

Then he saw it.

He had been focusing on ISPs, when he should be focusing on the time stamps. Because the program was supposed to be the safest out there, it only sent data when authorized users pinged the phone. They had to proactively log in and collect the data. Sean had already considered that Madison's phone may be compromised, but convincing her of that would be difficult. If he didn't find anything in the raw data on Jesse's phone, he would call Rick Stockton and go through proper channels to get access to Madison's phone—or walk the FBI cyber team through what to do.

Then he went back through all the data and saw the breach.

Every time Madison logged in to see where Jesse was, the data was sent to a blind account. The individual couldn't get into Jesse's program, but the breach was on Madison's end. And she had checked Jesse's location while they were at the Rib House on Wednesday, and again Friday night, an hour before Lucy was run off the road with Jesse in the car. At that point, they had still been at St. Catherine's. Someone had followed them from there and taken the opportunity to scare them.

Why would she compromise her son like that?

Carson Spade.

Spade could easily gain access to Madison's phone. If Madison wasn't checking Jesse's location, Carson could easily do it. Madison might not even know what he was up to.

He dialed Madison's cell phone number. It went immediately to voice mail.

"This is Sean. We need to talk. Call me."

He downloaded all the data and sent it to Rick. This was proof, as far as Sean was concerned, that Carson Spade had lied to the FBI and his handlers and that he should be put behind bars. Screw the plea deal. He was putting his son at risk and for what? Why would he do it? To get back into WITSEC? To get that clean slate? To keep Jesse away from Sean?

Of course, someone else could have set up the blind account, but it had to be someone with physical access to Madison's phone. Who else except her no-good husband?

Jesse walked by the den door, but didn't come in or even look at Sean. Bandit followed on Jesse's heels.

Sean got up and went to the kitchen. "Do you want me to make you something?" he asked.

Jesse shook his head and stared into the refrigerator.

"How are you feeling?"

"Fine."

He closed the refrigerator without getting anything.

Sean wanted to tell him what he'd found, but he didn't want to put any more stress on Jesse. He didn't know why he was so quiet, why he wouldn't even look at him.

"You remember Jack, right? Lucy's brother? He'll be here this afternoon."

Again, nothing. Sean tried to remember when his life came crashing down on him after his parents died. Duke tried to talk to him, and Sean had the same reaction. He didn't want to talk to anyone. He wanted Duke to leave him alone, to let him figure things out on his own. But Duke wouldn't leave him alone, and that had made Sean even angrier.

At fourteen, he had no idea what to do with his rage, so he got in trouble. A lot of it. He didn't want Jesse to go down the same path. Sure, Sean had cleaned up his act, he'd learned to channel his anger and develop healthier ways to relieve frustration, but there were times when he nearly got himself killed because of his rash actions. He'd been wild. He didn't get into drugs and drinking, but he'd raced cars—before he was legally able to drive. He risked life and limb to get a rush, to feel alive, when everything inside him felt dead and buried along with his parents.

Would Jesse go down a similar path? Would he rebel to the point of putting himself in mortal danger? How could Sean stop it? Lay down the law? Give him space? Talk to him? He didn't know. He didn't damn *know* what he was supposed to do. He was a father now, but he had no real examples. His own dad had been interesting and brilliant, but he'd never disciplined Sean. He was absentminded and more interested in work—that's why Sean had become interested in electronics and computers in the first place, because that was how he earned his father's time and attention. Sean's brother Duke was the opposite. He was strict and dictatorial. He knew Sean was going down a dangerous path after their parents were killed, and Duke's way of trying to prevent it was to go to the opposite extreme.

What was Sean supposed to do now? He had no real authority over Jesse. He had only what Madison granted him. He wanted more—he wanted it all—but he'd never have it. Jesse didn't have to listen to him. Hell, if Sean was in his shoes he'd say go to hell, leave me alone. The pushing and prodding that Duke tried in order to force Sean to talk had made Sean clam up or lie.

Jesse wasn't Sean, and Sean wasn't Duke—or his own father. But that didn't mean Sean had any answers. Hell, he had *no* answers. He was far out of his comfort zone and areas of expertise.

"Lucy likes my chocolate chip pancakes," Sean said. "Of course, Lucy likes anything with chocolate."

"Where is Lucy?"

"She had to work."

Jesse grabbed a banana and said, "I'm not really hungry. I'm going to play video games."

"Want a partner?" Video games. That was something Sean could do. A connection he could make.

"No. Don't you have things to do?"

Jesse walked away. Bandit looked at Sean and tilted

his head, as if he knew there was a strain between them. Sean scratched him behind the ears, then said, “Go with Jesse.” Bandit didn’t need to be told twice. He bounded out of the kitchen. Sean watched as his son and dog disappeared at the end of the hall into the game room.

He sat down at the island. He’d played the whole thing wrong.

But he didn’t know how to fix it.

CHAPTER TWENTY-THREE

Kane Rogan was used to working with a team—he had his core group of mercenaries, all former military, and while he was the commander, he listened to his men and weighed the pros and cons of any decision. Quickly, because when you were in the middle of the jungle or planning an op to rescue a hostage there wasn't time to pontificate or debate.

There were also times when one person could get the job done. Having backup was preferred, but not always required. He'd never tell Sean that—Sean could be reckless, especially when someone he cared about was at risk. Kane had never been reckless. When he went into a dangerous situation, he always knew what he was getting into. He always knew the threat, analyzed his chances of survival, and determined whether the goal was worth the risk.

Since Siobhan had moved into his heart and his bed, he had recognized that taking risks didn't just impact him anymore. And while he wasn't ready to give up his vocation, he had added another factor to the mix: Was the risk worth losing Siobhan?

For the first time in his life, he looked forward to going home. Hell, for the first time since he'd enlisted in the marines when he was eighteen, he *had* a home.

Because neither he nor Sean really knew what was going on in this situation or if it even connected to Carson Spade or Jesse, Kane opted for caution. Sean would do his thing with computers, and Kane would watch the players involved and figure out the threat. He wouldn't have been overly concerned except that Domingo had been assassinated to keep from talking. That told Kane whoever was behind this didn't want anyone to know the endgame. Vasquez was just another tool. But even if he was a tool, he might also be a threat.

It took Kane time to track down Vasquez, but soon he learned that the man had a standing golf date with three other men at eight a.m. every Saturday at a private club. Sean was much better at bribing or talking his way into these situations, but Kane had a few tricks up his sleeve, and speaking fluent Spanish helped. He found a young woman on the janitorial staff, gave her a short but believable story about how he was trying to get pictures of a deadbeat dad who spent thousands of dollars golfing but couldn't pay his ex-wife to feed their kids. He slipped her a hundred dollars and promised he'd keep her confidence. She let him in through the staff entrance.

From there, he just had to blend. He grabbed a staff polo shirt, a golf cap, and a clipboard so that it looked like he was working. Then he slipped into a golf cart and tracked Vasquez down at the twelfth tee.

There were two caddies and four golfers. He parked close, but not too close, and pretended to be checking a flower bed. He had no idea what people did to maintain these type of exclusive golf courses, but he imagined there were always things that needed fixing. And maintenance people were ignored by almost everyone. It was often the best cover.

He couldn't get close enough to hear anything that they said, but he did have a powerful little pocket camera that he used to discreetly zoom in and snap photos of everyone in Vasquez's party.

He sent the photos to Sean to run their identities. Kane didn't recognize any of the men, other than Vasquez. All white men, except Vasquez, who was Hispanic. All in their forties to early fifties. Anyone walking by would think they were businessmen playing golf on the weekend.

Kane left after twenty minutes and took the cart back. He earned a few odd looks from staff, but no one stopped him. How long before they were done? At least an hour. A couple, if they stayed at the club for lunch or drinks.

He'd checked on the house earlier. Full security and it appeared that the wife was home. If they needed to get into the place, Kane would have to wait until dark and when he had Sean to help. He didn't want to get his brother caught breaking and entering, and if it was an old-school security system Kane would have no problem getting in. But the high-tech systems were out of his league.

He left the neighborhood and drove downtown to Vasquez's PI office. He called Nate.

"You taking heat about last night?"

"Not too much. Need me? I'm sitting on my ass doing nothing."

"Do you have a solid contact with SAPD?"

"A couple."

"I want everything on Vasquez. Proven and unproven."

"I'm on it." Nate hung up.

Kane liked Nate Dunning and wished he could bring him into RCK. He was exactly the type of operative who would fit in well with their organization. Unfortunately, JT Caruso, Kane's partner, had an agreement with Rick Stockton that they wouldn't recruit out of the FBI. The only exception was former Sacramento FBI Agent Mitch Bianchi. However, there were extenuating circumstances: Mitch had wanted to quit, and he had broken a bunch of FBI rules—ridiculous rules, Kane had thought at the time—that had put him on the hot seat. They'd finessed it and it worked out.

No way in hell would Rick Stockton let Nate Dunning go. Rick had actively recruited FBI agents out of the military. And if Nate quit the FBI to join RCK, they would severely damage their relationship with the one person who could cover them when things went south.

Vasquez maintained space in a strip mall that was primarily destination businesses: a real estate office, a mobile phone dealer, a dry cleaner, a chain tax assistance business, a few others. A mom-and-pop Mexican restaurant had the largest space.

Why would a former cop—probably corrupt—who lived in a million-dollar house in an exclusive San Antonio community have his PI office in a lower-middle-class neighborhood? Might mean nothing. Lower rents. Certain clients. Maybe he wanted to help the little guy.

Kane was thinking that wasn't his primary reason.

Thugs like Domingo wouldn't stand out here. People could come and go at all hours and no one would bat an eye. At night, everything was closed—except for the twenty-four-hour gas station across the street.

Kane grabbed a plain, black ball cap and put it low on his head. He wore a black shirt and khakis and his hair was completely covered by the cap. He'd gotten tired of telling Sean to cut his hair, but it was probably a good thing because Sean was a taller version of Kane. He didn't need to look any more like him.

He walked down the strip mall as if he was heading for the Mexican restaurant. When he got to Vasquez's office, he slowed, took a couple of photos of the door—they were open by appointment only on the weekends. Nothing could be seen inside; the blinds were tightly closed. He couldn't even see how big the office was, whether there was a receptionist desk or waiting area or how many internal doors. There was a security camera above the door.

He walked down to the restaurant and entered. It had counter service. He ordered six street tacos and a beer, sat in a booth that had a view of the door, and considered his options.

He had an idea.

He called the number of Vasquez's business. He wasn't surprised that he had an answering service.

"Vasquez Private Investigations and Security, how may I help you?"

"I need to speak with Mr. Vasquez." He spoke with a heavy Mexican accent.

"The office is closed today, I can take a message."

"A message? Write this down. I know he ordered the hit on my boy Manny. Manny Domingo. If he wants to talk, call me, otherwise one good turn deserves another." He gave his burner phone number. Sean had set up a trace for it, just in case they needed it. He hung up before the answering service could get any ideas about asking questions.

He looked at his watch. One seventeen. How long would it take the service to deliver the message?

As it was, the message was delivered at the same time his tacos were. He let the phone ring three times before answering.

"We need to meet," Kane said.

"Who is this?" Vasquez sounded angry, not worried.

"I'm sorry," Kane said in a heavy accent, "did I interrupt your golf game?"

Silence.

"You're fucking with the wrong person."

"No, Mr. Vasquez, *you're* fucking with the wrong person. Your office, one hour, alone."

"Sounds like a trap."

"Be there, or I'll have some friends of mine in New Orleans pay a visit to sweet Maria and tell her what her father has been up to."

He hung up. He didn't generally like threatening the children of his targets, even adult children. Chances were that Maria Vasquez was innocent of her father's dirty work. But Kane couldn't use the man's wife—he didn't know anything about her, and she could be in as deep as her husband *if* they hadn't won the lottery or her rich uncle Roberto didn't croak and leave them the house. Until he knew more, he went with his gut, and his gut said Maria Vasquez was innocent and her father wanted her to stay that way.

Kane ate his tacos and waited.

CHAPTER TWENTY-FOUR

The search of Cassidy Roth's house was almost a complete bust.

First, it was immaculate. She was a minimalist. Her bookshelves were orderly, every book straight and in alphabetical order. She had no fiction—most of the books seemed related to science and the history of science, with a few thick world history books. Her linen closet was organized, every towel and sheet folded perfectly. She had an extensive DVD collection sorted first by genre then in release order.

The boxes she'd been described as taking from Charlie's apartment after the standoff were nowhere to be found. Her computer wasn't covered in the warrant, which had been limited in scope: They were looking for Charlie's computer, Paul Grey's cell phone, evidence from Charlie's apartment, and notes or an address book that could give investigators a clue as to where to find any of the above. They also had a warrant to track her cell phone, but they'd tracked it to her house—she had left it there, which told Lucy she had a second phone.

Lucy really wanted to get into Cassidy's computer because there could be more information, including information about Adam, Vince Paine, or what she was up to.

It seemed, the more Lucy thought about what Em Granger had said, that Cassidy had it in her head that the FBI couldn't help, that they de facto felt the case was over because McMahon was dead and the hostages were all safe. The young woman may be a brilliant scientist, but she had no idea how the FBI ran investigations. If she did, her first stop would have been *to* the FBI.

Still, Lucy understood that some people were skeptical of law enforcement, or they had a critical view because of bad press. All the political crap that went around—which was primarily focused on the DC region and high-ranking agents—had unfortunately affected the trust of local offices, which were mostly out of the political realm. Lucy and her colleagues did their job and did it well. But they were often painted with the same brush as their corrupt or high-profile colleagues. And it didn't have to be simply the FBI. Negative press about *any* law enforcement agency had a domino effect on *all* law enforcement. Without the public's trust, they would never be able to effectively do their job.

Was that Cassidy? Was she skeptical that the police could help? Distrustful of the FBI? The evidence from Charlie's apartment wasn't here; where would she take it? Why?

Leo came up to Lucy. "We got something—I don't

know if it's going to help." He handed her a sticky note. "A pad of sticky notes was next to where I suspect she charged her phone—there is a box in the wall for a USB plug, but no cord. She wrote down a name."

Leo had used the old-school method of shading the impression on the paper below. Cassidy had small, perfect block printing.

HOGTIED

"Hogtied? What does that mean?"

"Not what, where. It's a bar in Bandera."

"How far?"

"About an hour. She didn't write down a time, but it was the last thing she wrote."

"Definitely worth checking out."

Cassidy Roth didn't know what happened to cause her boss and mentor Charlie to lose his mind, but she knew the day it began. And now, unless Vince bailed on her, she might have another piece of this complex puzzle.

It had been the last Friday in March. Most people had left for the day, but Cassidy always worked late. She didn't have many friends, which was fine with her. She'd never been comfortable around people, even people she worked with. She much preferred working on complex problems—and right now she was working on stabilizing a chemical compound that had shown promise in slowing the progression of Alzheimer's.

Charlie stopped by her workstation.

"You should go home, Cassidy," he said. "It's after seven."

"I will. I'm working on a computer model, I don't want to lose my train of thought."

He smiled. "I completely understand," he said. "I'm going to be leaving in a few minutes, so good night."

" 'Night."

Charlie walked down the hall to his office. Cassidy continued working for another hour, then saved her data—she had a promising lead on her model, she couldn't wait to test it out next week—and shut down her computer. Medical research appealed to her because it was methodical. There were so many possible variables to any given problem, and she loved working through them one by one in order to solve an issue. One microscopic change could be the difference in finding a cure for a disease. She was proud of her job and company. CHR was at the forefront of cutting-edge research that would, ultimately, save lives.

She went down the hall to her small office—as a senior research assistant she had not only her own lab work space, but an office, which was very cool. She grabbed her satchel, made a note of something she didn't want to forget next week, and left. She hesitated when she heard voices coming from the bio-lab at the far end of the hall. She had thought she was the last one here.

She walked down and was about to call out when she recognized Charlie's voice, but she hesitated when she heard a female voice.

"You're wrong," the woman was saying.

It was Cortland Clarke. Few people intimidated Cassidy, but Ms. Clarke was one of them. She rarely came to the lab building, and it was after eight on a Friday.

"I can prove it, Cortland," Charlie said. "Why are you fighting me on this? If I'm right—and I think I am—lives are on the line."

"Stop being melodramatic," she said. "Clinical trials are heavily regulated, and we followed the rules to a T. Nothing is wrong with XR-10."

"It doesn't hurt to run another set of trials."

"It will cost millions of dollars!"

"Hardly."

"We're scheduled to go to doctor trials in six months! Another round of clinical trials will delay us by a year—so yes, millions of dollars."

"But if I'm right, we can't let XR-10 go wide."

XR-10 was CHR's newest creation, a drug that halted the progression of Alzheimer's in patients who had a certain gene. Though not everyone could benefit from it, the impact could be far enough reaching that they could gain a contract to expand trials to explore other remedies. It would be a game changer.

"Paul, you oversaw the trials," Clarke said. "Did you falsify data?"

"Of course not!"

Paul Grey never worked late. He must have come in while Cassidy was working in the computer lab.

"I didn't say that Paul did anything, only that some of the parameters are off. Something is wrong, I can't put my finger on it, that's why we need to go back to the beginning and verify all data. If we can do that, I won't push for more trials."

"Which you won't get," Clarke said. "Paul, you lead this."

Charlie said, "This is my division, I will verify the data!"

Cassidy had never heard Charlie so angry before. It surprised her, and she took a step back, made sure that no one could see her.

"Paul is in charge of this project," Clarke said. "He can put together an impartial team, one that wasn't involved in the original data collection. You have one week, Paul—I'm not delaying this unless there's a major flaw in the data."

"One week?" Charlie said. "That's ridiculous! It'll be a month minimum to pull together all the figures and compare computer records with written records."

"This is my company. If you don't like it, you can leave."

"Garrett would never agree to this."

"You're welcome to talk to him when he gets back from Japan," Clarke snapped.

Cassidy heard footsteps, and she ducked back into her office and shut the door without turning on the light. She waited and was about to leave when Paul and Charlie walked by, talking.

"Let me do this," Charlie said to Paul. "You know I'm better qualified."

"Charlie, don't put me in this position."

"You know there's something wrong here!"

"No, I don't. For what it's worth, I think you're wrong."

"I'm not wrong. Not about these trials."

Cassidy waited until they'd left, then she slipped out. It wasn't like she had been doing anything wrong, but she didn't want them to know that she'd been eavesdropping.

When she returned to work on Monday, Charlie was at his desk. He was rubbing his head.

"Do you need aspirin?" she asked.

"No," he said. He pulled out a bottle of aspirin from his drawer and swallowed three with coffee. "What do you need?"

"The computer model I was working on Friday is ready to be vetted."

"What computer model?"

"On the gene therapy? Remember? We were investigating possible blockers . . ."

"Oh. Talk to Vince about it. I'm working on something else, I don't have time."

She tried not to be hurt as she sought Vince's review. She remembered Charlie's argument with Paul and Cortland Clarke on Friday. Maybe Paul had tapped Charlie for help. Serious problems with a clinical trial would definitely trump a long-term research project.

She put everything out of her mind, but not for long.

A week later, Charlie had become forgetful and erratic. He let important things slip and acted short-tempered with everyone. A month later, Charlie was fired. And when Vince was fired for letting Charlie into the lab, Cassidy knew that she had to do something. She'd spent nearly two months pulling out as much information as she could about the clinical trial that Charlie was obsessed with, but Paul became suspicious of her. Then he, too, started to change. He had always been friendly; now he was quiet and spent most of his time in his office, with the door closed.

Last Monday, Cassidy had no answers, just a lot of suspicions. She arrived at work early and confronted Paul as soon as he drove into his assigned parking space.

"Something happened to Charlie the night you and he argued."

"What in the world are you talking about, Cassidy?"

"End of March. Late, in the lab. And after that, he changed. You know it, you had to have seen it, too! He's worse now."

He paled. "Lisa left him. You need to stay out of it."

"This happened before Lisa walked out. I've been trying to help him, but he doesn't want help. He's in pain, Paul—intense pain."

"He needs to see a doctor."

Cassidy had said the same thing, and Charlie said he would go . . . but he hadn't. She looked up all the possible chemicals he could have been accidentally exposed to in the lab, and while some might create some of the symptoms Charlie had, nothing would last this long—especially since he hadn't even been in the building in two months. And no one else at CHR had the same symptoms.

"There are holes in the XR-10 clinical trial, and I think you know exactly what went wrong."

"I don't know what you're talking about, Cassidy. There were no problems with the clinical trial."

"Yes, there were. I just told you—I heard you and Charlie arguing in March. Cortland Clarke was there. Charlie wanted to delay the expanded trials, and Cortland said that would cost millions of dollars."

"The problem with eavesdropping is that you only hear half of the conversation."

But he wasn't looking her in the eye.

"But Charlie doesn't remember it. And he doesn't remember anything he did before he was fired. And his day-to-day memory is spotty. Don't you think that's odd?"

"His personal life—Lisa—he has a lot to deal with."

Why did he keep blaming the separation for Charlie's behavior? "You know that's not it, Paul! Charlie forgets anything complex, and he has been writing in code—but neither of us understands it. It's like a made-up language."

"You've seen him?" He sounded surprised.

"He's your friend and he's hurting. I think he's dying, Paul, and I don't know what to do to help."

Paul glanced around, nervous and worried. "I can't talk about this here."

"After work."

"I can't—"

"I swear, Paul, I'll go to the FDA about the irregularities in the clinical trial if you don't help me figure out what happened to Charlie!"

Paul seemed torn.

"I mean it." She was scared to death, but she stood her ground.

"Five thirty," he whispered.

"Where?"

He gave her the name of a bar. "It's thirty minutes away. I met Charlie there a couple weeks ago. Are you bringing Charlie?"

"No. He's sick. He's in constant pain and eats aspirin like candy."

Paul looked sick himself. "I have to go to a meeting," he said. "We'll talk, Cassidy, but I can't promise I know how to help."

Cassidy watched Paul enter the lobby of CHR. She got back in her car and drove away. She called human resources and said she had the flu and wouldn't be in for the next couple of days. They didn't even question it—she had never called in sick in the nearly five years she'd worked here.

But there was something odd about Paul's demeanor, and she feared he would go to Cortland Clarke with her accusations. And if Cassidy was right—and Cortland had something to do with making Charlie sick—she didn't want to be in the building right now. She couldn't imagine what Cortland had done, or why Paul would help her if it was unethical or even dangerous.

Cassidy didn't have enough proof of anything to go to the FDA, but she had one thing that no one did—access to Charlie. She just had to convince Paul to help her. If she could get Charlie into a medical facility where they could do tests, they might find out what was wrong with him . . .

And maybe it had nothing to do with CHR. Maybe he contracted a virus or had a head trauma that he told no one about or . . .

She didn't believe it. If she hadn't overheard the argument in March, maybe she could buy that theory. But now? She was positive that Cortland Clarke had poisoned Charlie. But for the life of her, Cassidy couldn't figure out how or with what or why he was still having symptoms.

But maybe she could convince Paul to help her take Charlie to Baylor, a state-of-the-art research hospital in Dallas that had one of the best neuroscience departments in the country. They knew Charlie and his work, they would want to help him find the truth—and they had the clout to start a real investigation. At a minimum, they would find answers to what was wrong with Charlie. She was certain.

CHAPTER TWENTY-FIVE

Cassidy felt sorely out of place at the cowboy bar. Fortunately, it was early and the place was sparsely populated.

Vince was already there. She was never late for anything, but she had to make sure no one was following her—the FBI or someone from CHR. She still made it almost on time.

She sat down across from him. Vince was drinking a beer, though it was barely after noon. He looked awful. He hadn't cut his hair in months—probably since he'd been fired—and it fell in his eyes.

But it was more than his physical appearance. He was edgy, almost paranoid.

Very similar to how Charlie had acted at the beginning of his spiral down.

"What's going on, Vince? Why have you been avoiding me?"

His hand was shaking when he lifted the mug to his

lips. He guzzled a third of his beer before putting it down.

"I don't want anything to do with CHR or Charlie or you."

"You know what happened to Charlie."

"It was all over the news. I don't want it to happen to me."

Cassidy frowned. "Why would it? Are you . . ." She hesitated, assessed him. "You look strung out. Are you using drugs?"

"Blunt as always."

"Dammit, Vince, this is important. I need to know. If you're not using then maybe you were poisoned with the same substance that Charlie was poisoned with!"

"I don't know," he said.

"You don't know what? If you're using drugs?"

Vince rubbed his forehead. "I'm not using, but I feel perpetually hung over. At first I popped pain pills—so yeah, maybe that was a problem."

"What kind?" Charlie had eaten aspirin like candy. Maybe the acetylsalicylic acid had an adverse reaction with whatever he'd been poisoned with—though that seemed unlikely to have continuing side effects that lasted three months.

Vince looked into his beer. "Hydrocodone."

So easy to become addicted to. "Oh, Vince. How long?"

"I started right before I was fired—I had a splitting headache I couldn't get rid of, and I still had a prescription from when I had my wisdom teeth pulled, but had only used a couple. But the rest of them—I didn't realize I'd taken twenty-eight pills in less than two weeks. I was fired, and then I grabbed an old prescription from my sister—I went to stay with her in New Mexico for a few weeks. But I swear—I haven't popped a pill in three weeks. I just feel . . . not myself." He paused. "It's getting better, though. I haven't taken anything, not even aspirin."

"What happened? You have to know something."

"No more than you know."

"But you let Charlie into the lab that night."

"I never should have done it. But he said he had to pull some old files. I told him I'd do it for him, but he was totally paranoid. You remember, right? If I'd done it, he'd never have been caught—we'd never have been caught—and maybe I would have been able to figure it out."

"What files?"

"I don't think he even knew. He said he would know it when he saw it, but he couldn't even describe what he was looking for."

"I think you were both poisoned." It was the only explanation for these odd symptoms. But how?

"That's the only reason I agreed to meet with you. You still work there—you're the only one in the position to go through the files."

"I haven't been to work all week."

"Why not?"

"Because I met Paul Grey on Monday and I had a feeling someone in the building knew about the meeting.

People were watching me too carefully, and I didn't want what happened to Charlie—and you—to happen to me."

"Do you think I'm going down the same path?"

"No. You're getting better, but Charlie was getting worse. I think they found a way to continue to poison Charlie, or he had an unexpected reaction to whatever drug they used. And Paul knew what it was."

"He does? What did he say?"

"Paul's dead."

Vince's eyes widened. "How?"

"He killed himself."

"How do you know?"

She told him the truth. "I talked to him on Monday and he promised to help me. He said he knew what Charlie had been looking for in May when he was arrested for vandalism. He was supposed to bring it to me Monday night. I saw him sitting in his car under a streetlight. We were meeting in the middle of nowhere because he was paranoid." She closed her eyes. She'd never get what happened next out of her head. "And he—he looked up at me as I approached his car. Then he shot himself."

Vince paled. "Oh, God. Was he . . . poisoned, too?"

"I don't think so. I confronted him that morning at his car, at CHR. He agreed to meet with me that evening. I laid everything out and he said he knew what I needed to help Charlie." He'd also told her that her calling in sick had drawn attention to her, and that she might not want to go to work for a couple of days. Was that a warning? Maybe. She didn't know. She didn't trust Paul, but at the same time, she didn't *not* trust him.

"And?" Vince pressed.

"He said he would go back to the lab when everyone left and bring me proof. We were supposed to meet again at ten. When I saw his car there I was so optimistic, that he had everything I needed, and then he . . . he just . . . killed himself." Her voice faded. She couldn't tell Vince everything about that night. How she searched Paul's car for the information he had promised to bring. It wasn't there. How she'd hacked his phone, looking for proof of anything that would help. Then she'd left Paul there . . . just left him dead and hoped that someone would find him before morning.

She'd avoided Charlie because he knew about her meeting with Paul, and how could she tell him that his best friend and colleague had killed himself instead of helping to save Charlie?

"Vince, think about this, okay? At the very end of March, Charlie had a huge argument in the main lab with Cortland Clarke and Paul. It was about the clinical trials for the XR-10 memory drug. He insisted that there was a problem with the results, but Paul and Ms. Clarke said no, that Charlie was mistaken. Then Clarke agreed to let Paul review the data—which later he insisted was fine. But after that meeting, Charlie started getting sick—headaches, paranoia, memory loss. I know you saw the same thing I did."

"I thought it was because he and Lisa were separating."

"This all happened before that."

"But people don't just separate spontaneously. It was only two weeks."

"Because Charlie had changed. He'd become belligerent. Yelled at people. Maybe—maybe he hit Lisa or one of the kids. Lisa is pretty tough, she's not going to let Charlie do something like that."

He frowned. "I don't know."

"Think! There has to have been something that happened, something Charlie said to you before he went way down the rabbit hole, or something Paul said."

"That's the thing, I can't remember much about what happened around the time Charlie was fired. It's all a blur. I don't even remember letting Charlie into the lab. I sort of remember a conversation with him—where I told him I would look for the files—and that's it. My head hurt and I was popping hydrocodone."

"You don't remember," she said bluntly.

"I'm not lying!"

"I believe you."

"You do?"

"Charlie couldn't remember anything that happened for weeks, but he was getting worse. He had problems remembering *anything* that happened, even the day before. He could drive, recite the alphabet, work through complex math problems in his head, remember his wedding day and all the stats from the Texas Rangers, but he couldn't remember anything related to CHR or what he was working on or what drug might have caused this. Because he *was* poisoned. I'm certain of it. Only, I think he had to have been continually poisoned and I haven't figured out how when he lived like a recluse. He'd even moved out of his house into a crummy apartment downtown."

Vince didn't say anything for a second. "I think you're right. I still can't remember anything except vague things that happened those two weeks in May before I was fired, but I'm getting better now that I'm off the pain pills. I can finally focus. We need to go to the police."

"What are they going to do? To them, Charlie is a criminal, someone who took people hostage and shot at a cop. They don't care why, they just care that it's over and only Charlie died in the process. I need proof, and we don't have proof. CHR will deny everything, say it's sour grapes because both you and Charlie were fired and we're grasping at straws. I have a friend of mine running a bunch of tests on Charlie's hair samples to see if we can isolate the drug. But until we do that, I can't go to the authorities. If we tip off CHR they'll destroy any evidence they have."

"What do you want from me?"

"You already helped. You confirmed my suspicions. Now I need to get answers."

"Be careful, Cassidy. If you're right and someone at CHR poisoned both Charlie and me then you could be in danger."

"I'll be careful."

She had one idea, and now she had to figure out how to implement it. How could she get into the lab without using her own ID?

Lucy and Leo arrived at Hogtied at one thirty that afternoon. Lucy really wanted to get back home; she was worried about Sean and Jesse, and she was beginning to feel the effects of the accident, particularly in her back, which was sore and stiff. She took three ibuprofen and hoped it would take the edge off.

"Last stop of the day," Leo said. "That's the second time you've taken pain pills."

"They're over-the-counter."

"You should have taken the day off."

"I'm okay. But I'm not going to object to going home after this."

They walked into the cowboy bar. Country music—real country music, not the pop version of country—played out of an old-fashioned jukebox. There were peanut shells on the floor, a stage in the back, and a dance floor that looked well used. The bar itself was old, solid wood, and the bartender looked just as ancient and solid.

Leo introduced them. "We're looking for a girl who may have been in here last night or earlier today."

"Y'all have to be more specific," he said with a thick Texas drawl. "We get a lotta ladies in here."

Leo showed the bartender Cassidy's driver's license photo.

The bartender nodded. "Left an hour ago, or thereabouts."

"Alone? Was she with anyone?"

"She chatted with a guy for 'bout half hour or so, they had their heads together, then she left."

"Is he still here?"

"Nope, paid his tab, left right after her."

"Do you have his credit card receipt?"

"Yep. He ain't a regular, but I've seen him around now and again. Sort of sticks out, soft hands, pale skin. Most of my customers work outdoors, ya know. But he was okay, didn't cause trouble."

The bartender turned around and retrieved a small slip of paper from the cash register. "I need that for my books, so I'd be much obliged if y'all just take a picture."

Lucy did, then handed it back to the bartender. She looked closely. Vincent A. Paine. She showed Leo.

"They in any trouble with the law?" the bartender asked.

"We don't right know yet," Leo said, his Texas coming out through his voice, though Lucy rarely heard more than a light accent when he was working. "Let's just say she's a material witness to a possible crime, and we've been looking for Mr. Paine. You wouldn't know where he's living?"

"Can't say. We're not a big town here, but we get people from all 'round the hills, 'specially weekends when we have live music. I got a feeling, now that I think on it, he might know one of the girls in our regular band. They play Friday nights. I recall that's when I usually see him around."

"Was he here last night?"

"Can't right say, but I don't think so. But likely the week before."

"Would you mind giving us her name?"

"Well, I don't have a problem helping out law enforcement, but I don't really know what's with what here, and I ain't looking to jam up any of my friends." He glanced from Lucy to Leo. "How 'bout if I ask her to call you? Or you can just come back Friday and see her then."

Leo handed the bartender both his and Lucy's cards. "Please talk to her. And if you see Mr. Paine again, I'd greatly appreciate a call."

"He's not a dangerous fellow." It wasn't a question. "He's one of those, whatchacallit, nerdy types. Glasses and skinny and educated. Raised well, I'll tell ya, polite as they come. I'll call, just want you to know what's what."

"Sure do appreciate it," Leo said. "And if you can pass those cards on to your musician friend, that would be real helpful."

Back in the car, Lucy asked, "Why didn't you play hardball with him? There's no reason he couldn't give us her name and number."

"Because I know folks like him. He's old school, longtime Texan. He'll give her our contact info, find out what's going on, and tell her to call us."

"You sound confident."

"You have your strengths, I have mine. She'll call no later than Monday. If she doesn't, we'll come back on Friday. Coming any earlier to play asshole feds isn't going to give us squat."

CHAPTER TWENTY-SIX

Sean ran his facial recognition program in the background to identify the golfers Kane photographed with Vasquez while he analyzed the blind account information from Jesse's phone. Locating it would be next to impossible . . . but *not* impossible. He might be able to trace it with a virus, if he could break the coding of the tracker program. It was possible, he thought, if he had Madison's cooperation.

The alarm beeped once.

Sean glanced at his tablet, hit VIEW on the front camera. He'd heightened the settings so that if anyone stepped onto the property, he would know.

Jack. He wasn't alone.

Madison was with him.

Shit.

Sean went to the door and took a deep breath. Why was Madison here? Jack wouldn't have brought her without giving him a heads-up, would he? Why hadn't he texted him when they landed?

Jack knocked and Sean opened the door. Sean didn't say a word. He didn't really trust himself right now.

They entered and Jack said, "We were on the same plane."

Sean closed the door.

"You could have texted me," Sean mumbled.

"Where is Jesse?" Madison demanded.

"Playing video games." Sean motioned down the hall. "End of the hall to the right."

He felt defeated. Lost. Madison hesitated, then brushed past him and strode down the hall.

Sean went to the kitchen. Jack followed and asked, "What have you learned?"

"I know how we were tracked. The parental tracking app on Jesse's phone. Every time Madison—or someone with access to her phone," he added pointedly, "checked Jesse's location, the information was sent to a blind account. I tried to track that account but it's fluid. I sent everything to Stockton, but it can only be tracked real-time."

"Where's Lucy?"

"Working."

Jack frowned.

"She's fine. She has a complicated case, she can't step away. And what can she do here? Worry with me?" Sean looked out the window, but wasn't looking at anything specific. "So you brought Madison here."

"It was either bring her or she'd come here without me. I didn't know she was on the plane until I saw her at the airport. I'm sorry I didn't give you a heads-up, Sean. I should have."

"This whole situation is fucked, Jack, and I don't know what the hell I'm supposed to do."

Sean was rarely at a loss, but since last night he didn't know how to talk to Jesse or Madison or convince either of them that Jesse was safest here, with him.

And though Sean *wanted* Carson Spade to be guilty, it simply did not make any sense that Spade would go after Jesse. Even if just to scare him, or scare Sean. Was it to get them back into WITSEC?

If they go back to WITSEC, you'll never see Jesse again. At best, once a year.

Is that what Carson wanted? Simply to hurt Sean? Sean wouldn't put it past him.

Still, it didn't make sense. There were less dangerous ways to get Jesse away from Sean.

Spade had been a criminal; he still was, as far as Sean was concerned. He did a lot of things that made no sense considering he had a wife who loved him and a stepson who used to admire him. For money? For power? Or because he hated Sean for helping take him down? For exposing him as a criminal to the people who loved and trusted him?

Sean knew that a guy could do the wrong thing for the right reason. Some people felt trapped and the only way out was to work for criminal organizations. Some people, like Michael Rodriguez, would be killed if they didn't cooperate with drug cartels. Kids didn't think they had a choice. People did a lesser evil to avoid a worse crime.

That wasn't Carson Spade.

Spade was a lawyer and accountant. He came from a

solid middle-class family, had an Ivy League education, and could have made a damn good living *legally* in any number of industries. He *chose* to work for the cartels. He didn't work for them by mistake; he didn't start working for a business and later learn that he was laundering money for drug dealers. He went in eyes open and *willing.*

That was why Sean would never trust him or believe that he would change.

Madison walked into the kitchen. "I'm taking Jesse back to Sacramento. He's upstairs packing now."

Sean turned, stunned. "No."

"You have no say in this, Sean. You have no rights here. He was nearly *killed* last night on *your watch.*"

"Because of your husband!"

"I'm not listening to this. I trusted you, Sean. Against my better judgment, I trusted you with *my son.*"

"He's my son, too." Sean was hollow and torn apart inside. He didn't know how to stop this from happening. He felt like his life was spiraling out of control and he'd never find his footing again.

"Not legally, Sean. I've talked to a lawyer. With your background there is no way a court will give you any rights if I contest it."

"You promised me I could see him."

"*If* Jesse wants to see you, you can visit him in Sacramento one weekend a month."

"You lied to me for *twelve years.* You kept Jesse from me, lied to him, lied to everyone! I will fight you on this, Madison."

Madison glanced at Jack and frowned. "We don't

need to have this conversation in front of your brother-in-law."

"What? Think your perfect reputation is going to be in tatters?"

"You were a criminal hacker, Sean. You think you have friends in high places who have wiped your files? Think again. My father also has friends in high places, and when the court knows that you were once a hacker, that you have violated the law right and left, that you have a dangerous job, you'll never see Jesse again."

"You don't know what you're talking about."

"You can't deny that you went to Mexico last year and killed people *in front of my son*!"

"You hired me to find Jesse, and your husband brought him into that dangerous situation. I saved his life!"

"That will not matter, not to the court, especially when I told you not to go to Mexico. You defied me then and put Jesse in danger. I'm his mother. I raised him. I've tried here, I've really tried, but I can't do this anymore. It's tearing apart my family."

"Did Carson put you up to this?"

"Do not talk to me about my husband. You have no idea how you've hurt me."

"That's rich, coming from you."

Bandit ran into the kitchen and stood next to Sean. At least one living creature came to his defense.

"Just stop, Sean. Stop. I'm too tired and upset to have this conversation. Talk to my lawyer. We're leaving."

"It's too dangerous. The men who ran Lucy and Jesse

off the road, they tracked Jesse through your parental tracking app."

"You have no proof of that."

"I backtraced his phone and found out that every time you checked on Jesse's location, the information was piggybacked to a blind account. I can prove it—give me your phone and I'll show you how it worked."

"You are a liar, Sean Rogan. I haven't checked on Jesse's location—that app was for finding his phone only, if he lost it. Or if, God forbid, he was missing."

"You want to see the log? Of the twenty-six times your phone logged in to view Jesse's location, including an hour before he was run off the road?" Sean wasn't backing down, not on this. Not when his son's life was in danger.

"You falsified it." Her voice sounded strong, but cracked at the end.

"I sent the information to the FBI. They can verify it. Do you want to ask Carson? Do you think your husband is somehow a saint? He's behind this, and I will prove it."

"He's a better man than you. We are leaving."

"You can't! Dammit, you're in danger. Hell, Madison, I don't care what happens to you. You're blind when it comes to Carson. But you're Jesse's mother and he loves you, and that means something."

She stood there fuming, her eyes wide. "I don't give a shit about you, either. And you're not Jesse's father, not legally, and after this he'll realize he can't trust you or anything you say. I will destroy you, Sean."

"You're not leaving here—not without a marshal as

an escort. Not without protection. Dammit, Madison! If it's not Carson, then someone hacked your phone."

"You're paranoid." She turned and started down the hall again. "Jesse! We're going."

Sean started after her and Jack stopped him. "You can't, Sean. You can't lay a hand on her."

"I can't let her leave! We don't know what's going on, and he's safe *here*." His whole life was crumbling around him. He couldn't lose Jesse now, not when he'd just found him. His eyes burned, but he forced himself to get his emotions together. It wouldn't do Jesse any good if Sean lost it with Madison.

"I'll go with them," Jack said. "I'll protect Jesse with my life. You know that, right? You can't make this situation worse. We'll find a way to fix this, but right now you have to let them go."

Sean didn't want to, but Jack was right. Madison was Jesse's mother. She had every legal right and Sean had none.

"I'll call Jimenez and see if he knows anything. Tell him what's going on. Have him send marshals to meet you in Sacramento and take custody of Madison and Jesse."

"Keep me in the loop. Once we're at the airport, we'll be relatively safe, but I'll sit with them on the plane, make sure they are handed over to the marshals."

"Have Madison remove the battery on her phone. I'm keeping Jesse's—it's the only evidence I have that someone tracked him."

"Talk to him before he leaves. Tell him—well, just tell him what he needs to hear."

Sean had no idea what that was, but he couldn't let his son leave without knowing that he will fight for him.

Madison stomped back into the kitchen. "Did he come in here? He's not in his room or the game room."

Sean pushed past her and ran down the hall. Jack ran upstairs. Sean searched every room, then went to his computer and brought up the security panel.

Jesse had disabled the security—with Sean's passcode. The kid had watched him multiple times. Sean had given him his own code, but it wouldn't have disabled the whole system. It was so he could go out back without setting off the alarm. But Sean's code overrode everything.

He'd left fifteen minutes ago—while Sean and Madison were arguing in the kitchen.

Sean flipped through the cameras. Jesse had gone out the back door and through the side gate.

And then he was gone.

Jesse took some pride that he was able to slip out of Sean's super-secure house without anyone knowing. Of course, it was because Sean had told him how the system worked and gave him a passcode, and Jesse memorized Sean's because Sean used it so much. He'd once thought that Sean was paranoid about his system, but then he thought about the boys at St. Catherine's and what they'd gone through. And that his stepfather had worked for some really bad people. And that the US Marshals had gone through all the ways those same bad people could find them if Jesse broke the rules.

But now that he was walking, he didn't feel as great or proud of himself. He was sore from the accident, but he also felt sick that his mother had come to take him home.

He didn't want to leave. He was angry with his dad for calling his mother in the first place, angry that he seemed set on sending him home . . . but then he'd heard Sean stand up to his mother. He couldn't believe what his mother had said to Sean, especially since he knew that she was lying. She either lied to Jesse, or she lied to Sean. He didn't know.

What did Sean really want? Did he want him here . . . or not?

Jesse felt like a spoiled brat, but he didn't know what to do, and his mother hadn't asked him if he wanted to go home. She *told* him they were going back to Sacramento. And that maybe he shouldn't see Sean anymore.

"I don't want to go back." He didn't want to leave San Antonio. He didn't want to see Carson. He missed his mom, but right this minute he didn't. Right now, he was so mad at her he wanted her to leave.

"It's dangerous for you here! If anything happened to you—dear God, Jesse, you're my entire life. You're the only person I care about. I need you with me."

"Then stay here. I have two more weeks with my dad. I don't want to leave before I have to."

"Aren't you listening to me? It's too dangerous for you here! Sean is wild. He's never changed. He's irresponsible and he and his brothers are reckless. Dangerous. They brought this on themselves, and you're the one who's paying for it."

Jesse glared at her. "That sounds like something Carson would say."

"Don't call him that. He's your father."

"No. Sean *is my father. I'm changing my name to Rogan."*

She looked like he'd hit her. He probably shouldn't have said that when he was mad.

"Mom, please—don't make me go. Stay here, sure. Okay? But I want my two weeks. Dad and I are going to see the Astros next weekend. I don't want to miss that. And I've made friends, and I promised to teach this kid named Tito all the ins and outs of Destiny, *and I don't want to disappoint him. And—"*

His mom started crying. He hated when she cried. "Jesse, please. I need you with me. At home. We'll arrange another time for you to visit. Later, when the police figure out what's going on. It's Sean's fault, sweetie. He probably didn't mean for things to get out of control, he never does. He means well, but he's irresponsible. He hasn't changed since college, he's never going to change. Please, honey, don't argue with me, don't make this any harder than it has to be, just pack your things and we're leaving. I already have tickets for us."

He'd told her he would pack. And he'd started to . . . but he felt trapped. He didn't want to see Carson. He didn't *think* that Carson had anything to do with the accident, but he really didn't know. Sean was so certain . . .

Then he heard them fighting in the kitchen. He knew if he went with his mother she would never let him see his dad again. She hated Sean. Carson hated Sean. And Jesse was thirteen. He had no rights at all.

Yeah, leaving was a bratty thing to do. But how else could he get his point across? He was a kid. He couldn't do anything without his mom allowing it. And his grandfather hated his dad, too. He had a lot of money and he would use it if Sean tried to fight for custody. That wasn't fair to Sean, or to Lucy. Jesse knew how his grandfather operated. He would sue Sean and continue to sue him and the costs would pile up and there was no way Sean could afford the fight. Especially since he'd put so much of his money into a trust for Jesse. Jesse didn't want it, but Sean told him it was his responsibility as a dad, and had he known about him from the beginning, this was the money he would have paid Madison anyway for child support.

"It doesn't matter that Madison and her family have money. It's the principle of the situation. I'm your father, I want to take care of you in every way I can."

Jesse didn't want to wait five years to have a relationship with his dad and Lucy. He didn't want to never see his uncle Kane again, or Uncle Duke and his baby cousin Molly. He had a family here. His mom was his family, too . . . he didn't want to leave her. But why did he have to make this choice? Why did his mom have to be stubborn about this?

His mother would change her mind only if they didn't leave while she was angry. She allowed Jesse to spend part of the summer with Sean because she was so relieved they were out of WITSEC. She'd hated the program and felt trapped. But right now she would go back and Jesse would have no leverage, no way to convince her of anything. And Carson had influence over her.

He was talking about moving to Hawaii! His mom loved the idea. To get away from everything that had gone wrong in their lives and start fresh. That's what she'd said, to start fresh.

Jesse didn't want to live in Hawaii. Sure, it was fun to visit and they had a house there and everything, but he didn't want to live there. He'd be even farther away from his dad.

Carson just wanted to get them away from Sean and the Rogans.

Jesse had explored Sean's neighborhood a lot over the last month. It was hot and sticky out in the middle of the day, but he'd brought water in his backpack. He drained a water bottle and realized fifteen minutes had passed. They'd probably know he was gone by now, and he really didn't want to go back until he figured out what his options were.

But he wasn't stupid. He needed a place to go and think.

He walked to the bus stop. The bus was just pulling up. The scrolling display read: DOWNTOWN SAN ANTONIO. RIVER WALK. GUADALUPE STREET. BIRCH & VINE.

That would get him within a mile of St. Catherine's. He climbed in, put change in the box, and walked to the back. He sat and stared out the window.

Jesse didn't know what to expect. He didn't know what he expected to do or say. Maybe to just be with kids his own age who had it worse than him. Jeez, that sounded ridiculous. None of those boys had parents who cared about them, and he had two—two parents who hated each other, but loved him. If he knew where Lucy was, he'd go there—she always listened to him. *Really* listened. Sometimes he didn't understand her advice, but she made him think, and she didn't talk to him like he was immature or a little kid. She talked to him like an adult. He respected that.

Of course, he wasn't acting like an adult now. He was acting like the immature little kid his mother thought he was.

Jesse wanted everything to go back to the way it was before Wednesday when he and Sean were followed. When his mother wasn't worried, when he and Sean were having fun, when Jesse wasn't scared that he would never see his dad again.

He closed his eyes and tried not to cry.

CHAPTER TWENTY-SEVEN

Nate called Kane back less than an hour later. "I have no proof," Nate said in lieu of hello, "but my friend was very chatty about Vasquez. A lot of fodder for the rumor mill."

"That's all I need."

"He sold himself to the highest bidder. Looked the other way if someone paid him enough."

"Drugs?"

"Yes—but no specific allegiances. The only thing my buddy was certain about—again, no proof—was that Vasquez once killed a low-level drug dealer for money."

"A hit man?"

"Likely. It was a bust that went south and Vasquez was hauled up in IA and the investigation tainted his precinct. But there was no proof—he got a demotion, but a year later was back on his old beat, then retired at full pay. Tells me that he's willing to do just about anything for a buck."

"Still—his house is damn expensive."

"I pushed. The guy could still be taking hits, but my buddy says it's usually one criminal against another. His big deal is falsifying evidence. Rumor has it that a rich fuck who killed his wife paid Vasquez to lose the evidence during the last couple months he was on the job. Evidence disappears. Everyone thinks the prick killed his wife, but can't prove it."

"So he's a sneaky hit man and liar."

"Pretty much."

"Thanks."

"Need backup?"

"I'm good."

He ended the call. Damn, Nate was good. Very good and very fast.

So Vasquez fronts as a PI, but is actually a hit man? Did he take out Domingo himself? Or did he run a gunman or two?

That didn't feel right to Kane. Vasquez seemed more like a fixer. If someone needed killing, he'd kill him. But disposing of evidence, that sounded slimy.

Still, the potential to be whacked put a completely different spin on things and made the situation far too dangerous. A good sniper—like the one who took out Domingo last night—could take the shot and be gone in seconds. That put all of them at risk.

Kane sent Jack a message.

Vasquez a fixer. Possible hit man. Know the situation. Spread the word.

Sean was good with security, and there wasn't a car he couldn't drive or a computer he couldn't crack. But Sean had never been military. He'd never had to protect himself against a potential sniper attack. Jack would make sure Sean, Lucy, and Jesse—and now that damn bitch Madison—were safe, as long as everyone listened to him.

Kane should walk away from Vasquez's joint, but he needed more information, and this was his best chance. Where was this asshole? He was late, and that never boded well.

Five minutes later, he saw Vasquez drive up. Two cars came in behind him, each with two men. Not the men Vasquez had been playing golf with. Vasquez talked to them. One car left, but out of the corner of his eye Kane saw the vehicle go around to the back. The other car parked directly across from Vasquez's office door.

What did this guy take him for, an idiot?

Vasquez looked around, then went into his office. Kane slipped the cook a twenty and went out through the back. He called Vasquez.

"I'm here," Vasquez said. "Where are you?"

"I should know never to trust a corrupt cop."

"I will kill you if you so much as *look* at my daughter."

"Just remember: You wanted to play it this way. I'll see you soon."

Kane walked half a block away and slipped into his truck. He drove off, not being able to resist driving by the strip mall.

Vasquez was standing in his doorway, looking both angry and worried.

He should be worried.

No one fucked with Kane's family and got away with it.

Now it was time to find out what was going on with his nephew before the kid got himself hurt, or worse. Because something wasn't adding up here, and Kane always trusted his instincts.

Bart sat at his desk and called the man who hired him.

"Guy is a no-show."

"He spotted your men and bolted. I told you, if it's Rogan, he's not going to walk into a trap."

"Fucking Domingo. I wish I could have him killed again. He gave them my name."

"And nothing more. If they knew anything, they wouldn't concern themselves with you. Minor hiccup, but it actually works in my favor."

"He's going to be on alert."

"He was on alert as soon as he was tailed on Wednesday."

"I told you that was a stupid-ass idea, Robertson."

"Not my stupid idea, but Carson Spade has no idea what can of worms he's opened up. As soon as I get his wife and son, he'll give me everything he's hiding from the feds. Millions are at stake here."

"Maybe he won't. Maybe he'll say kill them both, good riddance."

"Then the FBI will have the proof that he lied and hid assets, and he goes to prison. My dear old friend Carson would not do well behind bars. And he will know by then that I can get to him anywhere."

"So what now?"

"My guess is that Madison will be on her way to the airport tonight, tomorrow morning at the latest. We grab her and the kid and make a deal."

"And Rogan?"

"I was hired to assassinate him as soon as Madison and Jesse are out of San Antonio, after all. Two birds, one stone. Don't panic, and the payday will be sweet."

"Not panicked, just pissed."

"Stay alert, Bart. I have everything under control."

CHAPTER TWENTY-EIGHT

Lucy ran into the house. "Sean!"

Madison Spade walked out of the kitchen, startling Lucy. "Sean is out looking for my son."

"I came as fast as I could. He will be fine. He's a smart kid."

Lucy was worried, but her fear wouldn't help alleviate Madison's. Jesse *was* a smart kid, but it had been reckless to leave the house, especially since they didn't know the reasons behind the hit-and-run.

Madison didn't say anything, just walked back to the kitchen.

Lucy followed. Bandit didn't greet her; Sean must have taken him.

"Sean and Jack will find him," she said.

"I will not talk to you about this," Madison said. She picked up a coffee mug. Her hands were shaking, and she tried to be stoic.

"There's no reason for you to be hostile toward me,"

Lucy said. "We all care about Jesse. We all want him back safe."

"No. I want him safe back in Sacramento with me. He'll never be safe with Sean."

Lucy had to swallow her temper in order to respond. "Madison, Sean risked his life to save both Jesse and your husband last year."

"I should never have gone to him. Never! None of this would have happened."

"Is that what you really want? To take back the last year, not tell Sean he had a son, your husband still laundering money for the cartels? Is that *really* what you want? You think that life is *safer* than a life with Sean?"

"Sean has turned Jesse against me! Convinced Jesse that he needs to change his name. Convinced Jesse that Carson is a bad person. It's insane that Sean thinks *Carson* is behind your accident."

"Sean has not said a word against you to Jesse."

"You wouldn't know. You're so blindly loyal. Sean is all charming and sweet and romantic, but underneath that facade he's a cunning and manipulative bully."

So much animosity. Out of guilt? Regret? Lucy couldn't let Madison get under her skin. She said, "If you force Jesse to go home he'll only want to return sooner."

"He will never be under Sean's influence again. *Never*."

"You don't mean that."

"I do. I regret letting Jesse come here. I regret bringing Sean into his life. It was a mistake, and one I will not make again."

"And you told Jesse this?"

"No. I just told him we were going home. But I told Sean, and dammit, I mean it."

"And Jesse heard."

"Of course not!"

"You're not stupid, Madison, so listen to me. Sean is a great father. Jesse loves him. Jesse calls him dad. It was Jesse's idea to change his name. Why? Because Sean is one of the good guys, and the man who raised him is a criminal who put his entire family in danger because of who he worked for. Sean has never said a word against Carson—even when he thought Carson was the one who tracked us, he didn't tell Jesse. Jesse is proud of Sean, and he should be. You raised a great kid who can think for himself, a kid who has a huge amount of compassion for others. You should be proud of that, in spite of Carson."

"Do not talk to me about my husband. Sean is no saint. Or didn't you know he was a criminal hacker in his youth?"

Madison evidently thought she would surprise Lucy with that information.

"None of us are saints, Madison," Lucy said. "Certainly not you."

She shouldn't have said that, but Madison was pushing all her buttons.

Madison looked down into her coffee mug. "I want my son back." Her voice was barely audible.

Lucy pushed aside her anger, reached over, and squeezed her hand. She repeated, "Sean and Jack will find him."

Lucy's phone beeped. She looked down. It was a message from Sean.

Jesse is at the boys' home. He's safe. Jack and I are heading there now. Tell Madison.

Lucy showed the message to Madison.

"Take me there. Right now."

Lucy raised her eyebrow.

"Please," Madison added in a whisper. "I just need to see my son."

Maybe this was actually a good thing, Lucy thought. Madison needed to see the truth, because talking to her certainly wasn't working.

Jesse had only been gone for three hours. But those three hours had been hell for Sean. He had compassion for Madison, but she'd made him so angry and hit him at his core. Saying that he wasn't good for Jesse. That Jesse shouldn't be with him at all.

Intellectually he knew it wasn't true. He loved his son, he knew he could be a good influence on him. But he couldn't shake that niggle of doubt, that insecurity that he didn't deserve Jesse.

Why had he gone to the boys' home? Sean knew he'd made a connection with a couple of the kids, and he wished he'd brought Jesse over sooner. He hadn't even thought about it until the barbecue last weekend when Jason Lopez brought his two kids, and Ryan Quiroz his two young boys, and a few other kids were over, that he realized for the first few weeks it had been just him and

Jesse—and Jesse was a kid. He needed time with other kids.

Jack was certain that Jesse had overheard Sean and Madison arguing, and Sean wanted to hit himself for not thinking about that when he reacted to Madison's demands. But was he supposed to let her just take Jesse? Not fight for him? It wasn't just that he wanted to be part of his son's life, but that there was a threat to his safety.

Unless it was all a lie. All set up by Carson Spade to make Madison *think* there was a threat so she'd bring Jesse back to Sacramento and ban Sean from future contact.

Why did Jesse choose to go to the boys' home? Lucy had tried to talk to him last night, but Sean honestly wasn't paying much attention. Now he wished he had. She had been talking about what Jesse was feeling, and maybe Sean dismissed it as psychology. He'd been so scared after the accident, and all he could think about was protecting Jesse and finding the truth. He owed Lucy an apology, because one thing she did well was get to the heart of a situation. She loved Jesse, but she didn't have the same fears that he did, so she could assess things with a clearer head.

But first things first.

"I'll check the grounds," Jack said when they arrived.

"Thanks, Jack. For everything." He motioned for Bandit to follow Jack; the dog obeyed.

Sean took a deep breath. He wanted to yell at Jesse for disobeying the rules and scaring him, and he wanted to hug him and never let him go.

He knocked on the door. Mateo answered.

"My brother-in-law is looking around," Sean said so Mateo wouldn't be suspicious if he saw Jack through a window.

"Come to the kitchen," Mateo said.

Sean wasn't a religious man, though he liked Mateo and had always felt comfortable here. But he was surprised when he didn't see Jesse. Sister Ruth and one of the boys, Brian, were prepping for dinner. They discreetly left when Mateo entered with Sean.

"Where is he?" Sean asked.

"I thought we should talk a minute."

"Mateo, I need to see him."

"He's fine. He's playing video games with Tito. He said you told him he could come over and visit anytime. I didn't know he left without permission, otherwise I would have called you sooner."

Sean rubbed his eyes. "He heard his mother and me fighting. She flew out here to take him home." His voice cracked and he took a deep breath. "I'm sure she's on her way here now, and I don't have any rights. It's killing me, Mateo. Just . . . just killing me that I can't fix this."

"What does Jesse want?"

"I thought he wanted to stay with me—for half the summer, like we planned."

"When two people love someone like you and Madison love Jesse, it's difficult to compromise. But you know I'm here to help. Just say the word."

Sean knew, but Mateo didn't know the whole story. "Did Jesse talk to you?"

"Not directly. I'm used to reading between the lines with teenagers. It's clear he's conflicted, and leaving as he did was something he felt was in his control. I sense he thinks nothing is in his control, and that can be difficult for a thirteen-year-old. Adults, making decisions, the child, having no say. He wants a voice, but I suspect he thinks no one will listen to him. That's why counseling sometimes works. It's a safe place where everyone has the opportunity to talk and everyone can listen."

"If I thought that counseling would help, I'd go." He certainly had changed over the years—he'd never have gone to a psychologist in the past. But he would do anything to fix this. "Madison never put me on Jesse's birth certificate. She has all the parental rights, I have no legal rights. I made her sign a legal document that I am Jesse's biological father, but that's all I have—I don't have custody, I don't have any say. She let him come here this summer because Jesse asked. I was willing to fly out to Sacramento to see him, but he told his mom that he wanted the time with me because we missed so many years. I think he guilted her into it, but I didn't stop him. I want her to feel guilty about what she did. She lied to me. She lied to Jesse. And I've had a real hard time forgiving her."

"You haven't."

"No. I haven't. Maybe you would, because you're a better man than me, but I don't know that I can ever forgive her." Sean stood. "I appreciate your help, Mateo. Really. But I want to see him before Madison gets here. It might be the last time I see him in a long time." His voice cracked as he realized this was it. He was losing his son.

Sean went down the hall to the family room. This was the place he spent most of his time with the boys—they had a pool table, a television, movies, video games, and a long, low table to play board games. When they needed to study, the landing upstairs had been converted into a library—several desks, a couple computers, a printer, books. And while there were three boys to a room, they all got along. They'd survived a nightmare, and were grateful and appreciative of everything they had.

Sean would have done anything to change the past so they never had to live through it. But living in the past was foolhardy. Just like he would do anything to turn back the clock and be a father to Jesse . . . except that choice had been stolen from him. The only option was to keep moving forward.

Jesse was playing *Destiny* with Tito, showing him some of the cool things about the game. Things that Sean had shown him, just weeks ago. He watched for a moment, then said, "Hey."

They turned around.

"Sean!" Tito jumped up and hobbled over to him. Sean picked him up—for a ten-year-old, he was small. He'd been grossly malnourished for most of his life, but he'd gained thirty pounds in the last fifteen months and grown three inches. Sean could still pick him up far too easily.

"Ugh, Tito! You're getting too big, kid! I'm going to need to start lifting weights to keep up with you."

He hugged the kid and put him down.

"Jesse showed me how to infiltrate the base! I can get to the next level!"

"That's great."

"Can he come back tomorrow? Please?"

Sean caught Jesse's eye. "Maybe," he said. "Jesse's mom is in town, so I have to talk to her first."

"Oh. Okay. But you can come, right? It's Sunday. You haven't been to Sunday dinner in *weeks*."

Sean had gotten into the habit of coming by the boys' home on Sunday after church. He didn't go to church, but the boys did—and in the afternoon, he would hang with them, play video games, and inevitably Sister Ruth would have him and Lucy for dinner. Sometimes Lucy was working, but Sean never said no. He enjoyed it.

But since Jesse had come to town, he had avoided the boys' home, and he just now realized that he'd impacted them as well as himself. He'd made this commitment when he bought the house; more, he *wanted* this commitment.

"If I'm not working, I'll be here."

Tito grinned. "Great! Can Jesse stay longer? Dinner's in an hour. You can all stay for dinner!"

"I don't think we can. Right now, I need to talk to him, okay?"

"In private?"

"Yeah."

"Sure." Tito limped over to Jesse and gave him a hug. "Thanks for playing with me. I had lots of fun." Then he left, closing the double doors behind him.

Jesse stared at Sean. "You're mad."

Sean was so relieved that Jesse was okay and nothing bad had happened. Yes, he was mad. But not as mad as he thought he'd be.

He walked over and hugged him tight. "Never, never walk out like that again," Sean said. "Whether it's safe or not, never leave without telling someone where you're going."

"I didn't know where I was going. Not until I saw the bus."

Sean stepped back. "If it was safe out there, I'd be angry; but it's not safe. So I'm angry *and* scared to death."

"You think it was Carson. He's not going to hurt me."

"You *are* hurt. Car accidents are unpredictable. There could have been a fire, the car could have rolled, you could have been seriously injured. Just because I think Carson is behind it doesn't mean that he has any control over what the people he hired are doing. When you deal with criminals, they can be unpredictable. *If* he's behind it, because I don't have proof. And I should never have said that to you—never blamed him."

"I'm sorry."

"So am I." Sean sat and waited for Jesse to sit next to him. "I don't know how to do this. I don't know how to be a dad. I want to. But I screwed this all up."

Jesse shook his head. "No you didn't. I did."

"Nothing that has happened is your fault—except you walking out. And even then, I can't completely blame you. I would have done the same thing if I heard my parents fighting about me."

"Did your parents fight a lot?"

"No. Never, really. They argued sometimes, but they

were never mean to each other. They lived in their own world. They were both smart, very focused on their work. Ironically, if I'd walked out they probably wouldn't have noticed, not for a while at any rate." Suddenly that made Sean sad. He had loved his mom and dad, but they'd been absentminded parents. They cared about their kids—but they raised them almost like free spirits. It was pretty surprising, he realized, that Kane was such a militant soldier and Duke had been an ultra-strict guardian. At the same time, Sean could see that he might be more like his parents—not when it came to safety and security, but when it came to just having fun. There had to be a balance. He just didn't know what it was—or where to find it.

"My mom told me that she wanted to take me home, and she said you could visit. But then she told you she'd never let you see me again, and I knew she meant it. I don't want to go back, and I didn't know what to do. I'm really sorry."

"Your mother's worried, too. She's had a lot on her plate with WITSEC and everything that's happened this year. She didn't mean we'd never see each other."

Neither Sean nor Jesse believed that.

"It's a lot of work," Jesse said.

"What?"

"Going up against my mom and grandfather."

"Your mother will change her mind. She's upset."

"Not on this—she didn't want me to come here in the first place."

Sean didn't think she'd been happy about it, but she hadn't tried to stop Sean from picking him up.

"I don't understand," Sean said. "I talked to her, we worked this out."

"When we were in WITSEC, the second time you came to visit, you said that there might be a chance that we could get out."

"I remember." It had been in February, Sean had jumped through hoops with the marshals and finally had twenty-four hours with Jesse in a hotel in Cleveland—far from where Sean lived, and far from wherever the Spades were living. "A lot had changed with the Flores cartel, and the marshals promised to run another threat assessment." It had taken nearly four months, but they determined there was no major threat. The family could stay in the program, but they chose to leave.

"My mom hated not talking to her friends, but especially Grandfather. And Carson felt trapped, and didn't know what to do because he couldn't do anything that he liked. They jumped at the chance, and I said I wanted to live with you now. My mom started to cry. And I hate that because it makes me sad and I don't know what to do. So I told her just for the summer. And she agreed. She tried to back out, but I told her she had promised, and she said I could stay for six weeks. I thought . . . well, I don't know what I thought. That she would move here and I could see you all the time. But now she wants to take me away and I know she'll never let me come back. She has a reason now."

Sean didn't believe for one minute that Madison had orchestrated the attack on Lucy and Jesse. For all of Madison's flaws, she loved her son and would never put him in danger.

Living with Carson Spade puts him in danger.

That was different, Sean told himself. She might look the other way. Such as with the evidence from Jesse's phone that someone with access to her parental tracking app had sent the data to a third party. But after she absorbed the truth, she had to believe it, didn't she?

"Jesse, I don't know what you want me to say, so I'm going to tell you how I feel. I want you. I would be the happiest man on the planet if you could live with me all the time. But that can't happen, and you would miss your mom."

"Not after today. She—she said no court will let you have custody."

"She says that, but she doesn't know that. She was upset. You were hurt last night. When people we love are in dangerous situations, sometimes we react without thinking because we're so worried about them. Like—last night. I'm sorry I walked away at the hospital. I was having a hard time processing what had happened, and I'd just talked to your mother and she was angry and upset. I should never have walked out on you and Lucy. But it's true—if I thought Sacramento was the safest place for you, I'd send you home. If I thought going back into the witness protection program was the only thing that would keep you safe, I would make sure you were in it. It would tear me up to let you go again. But to make sure you were safe, that no one could hurt you, I would do it. Because I love you."

"I love you, Dad." Jesse hugged him and Sean didn't want to let him go. He didn't know what was going to happen, but he would fight for this kid with his last breath.

Sean just held him, taken aback at how powerful a hug from his child was.

"Jesse."

Sean and Jesse turned to the doorway. Madison was there. She looked pale and scared.

"I'm sorry, Mom." Jesse got up and hugged her.

She held on tight, and tears fell. "You really scared me." She took a deep breath, stepped back. "I don't know what to do," she said, as much to Sean as to Jesse. "I'm so tired."

"Stay for tonight," Sean said. "Let the marshals do their job. And we'll figure out exactly what happened. You can stay at my house."

She looked at him oddly. "You'd be okay with that?"

He didn't want Madison anywhere near him, but he would do anything for Jesse's well-being. "I know you'd feel better if you were under the same roof as Jesse."

"What about—your wife?"

"We have plenty of room, Madison."

"Maybe she wouldn't be okay with it."

Did she want to start a conflict? "Lucy is fine," Sean said.

"Please, Mom. Please. I don't want to leave."

"For tonight," she said. "I really didn't want to get back on a plane right now anyway."

Sean couldn't believe how relieved he was.

"No promises about tomorrow," Madison continued. "I need to talk to the marshals myself. And I don't trust your assessment of that phone app. I want someone else to look at it."

Sean tried not to take it personally. "Of course."

Madison looked around and frowned. "What is this place? It's not a very good neighborhood."

"The neighborhood is fine," Sean said. "This is Saint Catherine's Boys' Home."

"A boys' home? Boys' homes are for juvenile criminals. You're having our son hang around with criminals?"

"Not this house. They're orphans."

Madison didn't believe him, and he wasn't going to explain that the parents of many of these kids were in prison—that certainly wouldn't go over well.

"Troubled kids. Problem kids."

"Mom, it's not like that," Jesse said.

She wanted to argue; Sean could see she wanted an excuse to take Jesse away. But Jesse continued, "Dad built this place for them. They needed it, because they didn't have any other place to go. I like coming here."

She looked skeptical, and Sean could see that she wasn't going to budge on her opinion. Simply, she said, "Can we leave? I'm really too tired to argue."

CHAPTER TWENTY-NINE

Madison hadn't packed much in her overnight bag because she'd honestly planned on bringing Jesse back tonight. But she *was* exhausted and she didn't know what else to do but stay here. In Sean's house. With Sean's *wife*.

She didn't have the energy to argue with Sean or with her son.

"I love you, Dad."

She would never get that image out of her head. Of Jesse telling Sean he loved him. Jesse calling him Dad.

Jesse wanted to be a Rogan.

Hadn't she, too? Nearly fourteen years ago she and Sean had a fun and wild weekend in Las Vegas. Sean had been a month shy of eighteen, she had been nineteen, they both had fake IDs. She never intended on getting pregnant. But this was Sean . . . she loved him. He was smart and sexy and fun and her dad hated him, which was an added bonus.

Then he was expelled from Stanford and she never

told him she was pregnant. She had been too much like her father, she supposed. The scandal of the expulsion, which everyone was talking about. And Sean was so angry . . . she wanted to believe Sean didn't want anything to do with her and Jesse, but she knew that wasn't true. Because even though Sean had been a wild young man, he was honorable. He would have stood by her. He would have stood up to her father. He would have done the right thing.

She hadn't given him the choice. Maybe because she didn't have the guts to defy her father.

Everything had just gotten out of control. Carson was right: She should never have hired Sean to find him and Jesse last year. But Carson also made her angry. She knew he didn't have a squeaky-clean job, but she hadn't known he was working for the drug cartels. She thought he was helping businesses hide money out of the country, and really, she couldn't care less. She'd convinced herself that Carson wasn't even breaking the law, not really—it wasn't *his* money he was hiding. It was for other people.

The truth was so much worse.

But Carson was her husband. Jesse was a toddler when they met, and he swept her off her feet. He loved her, loved Jesse, didn't care that another man had fathered him. Madison was happy. For ten years, she had been blissfully happy, content with a good man and a beautiful boy.

Now she was losing her son.

Her cell phone rang. It was Carson. She didn't want this conversation, but she couldn't avoid it.

"Hello," she said.

"Madison! I've been trying to call you. I got your text, why aren't you bringing Jesse back tonight?"

"It's a long story, and I'm too tired. Tomorrow."

"Where are you staying?"

"You're not going to be happy."

"Rogan." He said his name as if it was *Satan*.

"His guest room."

"You and Jesse should be in a hotel."

"It's fine. Really. Sean is right about one thing—it's safer that we're here rather than in public. They don't know what happened last night with the accident, but it was on purpose. Jesse is bruised. He's fine, but it could have been worse."

"It's Rogan! His lifestyle."

"I don't know."

"What do you mean you don't know?"

"Sean thinks that someone was able to track Jesse through the parental tracker I have."

"Those programs are foolproof."

"Sean doesn't think so." She didn't tell him what Sean said about Carson—Carson would be furious. And no way did Madison believe that Carson was behind this. He would never hurt Jesse.

"Rogan is full of himself. He's an arrogant prick."

"I don't want to argue about this, Carson. I'm exhausted."

"Maddie—sweetheart—I would be there if I could."

"I know."

"Do you want me to book your flight?"

"No—I need to meet with the US Marshals tomorrow. Make sure that everything is okay. I don't want to go back into witness protection, but I can't bear to think of anything happening to Jesse."

"But you will be home tomorrow."

"I'll let you know."

"I miss you, Maddie. And Jesse."

"I love you, Carson. I'll call you in the morning." She hung up. She didn't know what to do. She didn't have anyone to talk to. Her few friends had dropped her as soon as they found out Carson laundered money for drug dealers. Then in WITSEC she'd been too scared to make any friends—and if she did, what would she talk about? She had to lie to everyone. Now she had her dad back, but he was so angry with her she could barely have a civil conversation. He now despised both her ex-boyfriend *and* her husband. He wanted her to divorce Carson and move with Jesse back to Orange County to live with him.

She didn't want a divorce. Carson had protected her in ways she could never explain to Jesse, and especially not to Sean. Considering that Sean was hardly a saint, he'd really gotten on the high-and-mighty pedestal, hadn't he?

Besides, Carson loved her—and she loved him. Most of the time.

She just wanted everything back the way it was before . . . and that was impossible.

Carson dug out his burner phone—in case the feds were tapping his home phone—and called Jeremy Robertson for the hundredth time; finally, he answered.

"Where the hell are you? I've been trying to reach you all day!"

"Working. What's the problem?"

"Whoever you hired is the problem! Jesse was in the car last night. *My son.* Now Madison is in San Antonio!"

"Isn't that what you wanted? For Madison to bring Jesse back home?"

"Rogan convinced her that there is an actual threat. They're bringing in the marshals to work the case. What the fuck, Jeremy? This isn't what we agreed to. You promised me that Jesse would stay out of it."

"There were no serious injuries," Jeremy said.

"You're not listening to me. The fucking *marshals* are getting involved. They probably called the damn FBI. Rogan's wife is a fed, for shitsake."

"Working for those people all these years has turned you into a foul-mouthed jerk."

What the hell did that mean?

"Jeremy, I reached out to you because we've been friends for a long time. I helped you when you needed it. No questions. Now I need help—and I paid you well for it. Get it back under control."

"You need to calm down, Carson."

"Don't tell me to calm down! Promise nothing like this will happen again!"

"I've already dealt with the situation. You need to stop panicking."

"If Madison had gotten on the damn plane tonight, I'd feel better. But twenty-four hours with Rogan? He has a way of twisting everything around. I can't have her doubt me."

"Madison doesn't have her hands clean, Carson. Maybe it's time you reminded her of that."

Carson had thought about it, sure, but the single best way to get Madison to do the opposite of what he wanted was to threaten her. She had to come to the decision on her own . . . and then she'd be one hundred percent committed. They'd been married for nearly eleven years. The last year had been hell, but the first ten—they were amazing. He'd make the next ten even better.

"I'll call you as soon as I know Madison is on the plane. Stay away from her and Jesse—she's naive, but she's not stupid."

"I never thought she was, old friend."

"And as soon as my family is safe, take care of Rogan."

"My pleasure."

Lucy knocked on the guest room door. Madison answered it a moment later. "Here," Lucy said and handed her a small bag of toiletries. They always had plenty of travel-sized items, and the guest room was stocked with towels, shampoo, and soap. "If you need anything else, let me know."

"Thanks," Madison said. She looked tired, and Lucy didn't blame her.

"Sean's making dinner—well, breakfast for dinner because neither of us had time to go to the store today. It'll be ready in a few minutes."

"I'm not hungry. I'm going to lie down for a while."

Lucy left her and walked down the hall. Kane was

talking to Jesse outside by the pool. Jesse was listening intently. Probably giving him a security lecture. She didn't like that Jesse had to grow up so fast . . . but better safe than a victim.

Sean was standing at the stove cooking up a delicious-smelling egg dish with chorizo and bell peppers. Her stomach growled.

Jack was setting the table, and he laughed. "Skipped lunch again?" he said.

"It's been a busy day. I had breakfast."

Sean grunted. "Probably a bagel and gallon of coffee."

She kissed the back of his neck. "You know me well. I'll feed Bandit."

She didn't have to call for the dog; as soon as he heard his name he bounded in from the laundry room, where he had been watching the kitchen. He stopped at the edge of the island—Sean didn't allow him in the kitchen proper. Lucy went to the garage, filled his bowl with kibble, and brought it back to the laundry room. Bandit ate happily while she gave him fresh water.

Jack had six plates on the table. "I don't think Madison will be joining us," Lucy said. "It's awkward for her, considering."

"Probably a good thing," Jack said.

"How's Jesse doing?"

"Feeling guilty, which is healthy," Jack said.

"Spoken like a true Catholic," she said.

Jack grunted. "Kane is laying down the law."

Sean continued to cook. He was preoccupied about Jesse, and it had to be weird to have Madison here in the house. She glanced at Jack. "Hey, could you take Bandit out to do his business?"

Jack knew she wanted privacy and took Bandit to the backyard.

"Sean," Lucy said.

"Hmm?"

"Talk. It's just us."

"I don't have anything to say."

"It was very nice to invite Madison to stay."

He glanced at her. "You're okay with it?"

"Why wouldn't I be? She's Jesse's mother."

He frowned, went back to the stove. Turned off the burner and grabbed tortillas from the bread box.

"You think I'm jealous?"

"No. You don't have a jealous bone in your body."

"Well, maybe one small bone."

He looked at her, worried.

She smiled, touched his face. "I love you. We're going to get through this, like we get through everything. Madison was in your past—long ago. And you're bonded for life because of Jesse. I'm okay with that; you also need to be."

"I thought I'd forgiven her," he said quietly. "When I picked Jesse up last month, we were cordial. I was just so happy to get to spend real time with him—but then I saw her today and I'm so *angry* at what she took from me. I can't get that time back. I can't do anything about it. I'm trying so hard to just put it aside, to not let it cloud my relationship with Jesse. To not let anyone see that I'm still angry. And then she reminded me that I have no rights. Nothing that she doesn't allow. My anger jumped to the surface and I want to go to war. Which wouldn't be good for me, for you, or for Jesse."

Lucy wrapped her arms around Sean's neck and pulled him down into a kiss. "You're human," she whispered. "We're going to make this work, okay? Everyone is on your side, Sean. Me. Jack. Kane. My family. Your family. Our friends. But mostly, Jesse. He wants you in his life, and Madison will realize that if she pulls him away from you, she'll damage her relationship with her son. Right now she's emotional and worried. Give her tonight and it will get better."

"I hope you're right."

"I am." She hoped. "Consider this, though—she feels like she's in the lion's den. She's here, in your house, with your family and your wife. She's on the defensive. Try and cut her a little slack."

"You are far too forgiving and compassionate."

"Compassion is not a sin, Sean. And believe me, if she follows through on any her threats, my compassion will disappear."

She kissed him again and felt him relax, which was all she wanted. He had been so tense and worried, but now he was returning to his old self.

A beep alerted them that someone was approaching the front door. Sean reached over and checked the security panel. "Hey, it's Nate, want to let him in?"

"I didn't know he was coming."

"Neither did I, but I'm not surprised. Being on leave has messed him up. He doesn't relax well." He kissed her nose. "That was something you had to learn, too."

Lucy opened the door to Nate, then reset the alarm. Sean dished up huge bowls of food—eggs and chorizo, red potatoes, broccoli, fresh salsa, and a stack of warmed tortillas. Kane, Jack, and Jesse came in and everyone sat around the table.

"I know none of you are much for praying," Lucy said, "but I for one thank God that you are all here tonight and safe."

"Amen," Jack said. "I'm starved, pass the eggs."

CHAPTER THIRTY

First thing Sunday morning, Sean took Madison to the US Marshals' office. John Jimenez wasn't happy about being called in on the weekend, but he was there when they arrived.

He was surprised to see Madison. "Mrs. Spade, I didn't know you were in town."

"I came as soon as I heard about the hit-and-run."

"Of course. Please, sit down. Can I get you anything?"

"Just water, if you have it."

"Of course."

"Me too," Sean said as John walked out of the conference room. Sure, John was mad at him for what happened with Domingo, but Sean hadn't shot the thug, and it wasn't going to come back on John—Sean had made sure of that.

John returned with three bottles of water, handed them out, and sat down. He took a sip from his own bottle. "We are still reviewing all the evidence from the accident and consulting with SAPD. I don't know what else to say—we don't have answers yet."

"Is it safe for me to take my son home tonight?" Madison asked. She sat stiffly, almost regally, in her chair. She barely looked at Sean. He'd thought they'd had a truce, but she was still angry. Well, shit, how could he fix this? Why was she so angry? He had done everything in his power to save Jesse and her corrupt husband last year, and he'd done everything to protect and love Jesse now. That she was mad at him got under his skin.

"I don't see why not," John said cautiously, "though I don't necessarily think you have to take him out of town. There has been no chatter about your son or husband, and we've reached out to all federal and local law enforcement."

He seemed confused. "Did I misunderstand the dates of Jesse's visit?"

"No," Sean said. "Madison thinks he'll be safer in Sacramento. I think that someone has been tracking him through a parental tracking app that Madison has installed on her phone." He slid Jesse's phone over to John. "She doesn't trust my diagnostic abilities and won't let me access her phone, but said she'd let your department have a run at it."

Jimenez opened his mouth then closed it.

Madison frowned. "You make me sound downright awful, Sean. What I don't trust is your assessment because you will do anything to keep Jesse here with you." She turned to John and said, "Sean thinks that my husband had something to do with the accident."

"What I *said* was that I think your husband set up

your phone to send Jesse's location to a blind third-party account every time you logged in."

"And I told you that I haven't checked on Jesse through the app since you picked him up!"

Sean bit his tongue because it was so damn obvious what had happened but she would never believe it. Clearly Carson had the same app on his phone and used Madison's password to track Jesse. Why couldn't she see it? Why was she being so deliberately blind?

"I've done everything I can legally do," Sean said slowly and carefully. "But someone has been tracking Jesse through his phone and I'm hoping your office can trace it."

John looked at Sean and shook his head. Sean bit the inside of his cheek. He hoped John didn't spill the beans—he didn't have to lie to Madison, but Sean knew that the marshals locally used the FBI's cybercrimes unit when needed, and Sean had many friends in the FBI.

Fortunately, John simply said, "Well, I can definitely send the phones in for processing. We should learn within twenty-four hours if there has been any hack."

Madison looked relieved. "Thank you. So I can go home?"

"I'm still working on updating the threat assessment. The fact that someone followed Sean and Jesse on Wednesday, then another vehicle ran Agent Kincaid and Jesse off the road on Friday, tells me there could be a potential problem. I'm not at the point where I can recommend a protective detail—I simply do not know what, if any, threat there is. I'm hopeful these phones will give me something to work with."

"I don't want to go back into witness protection," Madison said, "but I will do anything to protect my son."

"Of course, but as you were told when you left WITSEC, it's not a revolving door. You could have stayed—regardless of the new threat assessment, we would have kept you in the program. But you opted to leave. There would have to be an immediate and verifiable threat directly related to Mr. Spade's former illegal business dealings against you or Jesse in order for you to be readmitted into the program."

"Or my husband."

"Actually, no."

"What?"

John seemed uncomfortable that he was the one sharing this news. "Mr. Spade agreed to turn state's evidence against individuals in the Flores drug cartel. However, all the individuals he had firsthand knowledge of are deceased. He has no information that would be of help to the federal government. Because he was forthcoming and shared an extensive amount of information with the FBI and the DEA, he was granted probation in lieu of prison when he was released, under specific terms. But he has no information that is valuable to the government at this time."

"But I thought if there was a threat—"

"If there's a threat against you in retaliation for something that Mr. Spade had or had not done, you would be protected, but de facto such threat would mean that he lied in his plea deal and thus would not be under the protection of the US Marshals. He was well aware of that when he signed the agreement—my office went over it multiple times."

"Of course he disclosed everything to you," Madison snapped.

She was lying. Sean didn't know how he knew, but Madison was lying about something. Maybe it was the way she averted her eyes, just slightly; or the way she was holding her fingers, just a bit too tightly. Those habits could be simply because she was nervous, but Sean had known Madison for a long time. And while he hadn't seen her in years until recently, he could still read her well.

John said, "I would suggest that you remain here until I get the report back on these phones. I'll expedite it, but I know I won't get anything before tomorrow morning, and more likely the end of day tomorrow. And if it's a complex hack, it may take cybercrimes longer to trace it."

"But I don't know what to do here. If there is a threat . . . how can I protect my son?"

Sean was about to jump down her throat; fortunately, John saved his ass.

"If I may, Mrs. Spade, Mr. Rogan here is trained in security and his wife is an FBI agent. I would heed their advice and they can keep you safe until we have more information."

"You and Jesse can stay at my house as long as necessary," Sean said. "My security is the best home security system that I could build and install."

She clearly didn't like that answer, but she nodded. "I have a new number Sean gave me while you have my phone," she told John, then wrote it down for him. "Please let me know as soon as you know anything."

"Of course. We all want the same thing."

Madison shook her head and left the conference room.

John looked at Sean. In a low voice he said, "What the hell was that?"

"She thinks I'm the problem."

"You're a pain in the ass, but you're hardly the problem. Do you really think there's a threat against Jesse or his mother?"

"Yes. I don't know who or why, but I'm going to find out. Both Kane and Jack are in town helping me."

"Where's Jesse now?"

"At the house with Lucy and our friend Nate Dunning, who's also an agent. Kane and Jack are running surveillance on the guy we believed ordered the hit on Domingo."

"I don't want to know—I'm still furious with you about that."

"I didn't kill the guy. He was going to talk to Kane but got whacked before he could say much of anything. We have other leads, and we're going to pursue them."

"You know, Sean, you need to watch your own ass. You've pissed off just as many people as Carson Spade."

"Do not compare me to that prick."

"Just saying—your motives were a whole lot purer, but that doesn't mean that you're not near the top of the cartel's Most Wanted list."

* * *

"Where are we going?" Madison asked Sean.

"We need to talk. And I'm hungry. So we're going to lunch."

"I don't want to."

"I don't give a damn, Madison. I need to talk to you without anyone else around. We need to work out what we're going to do about custody with Jesse, and we're going to do it in public so neither of us lose our temper."

He pulled into the parking lot of a chain restaurant and got out of the car. He walked around and opened her door. Not because he was being a gentleman, but because he was surveying the parking lot and making sure that no one had followed them or was giving them undue attention. They were clear.

It was busy—the Sunday brunch crowd. But within ten minutes, they were seated in a booth with a bit of privacy. It felt like ten hours because Madison refused to talk to him.

They ordered and when the waitress left, Sean broke the silence.

"I know this has all been difficult for you," he said, trying to remember all the things Lucy had told him about what Madison might be feeling.

"You have no idea, Sean," she said quietly.

The waitress returned with a glass of white wine for Madison and Sean's soda. He would have much preferred a beer, but he was carrying a concealed gun and while he didn't think there was a threat against Madison, he could be wrong. He needed to be on full alert.

"I have tried to forgive you for lying to me. About Jesse. About what you knew about Carson's activities—I know you told the marshals that you didn't know exactly what his business was, but you're not stupid, Madison. You never were. If you didn't *know*, you suspected and turned a blind eye. I know you lied to me about Carson's trip to Mexico last year—you covered for him. And you probably covered for a lot of the bullshit that he did. That was then.

"Jesse is my son. I will be part of his life. I would prefer to be in his life with your blessing. I love him, Madison. I can and will protect him every minute he's here with me. Please, let's work out an arrangement that's good for both of us."

"You want my son."

"I don't want to take him away from you."

"Yes, you do. You think that you're a better parent than me. You have no idea what being a parent really means, yet you have the audacity to look down on me for choices that I made for my family!"

Sean was so glad they were in public because he wanted to throttle Madison.

"You took my choice away from me."

"It was *my* choice to have Jesse. He's *my* son."

"I don't believe this. I would have been there for him, and for you. You didn't even give me the option! You stole it from me." They were going around and around on the same argument.

"Do we really have to argue about this?"

"Every time you bring up this conversation to lambast me for being a failure and I bring up the fact that you lied to me and denied me the right to be a father, you tell me you don't want to argue. Until yesterday when you threatened to take Jesse away from me forever, I thought we had an understanding. I was willing to play by your rules, Madison. I was willing to visit Jesse in Sacramento, and I was ecstatic that you let him come here for six weeks. Six weeks where I could finally get to know my son. And I knew it wouldn't last, that I would have to bring him back, and I was okay with that because I figured I could fly out for a long weekend every month and visit. That we could talk on the phone or Skype or email. Whatever he wanted, whenever he wanted. And then you threaten to take all of it away from me. Every minute, every contact. For no reason."

"You accused Carson of trying to hurt Jesse. Carson loves Jesse. Carson *raised* Jesse."

"Because you didn't give me the chance."

"*Really*. You were eighteen when Jesse was born and going to college three thousand miles away. You would have given up college—you would have given up everything—to be a father?"

"Yes."

"I doubt it."

"We'll never know, will we?"

"We keep having this conversation," Madison said.

The waitress came with their food, but neither of them took a bite.

"We keep having it because we can't come to an agreement that you'll keep."

"Don't put this on me."

"I was fine with the last agreement. I was thrilled that you let me into Jesse's life."

"That was my choice. And I can choose to exclude you."

"Is that what you really want? Is that what you really think is best for Jesse?"

She didn't say anything. She bit her lip, then spoke so quietly that Sean almost missed it. "No."

"Then let's work on this together."

She nodded, and Sean breathed easier. He would have been willing to fight hard for Jesse, and Madison would not like how he played hardball. He suspected there were more secrets that Carson kept from the FBI, secrets that Madison was privy to. She was putting her own freedom and security at risk for that bastard, but Sean wouldn't tell her that unless he had to. If he could get her to concede on just a few points, he would rest easily until Carson buried himself.

And Sean expected that to happen sooner rather than later.

Nate and Jesse were playing video games and Lucy was cleaning up in the kitchen when Sean and Madison walked in. Bandit, who'd been down the hall in the game room, bounded into the kitchen before the garage door even shut. How the dog always seemed to know when Sean came home marveled Lucy.

"Hey, buddy," Sean said and scratched Bandit.

"You'd think you were gone for a week," Lucy said.

"It was a week in dog years," Sean countered. He walked over and kissed her. "Everything good?"

"No problems. Nate and Jesse are playing that football game with the annoying voices."

Sean laughed. "You know, the back end of that game is really amazing."

"I don't need to know."

She could tell by Sean's mood that everything had gone well with Madison. Lucy asked, "Madison, can I get you anything?"

"No, I'm fine, thank you."

Madison still seemed out of sorts. Sean winked at Lucy. Yes, he was in a good mood, which meant that he was able to convince Madison to uphold her original visitation agreement. Which was good—as long as Madison didn't change her mind again.

The one thing Lucy was concerned about was Madison's habit of being persuaded by those around her. Right now, she seemed to be agreeable to this arrangement; what happened when she returned to Sacramento and started listening to Carson? What would happen when she visited her father, who wanted to deny Sean all visitation with his son? Would Madison change her mind yet again? What did she *really* think or *really* want?

Lucy wondered if Madison even knew.

"I'm going to talk to Jesse for a minute, excuse me," Madison said and walked down the hall.

"It went okay?" Lucy asked when she was out of earshot.

"I got her to agree to let Jesse come for six weeks every summer and the week after Christmas. And I can visit him in Sacramento at least once a month with forty-eight hours' notice. It's what she'd agreed to before all this happened, but she did agree to put it in writing, and we'll make it official with attorneys and the court. I'm not going to go through this bullshit of her changing her mind on a whim."

"Good." Though Lucy would believe it when Madison signed.

"The only thing that's not settled is whether Jesse's going back with her tomorrow. I don't want her here another two weeks . . . but I offered."

Lucy didn't want Madison living here for two weeks either, but she understood. "We'll make it work."

"She doesn't want to stay. She's uncomfortable here, and I don't blame her. Kane and Jack gave her the cold shoulder yesterday. And while you have been more than gracious, I think she's intimidated by you."

Lucy laughed. "Intimidated? Hardly."

"I'm serious. I just hope she gets her life together sooner rather than later. And all this may be a moot point if I'm right about Carson." He glanced down the hall to make sure no one else could hear him, then said quietly, "There is no way Carson would be allowed back into WITSEC. If Madison and Jesse are under a direct threat, they can go, but if they are in danger, that means Carson lied and his agreement is null and void. Madison didn't know that until today."

"Who's processing the phones?"

"My guess? Yancey. He's the best tech the FBI has locally. Other than me, of course. Yancey's annoying, but he's competent."

"Competent? High praise coming from you."

"He won't fuck it up, that's the most important thing. If I went through her phone, she would never trust the information I found, but an impartial third party? She won't have a choice."

Madison said hello to Jesse but didn't want to disturb his game. Nate Dunning, though she'd met him earlier, made her nervous. Like she knew he hated her though he was polite and showed little expression.

Maybe she was exaggerating. Maybe not. She was in Sean's house and Nate was Sean's friend and everyone knew exactly what had happened between her and Sean nearly fourteen years ago that resulted in her pregnancy and subsequent lie to Sean.

For so long, she'd convinced herself she hadn't lied. Not telling Sean that she was pregnant wasn't *exactly* a lie. He'd called it a lie of omission, and perhaps it was, but she'd really believed it was the best at the time.

At least, she'd convinced herself—let her father convince her—that it was the right thing to do.

Now? She didn't know anything anymore.

She went back to her bedroom and called Carson.

"Hello."

"It's so good to hear your voice. I was worried that the meeting was taking so long. Are you at the airport?"

"Marshal Jimenez needs until tomorrow afternoon to process the phones."

"What? Does that matter? Aren't you coming home tonight? I miss you."

"I promised him I would stay in San Antonio until he knows for certain whether Jesse's phone was compromised."

"You're still at Rogan's, aren't you?"

"It's safer this way. Until we know the truth."

"I told you, it's not Jesse, it's Sean! He's the one who put Jesse in danger."

"We don't know that." Madison rubbed her temples. "Jimenez said that even if there was a threat, that you wouldn't be allowed back into witness protection."

"He's wrong."

"I don't think he is. He explained it all very clearly. You told me that we could go back if anything became too dangerous."

"I'll fix it."

"You can't, Carson! Some things you can't fix. I'm scared."

"Madison, I will do everything in my power to protect you. Don't be scared, sweetheart. Haven't I always looked out for you?"

"There are some things, Carson. If Sean ever finds out everything . . ."

"He won't. Don't even say it in his house! He could have every room bugged."

"That's absurd." But was it? "I'll call you tomorrow when I hear back from Marshal Jimenez."

"This whole thing is ridiculous, you know that. Sean

is making you jump through hoops, and Jesse is *our* son. When you come home, that's it. No more bouncing back and forth. Sean has no rights."

"He does."

"He doesn't!"

"It's not fair to keep him from Jesse."

"You're listening to him again. He's twisted your emotions in a knot. He's a bad influence, and you know it."

"Maybe—"

"Certainly he is. After this fiasco we can easily get a restraining order against him."

"Carson. Stop. I don't think that would be a good idea."

"It's a great idea."

"If we push him too hard, he'll push back harder. If he digs around too deep . . . you lied to protect me. I love you for it. If Sean finds out about my antiques business—"

"He won't."

"But *if* he does, he'll be able to prove you knew about it, and then your probation will be revoked and you'll go to jail. I can't bear to think of that."

"Did he threaten you?"

"No. But if I keep playing hardball with him over Jesse, he will find something. He is tenacious, Carson. He's not going to let it go. Jesse has bonded with him. If I tell my son he can never see his father again, he'll never forgive me."

"I am Jesse's father, Maddie. *Me*. Sean has twisted up that boy something awful."

"Be that as it may, I don't know what else to do."

Madison hated conflict, and her life had been one conflict after another once Carson's illegal activities had been exposed.

She needed it to stop.

"We'll figure it out. Together. When you're home. I love you, Maddie."

"I love you, too."

Madison hung up, confused and sad. She really didn't know what the right decision was. It seemed only fair to include Sean in Jesse's life—she couldn't un-ring that bell—but at the same time, that decision could negatively impact her relationship with Carson. That wasn't fair, either.

She wished everything had been different. What would have happened if she'd told Sean that she was pregnant? Would he have really stayed? Would she have gone with him to MIT? What kind of life would that have been for Jesse, with her cut off from her father's money? How would they have lived? Sure, Sean made a good living for himself *now*, but back then when he was barely eighteen? She had no doubt her father would have held firm to his promise to revoke her trust fund. When he found out Sean was Jesse's father, he'd been livid. And Madison agreed not to tell anyone.

But look at her life now. What a mess!

She left the guest room and glanced again at Jesse and Nate before walking down the hall. She didn't know what to do with herself, but figured she could find a book to read. She saw Sean in his office at his computer.

He was on the phone and quickly wrapped up the

conversation. It was clear he was talking to his brother Kane.

"Can I get you something?"

"I was going to sit in the sunroom and read, if that's okay."

"Sure. And if you want to go swimming, feel free."

"I didn't pack for swimming. I really plan on going home tomorrow, Sean."

"I know. Let's just wait to hear back from Jimenez, okay?"

She nodded and was about to leave when she saw a familiar face on Sean's desk. She walked over and picked up a printout of a photo. She bit her lip. Something was not adding up.

"What is it?" Sean asked. He sounded all business.

"I should be asking you the same thing. Who are these people?"

Sean pointed to one of the men. "That's the private investigator who hired the goons to follow me and Jesse, and run Lucy off the road—with Jesse in the car."

"That can't be."

"You know him?"

"Nooo . . ."

"Madison, what aren't you telling me?"

"I know one of these men."

"Who?"

She pointed. "Jeremy Robertson."

"How do you know him?"

This could not be happening.

"He and Carson went to college together. He was in our wedding. This has to be a coincidence."

Sean didn't say anything, but he was angry. She could feel the rage pouring off him. "I need to make a call."

"Sean—please—"

"Madison, I promised that I would protect you and Jesse. I will. Let me do my job."

FBI Assistant Director Rick Stockton immediately called Dean Hooper when he got off the phone with Sean. "Sean unknowingly found the missing link."

"Why am I not surprised? He doesn't listen."

"This time, he did—he didn't find it because he was investigating Spade."

Dean snorted.

"Kane has been tailing the private investigator who hired the driver who followed Sean and Jesse on Wednesday, and who we now believe ordered the hit on the same driver on Friday as well as the hit-and-run that Lucy was involved with. Kane sent photos to Sean to run through facial recognition, nothing popped that was of interest, but Madison Spade identified one of the men. Jeremy Robertson. I saw his name somewhere in Spade's paperwork, but I don't remember where."

"Robertson went to college with Spade, he's the CEO of a company—sporting goods, I think—and Spade said he was helping him find gainful employment."

"Let's dig around on him. It can't be a coincidence that Robertson is meeting with this shady PI at the same time that there's a possible threat against Jesse Spade."

"Maybe the threat isn't against Jesse," Dean said.

"You think it's Sean?"

"Sean was followed one night, then Lucy was followed another night. Together they helped take down the Flores cartel. Lucy did the legwork, and Sean brought Spade back to the States to face the charges."

"You think that Spade is behind this."

"I did exactly what you told me to do last week when Sean first brought this to our attention. I started digging into Carson Spade's life. I had him in the office. Hovered, made him nervous. On his own he mentioned that he had drinks with an old friend about a job. There was no reason for him to do that."

"Except out of guilt. Preemptively, in case we were following him."

"Exactly. I pushed a bit, casually, asked who, I didn't know he had friends in Sacramento. And he mentioned Robertson's name, said he was here on business, that he used to do a little legal work for him, made a clear point that it was long before he'd started working for Flores."

"Get everything you can get without a warrant, and if you think something is there and need the legal cover, get it to me ASAP and I'll expedite the warrant."

"Rick, I think you're forgetting something."

"What?"

"I'm the ASAC in Sacramento and the local AUSA loves me. I'll get my own friggin' warrant."

CHAPTER THIRTY-ONE

Kane and Jack had been surveilling Vasquez all Sunday. He and his wife went to church. Hypocrites, Kane thought. He wasn't much of a churchgoer, but Siobhan was and he respected her faith—and detested anyone who played both sides of the morality coin. After church they went with another couple to brunch at a fancy hotel known for their overpriced meals. Kane couldn't risk being spotted, so Jack went in and took discreet pictures. Kane wanted to search their car, but they'd used valet parking, which had tight security and cameras everywhere.

Jack returned. "Best guess, they'll be here an hour then go home. Now's our chance."

"You can't be involved with that." With Jack married to a fed, JT had forbidden him from doing anything overtly illegal.

"I'll watch your back."

They drove to the Vasquez house. Kane called Sean

when he saw the security system, and his brother walked him through how to run the system through an automatic reboot that wouldn't alert the police. "You have fifteen minutes," Sean said, "and that's a hard fifteen minutes. You can't reboot it twice in a row. If you're still on the property, the cops will be alerted and the cameras will record."

"Can't you just disable it?"

"Yes, I can—if I were there. But you can't. Trust me on this—I know the system."

Kane hung up without comment. He did exactly what Sean said, and the red light began to slowly blink—exactly as Sean said it would. He set his watch for fourteen minutes, forty-five seconds.

Picking the lock on the side door was easy, and Kane was inside.

The house was cool, almost breezy, a nice reprieve from the humidity outside. He listened for a few seconds, any sound that he might not be alone. Nothing. He searched quickly for Vasquez's den and found it downstairs—clearly the man's space with dark colors and the scent of pipe tobacco and Scotch.

He wished he could have used Sean; though JT's rule extended to his brother as well, Sean was more willing to break it than Jack. Kane didn't take a stab at the computer; he wouldn't know how to easily hack in.

He focused instead on the desk. There was a pad with phone numbers—he took a picture of the numbers. Easy enough to trace those. Did Vasquez keep most of his incriminating stuff at his strip mall office? That seemed to be more a front and much easier to breach.

A stack of folders on the corner drew his eye. Kane glanced at them and saw one labeled ROGAN.

Hot damn.

He had eight minutes left. He opened the folder and took pictures of all the contents. He didn't have time to read everything, but he saw a photo of Lucy and Jesse taken outside of St. Catherine's. That had to have been Friday night before the hit-and-run. It had been printed from a computer. He needed to read all the notes more carefully, but didn't have time. He glanced at the other folders and didn't recognize the names, but took photos of the labels.

Next he opened the desk drawers. Nothing of interest, though the bottom right drawer was locked.

Shit. He had six minutes left. He picked the lock—something he was as good at as his baby brother.

Jackpot. Inside were financial records. There was a wealth of information here, but Kane focused on the most recent folder, pulled it out, and started taking pictures.

In his ear he heard Jack say, "Three minutes."

Shit, he needed more time. He flipped the pages rapidly, took as many pictures as he could, and shoved the folder back. He carefully closed the drawer and heard it automatically click into place.

As he was walking out, he hesitated and looked at a photograph in a frame on the bookshelf. A much younger Vasquez was in the picture, along with his wife, and four other men and two women. One of the men looked familiar, but Kane didn't know why—which was odd because he rarely forgot a face.

"One minute," Jack said in his ear. "Get out."

He took a picture and ran out of the study, down the hall, and out the door he'd come in on.

His watch beeped. He had fifteen seconds to get to the fence and scale it.

Running across the front yard of a pricey house in an exclusive neighbor was a recipe for disaster—neighbors noticed that sort of thing.

In his ear Jack said, "Get the fuck out here, now!"

But sometimes, you had no choice.

He sprinted as fast as he could and leapt up the stone column next to the wrought-iron fence. If he slowed down, he wouldn't make it, so he grabbed the top of the column and pushed off and up with his feet, giving himself the added velocity to push himself over.

It was still an eight-foot drop to the ground. In the past, he would have been able to land perfectly every single time. But he was crunched on time, and he didn't plan the roll. He landed on his feet, and his left foot hit something uneven. His ankle rolled and he bit back a stream of obscenities.

Jack was right there with the car. He leaned over and opened the door. Kane limped into the seat and Jack was pulling away from the curb before Kane closed the door.

"Fuck."

Jack was smiling. "Hospital or home?"

"Home. It's not broken. But *damn* does it hurt."

* * *

While Lucy was inspecting Kane's ankle to determine if he needed a doctor instead of ice and a wrap, Sean went through Kane's phone and downloaded all the photos to his computer. First thing he did was look up the two phone numbers that were scrawled on the notepad. Both were burner phones. He was able to trace them to the major retailer where they'd been sold, but it would take more time to narrow the purchase to a specific location and day. Though they were both San Antonio area codes, that didn't mean much—you could get a burner phone with pretty much any area code. But they were likely bought locally.

Tracing them would be next to impossible, but they were still operational and could accept text messages. A strategic call or text might get the recipient to respond with identifying information. Something to keep in mind, but still a plan that was dependent on the phone owner to respond.

He turned his attention to the ROGAN folder contents. His blood boiled when he saw the picture of Lucy and Jesse outside St. Catherine's. They were getting into the Mustang, and Jesse was in the middle of saying something, his mouth open.

He then enlarged and sharpened the photos Kane took so he could more clearly read them.

The first sheet had personal information about both him and Lucy. Their address. Where Lucy worked. Sean's affiliation with St. Catherine's Boys' Home. That address. The estimated number of boys who lived there. Information about Nate Dunning, that he was on leave after the shooting on Wednesday.

Wait. How the hell did they know that? The names of the officers or agents who had discharged their weapons was not public information.

There was another fucking mole.

The mole couldn't be in the FBI. Rogan-Caruso-Kincaid had been hired to completely vet and clear each FBI and DEA staff member in San Antonio—agent and civilian—after a corrupt DEA agent had been arrested early last year. One of the people who had been helping the bad guys had been an SAPD officer who was dating an FBI agent and got information through her computer. But SAPD had told the FBI that they'd cleaned house after their mole was uncovered.

Sean wasn't surprised they had Nate's name—any criminal worth their salt would want all of Sean and Lucy's known associates. But that he was on administrative leave, that wasn't common knowledge.

He snapped his fingers. *Vasquez*. He'd been a cop. He must still have friends. People flapping their fucking lips to a corrupt former cop. But the possibilities were limited to someone involved in the McMahon takedown who had also been been on staff before Vasquez left.

He sent Nate a text message that he wanted to talk to him in private—sure, he was right down the hall, but he didn't want to announce what he needed to everyone. He didn't trust Madison. She seemed to want to make things work, but she'd changed her mind so many times he didn't trust that she wouldn't share everything she knew with her husband. She might not be intentionally obstructing him, but if Sean was right and

Carson was behind the surveillance and hit-and-run, Sean didn't want Carson knowing what he was doing.

He flipped to the next page. It was Sean's financial statement. It showed that he was cash-poor right now, after putting the cash into Jesse's trust—which was untouchable by anyone until Jesse was eighteen *and* had graduated from high school. In the margin someone had done some math and had the number $100,000 circled. Then written down under that was:

RCK-$1M

Sean knew exactly what it was. The hundred thou was what he could liquidate in twenty-four hours if he absolutely had to. His net worth was higher, but he wouldn't be able to sell his property or plane that quickly—and blackmailers would know that. He could, however, get a short-term cash loan on a percentage of his equity fairly quick because of his credit and holdings.

Every principal—and spouse or child—of RCK had ransom insurance in the amount of one million dollars.

He rapidly flipped through everything else Kane had found. There were pictures of financial statements from offshore accounts under names Sean had never heard of. But he'd seen enough of these to know they were shell corps and likely where Vasquez was putting his money. Except . . .

Sean flipped to the last page. Everything was a little blurry because Kane had been rushing, but as on Sean's financial statement there were handwritten numbers in the margin.

“Sean,” Nate said as he entered.

Sean put up his hand as he flipped back and forth between the last three pages and made his own notes. These numbers were much bigger. They totaled twelve million dollars.

“Fuck!” he exclaimed.

Nate closed the door and sat down.

Sean said, “Vasquez—or rather whoever he’s working for—I think they were planning on grabbing Lucy and Jesse on Friday and ransoming them. I don’t have the money, but they know what RCK holds in ransom insurance. But this—this is twelve million. That’s far more than what RCK insures on us. I think it’s what Carson hid from the feds—either alone, or with Madison’s help.”

Nate was all business. “They didn’t try to grab Lucy. She said they disappeared quickly.”

“Because there’s a mole in SAPD. They must have known that they couldn’t get to them before the police arrived. They’d already been dispatched because Lucy was on the phone with the nine-one-one operator.”

“Another mole at SAPD?”

“Vasquez knows that you’re on administrative leave. Who else would know? Your FBI office is clean. But the McMahon hostage situation was officially an SAPD operation; FBI was supporting. And yet you were specifically mentioned because you’re my friend.”

“This is serious.”

“Damn straight. I can keep Jesse under lock and key, but Lucy? She’s in the middle of this case, she’s not going to step aside, not even if there was a clearer threat. And what if they go after you?”

"I can take care of myself, and there's no reason to grab me. I'm not worth as much money. I'm back on duty tomorrow. I'll have Lucy's back."

"I know, but—" What could he say? He was missing something here. "I'm going to send all this to Dean Hooper. Maybe he'll recognize these accounts." He emailed the information to Hooper and then said, "I have to brief everyone, and figure out how to tell Madison. Can you sit on Madison and Jesse while I talk to Lucy, Jack, and Kane and coordinate security?"

"Of course."

Sean's cell phone rang. It was Dean Hooper.

Nate left and Sean answered. "Faster than I thought."

"What am I looking at?"

"You're looking at a ransom worksheet."

"You're only worth a hundred K? That can't be right."

"I put money into trust for Jesse. Cash-poor until I catch up again. I'm not worried about that, but my financial statement was in the same folder as a photo of Lucy and Jesse. I think that the hit-and-run on Friday was a botched kidnapping attempt."

"A lot of work for a little money."

"RCK has ransom insurance."

"Oh. That explains it."

"But they were going to ask for twelve million. That's two million from RCK for Lucy and Jesse, and ten million from those three other accounts. Who the fuck controls them, Dean? That's who would get the call if they'd been successful."

"Well, shit, Rogan, that changes everything. Where did you get this intel?"

"I didn't get it."

"You're not going to tell me, are you."

"I can't." If Dean knew the details, it could compromise future prosecutions.

If anyone survived targeting his family.

"Is this related to Robertson?"

"Yes."

"You think it's connected to Spade."

"You're a smart man, Hooper."

"I'll see what I can find out. Are Jesse and Lucy safe?"

"Jack, Nate, and I are all here at the house—along with a partly immobile Kane."

"What happened to your brother?"

Kane limped in at that point.

"He didn't roll when he leapt off an eight-foot wall. He's getting stupid in his old age."

"Watch it, Little Rogan," Kane growled. "I'm better half mobile than most people are fully healthy."

CHAPTER THIRTY-TWO

As they drove to FBI headquarters in Nate's truck Monday morning, he came up with half a dozen ways Lucy could avoid telling Rachel about the potential kidnapping threat against her, including reading in Leo Proctor to what had been going on with Jesse this week, but in the end Lucy decided she needed to be completely honest with her boss. She didn't want to return to the months of distrust that existed between her and Rachel after Lucy lied to her about a family emergency so she could pursue a cold-case investigation in San Diego.

First thing, before the weekly staff briefing, she went into Rachel's office and closed the door.

Rachel looked up. "Lucy. Can this wait for the staff meeting? I'm still putting together my agenda."

"I'm sorry, it can't. It'll just take a minute."

She motioned for Lucy to sit.

Lucy had already worked out a cover story with Kane just in case Rachel wanted to verify the information. She certainly couldn't admit that Kane broke into a man's house, no matter how dirty Vasquez was.

"My brother-in-law has been investigating the hit-and-run because he was concerned that it might be related to RCK business, and in the process he uncovered a potential threat against me and Jesse, Sean's son," Lucy said before she changed her mind about coming clean with Rachel. "I don't believe that I'm in any danger to do my job here. Jesse is safe at the house, and now that Nate has been officially cleared he agreed to drive me to and from home until RCK neutralizes the threat."

"What kind of threat?"

"Kane uncovered a photo of Jesse and me that had been taken immediately prior to the hit-and-run, along with documentation that suggested the person who took the photo knew that RCK had ransom insurance."

"He should turn all that into our office."

"I told him the same thing." Not really, but Lucy needed to at least pretend she had. "When he told me about it, he'd already sent the information to the assistant director. I'm sorry."

"Of course he did." Rachel frowned. "I don't like this, Lucy."

"I know."

"I appreciate you being honest with me about it, however. What Nate does on his own time is his own business. How viable do you consider this threat?"

"I don't think I'm the target, I think Jesse is. But I'm taking it seriously."

"If you want permission to work at your desk until this is resolved, I can do that."

"No, I want to clear the McMahon and Grey cases. Leo and I are really close—we have several leads to follow up."

"I read Leo's report over the weekend. He's looking at Clarke-Harrison, correct?"

"Yes. We're treading carefully, we recognize that they are a multimillion-dollar company with ties to the community, but something odd is going on over there, and Cortland Clarke was less than forthcoming. In addition, we've been given the run-around regarding Garrett Harrison. He's been out of town, but either he's avoiding our calls or he's not getting our messages. We asked the New York office to visit him in person about McMahon, and they reported that he wasn't registered at the hotel that we were given by his company."

"I have no problem going after them or anyone for any criminal act, as long as we make sure that we have all our ducks in a row. We don't need the PR headache. But Leo makes a compelling argument, and while right now everything is circumstantial and we do not have enough cause for a warrant, over and above the limited warrant you executed over the weekend, there's enough to continue the investigation. As long as you feel safe enough to do your job without being torn between the case and your concern over your stepson."

"Jesse is in good hands."

"Very well." She hesitated, then said, "I don't have any immediate case for Nate, and I know you work well together. I'll assign him to the task force. Jason wrapped up his end of it with Detective Mancini, who is focused on the lost evidence, so I'll have him back.

And perhaps—just for the next couple days—it would be better to have backup. Just in case you should be more concerned about the threat."

"Well, I don't think it's necessary," Lucy said while silently relieved, "but I appreciate the backup."

She got up and opened the door. Rachel said, "And if Clarke-Harrison is guilty, make sure it's a damn good case and pass it to White Collar. I already told Leo that when this becomes more a white-collar crime than a murder investigation where we're assisting SAPD, then he needs to pass it along. I have the smallest squad in the office, and I need you back."

"Yes, ma'am."

Lucy caught up with Leo and Nate in the staff conference room.

"Nate filled me in," Leo said.

"Rachel approved Nate to work on the task force. In fact, it was her idea."

Nate smiled. "You're sneaky, Kincaid."

"I used the old Jedi mind trick."

Nate laughed.

Leo left in the middle of the staff meeting. As soon as Lucy and Nate walked out fifteen minutes later, Leo grabbed them. "I was right about the bartender at Hogtied. The musician who knows Vince Paine? She called. I explained why we wanted to talk to him, assured her that he wasn't in trouble but we were concerned about his safety because he might have information that would put him in danger, and she gave me his address.

Back to Bandera, but she said he'll be there all morning. He works nights as a grocery clerk."

"A far cry from research assistant at a prestigious lab."

They climbed into an FBI pool car. Leo said, "He has a master's degree from LSU in biology. The other thing Maya said was that he had a problem with Oxy for a while. He's been clean for a few weeks, but he'd started because he was having debilitating headaches and couldn't remember things."

"Just like Charlie McMahon," Lucy said.

"But he seems to be better."

"He didn't live up there when he was working at CHR. His address was in San Antonio."

"True, but he and Maya have been friends since high school and he'd go up to watch her band every now and then. When he was fired, he moved into the apartment above her garage."

Leo glanced down at his phone, which was charging in the dash. "It's Tia." He put the call on speaker.

"Tia, you're on with Lucy, Nate Dunning, and me."

"Full house. Where are you?"

"Heading to Bandera to talk to Paine."

"We found Paul Grey's car. It's a damn mess."

"Where?"

"Parked on the street two blocks over from McMahon's apartment. Street cleaning is on Monday. It wasn't there last Monday; it was there today. They were going to tow it, then ran the tags. I can't believe no one called it in. There were flies everywhere, his brains were blown out right there. There was some cleanup, but mostly just a wipe-down. And evidence that Grey's body was transported in the vehicle."

"This makes no sense," Leo said. "Grey committed suicide, then—"

Tia interrupted. "Julie Peters is good, but she can still make mistakes."

"But he was killed in the driver's seat."

"Correct."

"For a minute, let's assume he did kill himself Monday night after he went to the bar."

"Okay." Tia sounded skeptical.

Lucy knew were Leo was going with this. She said, "He killed himself in an unknown location, but in his car. What if he was supposed to meet Charlie—like Charlie believed he was supposed to meet him on Wednesday—and he intended to tell Charlie everything. But got cold feet. Maybe he was involved in some way as to what was wrong with Charlie, and couldn't live with the truth, so he killed himself."

"And while dead, drives his car to Charlie's apartment."

Lucy tried not to take Tia's sarcasm personally.

"What if he killed himself, but the evidence was in the car?"

"And? I don't see where you're going."

"Where was Paul for the hours between when he paid Charlie's debt and when he was killed? What if he went to the lab after hours to get the information or evidence that Charlie needed—and someone tried to stop him? Or found out about it?"

"A lot of what-ifs," Tia said.

"I agree," Leo said. "We don't know what was going through his head."

Lucy felt like she was grasping at straws. "What we know is that Paul intended to meet with Cassidy Roth."

"We assume," Leo said. "We don't know for certain."

She glanced at him and frowned. "Who else?"

"I'm okay with that assumption," Tia said.

"And according to Mrs. Granger, Cassidy was trying to help Charlie with his memory loss. Maybe Cassidy found his body."

"And moved it to Charlie's house? Why?"

"You're right," Lucy said.

"I didn't say anything," Tia said.

"No—she wouldn't. But someone who wanted to frame Charlie might."

"Who?"

"Someone at Clarke-Harrison," Lucy said.

"And we have not one shred of proof that anyone at Clarke-Harrison is involved," Leo said.

"Just our gut, and you know like I do that there is something weird going on there."

Leo rubbed his face. "Maybe Charlie himself did it," Leo said. "Found his friend dead and snapped."

"That's a long shot. That means he drove him to his house, put his body in his den, then drove the car back to his apartment? Why?"

"Because he was mentally ill," Tia said.

"But he *wasn't* mentally ill," Lucy said. "He had a hormonal or chemical imbalance that resulted in severe memory loss and debilitating headaches."

"We're back at square one," Tia said.

"No—you have Paul's car."

"Like I said, it's a mess. Everything has been compromised."

"Ash Dominguez is good. Let him work his magic."

Tia sighed. "Why do I feel like someone mixed three different thousand-piece puzzles together, then took out half the pieces?"

"Tia," Lucy said, "what's going on with the missing evidence?"

"It's gone. The shipping company doesn't know what happened. They think the packages were misrouted, even though there is no computer error. I think their driver was bribed, but he's sticking to his story. I can't prove anything—he hasn't bought anything extravagant, and there's no large deposit in his bank account."

"He could have been bribed with cash and he's holding on to it; he could have been blackmailed into turning the packages over," Lucy said. "What makes no sense is they allowed the clothing to go through and not the other two packages. They were all shipped together; it's more suspicious that the two most important packages went missing."

"Remember," Tia said, "your office took the Paul Grey case. As far as the lieutenant is concerned, we have the cause of McMahon's attack at the coffee shop. He's buying the theory that he had a brain anomaly, which contributed to his erratic behavior."

"Jordan knows there's more to it," Leo said, frustrated.

"Yes, and he's fine with you running with it. But we

need to wrap it up on our end. Look—it's still technically open. We don't have an ID on the guy who slipped out early and hasn't contacted the authorities. And we're going through Grey's car. Maybe the guy left a fucking suicide note. But they have to do preliminary work before we can really dig in there. Like I said, it's a mess. Ash Dominguez is more than meticulous, and I talked to Julie Peters this morning. Dr. Moreno is deep in his analysis of McMahon's brain. He hasn't issued a report but he understands the situation."

When Tia ended the call, Lucy turned to Leo and Nate. "Why would McMahon move his car? Put Grey's body in his house? He wasn't that far gone. I don't think he had anything to do with it."

"Then who? And why?"

"To frame McMahon?"

"Now you're grasping," Leo said.

"Maybe," Lucy admitted, "but nothing else makes sense right now."

Nate said, "Anytime you move a body or contaminate a scene, it creates doubt and confusion. Evidence is compromised. There's no clear chain of evidence or events, and even if there is, any good lawyer is going to be able to show reasonable doubt."

"But why?"

"Could be that the perception that McMahon killed his friend is enough."

"And who would that benefit?" Leo asked.

"It would discredit McMahon," Lucy said. "So if in the course of our investigation we uncovered something suspicious about CHR, it would be more difficult to prove they were up to something."

"Except," Leo said, "Grey died—and his body was moved—before McMahon took the hostages at Java Antonio."

"So we're back at square one," Lucy said.

"No—we're going to talk to Paine. Maybe he has answers, or can lead us to Cassidy Roth."

Vince Paine didn't give them the runaround. As soon as he saw Lucy and Leo, he knew they had come to talk about Charlie McMahon.

"I don't know why he took those people hostage. I don't know what he was doing or thinking—I haven't talked to him since I let him into the building. And I was fired for it."

"We're actually here to ask you about Cassidy Roth," Leo said.

"I told her to go to the police."

"About?"

"Look, she's a really smart woman, but not so smart. I mean, she's intellectually smart, but she thinks that you guys would never understand the work that CHR is doing, and wouldn't know how to investigate what happened to Charlie."

Lucy said, "Tell us what she told you. We want the same thing—to find out what happened to Charlie."

"Cassidy and I were never really friends, but I don't want her to get into trouble."

"She's already in trouble," Leo said. "We know she

removed evidence from Charlie's apartment after the SWAT standoff. She's called in sick at work and she isn't at home. Either she's in trouble—or she's in danger."

Vince said, "She's trying to prove a theory, but I don't know how. She said she thinks that both Charlie and I were poisoned."

"With what?"

"I don't know and I don't know how! I've been trying to think about what happened around the time I was fired, but like Charlie, I just can't remember. Except I'm better now. Almost better. I'm not forgetting things, but I still have this block of time where everything is just . . . fuzzy. It's like when you're thinking, and you know something, but it's on the edge of your mind and it never comes to you. If Charlie felt like I did, but worse, I can see why he went crazy. There were days I wanted to slam my head into a brick wall."

"What else did Cassidy say? Did she tell you where she's staying? Or what she took from Charlie's apartment?"

He bit his lip. "She told me—well, she said that on Monday she talked to Paul Grey and he was supposed to bring her something from the lab that would help Charlie—I don't know what. She didn't know what, she was just positive that whatever Paul had would help Charlie get better, or at least tell them what was wrong with Charlie. She saw him in his car and—and she said he shot himself."

Leo leaned forward. "Where was this?"

"I don't know. She said in the middle of nowhere."

"And then what?"

"She searched his car and didn't find anything that could help Charlie. Cassidy thinks it has something to do with a research trial we were working on in March. Paul and Charlie had a huge fight about whether the trial was tainted. I didn't hear anything about it—but I sort of remember this tension between them. But that whole month is fuzzy." He closed his eyes, thinking. "I'm not quite sure that I followed her train of thought. I still get these bad headaches, I'm just not self-medicating anymore."

"Have you seen a doctor?" Lucy asked.

He shook his head. "I was on Oxy for nearly two months. I didn't want to go to drug rehab—I got off on my own. I'm clean."

"We believe you," Lucy said, "but a doctor might be able to run blood tests, find out what you were poisoned with."

"After this long, it wouldn't be in my system."

"It could be detectible in your hair or some tissues. It could be important, Vince."

"Yeah. Okay. Maybe."

Why was he so hesitant?

Leo asked, "You said that Cassidy searched Paul Grey's car but didn't find what she was looking for."

"She felt bad about leaving him there, as much as Cassidy can feel bad about anything."

"Are you sure she left his car where he killed himself?"

Vince thought, rubbed his forehead. He might be better than before, Lucy thought, but he was far from a hundred percent.

"Yes—she said they were meeting in a parking lot of

a business that was closed or something, far from CHR. No one around. He parked under a tree. She approached and then he killed himself. She searched, and thought someone would find him in the morning when the business opened."

"Do you remember what business?"

"I don't think she said. Just that it was in the middle of nowhere. Why is this important?"

"Because Paul Grey's body was found in Charlie McMahon's house," Leo said.

"What? You think Cassidy is lying? She's odd, but she's not a liar. In fact, she can be *too* honest."

"I don't think she's lying," Lucy said. Leo glanced at her in surprise, but Lucy was pretty certain based on what she'd learned about this young scientist that Cassidy was somewhere on the autism spectrum or had Asperger's syndrome. Brilliant, logical, meticulous, had a difficult time communicating with people. Some doctors felt Asperger's was high-functioning autism, and this wasn't an area that Lucy understood well. But either way, after walking through her house and listening to Emmaline Granger, Lisa McMahon, and Vince Paine talk about her, Lucy suspected she was correct in her assessment. And someone like Cassidy wouldn't lie—but she would believe that the FBI or anyone who was her intellectual inferior couldn't begin to understand what was going on—especially when she herself didn't understand completely.

Leo didn't say anything, and Lucy showed Vince the photo of the man who'd left Java Antonio right before Charlie took the hostages.

"Do you know this man?"

"Yes." He frowned. "Dammit, I know him! But . . . I don't know why. I've seen him. I don't know where."

"Maybe at CHR?"

He rubbed his temples. "I don't know. I can't remember. I know I know him, but it's like the memory was cut out of my head."

Driving back to San Antonio, Leo was mostly silent. Lucy checked in with Sean. Nothing had changed at the house. She then asked Leo, "Thoughts?"

"I don't know what to think, to be honest."

"I want to pass on that information to Dr. Moreno—maybe it will help him."

"I don't have an objection."

Lucy called the doctor who was dissecting McMahon's brain. It went to voice mail. She left him the exact description that Vince Paine had given them, how it felt to know he was missing a memory. Then she hung up.

"Has Garrett Harrison called back?"

"No, and I confirmed that he was returning this morning. He should have landed by now."

"Maybe he didn't get the message."

"I didn't leave it at CHR. I left it with his wife. After the runaround we've been getting, I decided to bypass them completely. I was hoping she'd pass it on to him before he landed."

"Do you want to stop by his house?"

"No—I don't want to put him on the defensive. If he's not involved with whatever is going on at CHR, he'll reach out if only to ask about McMahon. If he is involved, he might reach out to see what we know—or try to avoid us altogether. If we don't hear from him today, we'll go to CHR first thing in the morning. I wish we could get a warrant—I've been going around and around with our legal counsel trying to find a way to get CHR records, but we don't have enough."

"Maybe when Ash is done processing Paul's car."

"I think you're grasping at straws with that theory, Lucy."

After lunch they headed to the SAPD lab. Ash Dominguez didn't seem happy to see them.

"I told Detective Mancini this was going to take time."

"We were in the area," Lucy said diplomatically. "We're not trying to rush you."

Ash frowned. "I can't find the gun. Mancini was pretty certain that one of the guns McMahon had was the gun that killed Grey, but ballistics was negative."

"If Grey committed suicide, someone else took the gun."

"I got the autopsy and ballistics report—the bullet isn't in our system. It came from a nine-millimeter and that's the same type of firearm that Paul Grey owned, according to his wife and insurance records. But I can't say definitively that he used his gun to kill himself. And guns can't just walk away."

"And cars don't drive themselves," Lucy said. She understood Ash's frustration that they were pushing, but it had become urgent in light of Cassidy Roth's parallel investigation and tampering with the crime scene.

"We may have a witness to the suicide, but according to our sources the witness searched the car after Grey killed himself."

"Did she take his phone?"

"We don't know if she took anything," Leo said.

"His gun is missing, his phone, and according to Mancini his laptop. But the car itself is a mess—the blood and biological matter in the vehicle needs to be processed, but it was sitting out in the heat and humidity for days. I confirmed that the body was transported in the trunk—whoever moved Grey's body put it in the trunk, tried to wipe down the blood from the driver's seat and window. They wore gloves and the steering wheel was wiped clean with Clorox wipes. There were some prints on the passenger door and glove box that don't match anything in the system."

"Could be Cassidy," Lucy said.

Leo said to Ash, "Can you compare the prints with Cassidy Roth's? Our ERT unit has some of her belongings from when we served the warrant."

"I'll call Jackson, see what I can get. Is this important? Because I'm not done with the car."

"It is," Leo said.

"Fine. Oh. There's one thing I found that's really odd. It was taped under the steering column." Ash opened a box and showed them a tiny vial that contained a lone pill. It had been bagged. "The only prints on the vial are Paul Grey's. I haven't tested it yet, but it appears to match this."

He opened another box of evidence and showed them a baggie with three white pills.

"Aspirin?" Lucy said.

"Maybe not. These three came from the pocket of McMahon's slacks when he was shot. They were deep inside, stuck in the seam at the bottom of the pocket. Remember how there was a bottle of aspirin that disappeared with the other evidence? Well, sometimes I'll put mints in my pocket when I don't want to carry around a tin. I need to be careful with the lone sample because I don't know what I'm testing for. I'm going to talk to Julie Peters, get some thoughts from her. But I'll have something for you in a day or two. Tia said to be meticulous, because the buck stops here. She's already been pulled onto another case."

"We appreciate it, Ash," Lucy said.

"Why don't you think this is aspirin?" Leo asked.

"Because the external markings are not any approved brand. Every pill that is manufactured has a unique mark, to identify it for a variety of reasons. This mark on the surface looks almost identical to a major brand, but it's not."

"A forgery?"

"Possibly. Which could cause a huge stink all the way up to the FDA, but I still have work to do. Verifying that this isn't a legitimate marking will take time, but I can do that while I'm running the tests."

"And it was affixed under the steering column."

"Yep. Definitely odd, and a good place to hide something. Now out, please, so I can do my job."

CHAPTER THIRTY-THREE

Leo and Lucy arrived back at FBI headquarters at three thirty that afternoon and Leo went in to debrief ASAC Abigail Durant and SSA Rachel Vaughn. Lucy called Sean again to see how he and Jesse were doing. He said everything was fine, but she heard the strain in his voice. Lucy rarely left work early, but she was looking forward to going home and kept one eye on the clock.

Leo approached Lucy's desk. "Garrett Harrison is here."

"In the office?"

"Yes. I had him brought back to the small conference room next to my office. Let's see what he has to say."

They walked down the hall and entered a conference room that was the size of a normal office—meaning it was cramped with a table that sat eight. A whiteboard had been mounted on one wall, but there was nothing else in the room except a phone.

Garrett Harrison was an attractive, well-groomed fifty-year-old with a full head of gray hair and dressed impeccably in an expensive and crisp suit and tie. He didn't look uncomfortable in the attire, or being here in the FBI office. He did look tired, however.

Leo introduced himself and Lucy. "Thank you so much for coming down this afternoon. We would have been happy to meet with you at your convenience."

Garrett nodded, then said gravely, "I spoke to my wife on Friday. If I could have changed my meetings, I would have been here sooner, but I had a critical seven o'clock meeting in New York this morning. I came directly from the airport."

"We tried to reach you at your hotel, but the information your office gave us was inaccurate."

"I don't know why—my itinerary is available in the system. I was at the Grand Hyatt, where I always stay."

Leo and Lucy exchanged looks. "We were told something else. Have you spoken to your office?"

"I have. But I would like to hear from you what happened to Charlie. My wife sent me news stories and we talked, but I am having a difficult time reconciling the man I knew and called friend with a man who took fifteen people hostage."

"And you didn't know we were looking to talk to you."

"Not until this morning when my wife told me you left a message at the house. She told me Friday about Charlie, but I didn't know you wanted to talk to me immediately."

Leo seemed to accept that answer. "Charles McMahon took fifteen people hostage on Wednesday morning at Java Antonio and he turned his gun on SWAT when they went in. He was shot and killed. It was a justified action. No hostages were injured by Mr. McMahon or police action."

"How is Lisa? I want to reach out to her, but I thought it best that I learn from you what happened and why you want to talk to me."

"Lisa has family," Leo said, "who have been a terrific support for her, but I'm sure she can use a friend."

Leo then told Mr. Harrison everything they knew about McMahon, including his erratic behavior that predated his termination. He concluded with Paul Grey's suicide.

Harrison didn't speak for a long minute. "You think," he said carefully, "that Charlie's behavior is directly related to something that happened at my lab."

They hadn't said that, but that was certainly their theory, and Harrison was astute to pick up on it.

"We do," Leo said. "In the course of our investigation, we've spoken to Mr. Vince Paine, who was terminated by CHR in May. He has experienced many of the same symptoms as Charlie, including memory loss and severe headaches. He is, however, getting better, and while he can't remember much from the month leading up to his termination, he doesn't have a continuing memory problem. Charlie's problem was escalating and getting worse. We're looking for Cassidy Roth, who worked for him, but she hasn't been to work in a week."

"Ms. Roth? She's one of our most diligent employees."

"When she wasn't at her house, we called human resources and learned that she called in sick last Monday.

We need to find her. We think she has information pertinent to this investigation."

"What you're saying is that you believe that my company is to blame for Charlie's behavior."

"No," Lucy said. "But perhaps someone in the company knows more than they're telling us. Cortland Clarke and the lawyer Mr. White were not very helpful when we interviewed them."

"Cortland is paranoid about our proprietary formulas leaking out. Corporate espionage is a serious problem in the medical research field."

"We understand that issue," Leo said, "and we have no intention of damaging your company's reputation, but if something happened—an accident in the lab, for example—it could have been a contributing factor to Charlie's actions. We need to know what happened and hopefully prevent anything like this from happening again. It could have been an honest mistake and these results were unexpected."

Harrison said, "I loved Charlie like a brother. He was a good man, smart as anything, one of the few people I respected for not only his brain but his character. I didn't want to fire him. It was one of the hardest things I'd ever had to do. I urged him to take a sabbatical, but he refused. He got belligerent with me, hostile even. I told him to take a vacation, get out of town, work things out with Lisa. It escalated from there and I had no choice."

He sounded pained.

"I liked Paul, he was good at his job, but he wasn't Charlie. He didn't have the vision or the natural talent.

Paul was good with data, but not making that leap—from the evidence to the possibilities. I tried to talk to Charlie a few weeks ago, before I left on my business trip, to find a way to get beyond what happened, but when I finally tracked him down he was a shell of the man he once was. I was certain he'd started taking illegal drugs."

Lucy pulled out the photo of the man who slipped out of Java Antonio before the hostage situation. "We believe this man was talking to Charlie immediately prior to the events on Wednesday, but we haven't been able to identify him or interview him. Do you know who he is?"

"Of course. That's Franklin Clarke, Cortland's brother. He works for CHR."

"In what capacity?"

"Security." Harrison looked from Lucy to Leo. "What do you need from me?"

"Access," Leo said. "We want to know exactly what Charlie was working on at the end of March or early April, which is when his behavior started to change."

"I will get you that information. Give me twenty-four hours."

"That would be extremely helpful."

"I may also be able to get Cassidy for you." He reached into his pocket and pulled out his cell phone. "If I may? I have her number; she will take my call."

"Would you allow us to trace it?"

"Certainly."

"Great—we just need a few minutes to set it up."

Yancey set up the trace program on Harrison's phone, and he called Cassidy on speaker.

She answered on the fourth ring.

"Hello?"

"Cassidy, it's Garrett Harrison."

"Dr. Harrison. Hello."

She sounded surprised and respectful.

"I returned to town today and was told that you have been out sick for more than a week. Are you okay?"

"Yes, yes I am, thank you. I didn't want to make anyone else sick. The flu."

"I understand, and appreciate that. I'd like to talk to you in my office. It's about Charlie."

"I know about Charlie."

"You were his most trusted researcher, I thought we should get together. I lost a good friend, and I'm trying to understand what happened."

"Me too," she said quietly.

"I'm in the office now."

"I can't."

"Tomorrow morning. First thing, nine a.m."

"All right," she said cautiously. She sounded suspicious. Why would she sound suspicious? There was no way she could know that the call was being traced. "I have to go."

"Cassidy—is everything okay?" Harrison asked.

"Fine. Tomorrow. Goodbye." She hung up.

Lucy looked at Yancey. He shook his head. "She turned off GPS on her phone. I did get a ping in New Braunsfel, but that's as good as we'll get."

"Thanks," Lucy said as Yancey packed up his equipment.

"She didn't sound like herself," Harrison said.

Leo said, "We believe she's trying to find evidence of what happened to Charlie on her own, which could put her in danger. We really want to talk to her, so would you mind if we came to your office tomorrow?"

"Not at all. I'll expect you."

Harrison left and Lucy said, "I feel like we've made a huge advance just having him helping us."

"He wants answers, just like we do. I was very concerned that he would put protecting his business ahead of finding the truth, but he seems genuine."

"I concur."

"I know you're worried about Jesse and what's going on at home, and we're done here for tonight. Besides, it's after five. I'll meet you at CHR at eight thirty tomorrow morning."

Cassidy hung up on Dr. Harrison and bit her lip. Charlie had trusted him. Cassidy liked him a lot, though he always made her nervous because he was so smart and serious and professional. He was rarely in the office anymore because he worked with labs all over the world to find ways to more cheaply produce their medical drugs in order to decrease the costs.

She'd known he would be back this week, but she hadn't expected him today. Why would he want to meet with her? Had Cortland said something to him? Could he have her arrested? Was it a trick? Was he part of the conspiracy into what happened to Charlie?

She couldn't believe that—didn't want to—but she

couldn't risk trusting anyone, not when she was so close to finding the truth.

She looked down at the blood-spattered report Paul Grey had with him when he killed himself. It was a bunch of numbers that didn't mean anything to her because there was no context, but there was a file name at the bottom of the sheet.

She would get that file and with that came the truth. It had to. And she would bring it all to Dr. Harrison—sending a copy to both Adam and Vince, just in case something happened to her.

But first, she had to get into the building.

She was waiting outside Nina Okala's house. Paul's assistant was new, but because she worked in his division, her badge would be able to access every secure room. Cassidy only had to figure out how to get into the computer system. Paul had written one thing down on a sticky note, and she suspected it was his password. At least she hoped. And she hoped that whoever was behind this cover-up hadn't already changed it.

Because if that happened, Cassidy was screwed.

She was still an employee of CHR, and her login should be able to get her in—as a backup. But she had adopted a lot of Charlie's paranoia. Maybe she was wrong, and nothing in the system had changed and she could just walk in and get what she needed. It was technically espionage, she thought, because she was forbidden from taking anything out of the building. But if it proved that Charlie was drugged? If it proved that what he did at the coffee shop wasn't his fault? She was willing to take the risk.

Ms. Okala arrived home at five thirty. All Cassidy had to do was find a way to sneak in and grab her badge without her knowing.

CHAPTER THIRTY-FOUR

Late Monday afternoon, Sean ordered two large pizzas from his favorite place that delivered—one with everything and one with only pepperoni for Kane and Jesse, who seemed to have the same taste buds.

Madison came into his office. "Has Marshal Jimenez gotten back to you? He hasn't called me." She was upset about it.

"He'll contact us when he has answers."

"It's after five o'clock!"

"Madison, calm down."

"I wanted to go home tonight."

"It's best this way."

"For who? You?"

"Everyone."

Madison wasn't happy to be on virtual lockdown. "Let's call him, okay?" Sean said. He had a headache; he was over-analyzing these financial reports. Maybe the diversion would be good for him.

"Jimenez."

"John, it's Sean Rogan. I'm here with Madison. She's antsy that we haven't heard from you. I explained to her that sometimes analyzing data can take time."

"Yes," John said slowly, "but we have some information. I was just waiting for more before I called."

"What?" Madison said. "Is Jesse safe?"

"I can't answer that yet. What I can confirm is that there is an ISP address in Sacramento, California, that has logged in with your information, Mrs. Spade, and checked Jesse's whereabouts two dozen times over the last four weeks. I don't know who has that ISP address. I've forwarded the information to my local office and they're working it. There appears to be an automatic piggyback on the data as it's pinged, but they don't know where it's being sent. However, they think they can trace it with enough time."

"We don't have time if my son is in danger."

"I'm aware of that, Mrs. Spade. But there's no way that anyone can trail your son now with his phone because it's in my possession. We're working as fast as we can, but this isn't our normal procedure, I hope you understand. You voluntarily left the WITSEC program."

"I know," she said quietly. "Thank you."

"Hang in there, I'll let you know as soon as I have anything definitive."

Sean thanked John and ended the call. "It's Carson. Why can't you see that, Madison?"

"He wouldn't. Someone could have planted a bug or virus in his computer—if it's his computer. Maybe it's RCK tracking him."

"Don't be ridiculous, Madison," Sean snapped.

She stood. "You just don't understand."

He stared at her. "I guess I don't."

She walked out and Sean breathed easier. Jack came in. "Trouble in paradise?"

"I'm not in the mood, Kincaid."

Jack sat in the chair that Madison had vacated. "Anything else?

"I sent everything to Dean."

"You didn't answer my question."

Sean got up and shut the door. "I found the original documents that set up these shell corps. They're the same structure as all Carson's schemes. But the signature is different. It's Madison's."

"She set these up?"

"I don't know what the hell is going on, Jack. It's a different name, but it's her handwriting. I know her writing."

"That's hard to prove."

"Not for the FBI."

"You told Dean."

"I can't."

Jack sighed. "Didn't we have this conversation at the RCK meeting in January? You're married to a federal agent, Sean."

"Extenuating circumstances."

"Tell that to the judge when you're being sentenced."

Sean waved the concern away. "I'm not a novice at this, Jack. Dean will find the same information, he just needs to wait for a fucking warrant. And I'm not going to say anything—what would that change? Carson Spade is behind all of this! It just tells me that Madison knows a hell of a lot more about his activities than she's ever said. It's one thing to justify hiding money from the government—I've justified much of my hacking over the years. But Carson was involved with the fucking drug cartels. Human trafficking. He was an accessory to murder. I'm having a real hard time now, knowing what I know, believing Madison didn't know any of it like she said."

"I never believed her. But she's Jesse's mother and it's not my place to tell the AUSA and the US Marshals that they're not doing their job right."

"Carson backed her up. That tells me she is loyal to him for more than marriage—he protected her against prosecution. And together they hid all that money, Jack! Money that could have—and should have—been used to pay restitution to the women who suffered under the hands of the Flores cartel."

"You're not getting an argument from me. But what do you want to do about it?"

"I don't know." What could he tell his son? That his mother was privy to Carson's money-laundering scheme? That she had as much at stake as Carson? That she lied to the government *under oath* about what she knew and how involved she was?

Jack said, "You said Dean can find this information."

"Yes."

"And he's as good as you."

Sean nodded. "Maybe a tiny bit better."

Jack smiled. "Then let him do his job."

Jack got up and walked to the door. He turned back to Sean and he wasn't smiling anymore. "You have more than yourself to think about, Sean."

"I know."

"I don't think you do. Every time you cross the line—and I mean jump ten feet over into the freaking dark side—you risk everything you love. Your wife. Your son. Your freedom."

"Sometimes, it's worth the risk."

"Sometimes it is. I've been in your situation, needed to weigh risk versus my marriage to a federal agent. I did not hesitate to go to Mexico to help you and Kane rescue Jesse and stop the Flores cartel. Lives were on the line. But this information you found? This isn't worth the risk. And you're smart enough to know the difference."

Sean nodded. Jack was right. "Point taken."

"When's the pizza arriving?"

"Between five thirty and five forty-five."

"I'll get it. You take five."

"And do what?"

"Breathe."

Bart Vasquez looked at the assembled group and showed on the projector the blueprints of Sean Rogan's house and how they were going to take it.

"That's easy," one of the men said.

"Don't be fooled by the fact that there are no gates," Vasquez said. "The front door and garage door are both steel-reinforced—going either way would be cumbersome and take too long. The security system itself cannot be easily breached. If anyone walks across the property, Rogan gets an alert on his phone and on every security panel in his house. If a window breaks, full alarms and the FBI and SAPD will be alerted. Because a federal agent lives in the house, response time will be fast, but unless there's a patrol car in the neighborhood—and there won't be when we go in—it's still a minimum five-minute response from SAPD and fifteen minutes from the FBI.

"We're timing this so that the minimum number of hostiles will be in the house. However, there are two highly trained former special forces soldiers standing guard twenty-four seven. If they are not incapacitated when we breach, shoot. They are not to be underestimated. If they are out, leave them alone—we don't have time to fuck with them. We go in from the rear, do not be put off by the alarms. I've talked to some of the best hackers out there and no one is willing to take a stab at Rogan's system without more time, so we're going in on a clock. I want the packages out in three minutes flat. That gets us out of the neighborhood before first responders. And I promise you—response will be swift. Fuck it up, I'll shoot you myself. Does everyone know their job?"

Everyone did. If they didn't, they would be off the team—and *off the team* meant dead.

Jeremy Robertson was standing at the edge of the room. Bart glanced over at him. He was on the phone. He didn't say anything to the caller but nodded to Bart.

"News?" Bart asked.

"I just got confirmation that Rogan ordered pizza, and my men are on their way to intercept the driver."

"Good." Bart looked at his watch. "Let's get into position. As soon as we have everything in place, we go on my order. There's a nice payday in this for us if we do this right."

Jesse was tired of walking on eggshells around his mom. She looked at him with sadness, and that made him feel bad. He didn't know why she was so sad. Because he wanted to stay? Should he want to leave? Should he do what his mother wanted . . . or what Sean wanted?

His mom wanted him to talk to Carson, and he didn't want to, but last night when she was on the phone with him, she put him on the spot and Jesse was forced to make small talk with the man he'd once liked and respected. He didn't know if he could find that again.

His uncle Kane and uncle Jack weren't as fun today. Something was happening, and they weren't talking to him. That bugged him. Were they still mad at him for leaving yesterday? He didn't think so—Kane talked to him last night, really talked to him like an adult, and Jesse thought everything was cool. As long as he obeyed the rules.

Jesse didn't know what to do. He went down the hall and saw his dad working at his computer, a frown on his face. Sean had promised never to lie to him.

"Everything okay?" Jesse asked. He was a little nervous and he didn't know why.

"Yes."

"You're not lying to me, are you?"

Sean looked up at him. "Right now, everything is fine. I told you last night that there may be a plan to kidnap you for ransom, so it's best that we stay inside the house for now. The FBI is working on it, and I'm working on it. Between me and the weight of federal law enforcement, we'll put an end to these threats. I promise."

"But for now—stay put."

"I'm sorry, buddy."

"Thanks for telling me the truth."

"You okay?"

"Yeah."

"I ordered pizza."

"Thanks. I'm going to the game room, okay?"

"Great. Nate and Lucy should be home in an hour or two."

"You don't have to have Nate babysit me."

"Don't think of it like that."

Jesse shrugged. He didn't know how to tell Sean how this all felt. The situation with Carson. How his mom was acting all sad and weird. How he was scared and he didn't want to be. He wanted to be tough like Kane. He wanted to be strong for his mom, to prove to his dad that he wasn't a little kid. But he couldn't say anything.

"Trust me, Nate loves playing games as much as I do. You know, when Lucy and I first moved to San Antonio and I met Nate, we spent nearly fourteen hours straight battling each other on *Call of Duty*. We bonded, what can I say?" Sean smiled. "I wish I could break away now—but I need to go through these files. It's important, and there's nothing I won't do to protect you. Okay?"

He nodded. "Okay. But Nate doesn't have to entertain me. I can entertain myself." He turned away.

"Jess?"

He looked back at his dad.

"I love you."

"Love you too, Dad."

He went down the hall. Sean was worried, and he was trying not to make a big deal about what was happening, but Jesse wasn't a little kid anymore. He hadn't been in the last year since Carson had taken him down to Mexico without telling his mom. If it weren't for Sean and Kane, Jesse didn't know what would have happened to him. Carson had told his mom over and over that everything had been under control, that they were never in danger until the Rogans got involved, but Jesse wasn't sure about that. There seemed to be a lot of things going on that even Carson hadn't known about.

Jesse played for a while, then his mom came in with two plates and canned soda. She put two slices of pepperoni pizza in front of him.

"Sean got pizza," she said.

"I'm almost done."

"You need to eat."

"I will."

"Don't you think you play too many video games?"

He glanced at her. "You never cared before."

She sat down and ate her own pizza. To humor her, he paused his game and took a big bite, washing it down with soda. Then he started playing again.

"You're not being fair to me," Madison said. "I only want the best for you."

He didn't want to have this conversation, because inevitably his mom would start to cry and then he would feel bad.

"I know, Mom," he said.

"You really like him."

"Sean? Yeah, I do. He's my dad."

"I wish you would forgive Carson. Give him another chance. He loves you. He raised you."

"Mom, I don't want to talk about Carson right now. I get it, okay? You love him, and he's not all bad. And I'm trying to forgive him for everything, okay?" Jesse didn't know if he could. His mom, yeah. What Lucy told him the other night, it made sense. Jesse had never thought about what his mother might have been thinking or feeling when she found out that she was pregnant in college. She'd done everything for him, he knew she loved him. So sure, he could forgive his mother. Sean said he was working hard to forgive her, and if he could, Jesse had to try, too.

"Okay," his mom said.

"Thanks for not fighting anymore."

"I hate that you heard all that."

"I just want to spend time with my dad," he said.

"Well, we agreed to a visitation schedule. I just never wanted you to be moved around from house to house. And now it's state to state."

"Maybe we can move here, to San Antonio," Jesse said, hopeful.

His mother didn't respond. He glanced over. She was curled up in the corner of the couch, her eyes closed.

"Mom?"

"Hmm?"

He didn't think she'd want to move to San Antonio, and Carson would never agree to it. Plus, Jesse didn't think he could leave Sacramento until his probation was up. "Never mind," he said. He took another bite of pizza, then continued his game.

He yawned, felt oddly tired. He drank more soda, even though it wasn't caffeinated.

He glanced over at his mom. "Mom? Mom, are you awake?"

She didn't move or respond. He got up and his limbs felt heavy. He sagged on the couch. "Dad! Sean!" His voice was a whisper, no matter how loud he tried to shout.

He remembered what Sean had told him the other day, about security and always being alert. Something was wrong, and he didn't know what. He took out the cell phone that Sean had given him to replace the one the marshals had. He called Lucy and as he pressed SEND he realized he should have called 911. It was hard to think.

"Kincaid."

"Lucy."

"Who is this?"

"Me."

"Jesse?"

His head felt heavy.

"Something. Wrong."

"Jesse, I'm coming. Jesse?"

He heard Lucy talking in his ear, but he couldn't respond.

The sound of shattering glass made him jump. "Wha—?"

"Jesse! Hide, Jess. Under a bed. Anywhere. I'm on my way."

He tried to get up but couldn't move. He was only vaguely aware of the room around him. Shouts. There was a gunshot.

"Dad . . ." His voice was weak. His dad would die for him. Tears leaked from his eyes.

"Jess, are you there? Nate, go faster—faster! Jesse?"

Then Jesse heard nothing.

CHAPTER THIRTY-FIVE

The nine minutes it took Lucy and Nate to get to her house felt like eternity. While she was talking to Jesse, Nate had called 911 to immediately dispatch multiple cars. By the time she heard the gunshot, Nate was on the phone with Leo Proctor to mobilize SWAT.

And still they were five minutes out.

Jesse's call disconnected and she tried him again; no answer. She called Sean; no answer. She tried Jack then Kane . . . no answer. Her chest tightened in an overwhelming agony of loss. To keep calling and not getting anyone to pick up a damn phone!

Two squad cars pulled up right before Lucy and Nate arrived. The officers were just getting out of their vehicles. The house alarm was shrill and constant, meaning that there were multiple breaches and no one was able to disable it. Nate and Lucy both put their badges around their necks and Nate flashed his ID. "FBI SWAT is en route, but we're going in."

"We need to wait for a commander, we could have a hostage situation," the responding officer said.

"I'm taking command until someone higher-ranked gets here," Nate said. "There are five people inside, three men, one woman, one teenager. We received an emergency call from the teen and there was at least one gunshot." As he spoke, he pulled on his vest.

Lucy already had hers on. "The front hasn't been compromised," she said.

"I'll go around back with two officers, you go through the front with two." He tossed her a communications bug for her ear. "That's just you and me for now," he added.

She clipped the com around her ear and went up to the front. She typed her code into the front door panel. The alarm stopped, the silence echoing in her ears.

She braced herself for the worst, and prayed for the best.

Lucy motioned for the two officers to take the hall to the left—more doors and hiding spaces that needed a backup. She went right, through the wide hall toward the kitchen. She quickly cleared the living room and dining room. They were open and airy with no place to hide. She saw Nate and two cops in the backyard—and that's when she saw all the broken glass in the living room. They came in through the windows—shattering the plate glass. By the size of the breach, it was a large team. Military? Tactically trained? Who were these people?

There was blood in the kitchen and her heart skipped a beat, but she entered, gun ready, visually scanning for any threat. Nate came in through the back.

A hostile was bleeding out in her kitchen.

"Cover!" she said and kicked away the .45 semi-auto that was inches from the man's hand. She bent over and felt his pulse. He moaned. "He's alive. Gut-shot. Hispanic male in his thirties." She handcuffed him.

"Kane," she heard Nate say over the com.

No. No, no, no. In the eating area off the kitchen, Kane was on the floor. For a moment she thought he was dead. He wasn't moving. But she didn't see any blood.

Nate squatted and felt his pulse. "It's strong," he said.

"Where was he shot?"

Nate rolled Kane over on his back. His gun was still in his hand, and Kane groaned and loosely aimed his gun toward Nate, but his eyes were closed and he was distinctly pale.

Nate immediately disarmed his friend—in Kane's condition he might not know friend from foe. "Kane!" Nate said and slapped him. "It's Nate and Lucy. Kane! Wake up!"

One officer came into the kitchen and said, "There's one unconscious male, Hispanic, forties, in the downstairs bathroom. He was armed." The officer showed the weapon, a Glock.

"That could be Jack's," she said. "My brother."

"Go check," Nate said. "I'll stay with Kane. You, you"—he pointed to the officers who had followed him in—"clear the upstairs *stat*."

Lucy went down the hall and faced Leo Proctor in the doorway. He was fully decked out in SWAT gear and had a full team behind him. "Status?" he asked.

"SAPD is clearing upstairs, I think Jack is injured. I

don't know what's going on yet." She went to the bathroom. Jack was on the floor. The cop had his gun out and aimed at Jack. "Put that down," she ordered. "That's my brother."

The cop hesitated, then did as she said. Lucy knelt. There was vomit all around the toilet, but Jack was still unconscious.

She grabbed a towel, soaked it in cold water, and put it on Jack's forehead. He was clammy. He jerked, groggy. Opened his eyes. They were unfocused and alarmed.

"Jack, it's Lucy. Jack. I'm here."

He didn't say anything for several seconds. He tried to stand and couldn't.

"Luce." His voice was thick and weak.

She had a million questions, but he couldn't answer them now. She helped him up and slowly made her way to the living room, where she put Jack on the couch.

Leo said, "An ambulance is on its way."

Jack shook his head.

"Kane got one of them, he's still alive," Lucy said. "And we don't know what they drugged you with." But it was clear they were incapacitated. A gas?

"Water."

Lucy was going to get it, but Leo waved her to sit back down and went to the kitchen.

"Make sure it's a sealed water bottle, we don't know how they were poisoned."

"Pizza," Jack moaned. "I'm never eating pizza again."

The officers came back downstairs and reported that the upstairs was clear. There was no one else in the house. When Leo returned with Jack's water, Nate followed with Kane, who was groggy and could barely walk. Kane collapsed in a chair. He took one of the water bottles and drank.

They tried to talk, but Lucy had a faster way of finding out what happened. She grabbed the main security tablet out of Sean's office and cued up the security feed ten minutes before the call from Jesse. She ordered four shots to show on the split screen—the kitchen, the living room, the outside front, and the game room, where she was pretty sure Jesse was when he had called because she'd heard video games in the background.

At first, nothing. Kane and Jack were in the kitchen eating pizza. Sean wasn't on any of the screens, but Lucy saw Madison walk down the hall with two plates. She paused outside Sean's office door—Sean must have been in there—and talked for a minute, then continued down the hall out of sight. A second later she entered the game room. Gave Jesse his pizza. They talked and ate. In less than three minutes, Madison had closed her eyes. Jesse made a call—that had to have been to Lucy. At the same time three white vans pulled up out front. Each driver stayed in the van and three teams of four—twelve people!—emerged. Two men stayed in the front guarding the front door, but didn't attempt to break it down. They wouldn't have been able to; it was steel-reinforced. How the hell did they know that?

The others went around back. While they were doing that, Jack staggered down the hall as if he were drunk. He had his phone in his hand, but dropped it. He disappeared from camera view and must have made it to the bathroom where they'd found him.

At that point, the plate-glass windows in the living room shattered simultaneously. They must have known that there was a clear safety film on them because they had tools to make breaking the glass easier. One man stayed outside with a semi-automatic weapon, and nine entered. Three went to the kitchen, three went upstairs, and three went down the hall toward Sean's office and the game room.

There was no hesitation, no looking around. They knew exactly what they were doing, knew the layout of the house, and had a plan.

Kane was on the floor in the kitchen, unconscious. One of the men kicked him, and then moved away. He stayed in the kitchen, while the other two went to inspect the sunroom. Kane rolled over and shot the man in the kitchen, then collapsed again.

The two men ran in from the sunroom, saw what happened. One was about to shoot Kane in the head, but the other hit his gun hand and said something. They left.

At the same time, three men dragged Sean out of his den. He was partially conscious, but obviously lethargic and not completely there. They took him fighting out the back door.

Another man carried an unconscious Madison out, followed by the last man carrying Jesse. They all left.

The entire thing, from vans pulling up to pulling away, took less than five minutes.

They were gone six minutes before SAPD showed up, and seven minutes before Lucy and Nate arrived.

"Ransom," Jack said.

"They planned the whole fucking thing. They breached this fortress," Leo said. "They had to know about Sean's security."

"They knew enough to know that they couldn't disable it easily, so they disabled the people inside," Lucy said.

"I'm sorry," Jack said.

"This isn't your fault. I'm glad you're okay." She hugged him. Her heart was beating so hard she didn't know how to make it stop. "We'll find them."

"Ambulance is here," one of the cops said.

"You may need to get your stomach pumped," Lucy told him.

"Fuck no," Jack said. "I'll make Kane puke."

Kane groaned. "Vasquez."

"Probably," Lucy said, "but we can't prove it. And no way would he bring Sean, Madison, and Jesse to his house. I need that guy in the kitchen to talk."

"Where's Bandit?" Nate said.

If anything happened to Bandit, Sean would be destroyed.

They searched the entire house. The dog wasn't there.

Lucy reviewed the security footage. She hadn't noticed the first time because she was so preoccupied with the smoothness of the operation, but Bandit had run after them. In the front, Sean, Madison, and Jesse were loaded into the same unmarked van. The three vans sped out together. They were identical. Smart. If anyone was trying to pursue them, they might not be able to tell which one had the hostages.

Bandit ran after the vans.

Nate hit the wall and made Lucy jump. He walked outside.

"We'll get them back," Lucy said, sounding more confident than she felt. "JT will get a ransom call, he knows what to do. We'll get them back," she repeated.

They had to.

"Call JT," Jack told Lucy. "Tell him everything, send him the videos."

"Right. Okay." Lucy felt a million times better now that she had a plan. She went to Sean's den, saw the overturned chair. His computer was on the floor, but fortunately it hadn't busted. She put it back on his desk. Saw what he'd been working on—the financial documents he'd sent to Dean Hooper last night. The ones about RCK ransom policy and the offshore companies that Sean thought Carson still controlled.

This was about money. And if it was about money, that was good because that meant Sean and Jesse were still alive.

And they'd better stay that way.

Jack put his head between his legs. He still felt like shit, but he tried to puke again and couldn't.

"We need a full SWAT team ready," he said.

"You think the ransom is bullshit? Did you just say that to calm Lucy?" Leo asked.

"No." Jack looked at Kane. He needed his partner now more than ever. The paramedics came in. He said,

"I need you to give this man something to puke. We were drugged with a heavy-duty sedative."

"We'll take you to the hospital and evaluate—"

"Do it," Jack ordered. He wasn't taking bullshit from anyone, not now.

The paramedic looked nervous, but approached Kane. Leo said, "He's a witness, we need him talking."

"I'm. Talking." Kane was still out of it.

"Explain, Kincaid," Leo said.

"Madison and Jesse. They're hostages. Sean is just insurance. When Carson pays, Sean is dead."

"But Sean has hostage insurance, so shouldn't—"

"Trust me on this. Sean knew from the beginning—Carson Spade set the whole fucking thing up but it got out of hand. And if I were Carson Spade, the one person I would want dead over all others is the man who ruined my life. And that's Sean."

Leo glanced down the hall toward where Lucy had gone.

"She's tough," Jack said, "but she needs to put things in motion before she figures this out. And she will."

Nate still hadn't come back in.

"I need Nate," he told Leo. "Talk to him."

A retching sound in the corner made Jack queasy again. Kane was puking into a biomedical bag. When he was done, he looked at Jack and said, "Screw you, buddy."

"Glad you're alive. Drink water."

"I think," the paramedic said cautiously, "that you should both go to the hospital—"

"Maybe you should check out the bastard bleeding to death in the kitchen," Jack said. "We're not going anywhere."

"New rule," Kane said. "When working, we don't eat the same food."

"Amen to that."

CHAPTER THIRTY-SIX

Sean felt sick. He recognized that he was in a dangerous situation, so he didn't make any sounds or movement to indicate that he was awake. He assessed his physical condition.

His head pounded, his mouth tasted like shit, and he was sore all over, as if someone had used him as a punching bag while he was unconscious.

He focused on his environment. He had to find a way out, any way he could. The ground he lay on was hard and rough, like cement. He breathed in as deep as he dared, felt a pain in his side, but also breathed in cement dust and metal and some sort of chemical. Not bleach, but something similar. It was also hot as hell, no air-conditioning. During the day this place would be a furnace.

He didn't hear voices. It seemed dark, so he opened his eyes just a fraction. Yep, dark, though he could see light along the floor for a couple of feet, indicating that there was a closed door.

He listened again. They wouldn't have left him in here without a guard. The attack was far too well planned for them to think it was safe to leave him alone.

That's when he heard a voice. A faint voice, crying softly.

Jesse.

Sean tried to move then realized that his hands were tied with zip-ties. He could get out of them, but he didn't have the strength right now, or the balance to stand up.

"Jess."

"Dad? Dad? I thought you were dead."

Jesse was crying. Oh God, Sean would have done anything to prevent this. How had he screwed it up?

They'd taken him and Jesse . . . who else?

"I'm okay," he said.

That was relative. He was better awake than unconscious, but he was in no condition to fight.

"Are you okay, Jess?"

"Yeah. I didn't eat much pizza. They put something in the pizza, I heard them talking about it in the van. But Mom isn't moving."

They'd taken him, Jesse, and Madison. Who else? "She's unconscious," Sean said. "If I'm awake, she'll be waking up soon." He had to figure out a way to get out of this. He was on to something at his house, something that was just on the edge of his memory. Something in those files he'd been staring at all day—the files he wasn't supposed to have. It would come to him when the pounding in his head stopped.

He tried to scoot over to where he'd heard Jesse's

voice. Jesse met him halfway. "Are you tied up?" Sean asked.

"They put these plastic things on my wrist."

Sean should have taught Jesse how to get out of them. He didn't feel the weight of his gun in his waistband; they must have taken it from him. But he had a small pocketknife in his shoe. It was under his sock, and he could still feel it against his skin.

"Jess, I need you to get my knife out of my shoe."

"You have a knife? Why didn't they take it?"

"They took my gun, buddy. They didn't find the pocketknife. It's a small Swiss Army knife, it's not going to get us out of here, but it will cut these binds."

"It's dark."

"I know. Your eyes will adjust." He felt Jesse turn around, his hands fumbling down his body until he reached his shoes.

"It's in my right shoe, under the sock. It slipped down a bit, but you can reach it."

It took Jesse a minute, but he got out the knife. "Got it."

"Come here and cut my ties."

"What if I cut you?"

"You won't."

"I'm scared."

"I know, Jess. But I'm here. We'll get out of this."

Sean had the best security for home defense, and that hadn't stopped this attack. The damn Trojan horse. Had they killed the pizza delivery guy or bribed him? Sean was going with bribing. Give the kid a hundred bucks to play a joke on an old friend. It would work as often as it would fail. Or they gave the kid a hundred bucks and had one of their men deliver the pizza. If he refused, kill or incapacitate him. Whichever way, Sean hadn't seen it coming, and that made him scared and angry. Scared because he could usually predict any plan and have a counter-plan for it. He wasn't as good as he thought. His brother and Jack could be dead because he hadn't thought things through well enough.

And he was angry. Because his kid was scared and tied up in a dark room, and Sean wanted to kill whoever put that fear into his son.

Starting with Carson Spade and working his way up to Jeremy Robertson, going through Bart Vasquez and all his goons.

Sean winced when Jesse nicked him. The blade wasn't sharp, but the tip was.

"I'm sorry!"

"It's okay. Get the blade under the ties, and saw rapidly back and forth in short, firm movements."

Jesse figured it out, and a minute later Sean was free. He took the knife and cut Jesse's ties in one stroke. "Where's your mom?"

"There's a bed in the corner."

Sean was getting used to the dark. The thin light under the door helped. The bed was actually a cot, and he realized they were in a break room of sorts. Mostly empty, maybe abandoned. A lopsided table, a couple of chairs, the cot, a sink, row of metal lockers. There could be supplies in the cabinet that he could use. If he had to MacGyver an escape, he would do it. While he wanted to take out all these bastards, the priority was getting Madison and Jesse to safety. And right now he didn't think he could win a fight against even one person, not when his body was weak and shaking from the sedative.

"Madison," Sean said and gently patted her cheek. "Madison, we have to wake up now. Come on, let's go."

She didn't move. He put his ear down to her mouth. Was she breathing? He couldn't tell. He searched for her pulse. He thought he felt something, but his heart was pounding and he couldn't tell if it was hers or his. He felt the carotid artery on the side of her neck. A very faint pulse.

Shit, shit, shit.

He had no idea what Vasquez drugged them with. Madison weighed probably between 110 and 120. But Jesse seemed fine. "How much do you weigh, Jess?"

"Um, a hundred thirty? Maybe more?"

Jesse was thirteen, healthy, and growing. He was five foot seven, half an inch shorter than Lucy. They had joked that when he came back for Christmas he'd be taller. Yeah, he was at least 130. Madison was five foot five and very thin.

"How much pizza did your mom eat?"

"A piece. Maybe a piece and a half. What's wrong with her? Is she okay?"

His voice went up in panic.

"Shh," Sean said. "She's still out. She weighs less than all of us, so it makes sense that she's going to be knocked out longer." He looked down at his watch—it was gone. Well, dammit, he loved that watch. What did they think, he had a secret communicator built into it?

That would be cool, but so far no one had developed the tech unless it was in close proximity to a phone or computer.

Sean was concerned about Madison. Some sedatives could compromise the lungs, essentially shutting down breathing function. But she was breathing, that had to be a good sign, right?

All he knew was that she needed a doctor. He turned her on her side in case she threw up in her sleep. That's when he noticed she wasn't tied up. Because they didn't see her as a threat? God, he hoped that was the case and not where his mind went: that she was part of all of this to get the money out of the hidden accounts so she and Carson could disappear with Jesse.

That's the stupidest idea you've ever conceived. There would be far easier ways to pull out that money and disappear. Carson certainly has the skill to do it.

Sean took a deep breath and walked over to the door. It was solid metal. Jesse was right on his heels. Sean tried the knob. Locked. No surprise there. He hadn't found a lock he couldn't pick. But what if there was a dead bolt on the other side? He heard voices. Not close, but in the same building. He couldn't make out what they were saying.

Sean quietly went back to the sink and looked in the cabinet. There were some unlabeled containers. He opened them and smelled. Cleaning supplies. Okay, those might come in handy. He lined them up from the ones that likely had bleach or ammonia to those that were less caustic. Next he checked the lockers. All empty. Except each locker had a hook on the back, and some of the hooks were loose. Sean took out his pocketknife and unscrewed two of them. He positioned them in his hands, so the sharpest point was protruding from the back of his hand. They could do some damage. He put them in his pockets.

But Jesse had the best find.

"Dad," he whispered. "Can you use this? I found a mop."

Sean felt the mop handle. Wooden. "Perfect, Jess." He then sat down and took off the foul-smelling rag bottom. Now, this was a weapon he could do some damage with.

"What now?" Jesse asked.

"We wait."

"My mom . . ." He looked over to where she was still lying. "We have to do something."

Jesse was right, but Sean didn't think that there was anything they could do.

Sean hid the tools and pounded on the door. "Hey! Hey! We need help in here!"

He kept pounding on the door until he heard someone approach. "Shut the fuck up," a deep voice said.

"Madison hasn't woken up yet. She needs a hospital."

"Who cares?"

Sean pounded on the door. "Dammit! Her son is in here with her! She's sick, her breathing is shallow—whatever you bastards drugged us with, she's having a reaction."

"She'll be fine. Grow a pair."

"I will kill you. I will break your fucking neck! Keep me, I don't care, just take her and her son to a hospital."

"You're in no position to make demands, Mr. Rogan. Now, if I hear anything else from you, I'll come in and put a bullet in her head, then you won't have to worry about her at all."

He walked away.

Sean pounded one more time and sank to the floor. Jesse was at his side. Sean put his arm around his son. "We'll figure something out."

Jesse put his head on Sean's shoulder and Sean closed his eyes.

He had no idea how he was going to get out of here. Save Madison. Save his son. Save himself.

FBI ASAC Dean Hooper pulled up in front of Carson Spade's modest house only a mile from headquarters. He had two agents with him, but told them to stay out front.

Dean rarely deviated from the rule book, but he would if he had to—and this was one of those rare instances when he would prefer not having a witness if he had to play hardball with a lying money launderer.

Carson was surprised to see him. He was also nervous. He hid it well, but Dean had dealt with hundreds of white-collar criminals. Most of them weren't violent. One touch of violence in their orderly, illegal lives and they went full panic.

Dean entered without being asked.

"This isn't a good time," Carson said.

"This is the only time," Dean said. He closed the door behind him. "Honesty from this point on is the only thing that is going to keep you from spending the rest of your life in prison."

"Excuse *me*?" False indignation. Over the top.

"I know you've gotten a ransom demand, and you will work with me on this or so help me God, I will make sure everyone on your cellblock knows you had your wife and stepson kidnapped!"

"That's not true!"

Dean stepped toward him. Carson stepped back. Dean walked him all the way back to the small den. "I've had it up to here with you, Spade. You're already going to prison. You lied to the marshals when you went into witness protection. You lied to the AUSA about your banking accounts, and you lied to me about what you were doing here, in Sacramento, with Jeremy Robertson."

"This is not happening." Carson's voice grew weak.

"It is happening," Dean said. He pulled an envelope from his breast pocket. "I have the proof. Half a dozen bank accounts under a shell corp. And when I saw these, I thought, *This structure looks familiar. Why does it look familiar? Because it's the same way Carson Spade set up the money-laundering operation for the Flores cartel.* And I got a warrant and was able to dig deeper and because this is for a friend of mine, I worked straight through the night and all day and finally traced all of these accounts back to you and Madison."

"Leave her out of it."

"That's sweet, coming from the man who had his own wife kidnapped!"

"I didn't! Please, I had nothing to do with it."

"But you're not surprised that they're missing," Dean said, his voice low and angry.

Carson's mouth opened then closed. He walked to his computer and clicked a button. A disembodied monotone voice spoke.

"I have your wife and kid. You have twenty-four hours to raise twelve million dollars. I will call this time tomorrow with instructions. You know better than to call anyone."

"You bastard," Dean said.

Wife and kid. No mention of Sean, and so far, neither RCK nor Lucy had received a ransom demand for Sean. Dean hoped that didn't mean anything.

Dean called his best cybertech. "I need you at my location with all your equipment to backtrace a VOI and set up a phone trace."

"No!" Carson said, finally finding his voice. "He'll kill them."

To his cybertech, Dean said, "Thanks, Liz." Then he hung up.

"What are you doing?" Carson demanded. "You're risking their lives."

"This is my operation, and you're going to do everything I say or I will bury you so deep in the system you'll never see the light of day."

"You don't know what's going on."

"Don't I?" He pulled out another piece of paper. "You can thank Sean Rogan for finding this. An account—also under this shell corp—for one million transferred over to Jeremy Robertson. Payment for this kidnapping scheme?"

"I didn't have my wife kidnapped!"

"You have five seconds to tell me the truth." Dean paused. "Four. Three. Two."

"Okay! Fuck, fuck!" Carson paced. "I just wanted Jesse back home. Madison was depressed, she should never have let the kid go visit Rogan. Never! And Rogan turned Jesse against us. And I can prove it—Jesse wants to change his name to Rogan! Madison was in tears when she found out. All I did was give Jeremy a little money to put a scare into Rogan so he'd send Jesse home. *No one* was supposed to go after Jesse. I love my son. I raised him! I was there for him! If Madison thought Rogan had a dangerous job, then she would insist he send Jesse home."

Dean believed every word. It sounded like a desperate and stupid plan, with just enough plausibility that someone like Carson would think it might work.

Carson continued his rant. "Rogan has no rights, none! And it would have worked, Madison went there to get him, and I would have gone with her but I couldn't because of my stupid agreement with your office. Ridiculous! And then . . . and then Rogan wouldn't let Madison leave. He manipulated her, brainwashed her that someone was after Jesse, and that he was safer there. Well, that was a lie, wasn't it? He wasn't safer there! He was in danger because of Sean Rogan! I will kill him, I swear to the Almighty God, Sean Rogan is a dead man."

"Threat duly noted," Dean said.

"I mean—I didn't mean it like that—"

"Let me tell you what I think. I think that one million dollars is a hefty payment for 'scaring' someone, but right in the ballpark of a high-profile hit. Considering that your good ol' friend Jeremy hired a known fixer and hit man to take care of this project tells me that you had one of two plans: Either you wanted to increase the threat to you so that the marshals would put you back into WITSEC, or you paid to have Sean killed."

"I would never put my son in danger!"

It clicked. "You wanted Jesse home first, then Sean would be assassinated."

"No." But his voice was weak.

"Your plan is a bust, Carson. So you'd better work with me because if Sean, Madison, or Jesse turn up dead, I will prosecute you for murder one, in the state of Texas, with special circumstances, and I will be very happy to watch you fry."

If Carson could go any more pale he'd be dead.

"I—I—"

"Tell me everything."

"Why would Jeremy do this? Why?"

"Because there is no honor among thieves. And it's about fucking time you realized it."

An hour later Dean Hooper called Rick Stockton, who brought Lucy Kincaid in on the call. "Lucy, hang in there," Dean said when she got on the three-way call.

"I am."

She sounded worried, but strong.

"Carson set everything in motion, just like Sean thought. And I can't wait until he gets out of this and tells me that he was right, yet again," Dean said, trying to bring levity to the situation before he dropped the bombshell.

"What did he set in motion, Dean?" Lucy asked.

"His goal was to push Sean into sending Jesse back to Sacramento, either Sean doing it himself or Madison insisting. It didn't work out like he thought."

"No shit."

Dean had never heard Lucy swear. He cleared his throat. "The original plan was to remove Jesse from the situation, then assassinate Sean. One million was paid up front to Jeremy Robertson to accomplish both goals. I have since convinced Carson that after Jeremy accepted the money, he realized that Carson was hiding far more from law enforcement—funds that both Jeremy and Carson knew would negate the plea agreement Carson made with the AUSA. Jeremy is blackmailing Carson into turning over all his other illegal funds for the safe return of his wife and son."

"He's going to do it, right? We can go after Robertson later."

"He wants to do it, but we're holding off. We have"—he glanced at his watch, which he put on a countdown clock as soon as he timed everything out—"a little less than nineteen hours to put together a rescue plan."

"But if he pays—"

"If he pays, Madison and Jesse will be released, if we can trust the word of Jeremy Robertson's hired gun, which I'm skeptical about. But if they *are* released, Sean will be killed—per the original agreement. If he doesn't pay, Madison and Jesse will die, and Sean will be freed. Carson wants to pay right now."

"Of course he does." Lucy took a deep breath. "But a child's life is at stake. Sean would never want us to play with his son's life."

"We have time," Dean stressed. "And remember—Jeremy Robertson already reneged on one deal with Spade; he could be blowing smoke up our ass about releasing Madison and Jesse. Rick—what's the game plan? You're the boss."

"We're looking for Jeremy Robertson now. We confirmed he's still in San Antonio, but he checked out of his hotel room yesterday—maybe he was worried Carson would talk, or maybe he wanted to distance himself from the kidnapping. We know who Robertson hired to put the plan in motion, a corrupt ex-cop named Bart Vasquez. Problem is, because Vasquez is an ex-cop he still has some friends in blue. We have two unmarked units out in front of his office, but my guess is that he's in the wind. We're looking for a place Vasquez controls where he can keep three hostages under wraps. They used three identical vans, which makes tracking them difficult, but we have our best cybercrimes people on the ground poring over camera footage. When the time comes, we already have a warrant in place—coming out of DC so Vasquez won't hear about it—to raid his house and office. But that's last resort—we don't want to spook him or his people into killing the hostages."

"How are Jack and Kane?"

"Recuperating. I've forbidden them to go out tonight, but I'm not their boss."

Lucy said quietly, "Kane has a severely sprained

ankle, he's not going anywhere. But Jack will be ready when we have intel."

"I'm not going to tell you to stand down, Lucy, but—"

"Then don't say it, Rick. I'm going to get them all back. Safe. Dean, keep your eye on Carson. I don't trust him. He may release the money just to have Sean killed, since he knows he's already going to prison."

"He's secured and won't be talking to anyone outside my presence."

"Thank you. But we have to be prepared to release the funds—if there's a chance we can save Jesse." There was a hitch to her voice, and Dean knew that this was far harder on her than she let on.

Rick said, "No one is releasing any money to that bastard. We're going to find them and everyone involved is going down. That's an order, Kincaid."

Lucy hung up and rubbed her eyes. She was sitting at Sean's desk. The office was a mess, but she'd sorted through the papers. He had been going through the shell corporations plus digging into Jeremy Robertson's finances. Dean probably knew about but turned a blind eye to Sean's snooping.

Lucy didn't know what she would do if Sean didn't make it out of this. Her greatest fear was losing him. She'd lost people she'd loved before, not least of whom was her nephew Justin. That loss had defined her in so many ways; it had in part made her who she was today. When her brother Patrick was in a coma for nearly two years, she'd feared he would be like that for the rest of his life, neither dead nor alive, just existing. It had tortured her because it was her fault he'd ended up that way. Though intellectually she knew she wasn't the one who planted the explosives that resulted in the accident, emotionally she blamed herself because Patrick had been looking for her. To save her.

She couldn't lose the man she loved, the man she expected to live with for the rest of her life. Sean made her whole, he made her a better version of herself. He had confidence in her, faith in her, and he made her laugh. They just hadn't had enough time! Time to love each other. Time to have fun. Time to grow old and, someday, adopt children to raise and love, children who needed them.

Everyone in the San Antonio FBI office was working on finding Sean, Madison, and Jesse. Everyone. She had to believe in her colleagues.

Jack walked in.

"I told you to sleep," she said.

Jack lifted her out of the chair and hugged her tightly. She took his love freely. She needed it.

"Sean spent all afternoon in here," Jack said. "He was working on something. What was it?"

"I think everything Dean told him not to do. These are Robertson's financial statements, and I don't quite know what this list means." She held up a list of names and numbers in Sean's handwriting

"Can you look at his computer history?"

"No—he doesn't save history." But she sat down at Sean's computer and logged in anyway. "But I can see anything he manually saved. Here—the last file he was looking at was exactly what I thought. Robertson's banking information." She frowned.

"What?"

"This—it's not Robertson's bank. It's Bart Vasquez. Shit, Sean's going to get into deep trouble for this. He downloaded Vasquez's banking information to his computer." She almost deleted it, but didn't. Sean always cleaned up after himself, because he never wanted to put her at risk. But he never let her see him do anything in the gray area—or anything blatantly illegal.

"He must have had a reason."

"Yeah, he knew that Robertson was working with him. But I don't see what—oh. This is his business information, not his personal information. Wait, wait, wait . . ." She scrolled through. "Payroll!"

"Sean was trying to find out who worked for him."

"This is completely illegal, but—"

"Lucy, just read it. We'll deal with the fallout when Sean is safe."

"Vasquez pays via direct deposit into six different personal accounts amounts anywhere from a thousand a week to two thousand a week—numbers to keep well below the IRS threshold. Sean has the list of those names."

"Let's go."

"You're not going anywhere, Jack. You still look green."

"I'm not letting you go out there alone, and Nate hasn't returned."

"I can call—"

"Dammit, Lucy, I'm going. And I'm calling Nate. I know he wants to find Bandit, but finding Sean is more important."

"Nate will be here when we need him."

CHAPTER THIRTY-SEVEN

The FBI split the list of names Lucy gave them. She didn't tell anyone where she got them, and hoped she didn't have to. One of the names was of the man who was currently in surgery, the man Kane had shot in the kitchen. The other five all lived in San Antonio.

They didn't have the time or manpower to coordinate a simultaneous raid on each of the five unless they spread their people too thin, so each team of four took two names, and Lucy took three that were clustered together.

She had Leo, one of Leo's best men, Rod Rodriguez, and Jason Lopez, who had been the first to respond to the situation when she called it in. She appreciated his show of support. Jack was with them as well but he was a civilian and not at full strength.

The first house was empty. The other two men lived in the same apartment building a mile from the house. While Jason and Rod watched the front, Lucy and Leo went to the first apartment, under the name Bruce

Anders. Bruce's girlfriend answered, insisted he no longer lived there, told them to go to hell and if they didn't have a warrant they could go fuck themselves.

Lucy looked around the filthy place. "You know, your boyfriend makes a cool thousand a week, but it doesn't look like he's sharing any of it with you."

"Fuck off, bitch."

She didn't believe her. Lucy didn't care, because she didn't get the sense that the guy was around. The woman slammed the door in her face.

They headed back downstairs. Through the com she heard Rod say, "Thompson is running!"

"Don't let him get away!" Lucy called and took the stairs double time, running out to the front and following Rodriguez.

Billy Thompson was a younger kid, in his early twenties, who lived in the same large apartment complex as Bruce Anders. He was fast and agile, but he still had to traverse a winding path through the buildings and leap over hedges.

Jason said in her ear, "I'll cut him off through the back."

Lucy could run well, but wearing Kevlar slowed her down. She kept up with Rod, though, and they burst out together into the back parking lot just in time to see Jason tackle the kid, slamming his body against a parked car.

"Let me go!" Thompson shouted. "Police brutality!"

"Shut the fuck up," Jason mumbled, rubbing his jaw from where Thompson nailed him as he flailed about.

He rolled him over and handcuffed him, then sat him back up.

Lucy shined her flashlight in his face. "Where did Vasquez take the hostages?"

"Who?"

"I'm not in the mood, Billy."

"I don't know whatcha talking about, ma'am."

"Fuck this," Lucy said. She pulled out her phone and scrolled through the security feeds at her house. She found one of the vans out front, and there was Billy Thompson leaning out of the driver's seat. She shoved the phone in his face. "The men who broke into the house to kidnap a man, woman, and child had masks. The drivers did not. You have the right to remain silent, but I swear, if you don't tell me what the fuck I want to know, I will forget where I put you for the next ten years."

No one said anything. Were they surprised by her outburst? She wasn't. All her rage had been pent up for so long that it was ready to explode.

"I-I-I d-don't know," he stuttered. "I-I don't. I swear. I didn't drive the van with the cargo."

That might help. They had tracked the vans to a point after the fact, but lost them. If they could focus resources on one trail, they might find Sean sooner.

"Which van did you drive."

"Um, it was white."

Lucy wanted to hit him. She refrained. "They were identical white vans. You left the neighborhood. Were you the van that went north on I-Thirty-Five, south on

I-Thirty-Five past I-Ten, or south on I-Thirty-Five then east on I-Ten."

He looked confused. "I-I don't know."

"No one is this stupid, Billy. Which way did you go?"

"S-south. South all the way to the bar on Guadalupe, where we were to meet and get paid."

"And did you meet and get paid?"

"Y-yes."

"Which van had the cargo?"

"Am I in trouble?"

"What do you think?"

"I was just a driver!"

"Tell it to your priest. Where was the cargo heading?"

"I don't know. But they went east on I-Ten. I don't know where, I swear, they never told any of us, only the driver of that van. And he didn't meet with us at the bar, he works directly for Mr. Vasquez."

"What is his name."

"Then I can go?"

"Sure."

"Bubba Dobbins."

"His real name."

"That is his real name. His mother named him Bubba after her brother. I swear. Now can I go?"

"Absolutely. You can go straight to central booking."

"But-but-but you said—"

Lucy was already walking away while Jason and Rod read Billy his rights. Leo said, "How did you know you had a photo of him?"

"I didn't remember the face. But that isn't a kid who can go into a house in full tactical gear and do what he's supposed to do, so I made a guess that he was a driver and lucked out." She looked around. "Where's Jack?"

"He was in the tactical truck."

She walked briskly back to the main parking lot. Jack wasn't there. He was coming down the stairs from the first suspect's apartment. "Don't do that," she told him.

He simply looked at her. He handed her a piece of paper. "That's the list of all the places her low-life boyfriend Bruce Anders who gives her nothing but shit hangs out." He smiled. "More flies with honey, little sister."

Nate found Bandit over near Dafoste Park, miles from Sean's house, limping and panting. He immediately stopped his truck and called the dog. Bandit came to him, and Nate hugged him, then gave him water. He drank all of it. Nate dug around for another bottle and Bandit drank all of that, too.

"Good boy. Get in."

Bandit didn't budge.

"You're looking for Sean. So am I. You need to get into my truck, Bandit."

Bandit whined.

They were in a residential neighborhood. Vasquez wouldn't be holding Sean and the others here. But not far off was an industrial area, and that was the direction Bandit was heading.

How did Nate explain to the dog that he wanted to find Sean, too?

He sat down on the ground. Bandit whimpered and looked down the road.

"Okay," Nate said. "We'll do it your way." He was about to lock up his truck and walk with Bandit when Bandit jumped into the passenger seat.

Nate shut the door and ran around to the driver's seat. He rolled down the window so Bandit could smell. Maybe it was something about the exhaust, or he'd seen the van in the area, or what, Nate didn't know. But Bandit had been going through search-and-rescue training, and maybe something in his dog brain told him they were going in the right direction.

Nate drove slow and Bandit had his head out the window. When Nate got to an intersection, Bandit barked. Nate had no idea what that meant. He went straight. Bandit barked again. Nate backed up—thankful there was no traffic after midnight—and turned right. Bandit seemed happy.

Nate couldn't believe he was letting the dog navigate, but he didn't have any other ideas, and Lucy would call if she needed him.

He continued east.

Sean wished he had his watch so he knew how much time had passed. He suspected a couple of hours. No one had come in to talk to them or give them food or water.

"Dad."

Jesse was sitting with his mom.

Sean walked over. He was getting his strength back but still had a bitch of a headache.

"Something's wrong with my mom," Jesse said.

Sean feared the worst. But he hadn't known what to do for her. He walked over, knelt on the hard floor. Found Madison's cool hand.

Too cool.

He felt for her pulse.

He felt nothing. When he let her hand go, her arm fell heavily.

He put his hand on her chest.

Nothing. No rise and fall. No heartbeat.

Tears burned.

"Dad?" Jesse's voice was full of fear. He knew. Instinctively, Jesse knew his mother was dead.

Sean was certain she'd slipped away sometime in the last thirty minutes, after he'd last checked on her. But he didn't know what to do! He had nothing here, no equipment, no skills. He wasn't even an EMT who might have known what was wrong with her. All he knew was that they had been drugged . . . and she never woke up.

"Dad." Jesse wrapped his arms around Sean's neck, his body shaking with silent sobs.

Sean clutched him tightly. "I'm so sorry." His voice cracked.

He, too, had lost his mother when he was a young teenager. He had seen her dead and broken body after the plane crash and the rage and pain that fueled him had stuck with him for many years.

He felt it again. It was hot, burning, powerful, and he didn't know how to contain it.

Except that he had someone—more than one

someone—to live for. And Jesse was counting on him to find a way out of here.

Sean would not let his son down.

And when he could, he would make everyone pay for the fact that Jesse was forced to sit with his mother as she died, trapped in a dark room with her lifeless body.

Sometimes, old-fashioned police work worked best.

Lucy had a team behind her, and realized that a team that she trusted was the single greatest asset she could have as a law enforcement officer. They were all of one mind, they all knew what to do, and they all worked and gave above and beyond to track down where Vasquez was keeping Sean, Madison, and Jesse.

The information obtained from Thompson and Anders's girlfriend led them to a bar—not on Guadalupe, but on the southeast side, where the two a.m. curfew didn't mean much of anything and several dive bars clustered together in a two-block radius. The truck that had run Lucy and Jesse off the road was in the parking lot, clear because of the dent in the front passenger side and the scrapes off the paint. A good forensics tech would be able to match the paint with that on her car. She ran the plates.

Bubba Dobbins. It was nice that they had him now on two charges.

They raided the place, and ended up with half of Vasquez's team in custody. Lucy and Leo pulled Bubba Dobbins aside while the rest of his gang were being cuffed and read their rights.

"You have one minute to make a deal," Leo said. "Where did you take the hostages?"

"What hostages? You're crazy, cop."

"We already flipped one of your guys, we know you drove the cargo. We know you took them somewhere east, and if you don't tell us, you'll be an accessory to special circumstances kidnapping—drugging and transporting a minor under the age of fourteen."

"What? That's a law?" Dobbins looked closely at Lucy. "I know you."

"You ran me off the road. That's attempted murder of a federal officer."

"Murder? Hell, it wasn't murder. We was just supposed to grab you and the kid, not hurt anyone. But we was told to back off, the cops were nearly there and you had a gun and—oh."

Not the sharpest tack in the box.

"Where are they, Bubba?"

He rubbed the back of his head. "What do I get out of it?"

"I don't tell Bart Vasquez that you turned on him."

"What? I mean, jail. I don't go to jail, right?"

"You ran a federal agent off the road and kidnapped three people, I don't think you're going to avoid jail time. But," Lucy said, "if you tell me right now, no more fucking around, I'll say something nice about you to the prosecutor."

"You'd do that for me? After I, like, totaled your car?"

"Yes. Now."

"It's an abandoned junkyard over off East Houston.

Don't have the address, but you can't miss it. It takes up the entire block."

"Where in the junkyard?"

"There's just one building in the middle. Crap all around, rusting and shit."

Lucy and Leo passed Bubba off to an SAPD officer, and Lucy called Nate.

"Nate, I know you're looking for Bandit, but I need you."

"I found him. He's okay. His paws are a mess, but he's going to be okay."

Lucy was relieved.

"We're heading out to a junkyard on East Houston. One of Vasquez's men gave it up."

"I know exactly where it is. In fact, I'm almost there."

"How?"

"Bandit. He was tracking the van. I don't know how, but he did, and we're just around the corner from that place."

"Wait for us, Nate. We're ten minutes out."

Sean went over the plan with Jesse for the third time. Jesse didn't want to do it. He didn't want to leave his dad. He glanced over to where his mother was on a cot, dead. She was dead. He felt numb. He didn't know what to do, what to think. He wanted everything back the way it was.

"But I don't want to leave you," he said. He sounded like a little kid, but he didn't care. He was scared and if he ran he didn't know what would happen.

"Jesse, listen to me, please," Sean said. "This is the only way it works. I'm the distraction. You slip out. Run, don't look back. Get out of the building. Hide if you have to, then at the first opportunity to get help, do it."

"But what if they hurt you? What if—what if they—I can't lose you, too, Dad."

"I know you're scared. I'm just as scared."

"You're scared? Then why can't we just wait? Wait for Lucy and Nate to find us?"

"Because we don't know exactly what's going on, if they have a good lead, if they even know where to start looking. They have to process clues and evidence and that takes time. Sometimes we have to save ourselves. I will be okay. I promise."

"You don't know that."

"Jesse, the only thing that matters is that you're safe, do you understand?"

"No. You need to be okay. You need to come with me. I'm not going by myself." He was crying and he didn't care.

"You have to. I know this is hard, Jess, but you need to be brave and step up, right now. If we sit here we're only going to get more tired, more dehydrated, and I'll never be able to fight them off. But I can buy you time, okay?"

Jesse hugged him tight. He didn't know what to do, but he trusted his dad. "Okay."

Sean took a deep breath. "Showtime, Jess."

He pounded on the door. "Someone! Help! Madison isn't breathing! For shitsake! We need help in here!" He pounded again. Waited. Pounded. "We need a doctor!

No one's going to pay ransom if she's dead! We need fucking help! Now, you bastards!"

Someone hit the door. "Back off, Rogan. All the way to the wall or I'll shoot you. I get paid either way."

"I'm backing off. Please, just get Madison to a doctor."

Sean turned to Jesse. "Be ready." Jesse was flat against the wall next to the door. Sean was standing next to Madison's body.

The door opened. There were lights outside, and for a second Sean couldn't see anything except a big hulking shadow. Then two shadows.

"Got out of your ties, I see. Turn around, Rogan, and we'll secure you."

"She's not breathing!" Sean picked up Madison's arm. "She's dying. Don't you get it? She's in serious trouble."

"Back away from her."

Sean took two steps back.

One of the men walked in. The other blocked the doorway.

The second man said, "Where's the kid?"

"Sleeping," Sean said. "By the lockers."

Both men looked. Sean took that moment to throw bleach cleaner into the face of the man closest to him. He grabbed the mop handle and jabbed him hard in the stomach.

The second man ran in and Jesse ran out behind him. Thank God he obeyed.

The first man couldn't speak. He was down on his knees.

"She's dead, you fucking bastards. You killed her." Sean took the mop handle and swung it at the second thug. He fought with Sean over it and Sean let go. The guy stumbled backward.

"Victor! We need help in here!" the second guy shouted.

Sean pushed him and the brute got a punch square in Sean's jaw. Shit, that hurt! But he needed to buy Jesse time to get out.

He collapsed to his knees by the door. Pulled the hooks out of his pockets. The first guy was still out of commission, and Sean could hear shouts of the other men outside the room. The brute pulled Sean and was about to slam him against the wall when Sean took the hook and aimed for his face.

He must have been right on target because the thug screamed and his grip on Sean loosened. Sean kicked his feet out from under him and turned to run, right into a guy much larger than him. Victor.

And Victor had a gun.

"You'll watch your girlfriend and the brat die before I put a bullet in your head."

One of the thugs said, "The kid. Isn't. Here."

A gunshot far in the distance, in the junkyard, had Sean enraged.

"If you hurt my son, I will tear you apart!" The rage made him blind. He had to be smart.

The second man stumbled out of the locker room, bleeding from his eye. He tried to hit Sean, but his aim was off and Sean used his momentum against him and shoved him toward Victor, then he ran. He wanted to kill them both, but self-preservation and the overwhelming need to find Jesse and make sure he was safe filled him.

He heard the gun at the same time he felt the burning in the back of his left arm. Thank God the guy was a bad shot—six inches or so to the right and it would have gone through his heart.

Sean ran.

Jesse ran as his dad had instructed.

Run and don't look back.

He had no idea where he was going. There was a lot of junk in the building, but it was mostly pushed to the side, and he ran down a wide hall, away from where he heard shouts. He could probably hide in here somewhere, but Sean said to get out, get out of the building.

A door was directly in front of him. He pushed at it. It was stuck. He pushed harder.

"That's the kid!" he heard far behind him.

The door had one of those sliding bolts on the top, and Jesse stood on his toes to push it up and out of the lock. The door opened and he stumbled out.

"Stop, kid! Stop or I'll shoot!"

"Don't kill him! We need him for the money. Shit, Conrad, you're an idiot."

Jesse missed the rest of the conversation because he was in the yard.

It was dark. He could see some lights far off, but everywhere around him were towering piles of rusting metal, broken cars, old pipes. He hesitated just a second, then turned to the right because that looked like it had the widest path.

Behind him he heard the door slam open again. "Go right, I'll go left."

Maybe Jesse could find a place to hide. But wouldn't they find him? The path was getting narrower. He turned and came right up against a fence. He was trapped.

A dog barked. Were there dogs patrolling? Was he going to be attacked by an animal? Could he climb one of the car piles? Hide above everything?

Then he saw a golden retriever. He barked again.

"Bandit?"

"Down!" he heard, though he couldn't see where the voice came from. Bandit dropped to the ground, and so did Jesse. He heard a gunshot, and then a guy grunted and fell into a pile of metal.

"Jess, it's Nate."

"Nate?"

This all felt unreal.

Bandit ran over and licked Jesse's face. Jesse hugged him tightly.

The sound of a gunshot from inside the building behind them made Jesse jump.

"Dad—Nate, you have to save my dad!"

Nate was talking to someone else.

"I have Jesse. He's safe, I'm taking him out."

"No, no, my dad is in there. He's your best friend. Don't leave him, you have to save him!"

There was another gunshot and Jesse screamed in frustration.

Nate grabbed him by the arm. "There's a team going

in to save Sean and Madison right this minute. They know you're safe, and my job is to get you out of here."

"My mom is dead. She never woke up. I can't lose my dad, too. I can't. Please, Nate."

Nate put his arm protectively around Jesse. "I'm so sorry, buddy. I'm so sorry." He relayed the information over the com and brought Jesse out the way he and Bandit came in, through a hole in the fence that he had cut himself.

The first gunshot came from deep in the junkyard, and Leo told his SWAT team to be ready on his order.

The men were in formation.

When Lucy heard the second gunshot, much closer, she knew that someone was in trouble.

She turned to Leo. He was fully decked out in SWAT gear and had his men ready. She had to go in behind them. She wasn't SWAT.

Leo was listening to his com. "Nate has Jesse. Delta team, meet Agent Dunning and one hostage at the south fence, stat. Beta team, go go go! Alpha team, go go go!"

Leo led the Alpha team from here; Beta team was set up at the other entrance. Lucy stood at the entrance with Jason Lopez, in protective gear but not part of the team.

Through the coms she heard orders as SWAT commanded everyone they encountered to get down, hands up.

She heard *clear, clear, clear*. Four hostiles were being escorted out.

"We have a body. Female. Medic, stat."

Two medics ran in. They were agents, but not SWAT. Once SWAT cleared the situation, the paramedics could go in.

Suddenly she heard Leo command everyone to stop.

"Put the gun down, young man," Leo said over the com.

Lucy went in.

"Don't, Lucy," Jason said.

She ignored him.

Lucy followed the path SWAT took and stood immediately behind Rod Rodriguez, who was holding position outside a room. His gun was trained on a large man who held a gun to Sean's head. Sean's arm was bleeding.

Leo was in front of his men. He was trying to talk the man down. "Everyone else surrendered. You're the only one holding out. Is Vasquez worth that? Is he worth your life? Because I guarantee that you will die if you pull that trigger."

"This prick will die, too."

"Don't be so sure of that," Leo said. "I've seen Rogan here get out of trickier situations. Like the time that lovestruck psycho held a kid and a DEA agent at gunpoint. *Right*, Sean?"

That wasn't Sean, that was her, Lucy realized. But Sean knew exactly what Leo wanted him to do—a command to go *right*. At the time, Lucy knew that there had been a sniper set up to take a shot, but she had to maneuver the shooter into his line of sight. This time, all Sean had to do was move so he wouldn't be in the line of fire.

Sean immediately understood, leaning to the right

and dropping to the ground so quickly she almost didn't see him act. Lucy couldn't see who took the shot, but it took the left side of the gunman's skull clear off as soon as Sean had moved. The man went down without firing a shot.

Sean stumbled away.

"Medic!" Lucy called as she ran over to Sean.

"Jess—"

"Nate has him."

"I thought I sent him to his death. I thought my plan wasn't going to work. I was so scared."

"You've been shot."

"I'm okay." Sean grabbed her and held on. "Madison is dead. I couldn't protect them, Luce. I promised they would be safe, and they weren't. I couldn't protect anyone."

"You did, Sean. Jesse is safe."

But he wasn't listening to her. He just held her tight, his entire body shaking uncontrollably as he silently sobbed.

CHAPTER THIRTY-EIGHT

Jesse insisted on staying with Sean while he went to the hospital to get stitches in his arm. Lucy recognized that Jesse was partly in shock and feared that he was going to lose another parent. He hadn't completely wrapped his head around his grief, and there was no way she was going to let him—or Sean—out of her sight.

Nate drove them home at dawn. While Sean had been in the hospital, Nate took Bandit to a vet, who cleaned his raw paws and stitched up a cut on his leg. Other than that, Bandit was in good shape. He sat in the backseat of Nate's truck between Jesse and Sean. Jesse had his head down on the pup and Sean had his arm around his son.

They were going to be okay, Lucy thought. Time. Time and love, which she had in spades.

The house was a mess, but Kane told Lucy he was taking care of it. She and Sean took Jesse upstairs to his room. He practically collapsed in exhaustion. They sat with him in silence for several minutes before leaving him, with the door open.

Lucy and Sean went to their room and Sean sat on the end of the bed. "You need to sleep," Lucy said.

"Madison is dead."

"Shh. We'll talk about this later when you've rested and eaten. Sean, you can't put this on your shoulders. You did everything humanly possible. Sometimes we can't plan for every possible scenario."

"I promised to protect them. He's never going to forgive me."

"Sean, Jesse does not blame you for any of this. There is nothing to forgive. You saved him, and if he had been in that room when Leo's team came in, you don't know that he wouldn't have been the one with a gun to his head."

She held Sean tight until he finally drifted to sleep. She lay there with him, dozed for a bit, but was never truly asleep. Noises downstairs drifted up, and she made sure Sean was still sleeping, then left, closing the door so he could have quiet.

She checked on Jesse down the hall. He was sound asleep, Bandit with him. It was as if the dog sensed that Jesse needed him more, because Sean had her. She walked over and gave Bandit a hug and a scratch. "Good dog," she whispered. She closed Jesse's door and went downstairs.

Kane was directing a work crew who were cleaning up the broken glass and boarding up the windows. "I ordered glass already. They came, measured, and promised to install by Thursday. They're rushing it."

"Thank you, Kane. Is Jack sleeping?"

"Finally. Why aren't you?"

"I did for a bit."

Nate walked out of Sean's office. "I didn't know you were still here," she said.

"I was ordered to take the morning off."

"Doesn't seem like you're resting."

"I was on the phone with AD Stockton. Jeremy Robertson was taken into custody as he tried to board a plane to Mexico. SAPD arrested Bart Vasquez as he was shredding files. They searched his house and found the plans for your house and how they intended to raid the place. He won't be getting out of prison—there are state and federal charges, and everyone involved is going to get a Murder One charge for Madison. Stockton is on top of it. I swear, that man doesn't sleep."

"Dean Hooper called me when I was at the hospital with Sean," Lucy said. "He arrested Carson Spade. He'll be arraigned sometime today on all the charges he got a pass on because of his plea deal—one of the agreements was that if he knowingly lied, he would be held accountable for everything he confessed to. Plus, there are additional charges, including hiring a hit man." She glanced upstairs. It could have been so much worse. Sean could be dead.

"How is my brother?" Kane asked.

"He has this deep guilt that he couldn't protect Jesse and Madison. I don't know how he's going to get through this. He's not listening to me."

"He always listens to you, Luce. It'll just take him a couple days to absorb everything. Um, is it okay that

Siobhan comes up tomorrow? When I talked to her this morning, she wanted to see you and Sean, make sure everyone is fine. She's a mother hen, I swear."

"I can't wait to see her." Siobhan had become a good friend, and she was the best thing to happen to Kane. Sometimes, Lucy thought that Kane was still in awe of his relationship with the photojournalist.

Lucy went to her kitchen. Someone had already cleaned up, and all remnants of the tainted pizza were gone. She took a deep breath. Then another. She hoped Sean could get past this, because she was torn up inside. The man she loved was in pain, and she didn't know how to fix it.

She drank a bottle of water, then brought another up for Sean when he woke. She climbed into bed next to him and fell asleep.

An hour later, at one that afternoon, Lucy's phone vibrated and woke her up.

"Hey," she said quietly. It was Leo.

"We have a development. Are you up for meeting me down at SAPD as soon as possible? I'm leaving my house now, it'll take me about thirty minutes to get there." Like Nate, Leo had been ordered to go home and sleep after filing his report early this morning on the SWAT action.

"I'll be there."

She turned to Sean, who was now awake. "Go," Sean said.

"Are you sure? Leo will understand."

"I'm okay."

"I'm not. I nearly lost you. Again."

He kissed her, then rested his forehead on hers. "I don't know how to help Jesse."

"Yes, you do. Love him."

Lucy took a quick shower. When she went downstairs, the windows were completely boarded up and all the glass was gone. Jack was dozing on the couch, and she tried not to wake him. "Where are you going?" he said without opening his eyes.

"Work."

"You get time off."

"It's the case I've been working. We have a break. Leo wouldn't have called unless it was important."

Jack sat up and stretched. "How's Sean?"

"Feeling guilty."

"He has nothing to feel guilty about."

Lucy glanced around. No one was about. "I told him that. He told Jesse and Madison that they were safe here, and then his house—the place he feels the safest—was attacked."

"He couldn't have known what would happen."

"He thinks he should have known and protected against it."

"He did. He brought me and Kane to help because he knew he needed help. Sean is a guy who hates asking for help, but will do it when it matters. We fucked up."

"Jack—don't. None of this is your fault or Kane's. It's the fault of the men who planned an assault against our home. Really—it took twelve men to take you all out *and* you were drugged. Still, Kane got one." She sat next to her brother and hugged him. "I'm glad you are okay. I was so terrified when I came in. They could have killed you all. Twelve against three—Madison and Jesse wouldn't have been able to defend themselves."

"Megan's not really happy with me right now—I didn't quite tell her exactly what happened, but Hooper has a big fucking mouth and I'm not going to be talking to him for a while. I'm flying back tomorrow."

"I'll miss you."

"Same here, kid. But Siobhan is replacing me."

"Kane told me."

"I eavesdropped on Kane's Skype call with her this morning and she forbade him to fly down and get her tomorrow. She's coming back with a church group or something, and she wants to be here for all of you. She's a good woman. Kane sure did nothing to deserve her."

He was joking, of course; Jack had a lot of respect for his partner.

"I'm glad. She'll bring joy back to the house."

"What's Sean doing about Madison?"

"I don't know what's going to happen. I suspect her father will take over the arrangements."

"And Jesse?"

"Sean's not letting him go. He'll fight his grandfather if he has to. He hasn't said anything about it, but I know him. We're in for the long haul."

"Good."

"I have to go. Keep an eye on them for me?"

"You don't even have to ask."

By the time Lucy got to the lab, she was surprised to see Tia Mancini, Julie Peters, and Dr. Moreno there with

Leo, along with a young man who looked extremely nervous talking to Ash Dominguez off to the side.

"I'm sorry I'm so late," Lucy said.

Leo waved it off. "We have more news since I got off the phone with you—I asked Julie and Dr. Moreno to come down to compare notes with Ash. And this is Adam Hornbeck. He's at the university as well. In fact, he works under Dr. Moreno."

"Adam—you mean the friend of Cassidy's?"

"Um," Adam said, obviously nervous, "are you looking for her? I'm worried."

"Yes," Leo said, "we have a BOLO out for her, but explain what you found. In layman's terms, because I didn't know what the hell you were talking about ten minutes ago."

"Cassidy was really worried about her boss—well, former boss—Mr. McMahon. And when he took those hostages—she brought me his hair samples to test because she was positive he had been drugged with something that affected his memory."

Dr. Moreno said, "After the evidence went missing, Julie insisted that I add an extra layer of security to my lab. That's how I learned that Adam had come in during the middle of the night to run specialized tests."

Adam looked nervous. "I'm really sorry about that, Dr. Moreno."

"We'll discuss it later. Your findings were rather amazing." The doctor sounded impressed. "Adam's friend Cassidy had given him hair samples from the deceased, and he ran all the standard tests to no avail, but developed a rather ingenious methodology to help him narrow the testing. As you know, a lab is only as good as what it can test for. But what if you don't know what to test for? With limited equipment and resources, most labs can't run every conceivable test on a limited sample. With a little help and refinement, Adam, I think your system can be adapted for all labs."

"You showed me what I was doing wrong," Adam said, sounding more starstruck than guilty now. "Instead of focusing on a more broad spectrum, I researched a bit and found drugs that could affect the acetylcholine level in the brain."

"Which is?" Lucy asked.

"Acetylcholine is the primary neurotransmitter for memory, and necessary for learning and retaining new information. The lack of it has been linked to Alzheimer's."

"Which is what McMahon was researching," Moreno said.

"Exactly, which I knew, and because in research we often look at the *causes* of what we're trying to cure, it made sense that CHR would be researching drugs that inhibited acetylcholine in order to find a combination of drugs that would prevent its breakdown."

Dr. Moreno said, "Once I started working with Adam, we were able to cover far more ground, and we determined that McMahon had been drugged with an anticholinergic. We weren't able to narrow down the exact drug, but we did break it apart into its components and would thus be able to compare it with a source. About four months ago—at the end of March—McMahon was given a large dose of the anticholinergic.

Common side effects are confusion and light-headedness, among others, but not generally headaches—which we know that he experienced. There was another compound that I have yet to identify that I think created the headaches so that he would continue to dose himself with the anticholinergic."

"You lost me again, Doc," Leo said.

"When I inspected Mr. McMahon's brain again and ran additional tests on the compounds, I realized that the initial dose had—essentially—zapped him. I know that's not a scientific term, but it is the closest I can come to how he felt. The nerves that transmitted information from one part of his brain to the other stopped transmitting information in a coherent way. He could function, but the recent memories—whatever happened to him in March—were inaccessible. But as that other gentleman—Mr. Paine—indicated, he felt as if he perpetually was unable to think of the right word. For Mr. McMahon, it was worse because with the continued small dosing, any hope that those nerves would regain their strength diminished. That's why he continued to spiral down over the months, and no doubt that he would have died from this. The effects of several minor strokes showed up when I enlarged his scans, but he may not have noticed them because of his other symptoms."

"And the pills did it," Ash said. "The aspirin. We lost two boxes of evidence, but we had his clothing, and in his clothing were several aspirin. Reports from witnesses at Java Antonio indicated that he had been eating aspirin."

"Which I confirmed in his autopsy," Julie said. "The

stomach contents were lost—or stolen—in transit, but I still had blood samples in my lab, which I hand-delivered this morning to Ash."

"Long story short," Ash said, "the aspirin were tainted with the anticholinergic. The one large dose he got would have had long-term effects, but probably wouldn't have killed him. The continual dosing would have."

"How did the poison get into his pills?" Tia asked.

"Someone he trusted," Lucy said.

They turned to her.

"Paul Grey. It's why he killed himself."

"That's a leap," Tia said.

"Not really," Ash said. "The single pill found in Mr. Grey's car is a concentrated dose of the three that I tested from Mr. McMahon's pocket. Maybe he wanted someone to find it."

"He should have left a damn suicide note," Tia muttered.

"I think he did," Lucy said, "and Cassidy took it. Or she might have taken something else that would lead us to the same conclusion."

"Another leap," Tia said, "but I might be with you on this one."

Lucy continued. "She's been helping Charlie try to figure out what was going on with him, and up until Monday she'd been working at CHR. Maybe trying to get into the records, see if she could find anything to turn whistleblower. We know that Paul Grey planned on meeting her at five thirty Monday evening. I think they met and something she said had him wanting to help.

But then what? He backtracks? He gets cold feet? He pays off Charlie's debt to the bartender, apologizes for him, then goes to wherever he's supposed to meet Cassidy and kills himself. According to Vince Paine, she searched the car but left him there. Paine didn't think she found what she was looking for, but she could have found something."

Ash spoke up. "With Jackson's help from the FBI, I was able to identify the prints on the passenger door and glove box as belonging to Cassidy Roth. So it does reason that she searched the car. But I have no way of knowing if she took anything."

"So her prints are in the car, which confirms what Paine said."

"Why kill himself?" Leo asked. "He could have turned whistleblower if he had any evidence that pointed us here—which he did, with that pill. Even his testimony would help. He could have been granted immunity."

"Guilt?" Lucy suggested. "Because he knew whatever they did to Charlie would result in his death? Blackmail? Maybe he helped, and didn't think he would get a pass—or didn't deserve a pass. Maybe CHR had something on him that he didn't want getting out. We may never know, but he intentionally taped that pill under his steering column either for the police to find, or because he planned on giving it to Cassidy, but changed his mind."

"Okay, I'm with you. But then who moved his body? Who parked his car near McMahon's apartment?" Tia asked.

"Someone who wanted to frame McMahon so that

we wouldn't look into Grey's death," Lucy said. "Divert attention or muddy the waters."

"We need to find Cassidy because she very well could have the answers," Leo said.

Lucy snapped her fingers. "Franklin Clarke. He spoke to Charlie at Java Antonio. What did he say that might have set him off?"

Dr. Moreno said, "Whoever drugged Mr. McMahon turned his memories to mush. It was cruel and painful."

"Why didn't Cassidy tell McMahon that his friend was dead?" Tia asked. "If she saw Paul commit suicide as her friend indicated, why didn't she tell McMahon?"

"Maybe she didn't know how he would react to the information," Lucy suggested.

"Why would Cassidy do all this on her own?" Adam said. "Why didn't she go to the police with all this information?"

"We'll have to ask her when we find her," Leo said.

"I've been trying to call her since early this morning when Dr. Moreno and I figured it out, and her phone is going straight to voice mail."

"Did you talk to Franklin Clarke this morning?" Lucy asked Leo.

"I attempted to. He wasn't at CHR. I spoke to Dr. Harrison, and he called a full staff meeting. Franklin Clarke and his sister are both in the wind—and Grey's assistant, Nina Okala."

"The lawyer?"

"Claims he doesn't know anything."

"You believe him?"

"No. That's why he's sitting down the hall in an interrogation room, and Dr. Harrison has waived attorney–client privilege. Since Mr. Robert White works for the *company*, he has no individual that he ostensibly protects. Let's go shake him up."

It took Leo and Lucy fifteen minutes watching White posture and pontificate before he realized that he had no leg to stand on.

Lucy was surprised he didn't ask for a lawyer. Even if she had done nothing wrong, she would have asked for a lawyer to protect her rights.

"I was only privy to this situation after the fact," White said. "I had no foreknowledge that Cortland Clarke and Paul Grey conspired to cover up a failed clinical trial."

"So noted," Leo said.

Why White thought that would give him a pass, Lucy didn't know, but Leo's comment seemed to appease him.

Maybe he just wasn't a very good attorney.

"What I was *told*—again, I don't know *exactly* what happened because I wasn't there—was that last spring, a year ago, Dr. Grey ran a clinical trial that resulted in some serious side effects. It had to do with a dosing error—which he quickly realized and corrected. So the drug itself is completely safe, but several of the participants had long-term effects. They realized this in March when they conducted a follow-up. So yes, Dr. Grey corrected the error, but if they had reported it they would have had to go through the approval process again, conduct another clinical trial, and that would have taken twelve to twenty-four months, to the cost of millions of dollars."

Lucy just stared at him. She didn't trust herself to speak at that moment.

"And Charlie found out about the error."

"Not exactly. He found the falsified reports. He didn't know what they were, exactly, and wanted to review all the documentation of three years of research and trials—and that would have taken a lot of time and money."

"And he would have uncovered the dosing error," Lucy said.

"That was the fear, yes."

"And then?"

"I don't exactly know what happened at that point, but Cortland ordered Paul to fix the problem. We, um, Paul, well—"

"Spit it out," Leo said.

"Paul had been having an affair."

"So he was blackmailed."

"It's a little more complicated than that."

"More complicated than blackmail?"

"Paul was bisexual. This is Texas. I didn't care if he was gay, but you know how some people are."

"And he was married," Lucy said. "His wife didn't know."

"Franklin is really good at finding dirt on anyone," Robert said quietly.

"Does he have dirt on you?"

"He did. But when my wife divorced me, my affairs didn't matter anymore."

Lucy was beginning to like people less and less. Paul Grey drugged his best friend to cover up his own extramarital affair. The lawyer had cheated on his wife. It reminded her of the lies Madison Spade told Sean, and her culpability in her husband's money laundering. And the hidden money that Carson Spade used to order a hit on Sean.

Lucy wanted to see the good in people—she really did—but right now all she saw was the worst. It made her physically ill.

"So Paul was blackmailed into drugging his friend Charlie," Leo said bluntly.

"I wasn't told about any of this until Charlie was fired. Paul didn't realize what the side effects were, but he also didn't know until then that Cortland had had someone in the lab—I don't know how—create aspirin laced with this stuff. She was afraid that when the drug wore off he would remember everything, and she just wanted it to go away. And we thought it had, until last week."

"Monday. When Grey killed himself."

"What? Paul killed himself? No. Charlie killed him."

"Why do you think that?"

"Because Paul's body was in Charlie's house!"

"That information was only released to his family. We kept it in house until the investigation was complete. Did you talk to Diane Grey?"

"No, but—"

"You were there," Lucy said.

"I wasn't."

"Who? Cortland? Franklin?"

White looked like he had dug himself into a hole. And he had. He started talking faster.

"Look, on Monday Franklin saw Cassidy and Paul talking in the parking lot. He asked Paul about it, he said she was sick and going home, but Franklin didn't believe him. He followed Paul that night when he left and saw him meeting with Cassidy. I think he planned on, well, I don't know, I don't want to speculate. But after, Paul came back to the lab and Franklin confronted him with photo evidence of his bisexual affairs. When I say bisexual, I mean—"

"We don't need to know the details," Lucy snapped. "Franklin confronted him."

"Paul gave Franklin an envelope and told him to shred it, that it was all the evidence of what they'd done to Charlie. But Franklin didn't completely trust him. When he didn't show up for work on Tuesday, he started looking for him, and thought maybe he had given something to Charlie, or was working with Charlie, so he went to Charlie's house out in Helotes. Found Paul's body, but no evidence from CHR. Figured someone would find it and arrest Charlie for murder."

"Paul committed suicide," Lucy said. "Because you blackmailed him and he felt trapped."

"How can you be so sure?"

"We are," Leo said. He slapped the photo of Franklin leaving Java Antonio on the table in front of White. "Franklin was seen leaving the coffee shop Wednesday after having a brief conversation with McMahon, immediately prior to McMahon taking hostages. What was the conversation about? McMahon was in no mental position to be blackmailed."

"Franklin hadn't been able to find McMahon for weeks, and was worried that he was putting together the evidence, that Paul found a way to help him, so he sent McMahon a text message from Paul's phone—"

"Wait," Lucy said. "How did he get Paul's phone? We haven't found it."

"It was there, at Charlie's house."

"He took evidence from a crime scene."

"Well—I guess, yeah. And he told Charlie to meet him there. Charlie assumed it was Paul."

"Because it was Paul's phone. But if Charlie killed him, he would know that Paul couldn't send the text message."

"Charlie's memory was bad."

Not that bad, Lucy thought.

"Franklin moved the body to frame Charlie. That's how he got his phone."

Leo looked at Lucy. "But that all happened *before* Charlie took the hostages. Franklin couldn't have known what Charlie would do."

"No, but eventually someone would have found Paul's body in Charlie's house—and the longer the body was there, the harder it would have been to pinpoint time of death or cause. They wanted Charlie to stop asking questions. They wanted Cassidy out of the building. If the police believed that Charlie had killed his friend, and Cassidy was helping him, nothing she said about CHR would stick. At least in theory."

Leo asked White, "What did Franklin Clarke say to Charlie?"

"I don't know. He just went to see what Charlie knew, realized that Charlie wasn't in his right mind, so he left. I don't know what he said, specifically. I don't think that Franklin moved Paul's body."

He didn't sound convinced. Lucy was positive that was the only logical explanation. Franklin wanted to frame Charlie, and nail Cassidy as an accessory.

"Where are they?" Leo demanded.

"I don't know."

"And Cassidy?"

"I don't know."

"I don't believe you," Lucy said.

"I'm serious! Garrett came back on Monday and all I've been doing is trying to cover my own ass. Cortland and Franklin are doing their own thing now."

"Where does Nina Okala fit in?" Lucy asked.

"Cortland thought that Paul might have second thoughts, so she brought in Nina to keep an eye on him. That woman is a cold bitch. Don't let her petite sweet act fool you."

Leo paced. "We're running property records and flights. They haven't boarded a plane. They haven't used their credit cards. We know that Cassidy was planning on getting into the CHR building on Monday night, but we don't know if she did. And no one has seen or talked to her in over twenty-four hours."

"Well," White said as if he had just thought of it, "Cortland's grandfather had a nice spread up on Canyon Lake. It's in the name of the Cortland family trust. Cortland was named for her grandfather, Andrew Cortland."

It was their best—and only—lead. Leo and Lucy left White in the room and asked Tia to process him.

Leo, Lucy, and a tactical squad were already on their way to Canyon Lake, which was an hour from San Antonio, when they got the address for the Cortland family property.

Lucy brought up the map of the area. "There's a small airport near the property," she said. "They could already be gone, or waiting for transportation."

"All legitimate charters and pilots have been sent a hot sheet on the Clarkes, but there are plenty of unscrupulous people out there who will do anything for a buck," Leo said.

Cassidy had screwed up big time.

She hadn't thought that Nina Okala, Paul's assistant, was all that bright. Sure, she was a competent secretary, but she didn't talk, always seemed so shy and demure. Cassidy didn't know she had brains between her ears.

When Cassidy got off the phone with Dr. Harrison, she almost called him back and told him everything that she'd learned. All her theories. The proprietary documents she'd stolen from CHR to try to figure out what Charlie had been poisoned with. That she'd found a friend at the university to help her run tests.

But she didn't have everything wrapped up. She had a lot of theories but no hard facts. She'd broken the law.

She didn't report Paul's suicide, and she'd taken documents from his car. She'd taken Charlie's research and computer in the hope that she'd be able to figure out what had happened to him.

She thought if she could just get inside before someone—like Cortland Clarke—destroyed the evidence, she could turn it over to Dr. Harrison first thing Tuesday morning. She didn't have a great plan, but with Nina Okala's pass, she could access everything in Paul's side of the lab, and find the proverbial smoking gun, and then be waiting for Dr. Harrison in his office. Charlie had always liked and respected him.

Charlie liked and respected Paul Grey, too. And look what happened there.

She could be wrong about Dr. Harrison. He could be just as guilty as everyone else.

So Cassidy waited until Nina Okala went to bed. All the lights were off. Women at CHR almost always wore their key card on a lanyard and after work put it in their purse or briefcase. Nina had never carried a briefcase that Cassidy had seen.

The house was small but very nice and on a large piece of property at the end of a long driveway. Cassidy walked through the grove of trees toward the house. What if Okala had a security system? What if she was caught?

Maybe that was okay. She would then tell the police everything. But if she could get into CHR, all the better.

One step at a time. Just like in research.

And her plan almost worked.

The doors were locked, but the door into the laundry room wasn't dead-bolted. The lock itself was basic. Cassidy first tried to pick it—she'd watched a YouTube video that made it seem so easy—but she failed. So she used a crowbar that had been in the trunk of her car and pried the door open. She didn't care if Okala knew in the morning that someone had broken in. By then Cassidy would have all the information she needed.

Unless it was already destroyed.

One step at a time, Cass.

She didn't hear an alarm or a dog. Good. She walked through the kitchen. It was immaculate. No purse. The dining room. The living room. The house was spotless, with lots of antiques and big pieces of furniture. There had to be a den or something—she didn't want to go down the hall to her bedroom. That would be just totally weird. Sneaking into someone's bedroom while they were sleeping was creepy.

Between the living room and the back hall was a double door. That had to be an office, right? She opened one of the doors. She was right. Ms. Okala's oversized handbag was sitting on the chair by the door.

She went through it, found the lanyard, and had a momentary thrill that she was right about where it would be, that she had it in her hand.

She started out and walked right into Nina Okala. She didn't see the Taser in her hand.

Cassidy was speechless. Then she pushed past her and started to run, but she felt a sting in her lower back and her body jolted in pain, then numbness. She fell to the floor, convulsing.

She heard Ms. Okala on the phone. "I told you Ms. Roth was a smart girl. She did in fact break into my house and tried to steal my key card. Get over here now and clean this mess up . . . I didn't sign on for this. She'll be incapacitated for about thirty minutes. I won't be here. So if you don't get her, I don't know where she's going, but it probably will be straight to Garrett Harrison because he has an appointment with her tomorrow morning."

Ms. Okala turned on the lights. That's when Cassidy, through her blurred vision, saw two suitcases by the doorway. "It wasn't personal, dear," Ms. Okala said. "I won't be seeing you or anyone else at your messed-up company again."

Leo had his tactical team surround the property. The sheriff's office had staked out the airfield. They determined quickly that no planes had landed or taken off that morning, but according to the regional traffic control, a small charter plane was scheduled to land at four p.m.

"That's for Cortland Clarke," Lucy said. They only had thirty minutes.

"They could kill Cassidy and bolt," Leo said.

"No."

Leo raised his eyebrow. "They drove Charlie McMahon crazy. They blackmailed Paul Grey into committing suicide. Cassidy knows too much."

"Cassidy doesn't know half of what we know. But they're not killers. They're greedy, selfish assholes, but they haven't actually *killed* anyone. Now, if cornered I think they *can* kill, but my guess is that they have Cassidy tied up in that house and they're planning to disappear. No one knows she's here, she'll die of dehydration and they don't have a problem with that, but they're not pulling the proverbial trigger."

"How sure are you? Because this all sounds like a guess."

"Police work is all about educated guesses based on evidence and experience," Lucy said. "You of all people know that; you've taught me that. This is what they're thinking—leave Cassidy, disappear. If someone finds her, it won't matter because they'll be gone. They have a plan B, a nest egg or secret account or money already embezzled from CHR. But they're not thinking that far ahead. They're thinking *escape. Disappear.* When Garrett Harrison came back yesterday I think they knew he came to the FBI office. Maybe Franklin was following him; maybe Garrett called it in, not thinking that someone was going to panic."

"Okay, I'm listening."

"So let the plane land. Have the deputies stand down and take cover. Don't let the pilot see them. He'll radio that he's landed, they'll come out, we'll arrest them before they board the plane."

"And Cassidy?"

"She'll be inside the house."

"You think this'll work?"

"I think that if they're cornered and we storm the house, that will put Cassidy in danger."

Leo thought for about ten seconds. "Okay. Rod will

lead the tactical team to find Cassidy in the house, once the suspects clear it. I'll lead the tactical team at the airstrip. As soon as they leave the house, alert me and I'll detain the pilot. In case he's armed or plans to disappear during the takedown."

He looked at his watch, then called his team in to relay his plans.

Then they waited. SWAT was used to waiting. *Hurry and wait* was built into their training, because sometimes they had to sit on a building for hours, alert, ready to act on orders at a moment's notice.

Lucy wasn't as patient, though she was working on it.

Lucy stood with Rod Rodriguez. He was part of the counter-terrorism squad and had been former military, just like Leo and Nate. She didn't know him well, but had learned he was one of the best on the team, and she was glad he was here now, especially when Nate wasn't. Nate was again on mandatory leave for the shooting in the junkyard, and this one wouldn't be cleared in three days. Two shootings in a five-day span was going to get him more than a basic psych evaluation and three days' administrative leave.

She heard the plane before she saw it. It sounded just like Sean's Cessna. Rod told his team, "Small craft approaching. Be ready for my command."

Lucy was tapped into Leo's communications channel. They switched to two channels to avoid any confusion.

Leo said, "Plane landed. Hold."

Two minutes passed. Cortland and her brother Franklin left the cabin, each carrying two bags. They jumped into an SUV and drove off.

Lucy told Leo, "The two suspects have left the house, en route to the landing strip." She looked at Rod. He said, "We go in ten."

Lucy relayed the information to Leo, and Rod counted down. At four, the Clarkes were out of visual. Rod waited for three more seconds, then ordered his team in.

Lucy followed behind. She heard the team report in *clear clear clear* as they swept the house.

Had she been wrong? Had Cassidy been in the SUV? She was about to alert Leo to the possibility of a hostage situation when Rod said, "Agent Kincaid, they found an unconscious female in the attic. We've called for an ambulance. But the house is clear, you can go up."

Lucy went up to the attic, escorted by Rod. Cassidy was tied on a cot. The attic was blisteringly hot and humid, like a sauna. The agent who found her had already cut off her restraints. Lucy knelt next to her. "Cassidy, it's Agent Lucy Kincaid with the FBI. Can you hear me?" Her skin was hot and dry, and her heartbeat was rapid. That she'd already lost consciousness was a bad sign.

"She's extremely dehydrated," Lucy said. "We need to get her out of here."

"I got her, Agent Kincaid," the agent who untied her said. He carried her down to the cooler house.

Lucy asked for cold, damp towels. She needed to lower her temperature, but if she did it too fast the girl might go into shock. If she got her to wake up, she could force her to drink water, but she would certainly need an IV as quickly as possible.

Rod said, "Ambulance is on its way, ETA eight minutes."

"Find bottled water."

An agent returned with damp towels and Lucy wrapped them around Cassidy's wrists and ankles, with another on the back of her neck. Cassidy moaned.

"Cassidy, it's Lucy Kincaid. Can you hear me?"

"Ya." Her voice was thick and slurred.

Rod stepped out of the house.

"Okay, that's good. An ambulance is coming. Can you drink a little water?"

Lucy held the bottle to her lips. Most escaped, but Cassidy swallowed some. She sat with her for five minutes gently feeding her water while another agent kept bringing in wet rags to lower her body temperature.

Rod came back in. "Both suspects in custody, no shots fired."

"Did you hear that, Cassidy?" Lucy said. "Cortland Clarke and her brother have been arrested. They're going to prison for a long, long time."

"They." She swallowed. "They killed Charlie."

"We know," Lucy said. "We know everything now. And when you're feeling better, you can tell us what you know so that we can keep them behind bars."

"Nina," Cassidy said. "She's in on it."

Lucy spoke into her com. "Proctor, what's the status of Nina Okala?"

"Hold." A minute later, he came back on the line. "She was detained at the Los Angeles International Airport while attempting to board a plane for Japan."

Lucy relayed the information to Cassidy. "Relax. Everyone who conspired to make Charlie sick is going to prison." *Or they're dead*, but Lucy didn't say that.

"I'm sorry," Cassidy muttered and closed her eyes. "I didn't think anyone would believe me."

"I would have," Lucy said quietly.

The situation could have been so much worse; but now, justice would be served. She just felt all-around sad that Charlie McMahon died in the process.

CHAPTER THIRTY-NINE

Lucy drove Jack to the airport on Wednesday morning. She was going to miss her brother, and wished he lived closer. She said as much to him.

"I'll miss you too, kid." He hugged her. "You can always visit Sacramento."

"I know. And I will."

"I love Texas. I miss my spread in Hidalgo, to be honest, but Kane and Siobhan are happy there, and I'm glad. And Megan likes to visit, but I don't think she wants to live here. She doesn't mind that I come out, though. She understands family—Megan and her brother are very close, and she respects our relationship."

"I'm glad. She's a good woman."

"No argument from me."

She hugged Jack again and watched him walk through the airport doors before she drove off.

When Lucy got home, the house was quiet. She looked at the security pad. Kane and Siobhan had locked themselves in the pool house. That was good—Kane hadn't gotten any rest since the attack because he was taking care of the cleanup and hiring contractors. Lucy couldn't wait to get the boards down and the windows in. *Tomorrow.* Tomorrow they would be back to normal.

Sean was in his office, but he wasn't working. "Can I get you anything?" she said. "I can make lunch."

He half smiled at her. "Are you mad at me?"

She sat in his lap. "That was mean."

"I'm fine. Jesse's sleeping again. Is he sleeping too much?"

"No. He's sleeping because he needs to sleep. He's going to be okay, Sean. He has us."

"I talked to Madison's father this morning. He's flying out on Friday. He wants to take Jesse back with him."

"You are Jesse's father."

"He knows. He doesn't care."

"What does Jesse want?"

"I don't know. I haven't told him."

"Are you willing to fight for him?"

"Of course, but—"

"No buts, Sean. Just yes, you're willing to fight for him. Jesse needs to know that. He lost his mother. Everything is going to come out, Sean. Eventually, everything is going to come out. We might want to shelter him, lie to him, tell him this was all Carson, but eventually Jesse is going to learn that Madison was just as involved in lying to the AUSA as Carson was. That she knowingly falsified records. That she knowingly hid assets from the government and in the plea agreement. Money that was illegally obtained."

"I can't tell him that."

"You don't have to, Sean, but if you lie to him he'll know. You found that information. That means Dean can find it, too."

"I don't know how to fix this, Luce."

"First, you have to stop blaming yourself."

"I think you, Kane, and Jack all conspired to gang up on me. At least you're nice about it. Kane told me to get the fuck over it, and Jack told me to grow a pair."

She kissed him, then held his face in her hands. "We all love you. This will pass, but I know it's hard. Kane and Jack both have their own guilt to deal with, they just do it in a different way. And none of you have anything to feel guilty about. One day at a time, okay?"

"One day." He rested his forehead on hers. "I love you, Lucy."

"I love you. Always."

To make Lucy happy, Sean went to the kitchen and made grilled ham and cheese sandwiches for lunch. He wasn't hungry, but he ate half a sandwich with her. "I'm going to bring a plate up to Jess, see if he wants to eat."

"Good idea. Talk to him, Sean. Just—be yourself, okay?"

Jesse had been sleeping a lot, which was no surprise, and he hadn't wanted to talk. Sean walked upstairs with the sandwich and stared at his son, who was lying in bed with his back to him. The poor kid had lost so much. His mother. His innocence. But hadn't all that started last year when Carson took him down to Guadalajara in the first place? Exposed him to the business of the drug cartel and human trafficking? All Sean wanted to do was protect his family.

Bandit was on the bed and looked at Sean as if to say, *Don't make me get down. Jesse needs me.*

Sean sat on the edge of the bed, put the plate on the nightstand, and scratched Bandit behind the ears. When Nate told him that Bandit had tracked one of the vans, Sean was brought to tears. It had been an emotional week.

Jesse rolled over and looked at Sean. "I'm not sleeping."

"I know."

"What's going to happen to me?"

"I want you to stay here. But I'll understand if you want to live with your grandfather."

Tears ran down Jesse's face. "W-why?"

"You know him. He's your grandfather."

"Why don't you want me?"

"Didn't you hear me? I want you! I want you here, with me. God, Jess, I love you so much. But I nearly lost you. I couldn't protect you or your mom. I'll never forgive myself for . . . for telling you you were safe. You weren't. I failed in the worst way, and I can't fix it."

"You don't believe that."

"Jess—"

"You can't believe that. Carson sent those men here."

"He didn't."

"Yes! He may not have *wanted* me and Mom to be kidnapped, but he *wanted* to kill you. Not just a figure of speech, but really, honest and truly wanted Mr.

Robertson to kill you. And then Mr. Robertson wanted more money because Carson lied about how much money he had hidden away, so he took me and Mom."

"But you should have been safe here."

"Am I going to be safe anywhere? Are any of us really safe, anyway? What about the boys at Saint Catherine's? When their dads get out of prison, are they going to be safe? Are you going to send them away, too?"

"That's not the same."

"It *is*. Is it because of my grandfather? Because he'll fight you? I'll make sure he doesn't."

"I would fight to the ends of the earth for you, Jesse."

"Then I'm staying. You're my dad. My real dad. There's no other place I want to be. I love you. I love Lucy. I want a family I can trust. I can't trust anyone else."

Tears fell from Jesse's eyes, and Sean couldn't stop his own tears from falling. He squeezed his eyes closed.

"Then you'll stay," he said.

"Thank you."

"Don't—there's no thanks. You're my son, you're my family. But your grandfather will be here on Friday. He wants to bury your mom in Orange County. You need to go to her funeral."

"I know. But . . ." He bit his lip.

"What?"

"Will you come, too? Please? I don't want to go alone."

"You want me to come?"

Jesse nodded. "I need you, Dad. And we can fight my grandfather together. Maybe he won't object."

"Do you believe that?"

Jesse shook his head, but then he smiled. It was a small smile, but it was there. "But we're Rogans and we're stubborn. He can't beat us, if we're fighting on the same side."

Sean hugged his son tightly. "I love you so much, kid."

Bandit maneuvered his head in between Sean and Jesse and licked them both.

Read on for an excerpt from
Allison Brennan's next book

NOTHING TO HIDE

Coming soon from Minotaur Books

CHAPTER ONE

FBI Agent Lucy Kincaid squatted next to the latest victim of a possible serial killer. The victim had been identified as thirty-four-year-old Julio Garcia, the head chef of a convention hotel in downtown San Antonio.

Tortured then shot in the face. Fast, efficient, brutal. It was a gruesome sight, but Lucy was used to violence.

"I can give you five minutes," senior crime scene investigator Ash Dominguez said. "Until Detective Walker gives me the thumbs up, this is still his crime scene."

Lucy bristled. Ash was doing her a big favor, but the entire situation would have been a whole lot easier if Walker didn't have a chip on his shoulder about the FBI. The Bexar County Sheriff's lead detective knew she was coming to the scene, it had already been cleared by their mutual bosses. That he had slipped away irritated her, but she wasn't surprised. The FBI offered to assist after the second murder four weeks ago, but Walker pushed back. He didn't like working with federal agents, that much was clear, but now he didn't have a choice. Three dead with the same M.O. put the murders in a whole new category.

Don't blow it.

Her boss, SSA Rachel Vaughn, hadn't actually said those exact words, but she had lamented that there was no one else she could send out to the crime scene, which was now a joint investigation.

"It's not that you aren't capable of running solo with this, Lucy, but you're still a rookie and it's a touchy situation."

Lucy visually inspected Garcia's body. The smashed hands. The gunshot to his face. If the M.O. from the previous two held, the autopsy would reveal that he'd been hit in the stomach and groin by the same object that shattered the bones in his hands—likely a large hammer. There were conflicting interpretations of the three murders and Lucy couldn't say exactly *what* they were looking at. On the one hand it seemed personal; on the other, sexual. Yet again, an act of revenge or retribution. The attention to the hands suggested a thief, that the victims had taken something from the killer. But so far—at least between the first two victims—there was absolutely no connection that law enforcement could find.

The Bexar County Sheriff's department didn't want to give up their investigation, and the FBI tried not to flex their jurisdictional muscle unless absolutely necessary. So Lucy had to work with Detective Walker, who hadn't given her the time of day or answered any of her calls over the last month. She'd wanted to keep up to date with the status of the investigation, but he was avoiding her. Now he didn't have a choice—and clearly he was so angry he disappeared from the crime scene before she arrived.

This was the type of crime Lucy had the most experience with: violent. What that said about her, she didn't know—other than she was good at getting into the heads of both killers and victims.

Ash said, "It's not pretty."

"I read your other reports," she said. "Does this victim present the same way?"

"Damn near identical. The killer got up close and personal—most likely used a stun gun, not a Taser."

Virtually all personal Tasers now had AFID confetti to track to the owner. That put the killer in the smart category. Smart and bold, because stun guns were close contact weapons.

"I can't say for certain that a stun gun was used here, but that was the conclusion in the first two autopsies so I reason it was used again. Seems that he was stunned in his car, then the body was dragged here." Ash gestured to faint marks on the hard ground. "I'm sure the ME will find bruising consistent with being dragged. Then *whack, whack, whack*, the killer used some sort of blunt object—metal, like a large hammer or steel pipe. I'm still working on it, I can't tell you exactly what yet. Hands mutilated, stomach and groin hit once or twice."

"It's unusual that the focus was on his hands," Lucy said. Extremely odd. "The groin suggests sexual, but the victims were all fully clothed, and the genitals weren't mutilated."

Ash shivered. "I don't know about you, but getting

hit in the balls with a hammer would hurt like hell." He squatted across the body from Lucy. "There just doesn't seem to be any reason. Nothing taken, no message, no purpose."

"You sound like a cop now," Lucy said.

She swatted flies away from the body and looked closely at the mouth, unable to avoid seeing the brain matter and blood from the close-range shot in the face. In the previous murders, duct-tape residue had been found on and around the victim's mouth, but no tape was found at the scene. The killer had taken it with him, likely to avoid it being traced back to him. Tape was a terrific medium to obtain prints, trace evidence, or DNA. She could make out the rawness on his skin from the tape being pulled off. If they could find the tape—was it a souvenir? Did the killer dispose of it between the crime scene and his home? Destroy it?

The killer was smart. Ruthless. Purposeful. Because even though these victims all appeared random, there was a reason.

Once Lucy figured out how the victims connected, the reason would be clear, she was certain of it. And if the killer was truly a serial murderer, there *would* be a connection. While the victims might *seem* random, there would be a commonality that made sense to the killer. She couldn't shake the feeling that this was retribution, which meant the killer might be done when he finished with his list. Who was on it? People who had done him wrong? Hurt him emotionally or physically? If that was case, these three men would be connected—

even if it was long ago. Even if they hadn't communicated in years.

Ash jumped up. "Hey, Jerry."

Jerry said in a deep Southern baritone, "Far as I know, this is still my crime scene."

Lucy slowly rose from her squat and turned to face Detective Jerry Walker. They hadn't met—because he had been avoiding her calls—and she assessed him. Tall, broad-shouldered, large all around though not overweight. In his late forties, maybe a bit older. He wore jeans and a white polo shirt with a sheriff's patch on the breast, his badge clipped to his belt next to his side arm. But it was his well-worn black hat that stood out. He looked like he came from another era. The era of cops who hated feds.

"Detective Walker," Lucy said. "I've been trying to reach you for weeks. I'm Special Agent Lucy Kincaid."

"I've been working, ma'am. No time for chit-chat."

She bit back a response that would have gotten her in trouble. Before she could form a more diplomatic comment, Walker continued. "Ashley, the coroner said he was ready to move the body twenty minutes ago but you told him to wait. It's not getting any cooler out here."

"Jeez, Jerry, call me Ash," he said.

"Nothing wrong with Ashley. Good Southern name."

Ash rolled his eyes. "Maybe during the Civil War," he mumbled. He glanced at Lucy.

"It's not her call, not yet at any rate," Walker said. "Agent Kincaid is simply assisting in this investigation."

It was more than an assist, but she didn't comment.

Ash glanced at Lucy and she could see his wheels turning. He probably regretted letting her get up close and personal with the victim—except that she *was* authorized to work this case.

"Now, ma'am," Walker continued, "let's let the good folks from our crime scene unit take care of this poor guy, and we'll establish some ground rules."

She wanted to play nice—she *had* to play nice—and though Detective Walker's tone was easygoing, his words were not. She had been lucky in her career that most local law enforcement she worked with didn't have a problem with the FBI. She'd learned from her sister-in-law who'd been an agent for nearly twenty years that such camaraderie hadn't always been the case, but in her time both working with her training partner in Washington, D.C., and then here in San Antonio, she'd made many friends among local police. She really hoped she was wrong about Walker, but she felt like she was under a microscope.

She nodded curtly and forced a smile. "Ground rules."

He grinned back, but it didn't reach his eyes, then motioned for her to walk in front of him toward the staging area. She took one last glance at the deceased. Julio Garcia. No kids. Early thirties, married, had his life ahead of him. She would find out why his life was cut short so tragically. While Walker flexed his authority, she wouldn't be put off or chased away.

Though it was late September and the worst of the summer heat was over, it was still uncomfortable at ten in the morning. She walked to the staging area with Detective Walker.

"Deputies," he said to the two first responders, "if you'd be so kind as to finish the canvass. Check for surveillance videos on the highway, if anyone heard or saw anything. I'm right sure the gas station a quarter mile down has one, though it would be sheer luck if it caught cars passing on the street, or if our killer or victim stopped there. No neighbors in the area, but check the closest homes for what they saw and heard last night between midnight and three in the morning."

"We're on it, Jerry."

He waited until they left, then turned back to Lucy. "I understand you're a rookie."

She bristled. "Yes, I'll be here two years come January."

"I've been a Bexar County deputy for twenty-three years, and a detective for more than half that time. I'll tell you this, every time the feds have gotten involved in one of my cases, they've screwed it up. I said as much to your boss. To be fair, I've only had to work directly with your people twice over the years, so I'm going to give you the benefit of the doubt. Because we have three victims who all match a specific M.O., I'm stuck with your assistance. It's not my decision, but I will live with it. However, just to be clear, our respective bosses agreed that I'm the lead. I don't want any misunderstanding about that, so if you have a problem taking direction, tell me now. Save us both time and headache."

Lucy bit back her first sharp remark and said, "I have no problem taking direction, Detective Walker, as long as you have no problem taking my assistance. I have a

Master's degree in Criminal Psychology, and have worked multiple serial-killer cases."

"Psychology," he said with a hearty laugh. "Might as well consult a psychic to find out who killed these men."

"With all due respect, the FBI's Behavioral Science Unit has established clear guidelines based on evidence, victimology, and psychology to help narrow the suspect field."

He looked humored. "And what does your crystal ball tell you?"

Don't react. Stay professional. "I've read the autopsy reports, viewed the crime scene photos and reports, and read the case notes. I'm up to speed, except on one thing: witness statements."

"No witnesses. Each of the victims was killed at night in a remote area like this." He waved his hand around them. They were in the middle of a county park.

"I'm talking about the wives of the first two victims, the friends, neighbors, colleagues. Your notes were minimal." She shouldn't have said that, but she didn't backtrack. His notes *had* been basic. Just facts that the women knew about the day leading up to the murders of their husbands. When they left the house, what they were doing, when they planned to return. No known enemies. Ditto from their employers and colleagues. Nothing substantive, and she had more questions. "After reflection, the spouses may remember something else. These men got on the killer's radar somehow, and when we figure out how we'll know more. Plus, I want to go deeper into possible connections between the victims."

"They aren't connected, Agent Kincaid. It may surprise you, but I'm good at my job." He looked her up and down. "You have less than two years as an agent. And you're too young to have come from local law enforcement or the military."

"I don't think age has anything to do with competence."

"But it has everything to do with experience."

"Is your problem with me that I'm young or that I'm a federal agent?"

"Both, ma'am. Like I said, the feds I've worked with mucked up my cases and I have a long memory. But I'm willing to give you a shot."

"Sounds like I already have two strikes against me."

"I'm a man of my word, Agent Kincaid."

She sincerely hoped he was, because she really tired of games and jumping through hoops with people who were supposed to be on her side—the side of justice.

"Then let me into this investigation. Don't push me aside as if I don't have anything to contribute."

"Well, you can repeat all the groundwork if you want, but I have dug around into the backgrounds of the first two victims and there is no connection. Sometimes, a crime is exactly what it seems to be: random."

"The killer has a reason."

"Could be he's getting his rocks off."

"He picked these victims specifically. Knew they would be alone. Had the tools with him—stun gun, duct tape, hammer. Pre-meditated."

He nodded. "Yes, I'll give you that."

"He didn't stumble upon them and decide to kill them. He picked them out. Maybe at random, but he stalked them—got them alone. *Knew* when they would be alone. Knew their routines, and how to best approach them."

For the first time, Walker looked at her as if she had a brain. That angered her and relieved her.

More flies with honey.

She almost smiled when she heard her brother Dillon's wise words pop into her head. She'd use the honey as long as it worked, but she wasn't going to be demoralized or dismissed.

"I pretty much came to the same conclusion, especially since the only thing Billy Joe Brandish and Steven James had in common was that they were married, white, and under forty. And now Julio Garcia throws race out the window. He's Hispanic. They weren't even all born in Texas. Brandish is from San Antonio, Garcia is from Houston—I did a quick run on him when we ID'd him—and James is from California, relocating here with his wife six years ago to take a position with a large accountancy corporation. Brandish is blue collar—in construction and travels a lot to find work. James is wealthy white collar work. Garcia was a chef, worked himself up from prep work to running a kitchen at a busy hotel."

"What about where they live? Go to church? School? Where their wives work? Truly random victims are rare. Men as victims of a serial killer are rare. *Something* connects them, maybe even a location where the killer picked up their scent."

"I base my conclusions on evidence, little lady. Facts."

She didn't comment; she wasn't going to take the bait.

He continued. "They all live in different areas. James,

upper middle class in Los Olmos, Brandish barely holding on to his small house in an old neighborhood in the city. Garcia here lives on some acres in Bulverde, about five, six miles up the road. Cheaper to live up here and find some land for elbow room."

"So he was on his way home."

Walker nodded. "He left his restaurant at eleven-thirty last night. His wife was asleep—woke up at three-thirty and realized he wasn't home. His body was found just after seven this morning by a park patrol officer."

She did a mental calculation. "It would take what, thirty, thirty-five minutes at night to get from downtown to Bulverde?"

"Thereabouts."

"This just seems personal to me."

"Personal?"

"Why the focus on the hands? Why beat the victim with a blunt object, then shoot them? Why not simply shoot him in his car? Did the killer want information? But if the victims were interrogated, the killer wouldn't use duct tape on their mouths. Or did he beat the victims out of a rage? Yet—there wasn't rage here. Not uncontrolled rage, at any rate. It was . . . methodical. Planned."

"Beating a guy to a pulp tells me there is plenty of rage in this killer."

"But they weren't."

"Excuse me?"

"Beaten to a pulp. The damage to their hands was extensive, but very specific. Very focused."

Then it came to her. "The hands were restrained."

"No evidence of that."

"They had to be. What would you do if someone hit your hand with a hammer?"

"I don't see what you're getting at."

Lucy was on to something, though she didn't know exactly where she was going with it. "Victims are stunned. But that doesn't make them completely immobile. Temporary, but they may have some fight in them. They were dragged from the car, but not far. Thirty, forty feet. By that point the victim knows he's in danger. Might think he's being carjacked or robbed, or maybe he knows the killer and suspects he's going to be killed. He's going to try to crawl away."

"So the killer hits him in the groin. I can tell you that would incapacitate any man."

"And the first thing you would do is bring your hands down to protect yourself—unless they were restrained."

"If the killer hit the victims in the groin first. And there was no duct tape residue on the hands or wrists."

"We need to talk to Ash—he can look closer at the clothing. Maybe the wrists were bound through their shirts. Something to keep the hands on the ground—there was evidence of dirt and rocks embedded in the hands. The restraint wouldn't even need to be that secure—the killer didn't keep them alive long. Less than five minutes between first blow and the gunshot to the face."

"Well, now, your theory makes sense, but that still doesn't tell us anything about these victims or the killer."

"It tells us everything about the killer."

"Well, unless you know his name, it doesn't. Guess your crystal ball didn't tell you that."

"Detective Walker," she said as calmly as she could,

"I am doing my best here to work with you, but this animosity has got to stop. I'm a good cop, and I read your service record—I know you're a good cop, too. You said you were a man of your word and would give me a real chance—so start now."

He stared at her for a long moment, then nodded. "Very well. What now?"

"Talk to Garcia's widow, go back to the other widows and re-interview now that we have more information. Ask the lab to reinspect the clothes. But something else is bugging me, and it slipped away." Likely because she was spending all her time battling this detective.

"Well, if the thing that's bugging you is bugging me, then we're on the same page."

"Excuse me?"

"The victims all rolled down their windows before they were stunned. They were all stunned in their cars."

She felt the blood drain from her face. "You're thinking a cop."

His face hardened. "Yes, I am, Agent Kincaid. But for now, I'd like to keep this between you and me."

A cop. It made sense. Drivers would pull over, off the road, or into a parking lot if they were being pulled over.

She hoped and prayed that they were wrong.

"Maybe," she said slowly, "it's someone impersonating a cop."

"May just be that," Walker said. "But we have to look at the evidence wherever it takes us, and right now, I don't like where it's leading."

They watched as the coroner finished loading Julio Garcia's body into the back of the van.

"I need to notify Garcia's widow," Walker said quietly. He wasn't a soft man, but she heard the compassion in his voice and she pushed aside her earlier frustrations.

"I'll join you, Detective."

"You don't need to do that. Death notifications are never fun."

"Another thing we agree on. But I'll do it with you. It's never easy, but it's easier with a partner, Detective."

Walker looked at her. "You can call me Jerry."

"I'm Lucy."

"Short for Lucille?"

"Lucia. But I only respond when my mother calls me Lucia, so call me Lucy."

He grinned. "If you want to leave your vehicle here, we can go to the Garcia spread together and I can fill you in on the details."

"Thank you."

Dillon was right. More flies with honey—honey and a whole lot of spine.